James H. Graff, F. C. Armstrong

The Queen of the Seas

A Tale of Sea and Land

James H. Graff, F. C. Armstrong

The Queen of the Seas
A Tale of Sea and Land

ISBN/EAN: 9783337122157

Printed in Europe, USA, Canada, Australia, Japan

Cover: Foto ©Andreas Hilbeck / pixelio.de

More available books at **www.hansebooks.com**

THE QUEEN OF THE SEAS

A TALE OF SEA AND LAND.

BY

CAPTAIN C. F. ARMSTRONG,

AUTHOR OF

"THE TWO MIDSHIPMEN," "CRUISE OF THE DARING," "SAILOR HERO
"THE YOUNG COMMANDER," ETC., ETC.

LONDON

CHAPMAN AND HALL, 193, PICCADILLY.

1866.

THE QUEEN OF THE SEAS.

CHAPTER I.

SOME twelve miles from the now flourishing seaport of
Swansea is the town and port of Llanelly. Fifty years
ago the latter could scarcely be said to exist, but at the
present day is rapidly rising into an important place for
trade, with its copper works, docks, coalpits, and good
agricultural prospects. We cannot, however, speak about
either the beauty of the situation or the construction of
the streets, which are on a swampy flat, till lately ill-
drained, and with its houses and cottages scattered and
facing in every possible direction. The country along
the sea coast to the north is hilly and picturesque, and
many of the villas and country houses on the hill side,
leading to Pembray and the ancient borough of Kidwelly
(the latter having the handsomest church and castle in
the principality), can boast of magnificent sea views,
taking in the whole range of Carmarthen Bay to Caldy's
Tenby to the westward, and Wormshead to the southward.

At the period of our story, Llanelly was scarcely known,
for there were not ten houses in the place. The flat,
where the railway station, the harbour, docks, colleries

1

and copper works now stand, was then, in truth, a mere swamp. But everything must have a beginning, and so had Llanelly.

Welshmen are proverbially fond of the place where they were born, and a certain Joseph Lewellen was born within two hundred yards of where the church now stands. He was the son of a respectable farmer, and at the age of sixteen took to a seafaring life. It is not, however necessary to the interest of our story to follow his fortunes. It will be quite sufficient to say that he returned to the place of his birth, at the age of fifty, hale and hearty, with an amiable wife, a son and daughter, and a fortune of £100,000, made by mercantile speculations.

All his father's connections were dead; he could not find even one near relative. He purchased a fine tract of land facing the sea, between Llanelly and Pembray, another little village now rising into importance.

As nature had done much to make Llanelly a sea-port, Mr. Lewellen was resolved to assist her, and he set to work right heartily to do so. Money will do wonders when judiciously applied. Houses were built, docks were began, coal discovered, and trade commenced, and at the end of five years Mr. Lewellen began to reap the reward of his exertions and endeavours to bring trade to his native place. And to crown all, to the delight of the rapidly-increasing population, a remarkably fine ship of 600 tons was built and launched, and named by his fair daughter, "The Queen of the Seas." This vessel Mr. Lewellen destined for what was considered in the year 178— a most enterprising voyage. She was to sail for the land so universally known as Australia. Mr. Lewellen's only son, whose health was rather delicate, was to make the voyage in her, and he was to be accompanied by a dear friend and companion, named Cuthbert Gordon. As the future hero of our story, this young gentleman requires an introduction, with a brief mention of his early career, and a slight sketch of his family.

Mrs. Gordon, his mother, at this period a widow, was the daughter of an officer who held a lucrative situation in India under the East India Directory. Amy Ludlow, was just sixteen years old when she left England to join her father, then a widower, in India. No expense had been spared in her education. Her father, Colonel Ludlow, even before she left England had fixed upon a suitor for his daughter's hand, a man of great wealth, but nearly old enough to be her father.

On board the ship in which Miss Ludlow took her passage to India, under the care of a married lady going out to her husband, was a Lieut. Gordon, on his way to join his regiment in Calcutta. He was young, handsome, and amiable; Amy Ludlow lovely, innocent, and inexperienced.

A voyage to India in those days was a very tedious one, generally taking eight or nine months. Before reaching Calcutta, the young couple had exchanged vows of everlasting attachment, and when Amy entered her father's princely mansion and he gazed at her, proud of her extreme loveliness, she had no heart to bestow upon any suitor, save the handsome but poor lieutenant.

As soon as Colonel Ludlow, a most worldly-minded man, considered his daughter sufficiently recovered from the effects of the voyage, he became anxious to introduce her to the gentleman he had selected for her future husband.

Amy trembled when her father hinted his wishes and introduced the Honourable Alfred Gordon. She turned pale at the name; it acted like a spell upon her. Afterwards her father told her he was next in succession to the estates and Lordship of Dunskelling. He was a handsome portly man, but he was forty and Amy not quite seventeen.

Mr. Gordon became greatly enamoured of the young and beautiful girl, and she, seeing how things were likely to turn out, threw herself at her father's feet, implored his forgiveness, telling him she had exchanged vows with Lieutenant Gordon and could never marry the gentleman he proposed to her. In vain the father stormed and threatened; in vain Mr. Gordon implored her to alter her determination, offering her a princely establishment and unlimited control over a Nabob's fortune,

Amy was firm ; with tears in her eyes she thanked her suitor, and implored him to cease thinking she would ever change her mind, and begged him to show his generosity by refraining from a vain pursuit.

Lieutenant Gordon in the meantime had been despatched with his regiment into a most unhealthy and dangerous locality, and had distinguished himself in several encounters with rebellious native chiefs. Not long after, Colonel Ludlow was suddenly seized with a fatal disease, so common in that burning clime, and in eight and forty hours ceased to exist.

By the bewildered and distracted daughter's consent the Honourable Alfred Gordon, as the nearest and dearest friend of the deceased, undertook the melancholy task of seeing his friend's body to its last resting place, as well as the arrangement of the late Colonel's affairs, which when they came to be looked into, were found to be woefully embarrassed ; his liabilities great, and a very large amount due to the Honourable Alfred Gordon himself.

This debt, Mr. Gordon hinted, might be arranged, and several others struck out ; but Amy, who went to reside with the lady she had come out to Calcutta with, and who took great interest in her, insisted that all her father's debts should be paid as far as the means left permitted.

After every debt was settled, there remained for Miss Ludlow, out of her father's once splendid fortune, only a small income of £130 a year.

She gratefully and gracefully thanked Mr. Gordon for the trouble he had taken ; but firmly resisted all overtures to further intercourse in a matrimonial point of view.

Mr. Gordon was a proud, haughty, but a highly honourable man. Nevertheless, he took Miss Ludlow's determination much to heart.

Twelve months after the death of her father, Amy became the wife of the then Captain Gordon, and accompanied her husband and his regiment to Alemhabad.

In her married life Mrs. Gordon was most happy. Time rolled on, and she became the mother of three children—a fine boy named Cuthbert, and two girls— twins. Alas ! here ended Mrs. Gordon's felicity. Capt.

Gordon fell, leading his regiment against overwhelming odds. He was deeply regretted by all who knew him, and high encomiums were bestowed upon him by the Commander-in-Chief and his own Colonel. The distraction of the young widow was terrible. We pass over months of agonized sorrow. The devoted wife became the devoted mother, and she prayed to God to give her strength and resignation for the sake of her children. Every attention and kindness was shown her by the colonel and officers of the regiment, and finally she returned to Calcutta.

The Hon. Alfred Gordon had left India several years, and had succeeded to the title and estates of Dunskelling. She sighed as she thought of her beloved husband, who had often declared to her that he was the real heir to the title and estates of Dunskelling.

Mrs. Gordon soon left India, and on reaching England with her children she found that her limited income required great care to make it of use towards the education of her children. She was recommended Wales as being cheap in all the articles of life. By the upsetting of the old-fashioned six-inside coach she became acquainted with Mr. Lewellen, of Llanelly. Her children were unhurt, but she received some slight injury, and was obliged to remain a few days at Cardiff. Mr. Lewellen, a kind-hearted generous man, was interested in the still beautiful widow and her lovely children. He was transacting business in Cardiff, and he showed Mrs. Gordon every attention, and having ascertained her motive for coming into Wales, he instantly offered her one of several pretty villas he had built near his own handsome mansion, and at a rent that quite astonished her. The fact was, Mr. Lewellen contrived, without being importunate or intrusive, to learn her little history. His own family consisted of a son and daughter, nearly the same age as the young Gordons. He saw at once that Mrs. Gordon was a lady by birth and station, highly-accomplished and most interesting. He, therefore, offered her his villa, on the hill side, near Llanelly, and facing the bay, and commanding the most extensive and beautiful sea views imaginable.

Leaving Mrs. Gordon at Cardiff, Mr. Lewellen proceeded to his own home, promising to have the cottage ready by the time she expected to reach Llanelly, for she intended staying a week or two at Swansea.

Mrs. Gordon, when she did reach the cottage, was delighted with it, and thanked God she had succeeded in gaining the friendship of so worthy and good a man as Mr. Lewellen.

A constant intercourse took place between the two families. The children grew up together like brothers and sisters.

Mrs. Gordon's children participated in all the advantages of education that Mr. Lewellen's received, and Mrs. Gordon, herself a most accomplished woman, and a splendid performer on the piano and harp, taught her daughters to play well on both instruments ; and with untiring anxiety and industry, endeavoured, and with success, to render them as accomplished as herself.

Cuthbert Gordon and George Lewellen studied together under the tuition of a most amiable gentleman, the curate of the parish. Curates salaries in those days, and God knows they are but miserable stipends even in these days, were very limited. Mr. Edgehill, having a wife and children was very grateful for the munificent remuneration he received for superintending the education of the two boys.

Both, before they were ten years old, became excellent swimmers ; in fact, Cuthbert by far the most powerful and enduring of the two, and the most expert, had saved the life of his comrade whilst swimming from one sand-bank to another. George was seized with cramp, and would have sunk, had not Cuthbert, with singular coolness and courage of his age, took him on his back, and, after a terrible struggle, reached the shore. This act endeared the young man more than ever to Mr. Lewellen.

Both showed a great predilection for the sea, everlastingly out in the pilot boats, even in severe gales. They very early acquired the art of steering and managing a boat, and young as they were, they often assisted in saving life from the many wrecks that took place in the dangerous and far spread sands that stretched for miles out to sea.

With Mrs. Gordon's reluctant consent, through Mr. Lewellen's great interest, both boys were placed as midshipmen on board the Magician, 36-gun frigate, commanded by Captain Granby. Mr. Lewellen did not intend his son to remain when his term of midshipman should expire, but he wished him to acquire a thorough knowledge of seamanship, as he was then projecting the building of his "Queen of the Seas," and he intended his son should, in after years, be able to take the command of even a larger ship.

In the Magician the two boys sailed for the East. They were both handsome lads, but Cuthbert Gordon was a tall and very striking looking boy, with an enduring and high spirit, rather tenacious of control, if severity was meted out to him, but easily won by kindness. The royal navy in those days was very unlike the royal navy of the present time. It was always a glorious service, and made its flag respected by all nations, and in the battle and the breeze the Sons of Britain were almost always conquerors. George Lewellen was a fine, handsome lad, less robust than his comrade, and with a milder nature and temperament. The one would bend to the storm, the other would fiercely brave it. Kind, generous, and brave to excess, Cuthbert Gordon was the sailors' favourite and pride.

After four years' service they returned to England. George Lewellen was in delicate health, and he went home. Cuthbert was in full health and vigor, and wonderfully grown. He was now nearly seventeen, and was five feet ten, strong, active, and as clever a youth as any in the service. His captain delighted in him, and promised when he again commanded a ship to take him with him till he should have finished his time. But Cuthbert in an evil hour, not to lose time, entered on board the 'Pelican,' a frigate commanded by one of the greatest tyrants in the Royal navy. This man was originally master's mate, of very low birth. It is not our business to say how he rose to command a ship. But he did. His was by no

means a solitary case of good fortune, if it was through
good fortune, for at that period several similar cases
occurred.

The Pelican sailed for the Chinese seas.   This ship soon
became a Pandemonium ; her first and second lieutenants
were equally as tyrannical as the Commander.   It was flog,
flog, from morning to night.   The spirits of the men
were broken, and instead of the discipline of the ship becoming improved by the severity exercised, there was
scarcely a ship in the service so badly worked, and the
duties so negligently performed.

The Pelican joined the Lion, 64-gun ship, conveying
Lord Macartney to China, but very shortly after proceeded
to attack a pirate fleet that infested the coast of Macao.

Cuthbert Gordon had several times attracted the particular attention of the Commander of the Pelican ; he
was known to be a favourite of the men, and the only
officer on board, except the 3rd lieutenant and a very
young midshipman named Hope, who was obeyed with
anything like cheerfulness.

Captain —— saw this, and he took a most violent anti-
pathy to Cuthbert, and insulted and grossly threatened to
flog him on several occasions ; but Cuthbert did his duty,
and carefully avoided giving his commander the opportunity to illuse him ; but when the wish existed the power
was at hand.

On the 26th of June the Pelican came in sight of the
Chinese Piratical fleet, consisting of some very large war
junks and numerous smaller ones.

Falling stark calm the frigate could not approach
within gun shot of the pirate fleet; but instead of manning
her boats the captain simply ordered the gig to be
manned, and, to the surprise of all, ordered Cuthbert
Gordon to board the largest junk, much the nearest to
them, and declare if they did not haul down their flags
and surrender, he would blow them all out of the water.
At this time the junks were moving under immense
sweeps, and making the best of their way into the harbour of the Ladrones, where it would be quite impossible
for the frigate to follow or watch them with her boats.

With six men in the gig, Cuthbert Gordon pulled away for the principal junk.

"This is a mad expedition we are going on, Mr. Gordon," said an old Salt, respectfully ; "it's more likely they will blow us out of the water. Why not have out the boats and tow the ship within gun shot ? She would move faster than these lumbering junks do now under their sweeps."

" It's very possible, Jenkins," returned young Gordon. " Still it's my duty to obey orders."

" Well, it's all one, sir," returned the man. " I myself would just as leave become a prisoner to John Chinaman as—"

" There, Jenkins, say no more," returned Cuthbert, "give way, and we shall see what those piratical rascals will say to our captain's message ; but the thing is now to make them understand me."

After a four miles pull the gig, with a flag of truce flying, went alongside of a castle of a junk, over a thousand tons burden. She was crowded with men ; but they offered no opposition whatever to the young midshipman's ascending the side, leaving his crew below in the boat.

As soon as Cuthbert Gordon set his foot upon the deck he was seized, his hands bound, and then he was hurried below.

The commander of the junk, a Chinese who spoke English, ordered a cannon to be pointed down at the boat, whilst he desired the men to return to the frigate, and tell her commander that the very first shot he fired into the pirate fleet they would hang their prisoner from the fore yard.

The exasperated men could do nothing, they were forced to pull back and deliver their message.

Captain —— was standing near the gangway, as Jenkins, a captain of the fore-top, with rather a dissatisfied air and manner, delivered the message. The commander, in a bantering tone, said to the first lieutenant, " The young fool had no business to go on board, he must take his chance ; he's very likely to swing, for by—ha ! here's the breeze."

Jenkins, a hot-tempered man, and greatly attached to young Gordon, as he retired muttered some words that caught the captain's ear. He immediately ordered him to be arrested, and put in irons, with the intimation that his back should feel the cat the next day, and that pretty sharply too! and then orders were given to crowd all sail after the pirates.

CHAPTER II.

Two or three days before the Pelican came in sight of the Pirate fleet there were symptoms to be observed, by those accustomed to the Chinese Seas, of the awful approach of one of those terrible storms called Typhoons. But Captain —— laughed at the advice given to one of the lieutenants by an old quarter-master, who was well accustomed to the Chinese waters when the breeze sprang up. After the return of the boat from the pirate junk, the sky looked singularly threatening; nevertheless the captain crowded all sail in pursuit. The crew looked sulky; two were flogged that morning for a mere trifle, and five were, besides Jenkins, in irons below.

The Pelican made sail and dashed on in pursuit—the guns double shotted and all ready for blazing into the pirates.

The frigate had her top gallant sails and royals set. They were about eleven miles off the coast, and, to a certain extent, should the wind shift a point or two, they were imbayed by a tremendous reef of rocks, stretching out to the southward like a breakwater.

The heat was intense, and the sky to windward of a dense blackness. On flew the frigate and so did the junks, for they sail remarkably fast before the wind. Still the Pelican came tearing through the water. The smaller piratical junks steered through a narrow, shallow passage in the middle of the reef, but the four principal vessels had to weather it.

The pirate Captain, Stoppo Ochna, ordered Cuthbert Gordon to be brought upon deck. His hands were unbound, but several of the pirates stood round him ready to execute their chief's orders. The pirate captain spoke English, having at one time been an interpreter at Canton, and who claimed a descent from the famous pirate Koshinga, who won Macao from the Portuguese.

The pirate looked at the advancing frigate, and then at the unshrinking, calm countenance of his prisoner.

"Your commander must have been very careless of your life," said he, "to send you with such a fool's message; in twenty minutes your ship will be within gun shot. The first shot, and you swing there," and he pointed to the rope already prepared ominously with a noose at the end of it from the fore-yard.

"And what benefit," said Cuthbert Gordon, "will the cowardly act of putting me to death be to you? Do you imagine that the commander of a British Frigate will be stayed in the execution of his duty, because you threaten the life of a poor midshipman? No; if you hang me, he will annihilate the whole of you."

"Up you go, nevertheless," said the pirate, "I will teach you barbarians wisdom."

As he spoke, there came a flash from the frigate's bows. Almost at the same moment, a round shot tore through the high bulwarks of the war junk, knocking huge splinters from the timbers right and left. The pirate captain and three men were dashed dead upon the deck, and Cuthbert, who was standing amidst the group, was knocked down by a splinter, and half stupified. Before he could rise, a scene of undescribable confusion ensued. The typhoon had burst upon them with appalling fury; away went the sails and masts like reeds, the thunder rolled in awful peals over their heads, and the wild sea, torn from the surface, passed over the helpless junk like a snowdrift. She was dashing madly upon the reef. As to the frigate, she was not to be seen in the clouds of spray that covered the ocean.

Cuthbert recovered his legs; he was fortunately only slightly bruised. The dead pirate captain was transfixed by a huge splinter. No one heeded the young midship-man, for in ten minutes they would be on the reef, over which the sea broke in sheets of foam.

To avoid her doom was impossible ; the other three great junks being considerably nearer to windward, had weathered the reef, and partly dismasted and without a rag of sail left, were driving before the furious tempest. At length, with a hideous crash, the vessel struck.

This reef, in the form of a half-moon, was, where the junk struck, some four to six feet above the sea. In parts it was three or four feet under water, and its extent a mile and a half or more ; the extreme end some five miles from the coast, but the channel in no part of the five miles was more than five or six feet deep, and in gales it was all broken water.

The panic amongst the hundred and fifty men the junk contained amounted to madness, as she heeled over towards the rocks. Numbers threw themselves headlong overboard, many perished, some scrambled upon the highest parts of the reef and held on with the spray falling in sheets over them. Some contrived to launch the boats, two were smashed to pieces, and two got, with some eighteen or twenty men in them, through a channel into deep water, and were driven before the furious storm.

The junk, however became firmly jammed, and though short seas broke and dashed over her, and her bottom was at once stove in, yet it was not probable that she would go to pieces for several huge masses of rock broke the sea from the deep water ; yet, strange to say, such was the panic, that in less than an hour not one man remained aboard, save Cuthbert Gordon. In three or four hours the fury of the typhoon was spent, and before the sun set the sky opened, and a flood of sunshine was poured out upon the troubled deep, and as the sun dipped beneath the wave the tempest ceased, and nought remained but the heavy sea to tell of the past storm, so terrific in its fury, and so short-lived !

When the Pelican fired her first gun, which was double-shotted, and most accurately aimed, she was inattentive to the approaching hurricane which struck her with all sails set. Away went sheets and tacks, but the mighty whirlwind took away sails and topmasts, as if they were bamboo canes and rags, whilst the frigate heeled over till her bulwarks were under water. She, however, righted, and as she was running dead on the reef, her commander determined to wear to avoid it, as he could not weather it without getting on the other tack. Sail was attempted to be set to clear the land on the other tack, but such was the incredible fury of the typhoon, that the stout canvass was blown out of the bolt ropes, and the frigate paid off and got before the tempest. The anchors were then let go, for she ran within four miles of the shore; they held only a moment, and then nothing could save the ship. Throughout all this, the men, though their own lives were at stake, were sullen and slow in their movements. The captain swore he would make an example of the crew, he'd make their backs smart. The men knew that the ship would be ashore before long. Suddenly the noble frigate came with a terrific shock against a sunken rock, passed over, and then rapidly began to settle down, and finally sunk within three miles of the shore, and the sea about eight feet over her decks. Before this took place, several of the boats were launched, and just as she went down, the captain, first lieutenant, and the master and nine men, pushed off in the cutter; but the frigate suddenly heeled over, the foreyard struck the cutter, and sank her. Whether the captain was injured or not no one could say, for he was seen no more; but the lieutenant, master, and five men were picked up by the launch, and driven towards the land. The two other boats carried away sixty men; the rest, having released those confined below, finding the vessel sinking, took to the rigging and tops, and held on easily till the hurricane ceased. Of those who drove ashore in the boats, the first and third lieutenants, three midshipmen, the master, and forty-five men were saved, but the boats were stove in pieces.

The frigate lay about thirteen miles from the spot where the piratical junk remained stranded upon the reef, therefore those upon the rigging and tops of the frigate could not see the junk.

It was not till morning that the men on the tops and rigging were relieved by boats from the shore. In the meantime, Cuthbert Gordon remained in the pirate vessel which was full of water, but, during the evening, as the tide receded, her stern becoming much higher out of the water than her bows, he penetrated into the cabin in search of food.

The upper cabin he found had scarcely any water in it, but everything was knocked to pieces. After a search, he discovered materials for getting a light, for the lockers were full of articles of almost every description. As the water was rapidly receding from the cabins, Cuthbert thought it not improbable that the Chinese on the reef would return, and not unlikely take his life. On a further search he found abundance of biscuits, and jars full of strong drink, not very pleasant to the taste.

He then ascended upon deck ; it was a bright moonlight night, and he thought he could perceive groups of men upon the reef, some three or four hundred yards off, but he also perceived that they could only reach the ship by swimming across a narrow channel about one hundred yards wide.

Cuthbert passed the night without sleep, puzzling his brains as to how he might escape, but just as the grey light of dawn made, he perceived, to his great delight, a vessel within hail, and evidently lying-to, for the purpose of examining the wreck. As the light increased, he saw at once she was a British man-of-war schooner, and soon a boat left her side and pulled in for the junk. On the highest part of the reef numbers of the pirates were assembled, and coming out from the shore, he saw several small junks and rowing boats. As soon as the schooner's boat came close in to the reef, Cuthbert hailed, and, as the tide was rising, the boat, in which was an officer and six men, pulled up alongside, and Cuthbert, throwing over the side some ropes, they speedily gained the deck.

The officer was the lieutenant of the schooner Perseverance, a very young man, who listened to Cuthbert's account with surprise.

" What has become of the Pelican ? " he asked, " If

she did not drive ashore, she would surely be within sight, for the typhoon was only of four hours' duration. The schooner had prepared for it, and rode it out safely."

With his glass the lieutenant examined the numerous boats coming off from the shore, and at once resolved to burn the junk. In a few minutes she was set fire to, and they all entered the boat, and pulled away for the schooner leaving her in a blaze.

Captain Gardner, who commanded the Perseverance, received Cuthbert Gordon very kindly. He was bound to Singapore with despatches, and as the ship stood out to sea they failed seeing the masts of the Pelican, and the man clustered in the tops.

On reaching Singapore, they found the Badger, gun brig, about to sail for the Cape. The captain kindly offered Cuthbert a passage. At the Cape, our hero was introduced to Captain Richardson, of the 36-gun frigate Urania, who seemed greatly pleased with his appearance, and he offered to place him on the frigate's books as senior midshipman, as he had only about a year and a half to complete his six years' term. Cuthbert was delighted with this offer, and expressed his gratitude. Accordingly, furnished with funds by Captain Richardson, he resumed his situation of midshipman on board the Urania.

Intelligence of the breaking out of the war with France reached the Cape before the Urania sailed. The frigate was homeward bound, and her captain hoped before reaching England, to capture a prize or two.

In this he was exceedingly fortunate. After a desperate engagement of six hours, and a chase of twenty-four, a fine French frigate, the Brutus, of forty-four guns was captured. In this fierce fight Cuthbert Gordon distinguished himself; twice he boarded the Frenchman. On the second assault the third lieutenant was killed, and our hero, cheering on the men, forced his way to the quarter deck, hauled down the revolutionary flag, and held his position till the fall of her gallant captain and the surrender of the ship.

Captain Richardson was severely wounded, the third lieutenant, and two midshipmen, and nine men killed, besides seventeen disabled, in this severely contested engagement.

The commander of the Urania at once appointed Cuthbert Gordon acting third lieutenant, making no doubt but that the promotion would be confirmed. The Urania reached England with her prize, and anchored in Plymouth Sound.

Here a most unfortunate occurrence took place, which deprived our hero of all the advantages his courage and gallantry had gained him.

At a dinner party given by the first lieutenant of the Urania, there chanced to be a Lieutenant Thurton, a cousin of the first lieutenant of the Pelican. We forgot to mention that whilst the Urania remained at the Cape, a 10-gun brig on her way from Canton to England, brought the intelligence of the loss of the Pelican, the death of her captain, and the saving of the first lieutenant and all the crew excepting five men, and that there were great hopes of being able to raise the Pelican. This intelligence reached England, before the arrival of the Urania.

As the conversation turned upon the loss of the Pelican and its cause, Cuthbert Gordon was naturally referred to, as being on board at the time, for full particulars. Though he gave the account exactly as it occurred, as far as he knew, for as to how she was wrecked he could only surmise, but he stated that the ship was unhappily in a state of great insubordination, from the severity of the captain and the cruelty and injustice of the first lieutenant, the latter getting the men flogged for the merest trifle, and that her wreck might be attributed partly to the want of energy and willingness of the crew, whose spirit's had been crushed by undue punishment.

The next day, to Cuthbert Gordon's great surprise, Lieutenant Thurton, and another officer both belonging to the same ship entered his private apartment.

" Sir," said Lieutenant Thurton, in an arrogant manner to our hero, " you have, in an unwarrantable manner, cast a slur upon a gentleman, a near relation of mine, I mean Lieutenant Carpenter of the Pelican. I have now called upon you to insist upon your writing a complete contradiction to your statement of yesterday before this gentleman, Lieutenant Roberts."

"And suppose, sir," said Cuthbert Gordon, with a flushed cheek, and his dark eyes flashing with indignation, " I do not choose," and as he stood up and faced the haughty lieutenant, the contrast between the two figures was remarkable. "Suppose I do not choose to retract what I have said, thereby stating a falsehood, what then ?"

" What then ?" repeated the lieutenant fiercely. " I will horsewhip you the first time I meet you in the street, for you cannot suppose I will fight a duel with an unpassed lying midshipman."

Cuthbert Gordon as we have stated, being of a fiery impetuous nature, could no longer restrain his temper. Striding up to Lieutenant Thurton, he said, " Since you consider me beneath a gentleman's notice, and unfit to meet you as your equal, and degrade yourself by resorting to conduct unbecoming a gentleman, be it so. I now tell you, if you do not quit my room, and that instantly, I'll kick you into the street, and if ever you dare to use a whip upon me, I'll cut the coat from your back with another. Now go."

Furious with passion Lieutenant Thurton made a blow at Cuthbert Gordon's face ; our hero struck it up, and seizing the lieutenant by the collar, swung him off his legs, despite his struggles and the interference of his friend, and in the heat of his passion hurled him down stairs, where he lay stunned and senseless. This took place in the hotel, and in a minute landlord and landlady, several gentlemen, some naval and military officers, crowded round the fallen man, lifted him up, and carried him into an adjoining room.

Cuthbert Gordon was at this time only twenty years of age ; flushed with passion and excitement he entered the coffee-room, he knew several of the gentlemen present, and, curbing his passion, he simply stated the cause of the scene they had witnessed, and on Lieutenant Roberts entering the room, he repeated his statement, and facing that gentleman, who was pale and agitated, demanded if every word spoken was not the truth.

2

Lieutenant Roberts hesitated, but a Captain Harding, of the Racehorse, said, " I believe every word Mr. Gordon has said, and I state here before all present that I consider Mr. Gordon to have been treated in a most disgraceful and ungentlemanly manner, and I request, Lieutenant Roberts, you will speak out, as you were present the whole time."

Lieutenant Roberts then said that he considered his friend, Lieutenant Thurton, had acted hastily, but the facts were as Mr. Gordon had stated.

" I thought so," said Captain Harding, offering his hand to Cuthbert, " you could not have acted otherwise. If you want a friend at any time count me as one, I have heard that short as your career in the service has been, you have always acted as a gentleman, and with gallantry and spirit."

All present shook hands with young Gordon, and so the affair appeared to end, but four days afterwards Lieutenant Thurton insisted on a meeting ; they met, and Lieutenant Thurton fell dangerously wounded.

The result of all this was, that although our hero passed his examination with great credit, he received no appointment or promise of one. Those he had offended had powerful interest. So, thoroughly disgusted he resolved to return home, and after a time enter the merchant service. He was entitled to a considerable amount of prize money, therefore he would be no burden to his dear mother, on the contrary he felt proud of being able to be of assistance to her and his sisters. They were already aware of what had occurred ; the fond mother could not blame her son if he inherited the same independent spirit of his never to be forgotten father, and his sisters Amy and Lucy received him with every mark of affection. Mr. Llewellen, and his son and daughter George and Mary, soon joined the happy party.

" Never mind, my brave boy," said Mr. Lewellen, as he embraced him with the affection of a father, " never mind, you acted as all your friends would have wished you to act. I'll build you a 600-ton ship, make two or three voyages, and then you shall command her with five times the pay the Royal Navy affords the brave men who up-hold the honour and glory of our flag."

It was determined that Cuthbert should accompany George Lewellen, who had become tenderly attached to Lucy Gordon, to Australia. We will therefore in our next chapter commence the adventures of our hero from the period of his sailing in the " Queen of the Seas," on what was then considered a long and adventurous voyage.

CHAPTER III.

AT this period Australia was just beginning to attract the attention of speculators. It was, however, unknown as a great gold country. The natives of New Zealand were known to be a fierce, warlike race, and cannibalism existed among certain tribes.

The " Queen of the Seas " was fitted out with every attention to comfort, so that George Lewellen, and his friend, Cuthbert Gordon, might enjoy the voyage as one of pleasure and information. The vessel was commanded by a Captain Evans, a skilful and enterprising commander, who had sailed round the world as first mate, as well as having made two successful voyages to China and the East Indies.

The ship was laden with every article of commerce likely to bring good returns.

On the 25th of August, the Queen sailed from Llanelly, the pier head and new dock crowded with the good people of the town, and a cheer rang through the air, as she dropped her courses; and gathering away with a fine easterly breeze, quickly receded from the pier, Cuthbert and George Lewellen waving their hats as long as a certain party standing on a particular spot kept waving their kerchiefs in return. On reaching the bar, Mr. Lewellen bade the young men and Captain Evans an affectionate farewell, and entering the pilot boat returned to Llanelly.

A quiet passage to Madeira was enjoyed, and on the

2—2

17th of September, after a pleasant stay of a few days, the " Queen " shaped her course for the far distant land she was bound to. It was not Captain Evans's intention to touch at the Cape. Before they had been months at sea, and having encountered some short but heavy gales, Captain Evans perceived that Cuthbert Gordon was well able to take the command of the " Queen," should any accident happen to himself. He became attached to both young men, but particularly to Cuthbert. There were eighteen men before the mast, all well-chosen hands. Our hero soon convinced the crew that he was a thorough seaman, and that he shirked no part of a seaman's duty. Young Lewellen's health rapidly improved, and there appeared every prospect before the voyage ended, that he would be as well as ever.

It is not our intention to linger on details of the voyage. It will be sufficient to say that the " Queen of the Seas," being an admirable sea boat, weathered several tremendous gales, and was under Cuthbert Gordon's command for five weeks, owing to an accident that happened to Captain Evans, which confined him upwards of a month to his cabin; a tremendous sea striking the " Queen " when lying to, swept the deck, bruising several seamen, and dashing Captain Evans violently against the companion, breaking two ribs, and would inevitably carried him overboard had not Cuthbert Gordon, who had seized a rope, caught him by the leg, and pulled him back, getting some sharp bruises himself. At length, after what may be fairly called a prosperous voyage, having lost neither spars nor sails of any consequence, the anchor was let go in Port Jackson, now called Sydney Cove.

Port Jackson at this period presented a very different aspect to what it does now ; most of the houses were built of logs, and plastered, and thatched ; the governor's house alone being built of stone, and tolerably handsome in appearance.

Whilst Captain Evans was busily disposing of his cargo, to great advantage, the two young men, who had enjoyed the voyage exceedingly, set about seeing all they could find worthy of observation. They were invited to the governor's house, and received every attention from his amiable wife and daughters. Here they became acquainted with a most agreeable person of the name of Hunter, who had formerly commanded a fine ship; was once a master's mate in the royal navy, and delighted in paying attention to officers, when any vessel of war touched at Port Jackson. When he heard Cuthbert's history from Captain Evans, he took a prodigious fancy to the young man, and paid him all kinds of attention; accompanied the two young men into the interior, and showed them the aborigines of the country in their primitive state.

Captain Hunter was an enterprising man, and had discovered some particles of gold in the rivers he explored, though not in sufficient quantities to make any stir, though he was fully persuaded in his own mind that gold was to be had in large quantities. He owned a small fast sailing cutter, in which he made frequent voyages.

"I tell you what, young gentlemen," said Captain Hunter, one morning to our hero and his companion. "You must take a cruize with me to my Island, it is only a run of twenty miles. I will show you splendid shooting."

"Very well," said Cuthbert. "I should like nothing better Let us go alongside the Queen, to get our guns and a few things beside."

"Aye, aye; I'll run you alongside."

Captain Evans was ashore as the Musketo, a cutter of some five and twenty tons, ran alongside the Queen, and the two young men proceeded to take their guns.

"I'll take Tom Darling with us," said Cuthbert to the first mate. "It blows fresh, and Hunter has only two men and a boy with him."

"Do so, Mr. Gordon," said the mate, looking up at a somewhat unsettled sky, "Captain Hunter ventures too much with his little craft."

"Oh, he says there is a perfectly safe anchorage in the island, it will only be a single-reefed mainsail breeze."

"Aye, aye, Mr. Gordon," said the mate. "You fear

nothing; you may run to the island with a single reef, but you won't come back with three."

Gordon laughed, called Tom, who was a great favourite of his, and who was delighted at the idea of the trip, and jumping aboard the Musketo the sheets were slacked and away went the lively craft at a spanking rate.

The little cutter was well manned, lots of ammunition, and plenty, as her captain said, of grog for six days; they did not intend returning till the next day.

"By jove! won't we slaughter the ducks, lads," said Captain Hunter. "I reckon on one hundred and sixty brace, at the least; they are in clouds in the coves of the island." Then looking at the wake the little cutter left behind her, he rubbed his hands in great glee.

"Ain't she a beauty? She walks and no mistake."

"Yes," said Cuthbert. "She is a smart and stiff little craft, and as the Yankees say, I reckon she will have enough of wind to try her by and bye."

"Ah," replied the Captain. "She will show you what she can do."

"Are there any inhabitants on the island?" inquired George Lewellen.

"A family of Indians, who came and settled there some ten months ago. There's plenty of fine fish in the cove, and I am quite sure sheep would thrive well there. I'm thinking of stocking it."

"Stand by there some of you," shouted the man steering, just as Captain Hunter and his guests had descended to the cabin to partake of some refreshment.

"Hallo, what's the matter?" exclaimed the Captain to our hero, and both hurried on deck, which they had hardly gained when a heavy squall struck the cutter suddenly and violently, veering round three or four points at the same time.

Tom Darling had let go the peak haulyards, nevertheless the mainsail gibbed, knocked down the man at the helm, carried away the lee backstay, and broke the gaff into three pieces.

Cuthbert seized the tiller, whilst Captain Hunter and the rest tried to secure the boom. Every moment the gale (for into a gale it turned) increased in violence, the sea already rough was lashed into foam, and flew over the little cutter in showers of spray.

"This will not do, Captain Hunter," said our hero, as the owner of the Musketo came up, shaking himself like a Newfoundland dog. "There's a thick mist rising, and the gale will become a hurricane. You will not be able to make the island, as the wind now stands ; better get a trysail up and either lie to, or try and beat back, if it does not increase."

"It will soon blow over," said the Captain. We are subject to these sudden squalls ; but I'll have the trysail up at once."

With his two men and his boy and Tom Darling, a trysail was hauled up, and with some manœuvering set, and the boom secured along the deck; for nearly an hour, Cuthbert Gordon steering, the little cutter bore it bravely ; but the fury of the gale kept increasing, so that in two hours the Musketo was unable to face it : her sails were split, and the little vessel smothered in the breaking seas, that they threatened every moment to overwhelm her.

"We have nothing for it but to scud," said Cuthbert to Captain Hunter and George Lewellen, as he shifted the helm, and with great skill got the little craft before the gale.

Shortly afterwards they had to cut adrift the boom, and one of the small boats stowed upon deck ; the next moment the mast, which Captain Hunter confessed was already sprung, went over the side in a tremendous pitch the little cutter gave, as she ran down a heavy sea.

Cuthbert thought she would never rise to the next sea, but lightened by the fall of the heavy mast, she drove before the gale more steadily. With knives and hatchets they cleared away the wreck of the mast, saving rigging and the little light gig she carried. They now scudded right before the gale, the night intensely dark, and every now and then a sea would break over the deck, and only that all held ropes secured to ring-bolts, and fastened round their waists they would have been swept overboard.

"I have never encountered in all my voyages," said

Captain Hunter, "a severer gale than this. Luckily, the way we are steering, due east, we are safe from running on any land during the night; in fact, no land save New Zealand lies in our course, and long before we could reach there this gale will break up."

"Well, I hope so," said Cuthbert, cheerfully giving the helm to Captain Hunter's man, "but I fear it will be a long and a sharp gale."

They had managed to set a small boat's sail on the stump of the mainmast, some six or seven feet above deck, which enabled the man at the wheel to steer with more accuracy.

Our hero and his friend Lewellen, though not frightened, were still uneasy ; they knew that Captain Evans would be greatly alarmed, for, even if the gale should cease, in their crippled state, it would take several days to get back to Port Jackson ; there was, however, no help for it, but patience and a firm reliance in Providence.

The little crew were divided into two watches, and towards morning, no signs of the gale abating, Cuthbert and George and Tom Darling went below for a short nap and to change their garments, luckily all having brought a change with them. Gordon and George Lewellen slept notwithstanding the gale, and it was full daylight when they jumped up, put on their jackets and proceeded on deck with Tom Darling to relieve Captain Hunter and his watch.

The gale continued to blow as strong as ever, but with a regular, long, heavy sea breaking at times, and driving the little cutter that floated like a cork upon the summit of the tremendous billows before it.

"We can do nothing else than go before it," said Captain Hunter with a rueful countenance, "and by Jove we have only six days' provisions."

"Oh ! before that period has passed, we may fall in with some ship," said Cuthbert Gordon, cheerfully. "At all events we must husband our stores, and instead of six days, make them last twelve."

Captain Hunter, who was a very jovial personage, and fond of creature comforts, looked serious.

"Take a turn in, captain, and after a nap we will con-
sult your chart, and see where New Zealand lies. The
Musketo swims like a duck."

" Yes, by Jove, she's as good a little craft as ever threw
spray from her bows. It was my fault keeping a sprung
mast in her. If she had a good stick in her she'd face
this gale now."

The watch then turned in. Tom Darling thinking as
little about their really perilous position as a Thames
waterman sailing across Chelsea Reach.

Tom took the tiller, whilst Cuthbert Gordon and George
Lewellen, seating themselves on the companion, gazed
out over the really grand scene before them.

" What a speck we look, George," said our hero to his
companion. " What a magnificent spectacle the ocean is
in its present disturbed state."

"Faith, Cuthbert," returned George, with a smile, " as
far as the picturesque goes it's all very well, but the state
of our larder is anything but picturesque. Whereabouts
do you think New Zealand lies."

" Well," returned our hero, " right before us due east,
I think, about a thousand miles from us. We are running under this bit of canvas fully nine knots, but the
smashing of our compass by the fall of the mast was a bad
job. Apparently the wind blows from the same quarter.
Still it may have shifted two or three points and thrown us
out of our previous course. We shall see by-and-bye when
Hunter shows us his chart."

" It would take us a week to get back, even if the gale
ceased and a favourable breeze sprung up. We have not
a spar left but the bowsprit," said George Lewellen.

" In my opinion," said Cuthbert, "we must make New
Zealand if we can and cut a spar, Captain Hunter says
there is a set of new sails stowed away."

" What a state of terror and alarm," said George Lewellen, " our dear parents and friends would be in if they
could only imagine we were careering before such a gale,
and in such a cockle shell, with only six days' prog."

" Columbus crossed the Atlantic in a much worse boat
than this," observed Cuthbert, " and a half-decked craft

of fourteen tons accompanied him. If we can get ashore anywhere we shall soon get provisions enough with our guns."

"But the natives of New Zealand are a fierce savage race," said George.

"Oh, our fire-arms will keep them off," observed Cuthbert Gordon.

When Captain Hunter came upon deck he brought his chart. After looking at it, he said, "This gale abates nothing of the violence, and the sky looks threatening still."

"It will scarcely cease," said Cuthbert, "till rain falls."

Their stock of provisions was then examined and carefully divided; fortunately, Captain Hunter had put on board a good stock, intended as a present to the Indian family on the Island.

As all things in this world are destined to come to a close, so the gale, the Musketo ran before, blew itself out, but not till the morning of the seventh day. After ten hours heavy rain, the sky cleared and the sea began to go down; this was on the eighth day; two days' provision only remained and no land in sight.

Cuthbert Gordon proposed lashing the bowsprit, the only spar remaining, to the stump of the mainmast, and setting more sail; they were, he considered, to westward of New Zealand, and the islands off that coast, at this period, rarely visited by any ship, excepting some vessel of war, sailing round the world.

"To tell you the truth, Gordon," said Captain Hunter, "I have no fancy for making the coast of New Zealand; I should not like to be made a roast of."

"Neither should I," said out hero, with a smile. "Still, in our crippled state, it will take us fully ten days to make Port Jackson, and a shift of wind would starve us out. Therefore it is a toss up between roasting and starving."

The next day decided Captain Hunter, for the wind returned to the old point, but with fine weather. All the sail they could set was clapped upon the little Musketo, and her course shaped for New Zealand.

"Faith, Cuthbert," said the jolly captain, lifting his

waistcoat, "a few days more, and this will be big enough for a great coat."

Tom Darling was very quietly rigging out a line, having plenty of hooks, so sticking on a piece of objectionable meat, Tom began fishing. With the limited canvas the Musketo carried, she made slow progress upon a wind.

"Thanks!" shouted Tom Darling. "I have him."

All turned to look at Tom's prize. It was a small shark, some four feet long, which was soon on deck, and a blow of a hatchet finished his struggles.

"He's capital eating," said Tom, "especially when the lockers are empty;" and so he proved. There was plenty of wine and spirits on board, but the biscuit and meat were finished. There remained a quarter of a sack of flour; water, they had saved in abundance during the rain. Tom stuck to his fishing, and before night, using pieces of shark for bait, caught five fine fish, and one shark; the latter was killed and cast away.

Birds were then seen, and the next morning, to their great joy, land was discovered right before them, and not more than fifteen miles off.

"Hurrah, my lads!" said Captain Hunter, there's New Zealand. In five hours more we shall be close in."

All on board gazed upon the land they were approaching with intense curiosity; their provisions were exhausted. A strong breeze against them would drive them back into the vast ocean around them; and the look of the weather was far from promising.

The land stretched away to the east and west, far as the eye could reach. As they drew nearer they observed several islands scattered along the coast. Early that morning the beautiful white albatrosses, with black tipped wings, sailed majestically over and after the little cutter, and numerous porpoises passed and repassed them, as if they lay at anchor.

"What a magnificent looking country," said Cuthbert to George Lewellen; "see how covered with evergreens the islands are."

"I wonder if the natives are really cannibals," said George.

"In Cook's voyages, they are described as such; some of the tribes, at all events, eat their enemies taken in battle; but that is no reason why they should feast upon us. We have guns and plenty of ammunition, we need not be delayed here; all we want is a good stick for a mast, and some provisions. Look, what magnificent trees are growing on yonder hills."

They were just passing a very beautiful island, and right before them they beheld an inlet, well wooded on both sides, and completely sheltered from wind and sea by the island, and into this inlet they steered. The water was so beautifully clear that they could see the bottom, though four or five fathoms deep. Shoals of fine fish were swimming along in all directions. This inlet appeared several miles long, and not more than a mile or a mile and a half broad, the bottom fine sand. Up this beautiful sheet of land-locked water they steered for a couple of miles, and then anchored within half-a-mile of the western shore.

"What a lovely cove, George," said Cuthbert to his friend, "and how delightful the climate; nothing near so hot as at Port Jackson, and not a cloud in the sky."

Tom Darling, as soon as the cutter swung to her anchor, commenced rigging out his lines for a meal of fish, and in a very few minutes, a dozen fine fish, the names quite unknown, many with brilliant colours like the mackerel, were floundering about the deck.

As the sun wanted three hours of setting, Cuthbert Gordon proposed to George to launch the gig, and take their guns, and go and get a shot at some ducks, which were flying in all directions.

"Do so," said Captain Hunter, "and take Darling with you; how fortunate our little gig escaped being crushed or washed overboard."

"Exceedingly so," returned Cuthbert. "As yet I see no sign of inhabitants; but a few ducks will be a treat."

Tom Darling, who delighted in all kinds of sport, soon had the gig overboard, and casting in a fowling-piece, jumped in and pushed off; Captain Hunter and his men employing themselves in getting everything ready to get up the stump of the mainmast, so as to cause as little delay as possible.

In the meantime the young men pulled up the cove towards a large flock of ducks, who seemed to be quite unconscious of approaching danger, till fire was opened upon them from three guns, when a vast cloud of wild fowl, of all kinds, rose screaming into the air.

"Come, I see nearly a dozen," said Cuthbert.

"Blow me, isn't this glorious, sir," said Tom, reloading. "This is a fine place to live in. I would not mind having a hut, and a squaw for a wife, on yonder hill."

"Well, it would amuse you for a time ; I mean teaching her English, but you would soon be wishing for a sight of old England, a lazy do-nothing life would soon pall."

Having picked up eleven fine ducks they pulled in for the land, Tom declaring he saw several goats climbing up the cliffs, and true enough, just as the boat's keel touched the sands, Tom jumped out with his gun, and made a rush after a full-grown goat, and two kids.

Cuthbert slipped a ball into his gun and followed, leaving George Lewellen to keep the boat afloat. Tom's gun being loaded with shot, only frightened the goats, but Cuthbert brought down one of the kids with his charge. Tom picked it up with great glee.

"I'm blessed if it ain'tas good as mutton, sir, and quite fat," said Tom, " we can victual our craft easily here."

They were about to follow the goats when a shout from George Lewellen attracted their attention ; he waved his hat for them to return.

Throwing the kid over his shoulder, Tom walked on to the boat, our hero following.

As he approached, George pointed towards the side of the hill above them, and looking up, our hero, to his surprise, beheld three figures standing on a flat rock, some eighty or a hundred feet above them.

It was quite light enough to distinguish the natives ; there was a man and two women. The man had only a cloth round his loins, the women a very short petticoat thickly plaited. They had various coloured feathers in their hair, and all carried spears. When the man beheld our party gazing up at them, he uttered a most uncommon shout, and immediately he commenced a wild dance with one of the women, brandishing their spears, and uttering various cries.

" Well, l'm blowed," said Tom Darling, taking up the kid which he had laid on the ground to look at the natives. " They looks, sir, as if they wanted to frighten us. They baint black, sir."

"No, Tom, the New Zealanders are very far from being black, and it is said the women when young are very comely. Perhaps the antics they are amusing themselves with may not mean anger. At all events let us go back to the cutter, and now that we know there are inhabitants about this inlet, we ought to be prepared ; they have no fire-arms at all events."

" You see we shall have visitors," said George Lewellen, as they pushed off the boat. " I wonder they did not come down to us : they are gone back into the wood."

" I suppose the sound of our firearms attracted their attention," returned Cuthbert, " to-morrow we shall see more of them."

" If they try to prevent us cutting a tree it will be a bad job, Cuthbert," said George.

" There's a handsome brass four-pounder in the hold of the Musekto," said Tom, " carriage complete. I daresay Captain Hunter keeps it for firing salutes ; a shot or two from it would make them scamper in double quick time."

"I do not know that, Tom," said our hero, "they are said to be a very fierce, warlike race, but no doubt we may deal amicably with them."

Captain Hunter was in high feather when he beheld the ducks and the kid.

"Come, Mr. Gordon, that's cheering, we'll broil a few of those fellows for supper, we have not had a blow out for these ten days," and the ducks' feathers began to fly about in all directions. Living six days on half a pound of flour each made into cakes left plenty of room for a more abundant supply, and that night there was a choice banquet on board the Musketo, for Captain Hunter produced a keg of sound rum from his store.

"We will get my brass four-pounder up to-morrow," said the captain, looking quite happy after finishing a fine duck for his individual share. "They may talk of hanging ducks for a fortnight to make them tender, that's all my eye. Just fast five or six days and put a brace of roast ducks fresh killed under a fellow's nose, he'll tell you whether they require hanging or not; by Jove, they were as tender and young as chickens. But talking of the four-pounder, just mix a second tumbler, and I'll tell you how I got it."

The little cabin of the Musketo was an exceedingly comfortable one, and for a thirty-ton craft a large one. It had six berths, and a man of six feet could stand up, and have six inches to spare. Filling their glasses, and drinking the healths of all dear to them, Captain Hunter, as happy as a king, and happier, as kings go now-a-days, lit his pipe and commenced—

"About three years ago there was a fine American brig wrecked about two and twenty miles from Port Jackson in a reef some six or seven miles from the coast. Every soul perished from their own fright or want of presence of mind, for when the fog cleared off there ,was the brig with her masts standing, and her bows and part of the deck dry. When we heard of this in Port Jackson, the governor ordered out the government cutter to go and see, and save life and property if possible. I started also, with a crew of the little Musketo to assist; but we had no sooner come up with the wreck, than we observed a small schooner actually alongside plundering. She saw us, and made sail; she was full of men, so the Wasp gave chase, for they recognised her crew as a notorious set of wreck plunderers from ————. The water was so smooth that I got up alongside, with three or four feet of water to spare. Her deck was dry to the mainmast. Lying turned over on the deck was the brass 4-pounder they had evidently been firing to attract attention. We bundled this into the Musketo, and were making preparations to see what her cargo was, when we observed the vessel to have motion, and looking up we perceived a swell of ground-sea setting in, and so rapidly did it increase that

we had to rush aboard the Musketo, and east off for fear
of striking. There was very little wind, but so wonderfully did this ground-swell increase that the brig began to
roll desperately, and old Peters, a pilot said to me, ' We
shall have a heavy gale before night, and had better make
the best of our way back ; this is the highest spring tide
for the year. There will not be a vestige of the brig by
sunset.' By Jove, just as he spoke a tremendous roller
broke over the brig. The next instant she was swept off
the reef into the very deep water on the other side, gave
a heavy lurch, and down she went. We cracked on all
sail for port, and, by Jove, just made it, for a tremendous
hurricane set in just as we rounded the point, and we drove
across the harbour to our anchorage with such violence
that our cable when we let go, parted, and running, we
went foul of a bark, who slipped a hawser aboard us, or
we should have made a mess of it.

"The Wasp was driven into a bight some sixty miles
from the reef, and the schooner was wrecked further down
the coast, and the plunder they had taken out of the hold
scattered over the rocks. What became of her crew, was
not known. The Wasp did not reach Port Jackson until
seventeen days after her chase of the schooner. So the
brass 4-pounder remained with me ; I bought it, claiming
the salvage, but, to this day, we never heard of the owner
of the brig. She was known to be an American and that
was all."

" Come, spin us a yarn, Mr. Gordon," continued the
captain, " it's jolly. Let us have something about your
midshipman's life. You mids are everlasting meeting adventures, or getting into scrapes ; but you are a gallant
lot of young fellows, and here's your health. May you
never have a worse supper than this ! By Jove, we were
nearly in for a starve."

"Providentially we were saved the trial," said Cuthbert
Gordon, " and now, as you wish it, I'll spin you a yarn,
and show you how a fine frigate was all but lost, and only
saved by the gallantry and courage of her captain.

"I was about fifteen years old at the time the occurrence took place, and was then midshipman aboard the

Magician. She was commanded by as brave and gallant
an officer as any in the service. We were working
through the Straits of Malacca, the wind falling, and the
current being strong, the anchor was let go for the night
in a sheltered bay, not many leagues from the town of
Malacca. In the morning it was still calm when twelve
or fourteen large prows full of Malays were observed from
the look out, trying to steal out between a small island
and the main. Our captain said that they were pirates,
and a shot was fired to attract their attention, or at least
to let them know they were seen. At the same time two
or three of our boats were lowered and manned, but as
soon as the sound of the gun reached the crew of the
prows, six or eight of them immediately altered their
course, and pulled right for the frigate. They were full
of men, but not the slightest attention was paid to their
numbers, as all aboard naturally thought that our captain
was mistaken, and that they were merely the country
boats going on their own coasting trade. They arrived
alongside just a short time before the men were about to
take their dinners.

" Why I cannot say, but our captain allowed them to
come alongside, and permitted a number of them to get
on board. Their boats were then dropped astern, and the
ship's company were piped to dinner. They are a well-
built race of men these Malays—slender at the waist and
ankles, their complexion tawny, with long black shiny
hair. They are an adventurous race, passionately fond of
war ; but, at the same time the most treacherous and
ferocious in existence. It seems but little attention was
paid to these men who crowded our deck. The men
went to dinner, the officers were in their cabins. I know
I was below with Middleton,—he joined us after you left
us, George ; he was a fine young fellow, full of spirit and
daring—besides Middleton there was Eccles, the master's
mate, and two other midshipmen. We were all occupied as
suited us best, and little dreaming of the fate intended us.
Middleton said to me, ' I know our captain thinks these
Malays are pirates ; he has some project in his head or he
would not keep the rascals aboard, and their boats alongside,

"'Perhaps,' said I, 'he wants to lure the rest of them alongside. Who's on deck now?' The quarter-master, third lieutenant, and mate of the watch.'

"'What's that?' said Middleton, and he sprang to his feet, seized a cutlass from the rack, and was rushing up on deck. I seized another, and luckily stuffed a brace of loaded pistols into my breast, for it was no mistake there was something wrong on deck. I followed close on Middleton's heels; but no sooner did he reach the deck than he was stabbed by several Malays, and pitched back through the hatch, knocking me down the flight of steps, and, of course, I upset those following me.

"'Good God,' I exclaimed, as I regained my legs; 'Middleton is dead.' A tremendous noise—shouts, cries, fierce yells, and shrieks, and shots sounded from the deck. Again I rushed up the stairs, this time with a cocked pistol in my hand, and, as I leaped out two Malays made cuts at me with their terrible creeses; but the foremost I luckily shot dead, and then made a rush for the quarter-deck, escaping by a miracle. The Malays knew all the boats had got on board. The sailors were hurrying up from all parts, having seized pikes, cutlasses, and tomahawks. The first lieutenant was lying dead, with seven or eight men scattered round him. Just as I leaped over the body and got on the 'quarter deck,' the captain rushed up from the cabin, armed with a heavy sword. He was a very powerful man, and calling on his officers and men to throw the rascals into the sea, he leaped in amongst them. Five of the officers, myself included, followed; and one of the most frightful hand to hand encounters took place you can imagine. I am satisfied had our captain fallen we should all have been slain, so ferociously did these pirates fight. They gave no quarter, and asked none. But the captain hewed a lane through these tawny fiends till he joined his men, then, with a cheer he set on them and cut them down by the dozen. Numbers leaped overboard, some got into their boats and cut them adrift, others were drowned.

"At length our decks were cleared; but what a spectacle—four of our officers and fifteen men lay dead, cut and gashed in a fearful manner. Above fifty Malays lay stark and stiff, not one wounded man amongst the lot. Furious at our loss, fire was opened upon the retreating boats ; the guns loaded to the muzzle with grape and canister. Four of the boats were blown to pieces, and their crews, wounded and mangled, were drowned.

"I shall never forget that morning ; the decks were slippery with blood, and scarcely a man amongst us but had gashes and stabs. I had three, and could scarcely move. To add to our confusion, the men said these creeses were poisoned, but as only two men died of their wounds that could not be the case. I was a week or ten days before I could leave my hammock. We all knew that our lives were saved, and the ship rescued, by the extraordinary courage and strength of the captain. It appears that the Malays on board, then twenty or thirty contrived to make some signal to those in the boats. Those of the crew on deck were quite heedless to what was going on, thinking nothing of twenty or thirty half-armed Malays ; but with wonderful courage and dexterity they contrived to draw their boats under the frigate's quarters, and in a few minutes full two hundred of these fiends were on our decks. Thus, you see, in less than twenty minutes this fine frigate might have been taken, and her crew murdered by these daring and ferocious pirates." *

"You forgot one thing, Cuthbert," said George Lewellen, looking affectionately into the animated features of Gordon.

"What was that, George," asked our hero.

"Why," returned young Lewellen, "that the captain, be-before all the officers and men, shook you by the hand, and said he owed his life and the safety of the ship to your coolness and courage."

"Now, Mr. Gordon," said Captain Hunter, grasping our hero by the hand, " you are as modest as you are brave ; here's your health and glory to you."

"By jove Captain Hunter, if we go on drinking healths your stock of rum will be exhausted, and recollect we have a long run to make from here to Port Jackson, and I think I can safely assert there's none to be had here, so let's be off to bed,"

* The ship's name was the " Samaray."

CHAPTER IV.

THE next day all on board the Musketo were on the alert. They hoped to be able to get the stump of the mast out, and before evening saw down a pine to replace it. They also looked out for a visit from the natives, and for fear of accidents the 4-pounder was hauled up upon deck, thoroughly cleaned, and ammunition hunted out. Some bags of broken iron, used as ballast, were found, and several balls, two bags of good powder, and a bag of blasting powder completed their stock.

Whilst working away at the stump (not a very easy job, as they had no shears), the inlet appeared like a beautiful lake, covered with wild fowl. The woods looked lovely, and as the sun cleared the hills it threw a flood of gorgeous light upon those opposite, whilst the shadows of the wooded cliffs under which the Musketo lay, offered a strong contrast to the brightness and beauty of the opposite shores.

Suddenly two canoes were seen approaching the cutter, coming from the upper end of the inlet. All ceased work to watch them. As they came nearer, those in the Musketo could see that one of them contained four nearly naked Indians; the other, two Indians, and two women and three children.

"Well," said Captain Hunter, after a steady look at them through his glass, "there's nothing to fear from these, five are women and children, and I must say with remarkably scanty clothing; however, the climate is warm enough to do with less."

" By Jove, one is a very young and handsome girl," said Cuthbert, after a look through the glass, and the other's a comely woman; as to the children, they're not troubled with any kind of clothing."

"There's no money thrown away upon tailors, at any rate," said Tom Darling to a comrade.

As the canoes approached the cutter, the Indians all stood up, and whether intended as a friendly cheer or a shout of defiance the crew of the Musketo could not say, but it was a yell of a most discordant kind ; besides yelling, the men all brandished their spears, using the most violent gestures.

" Well," said Captain Hunter, " they may yell as much as they please, but I shouldn't mind fighting the lot by myself."

" We'll pepper their jackets, sir," said Martin, one or Mr. Hunter's crew, " if they prove saucy."

" Well," laughed Tom Darling, " you may pepper their hides, but blow me if you'll hurt their jackets."

Having yelled and gesticulated till they were or ought to be hoarse, the canoes paddled quite close, and then both parties took a good look at each other, the three children jumping into the water tumbling and diving, and standing on their heads like ducks, and quite as much at home in the water, as those web-footed birds.

The men were tatooed in a remarkable manner, over the face, arms, and breasts ; they were tall and well-shaped, and had features resembling Europeans. The youngest of the two females Cuthbert thought singularly pretty and interesting, and evidently not more than sixteen or seventeen with jet black hair, neatly tied up with a bunch of red feathers in it. Their only attire, a very short petticoat like a Scotchman's kilt. The young girl would have positively been beautiful, but that her face was daubed with red paint. All on board the Musketo made the most amicable signs to them, and the Indians on their part held up some fine fish, and two young kids, and some fresh meat that looked like pork.

" What shall we barter with ? " said Captain Hunter to our hero. " They seem inclined to be agreeable, and by jove the women are decidedly good looking, only their faces want washing."

" Have you any glass bottles, or broken pieces of looking-glass, or pieces of iron ? " asked Cuthbert ; " they will take those kind of things eagerly."

The next moment the canoes paddled alongside, and the

whole party, men, women, and children, jumped on to the deck of the Musketo.

As the elder woman passed Tom Darling, she said something in her own language, and looked very hard at him.

"Come mong vous porte vous," said Tom, making a bow, "now give us your flipper."

The woman saw Tom offer his hand, took it, and drawing him close, rubbed her nose against his, leaving him with as red a nose as herself. Tom laughed, but retreated from a second salutation.

Sundry glass bottles were produced and pieces of iron, which they eagerly grasped, giving in return all the fish and meat. The whole party, excepting the young girl, then executed a most singular dance, much to the admiration of the Musketo's crew.

Cuthbert and George Lewellen felt quite a lively interest in these proceedings, for the young Indian maid greatly attracted their attention. She stood quite still, gazing upon all the crew of the little cutter, till her gaze became fixed upon Cuthbert and George. After a moment she came up to them, and taking the beautiful crimson feathers from her head, she divided them, and with much grace of manner she placed one half in Cuthbert's cap, saying something in her own dialect, the only words Cuthbert heard, or could remember, was Matoo Patoo, which he supposed was the maiden's name.

This distinguished mark of the pretty Indian's favour, caused some merriment amongst all parties.

Cuthbert returned the compliment by kissing the Indian maid on her forehead, where there was no paint. Then commenced another dance round Cuthbert and the young Indian girl.

"By Jove, Mr. Gordon, you're the accepted lover of this handsome Indian. I wish we could manage to express our wishes and wants."

"I will try what I can do," said Cuthbert Gordon, "with the young girl. If her intelligence is half as bright as her eyes we shall do."

To the great surprise of our hero and all aboard, the

young girl laughed, and looking with a pleased expression of countenance into Cuthbert's features, she said, "Matoo Patoo talk little English."

"By Jupiter, how lucky and how strange," said Captain Hunter.

Cuthbert Gordon was surprised, but greatly pleased. "How have you learned English, Matoo Patoo?" he inquired.

"Matoo Patoo talk little English, but she know what you say. More better."

Captain Hunter had dived down into the cabin and soon returned with his bottle of rum and a glass. The Indians, even the children, surrounded him, making all kinds of gestures to express their delight, and suiffing and twisting their noses in a strange way; they evidently knew what rum was. They all had a glassful except Matoo Patoo. She smiled, shook her head saying, "No rum, no rum for Matoo Patoo."

Cuthbert Gordon then explained, speaking slowly to Matoo Patoo, how they had lost their mast, and that they wanted to cut another from the trees ashore.

She explained this to the men, and they replied at some length ; then the Indian girl (we shall cease giving Matoo Patoo's broken English for the future, as the young girl, though she rapidly caught what was meant in speaking English, found it difficult to explain herself without signs and a mixture of dialect.) The Indian girl said that if they came ashore, they would be assisted in getting whatever they wanted, and that her people, who lived up the inlet some three miles would be kind to them, and that her grandfather spoke English better a great deal than she did, and was once in England with Captain Cook, and she learned the little English she knew from him.

Our hero and Captain Hunter and George Lewellen were greatly interested, and Cuthbert Gordon told Matoo Patoo that they would visit them early the next day. He then went down into the cabin and brought up a small pocket mirror, and gave it to the Indian girl, who looked delighted with the gift. Several clean glass bottles and pieces of iron were then given to the men, and a bead necklace to the elder woman, which delighted her beyond measure; the necklace and several other trifles were intended for the Indians in the island they failed to reach, as presents from Captain Hunter.

After a variety of salutations, rubbing noses included, a ceremony which greatly amused the visitors—the Indians entered their canoes and paddled away up the inlet, and were lost sight of, round a bluff projecting rock.

"By Jupiter, Mr. Gordon, we are in luck," said Captain Hunter. "We have stumbled upon the very spot suitable to relieve our wants, and a friendly family of Indians."

"But how thinly inhabited this part of the coast must be," said George Lewellen.

"Most likely," said our hero, "their villages may be for the most part, inland. Captain Cook, as well as I remember, says all the young and handsome women in New Zealand are coquettes, and that their complexions are very little darker than the Spaniards in Mexico."

"By Jove, that Matoo Patoo is a specimen," said Captain Hunter. "You saw what an eye the girl had, she selected you at once; faith you must take care of yourself Mr. Gordon."

Cuthbert laughed. "Oh faith, you may laugh; but I will tell what happened to a young friend of mine at Madagascar. The Black Queen there, who is or was a cannibal, took a prodigious liking to him; he was a tall fine looking youngster; he was my first mate, at the time I commanded the Sylph brig, and by Jove, she sent a party of natives and seized him, to take him to her residence. By great good luck I was returning to the brig after some hours, hunting in the wood with eight of my men, and came across the blacks carrying off William Jones, and rescued him. I saved him from becoming King of Madagascar, and very probably when the Queen got tired of him and was looking out for another husband she would have had him roasted and served up for her own and her new spouse's supper. You may all laugh my lads, but what I tell you is a fact, so now let us get this stump out, and to-morrow we'll cut down a stick and turn it into a mast."

The next day the little boat was loaded with tools, a sail for making a tent, and with fire-arms, Captain Hunter, Cuthbert Gordon, George Lewellen and Tom Darling and one of his shipmates, pulled away up the creek to look for a good spot to make the mast, after they should select a stick. They did not intend pitching their tent out of sight of their little vessel, on board which remained one man and a boy.

Selecting a nice sheltered spot under a bank, above which were numbers of straight beautiful pines, all fit for their purpose, the party commenced cutting down some slight straight firs, with which they soon made a comfortable tent. Cuthbert Gordon and Lewellen, then taking their guns proceeded up the creek to look for ducks and kids, and to see if they could find Matoo Patoo's residence.

"I tell you, George, what we want greatly," said our hero, "some substitute for bread or biscuit. I wonder what the Indians use?"

"They may have yams," said George, "but there go several kids," and raising his gun he brought down one, and Cuthbert Gordon another.

Leaving their game where they lay, the two young men wandered on for a mile or so, and turning the bluff rocky head, they perceived that the creek narrowed exceedingly, and that the country on each side was fine pasture land; and further up the creek they traced several habitations amongst a fine grove of trees, and several canoes afloat upon the calm water of the creek.

"You see, George, that they do grow some kind of root, and how very well they cultivate the land. Ho, here comes some of the inhabitants, six or eight, and Matoo Patoo amongst them."

There were four men and four women. Matoo Patoo came on, and with a pleasant smile welcomed them to their village, and instead of rubbing noses, she presented her forehead to Cuthbert to kiss; the other woman doing the same.

"So, Matoo," said Cuthbert, with a smile, "you have rubbed off all your paint."

"Yes," said the Indian girl; "you don't like paint and grease."

"No, in truth, Matoo," said Cuthbert; "it spoils your pretty cheeks. Are you taking us to your grandfather's?" Only two of the women stayed with them, the rest went on, Matoo said, to see the place where they landed, and to help the cutter's crew to carry the mast when cut down. As they proceeded, Matoo suddenly caught our hero's arm, and pointed to a bird on a high rock, with his plumage bright crimson. Cuthbert at once raised his gun and brought the bird down. Matoo clapped her hands, and ran and picked it up. None of the women seemed at all afraid of the report of the gun.

Matoo brought the bird, and selecting two of the beautiful tail feathers, put them into Cuthbert's cap, and two into her own abundant glossy hair. The other Indian women laughed and said something in their own language, and one of them, a comely girl, took some of the smaller feathers and gave them to George Lewellen, but did not put any into her own hair.

"What did your companions say, Matoo," asked Cuthbert, "when you put those feathers in my cap?"

Matoo Patoo looked serious, if not sad. "Why do you ask," said she.

"Because," returned Cuthbert, "I am sure it means something, giving me those feathers."

"Giving you the feathers means nothing, except that we are pleased; but when I put the same number of feathers in my own hair it meant something, and my companion said—"

"What!" asked our hero, seeing the girl hesitate.

"That a great chief's intended," said Matoo, looking down, " could not have another." She hesitated, and then said—

"Love."

" Come," thought Cuthbert, " these New Zealand women are coquettes, and dangerous ones, too." But he wronged the gentle Matoo Patoo, as our future pages will prove.

As they approached the houses there came towards them a tall man, much more clothed than any of the other natives, and carrying in his hand a very old English musket ; and as he met Cuthbert and George, he held out his hand saying—

" How you do, sar—very glad see you in my house."

The two young men shook the old man's hand heartily, and complimented him on his speaking English, and how glad they were to hear their own language so far from home.

He then conducted them into his dwelling, passing a good number of women and children, who were anxiously regarding the strangers.

The old chief, who called himself Hanygahewra Matoo, was Matoo's grandfather. The dwellings of the chief's people were scattered over the side of the summit, covered with a magnificent wood, with a beautiful clear stream of water running down the side of the hill, and emptying itself into the creek. The house of the chief was composed of logs and roofed with a magnificent species of flags, and thatched much after the English fashion, only crossed and recrossed with strong reeds as thick as a man's wrist. Matoo Patoo and another woman anxiously prepared a table on which they placed yams, roast dog's meat, and a very strong drink, extremely agreeable to the taste. Whilst Matoo Patoo was doing the amiable, the old chief laid his musket in a corner, and then Cuthbert asked him how he came to speak English so well.

He said he was the son of Llaneg Yahew, who had sailed with Captain Cook to Otaheita, and that his father was present when they killed that great chief. That he was a little boy at that time, and that he went to England with his father.

On their return home, his father died on the passage to Cape Horn, but the captain of the ship landed him, in that very cove where the Musketo lay, with many presents, and guns, and powder, and ball, trade goods, four sheep, and two pigs ; he there joined his tribe, and finally married and settled in the place where they then were; but the wild fierce tribe on the north side of the hills came and killed Matoo Patoo's father, and most of his people, and all that now remained were about sixty men, women, and children. The old man said the Tolenza tribe were terribly ferocious men, that they ate all their prisoners, for they were afraid the great spirit of the mountain would burn their canoes, if they did not.

Cuthbert Gordon and his companion, after partaking of the things offered them, prepared to depart; and thanking the old chief who promised to visit the cutter, and bring his young men to assist them in getting their vessel masted, they left, Cuthbert saluting Matoo Patoo as he would a sister.

On returning to the tent, they brought three kids and four ducks with them, and Matoo Patoo promised to bring them some yams and poultry the next day.

Captain Hunter had cut down a fine straight pine, so near the size required, that it merely wanted the bark stripped off, and made to fit the cap.

The next day was passed very pleasantly. The old chief came with six men, Matoo Patoo, and two other Indian maidens. They brought their canoes and a great net, and baskets of yams, and pork, and several fowls.

"By Jove! this is jolly," said Captain Hunter. He had anchored the Musketo just opposite to the tent. Lots of fine fish were caught—fires lighted—and a regular feast took place. The Captain producing his keg of rum, and all their little stores such as clasp knives, &c. Cuthbert observed that Matoo Patoo had a kind of vest, besides her short petticoat, and that her sandals were prettily laced up a very well-shaped leg; she wore the red feathers in her hair, and carried a bow and a quiver of arrows, and showed Cuthbert her skilfulness. She shot with her bow, bringing down several large birds at long distances. In the evening the children, and a number of dogs, paid them a visit, and though these last visitors shouted and screamed and the dogs barked and yelled, still they were by no means troublesome.

Nothing could exceed the kindness of this amiable tribe of New Zealanders. What particularly delighted the

Indians was a large iron pot, which Captain Hunter presented to the old chief, to his immense satisfaction, for they had no utensil in which they could boil fish in water. Two or three days passed, and the mast was just ready to haul alongside, and slip the rigging over. A new boom was made, and provisions were stowed away for their adventurous voyage. Our hero frequently passed hours with his friend Lewellen, and Matoo Patoo, who was in truth as innocent as a child, rambling over the country collecting strange plants, and shooting birds with beautiful plumage, which they intended taking back to England with them. They were not afraid of Captain Evans having sailed for England, his stay at Port Jackson was always intended to be three months, and only one month was as yet expired, and before another fortnight had passed over they hoped the Musketo would be safely at anchor in her old berth.

One morning Matoo Patoo and two other Indian girls had paddled out beyond the island in their canoe, but came back to the tent looking greatly frightened.

"What is the matter, Matoo?" asked Cuthbert, as the young girl sprang out of her canoe, "you look alarmed."

"Two war canoes from Tolonga," said Matoo, looking anxiously into Cuthbert's features.

But Cuthbert Gordon showed no alarm.

"Tolonga men, bad, bad men," said Matoo. "What you do?"

"Oh, we will drive them away, Matoo," said Cuthbert, as Captain Hunter joined them.

"Tolonga, Tolonga," cried the two maidens from the canoe, and away they paddled up the inlet.

Our hero and Captain Hunter looked round and sure enough, they beheld an exceedingly long canoe, more than fifty feet long, and full of men, come into view, paddling round the island that blocked the cove from the sea.

"Faith, this looks serious, said Captain Hunter to our hero and his friend Lewellen, "what do you think we had better do?

"Warp the cutter close into this steep bank," said

Cuthbert, "and let us get on board and prepare for them if they are inclined to be hostile."

"Matoo Patoo did and said all she could to induce our hero and the rest to abandon the cutter, and seek safety with her grandfather's people ; but Cuthbert told her that would never do, for if the Tolonga men were bad men, they would burn the cutter ; that they had no fear, and that they could sink the Tolonga canoe, if she came near, and told Matoo to hurry home.

"No," said the maiden, calmly, "I stay ; I know the Tolonga chief, he wants Matoo Patoo for wife. Matoo never be wife to Tolonga chief ; he bad man, eat prisoners." So on board the cutter Matoo would go, for her canoe was gone with the two frightened Indian maidens.

In the meantime, whilst all were getting on board the Musketo, the canoe came rapidly up the inlet, impelled by twelve paddles a-side. When within a hundred yards of the cutter they ceased paddling, and, standing up, they uttered the shrillest of war whoops and brandished their spears in the most frantic manner, uttering frightful yells.

Matoo, who had learned to look through a telescope, said, turning to Cuthbert—

"The Tolonga chief is there ; they are all in their war paint; better fly."

Cuthbert Gordon made light of the fifty Tolonga men. He told Matoo that one discharge from their gun would either put them to flight, or sink the canoe ; but Matoo shook her head, saying—

"Tolonga men never afraid."

The cutter was now warped into a good position, and Tom Darling and Bill Jones had loaded the four-pounder nearly to the muzzle, and all the guns aboard were loaded with ball, and placed ready at hand.

The Indians, finding the cutter's crew paid no attention to their yells and shouts of defiance, paddled within sixty yards, and then recommenced their signs of defiance, and sent a flight of arrows at them, many of which lodged in the sides and bulwarks, and one hitting Captain Hunter on the leg, but having struck a stanchion first its force was spent. The worthy captain snatched up a fowling-piece and fired ; and all could see one of the Indians fall back, wounded or killed.

"Ah," said Matoo Patoo, "they will come."

"Hold your fire now, Tom," said Cuthbert Gordon, " be cool and steady ; just let them come within twenty yards then blaze away. Taking his own double-barrel fowling-piece, he prepared for the contest that it was now very evident could not be avoided.

CHAPTER V.

On came the war canoe full speed ; those not employed paddling, hurling stones, spears, and arrows at the cutter, but sheltering under the bulwarks as they saw the Indians prepare to shoot, the crew escaped being hit. Gordon's first thought was, that the arrows might be poisoned ; but Matoo told him the Tolonga's never poisoned their arrows, for they ate their prisoners.

"Remarkably pleasant enemies to fight."

"I hope I may be killed, sooner than become a captive to those wretches," said George Lewellen, shuddering.

"Now," said Captain Hunter, to our hero, starting up, " now Tom Darling, stand by. Do you, Mr. Gordon, point the gun."

The 4-pounder was loaded with musket balls, small bits of iron, and some rusty nails, there being half-a-dozen bags of the latter on board the Musketo.

Bang went the gun, and being well directed, the shot scattered death over the canoe, killing several, and wounding double as many. With furious yells and screams of rage, the Tolonga men pulled rapidly back out of shot, but still uttering defiance.

" Haven't the beggars got something to tickle their

brown hides," exclaimed Tom, as all hands hurried up some more nails from the hold, and a four-pound ball.

"Cram in the ball, Tom," said our hero, "we'll sink her next time."

Just then Matoo caught his arm—

"Two more Tolongo canoes," said the maiden; "come, let us all go."

"No, Matoo," said Cuthbert Gordon; "but you must, you can easily reach your people before a fresh attack; we must fight it out to the last; we cannot, must not, lose our little vessel."

"No," exclaimed Matoo; "I stay; I may save you yet."

Cuthbert did not or could not understand what she meant; but there was no time to lose, for the two boats had joined the other, and all three, with cries of vengeance, and frantic yells, paddled together to board the cutter.

"It's a bad job, Cuthbert," said George Lewellen; "there's over a hundred of those dark fiends; our case is hopeless."

"Never lose hope, dear George; with God's blessing we'll get out of this scrape yet. Take steady aim when you fire, and pick off a chief; you'll know them by their feathers."

"If we cannot drive the devils off," said Captain Hunter, "mind, my lads, we must get on land and make a running fight of it to the village, we can jump ashore as the tide now is."

This was a serious moment for the crew of the Musketo, with only six men and a boy, and over a hundred furious Indians to contend against. But not one lost heart.

The large canoe led with a diminished crew, the other two close after; a bad form of attack luckily for the Musketo's crew, for had they separated and attacked on both sides at once they would surely have massacred them all.

Before the four-pounder was discharged the Indians in the canoes lost several of their comrades by the fire from the fowling pieces, which increased their fury and excitement. They did not now stop to discharge their arrows or spears, but on they came. The cutter, it being high tide, was hauled in by the shore warp, close to the perpendicular bank, so that the crew could leap ashore from her. As the large canoe came within fifteen yards Tom Darling put a match to the loaded gun, the next moment beheld the large canoe with its side knocked out, and all its wounded freight in the water, where the dead and the injured for an instant floated. Many were desperately wounded in the other canoes, and yet, regardless of all, so frantic was their desire of vengeance, that without stopping even to pick up the wounded, they rushed alongside.

Active and powerful, Cuthbert Gordon and Tom Darling each armed with a hatchet, defended the cutter to the last. George Lewellen and Captain Hunter, both hurt from spear wounds, could only do their best to help. As to the poor boy, he leaped overboard and ran away.

The next instant some thirty or forty Indians gained the deck, Matoo Patoo seized Cuthbert by the arm and prevented him from slaying a tall, ferocious looking Indian with a crimson plume fastened to his head dress. Matoo Patoo and Cuthbert Gordon were now alone on the deck of the Musketo. Captain Hunter, George Lewellen, and the rest of the crew were driven over the side by the rush of the Indians, and thinking Cuthbert slain, and in despair, knowing the utter madness of attempting to regain the deck from the banks, made the best of their way to the old chief's village. In the meantime Cuthbert Gordon stood, hatchet in hand, surrounded by furious Indians. The young man's tall and powerful form was erect, and defiant as he gazed from one to the other of his frantic foes. But to Cuthbert's intense surprise they all fell back. As Matoo Patoo, with her slight, graceful figure erect, gazed into the Tolonga Chief's face, and uttered some words in her own language, the chief moved his hand and the men dropped their spears. The chief was bleeding from his breast and from the leg ; he sat down upon the companion, and looking into Matoo's face, said something, and then raised his tomahawk and held it towards Cuthbert Gordon. Matoo stamped with her foot, and uttering some rapid words, she made some strange gestures with her hands.

The Tolonga chief thought for a moment, playing with his terrible weapon, but at last he looked up, took a red feather from his strange head dress, and gave it to Matoo, she took it, and taking one from her own hair, gave it to the Chief. He then nodded his head, Matoo then approached the surprised and attentive Cuthbert, and looking down upon the deck, she said : "Go, your life is spared—go," and then without a look she turned round and sat down beside the Tolonga Chief.

Cuthbert, though he partly understood this strange scene, for a moment hesitated ; he saw the eyes of the chief glare upon him, and the wild, fierce savages round him seemed waiting for a sign or a word to fall upon him and slay him. Matoo did not even look towards him ; so walking calmly across the deck, he leaped ashore upon the bank, saying as he passed the Indian maiden :

"Farewell, Matoo, I can never forget you or the sacrifice you have made to save my life."

Whether the Indian girl understood all he said or not he could not tell, she remained as motionless as a statue. No sooner had he reached the bank than the Indians set up the most horrible outcries and yells, and then began a dance round their chief and Matoo, striking their spears and dashing their clubs upon the deck, and then began the plunder of the Musketo.

Immersed in thought, Cuthbert Gordon pursued his way along the shores of the inlet after his comrades ; the projecting rocks jutting into the inlet, shut them from his sight, but quickening his steps, he passed the rocks, and then beheld his friend Lewellen and Tom Darling, and half a dozen friendly Indians from the village coming towards him.

As soon as they recognised Cuthbert Gordon they raised a joyful cheer, and George Lewellen and Tom Darling ran towards him.

"Oh, Cuthbert, I thought you were slain when I saw you fall ; at the same moment we were all hurled overboard by the shock of those ferocious Indians. Poor Hunter can scarcely walk; he has a spear head in his side.

There is not one of us without gashes and spear thrusts. But where is Matoo Patoo ? ”

Tom Darling expressed his delight at our hero's escape ; they were all proceeding to see if a remote chance existed of his being a prisoner in the hands of the Tolonga Indians. The old Indian chief and all the females and children were fled to the caverns in the hills, and Captain Hunter was in a state of distraction about Cuthbert, lamenting his own folly in having induced him to accompany him in his mad excursion.

As they proceeded to the village our hero briefly related what had occurred.

“ I fell,” he said, “over the body of an Indian that I had slain.   Matoo had in some strange way saved my life, and she remained with the Tolonga chief, who was a remarkably fine looking Indian.   In fact, I imagined that the Tolonga Indians had come purposely to carry off Matoo Patoo, to make her the wife of the chief, and probably she had consented to his wishes on condition that he would spare my life, for otherwise I must have been sacrificed.”

“ Poor Matoo,” said George, mournfully, “ what a pang her generosity and devotion must have cost her.”

“ Yes,” returned Cuthbert, bitterly ; “ and I possess no earthly means of rescuing her from a fate I know she abhors, for we are far too few in numbers to attempt her rescue.   What we are to do now, I know not.   We have lost all our fire arms, and no doubt they will burn the cutter after plundering her.”

George Lewellen, far more gentle in spirit and feelings than Cuthbert, looked the very picture of despair, and his thoughts reverted to his home and Lucy Gordon, and the tears rose in the young man's eyes as her bright lovely features rose like a vision before him, and there he was in a wild savage land, condemned perhaps to linger years amongst a savage tribe of Indians.

On entering the old chief's residence, they found Captain Hunter reclining on a very rough couch, and in considerable pain ; but so rejoiced was he to see his young friend Gordon, that he would have jumped up had not Cuthbert restrained him.

" You must let me look at your wound, Captain Hunter," said our hero ; " there may be a piece of their boneheaded spear left in it.   I have often assisted our worthy surgeon in times of trouble, and if it is near the surface I am sure to get it out."

"I am so thankful to see you alive and unhurt.   You are quite right; there is, I am certain, a sharp piece of bone in my wound, for every time I move my body I feel it like a knife.   Old Jones looked at it ; but his sight is not keen enough, and, by Jove, he pokes his pincers in as if they were a toothpick."

The pincers were certainly clumsy ones ; but Cuthbert Gordon, nevertheless, after a patient investigation, pulled out a piece of sharp bone an inch long.

" Ah ! " said the captain, as he looked with great satisfaction at the splinter.   " It wasn't pleasant.   You're a capital surgeon, Gordon.   Now tell me, for I feel easier already, all about our late disaster.   Have the devils burnt the cutter ? "

" I cannot tell," said our hero.   " We have lost all our arms and ammunition, and poor Matoo remains with the Tolonga chief."

He then explained how he escaped.

" By Jupiter, we're in a precious fix ! " said Captain Hunter, ruefully.   " Few ships touch anywhere on this island except vessels on voyages of discovery for scientific purposes.   We may be here for years."

" We might build a craft large enough to cross the ocean to New South Wales," said Cuthbert Gordon, " here, with the tools the Indians possess ; but where are all the inhabitants ? "

" They are so terribly afraid of the Tolonga tribe, that they have retired with everything they possess to the mountain caverns."

" As soon as it is dark," said our hero, " Tom Darling and I will go and have a look to see if they have burned the cutter, and whether they have sailed away from the cove, for having succeeded in carrying off poor Matoo Patoo, I do not see what would detain them here."

Leaving George Lewellen and the rest to keep the captain company and watch, our hero and Tom Darling set out for the place of their disaster. It was a calm, quiet night, with the moon just shewing above the summit of the wooded heights on the other side of the creek. Keeping close under the hill side, they pursued their way till they came to the point. The moon had then risen sufficiently high to throw a flood of glorious light over the whole inlet, making every object distinctly visible. The moment they turned the bluff head Tom sung out in a joyful tone :

" Blow me, sir, if there isn't the cutter high and dry, and safe and sound ! "

Cuthbert Gordon uttered an exclamation of joy. There lay the dark hull of the Musketo, and not an Indian or canoe was to be seen.

" They are gone, Tom. I daresay they have cleared her out ; but thank God if she is uninjured, we shall be all right. The tide will soon be flood "

They had now reached the spot where the tent had been erected ; the sail that covered it was gone.

" How fortunate it was," said our hero, " that we carried the cutter's sails to the hopha or village, or we should be in a bad way. The mast and boom are quite safe, but the tools are gone. Let us go aboard before the tide surrounds her. I wish we had brought a canoe."

Having climbed on board, they perceived that the Indians had completely gutted the vessel, not leaving a warp of any kind aboard.

" I tell you what you must do, Tom, go back as fast as you can, and get Jones and Diggs to help you to bring the great net rope—the anchor and kedge are both here, they were too heavy and awkward for their bark canoes. I will wait here till you return ; we must move her off, for this is the last of the springs, or we shall lose a whole fortnight."

" I won't be long, sir," said Tom, " and I think it would be as well to bring a canoe with us ; the infernal devils have taken our gig, which will be a great loss."

" You are right, Tom ; bring back a canoe and the strongest grass rope you can get."

Tom got over the side just as the tide rippled up to the bows of the Musketo.

It was full three miles to the village, so that our hero could not expect his companion back under two hours; he paced the little deck full of thought. Unlike his friend Lewellen, our hero was not in love, but he thought of his fond mother and sisters, and of their quiet home; he gazed at the silvery planet, whose placed light shining over the tranquil waters gave to the really beautiful a look of divine tranquillity; nought was to be heard but the various calls of the wild birds that covered the water, or flew in clouds here and there. Stretching himself on the deck, for he was tired, and something unnerved by the fatigues of the day, he insensibly in the midst of his thoughts, fell into a profound sleep. How long he slept, he could not say, certainly not more than half an hour, when he was suddenly awakened by a heavy pressure on his chest.

Gasping for breath, he opened his eyes, and made, at the same time, an effort to rise, and then he faced two naked Indians pressing him forcibly down and binding his hands, whilst two or more were performing that operation to his feet.

"Ugh! ugh!" cried the Indians, as he shook them off, and one raised a hatchet, and made a gesture, as if he would slay him, if he stirred, but Cuthbert Gordon had no power to stir, for hands and feet were firmly bound. The six fierce-looking naked savages uttered gutteral sounds, denoting their great satisfaction.

The young captive was furious, first at his own rashness or folly in permitting sleep to overtake him, and next for sleeping so soundly as not to hear the Indians approaching. However, regret under the circumstances was useless; the Indians lifted him up, and carefully lowered him into a long canoe lying alongside the cutter, and getting in themselves they seized their paddles, and rapidly made way for the open sea, but when they came near the island they paddled in shore, and four more Indians got into the canoe from the beach, and then they continued as the sea was perfectly calm, to paddle swiftly along the coast.

The Indians said but few words to each other, but when Cuthbert offered to stir, they struck him with their paddles. There were a great many things in the canoe, evidently plundered from the Muskueto sailors, garments amongst the rest.

Our hero lay stretched along the bottom of the canoe suffering considerably from the small grass rope that confined his feet. His wrists were less tightly fastened, for he was struggling when they bound his hands, and he almost fancied he could burst the cords ; but he thought it prudent to remain quiet, knowing it would be certain death to attempt to free himself.

Just as daylight dawned, a light breeze sprung up, a mat sail was hoisted, and the canoe ran before it for two or three hours, as well as our hero could compute. The savages eyed him, at times, with most ferocious looks. What they intended doing with him he could not imagine ; at times he thought, from their savage looks, that they intended to roast and eat him in revenge for their comrades killed in the fight on board the cutter, but he dismissed this thought with a shudder. Suddenly they lowered the sail, and taking their paddles pulled in shore, for the sound of a gentle surf breaking on a rocky shore was plainly heard, and presently, as he lay on his back, he beheld a high cliff above him. The canoe passed round this, and shortly after was grounded on a soft sheltered beach. The ten Indians leaped on shore, and lifted the canoe out of the water, and then leaving their prisoner where he was, they proceeded up the beach.

Cuthbert left alone at once made an effort to free his hands ; but after exertions that covered his wrists with blood, he found to his intense vexation that the thin grass rope was ten times stronger than he thought. Casting his eyes over the canoe, he perceived the head of a bone spear under one of the benches. The edge was as sharp as a knife, and with a joyful feeling in his heart, he worked his hands against a sharp edge, till two strands gave way ; with a thanksgiving to Providence, he burst the rest; and then with the bone he freed his feet.

Raising himself gently up he perceived that only **half**

the canoe was out of the water ; but the tide was on the turn, and in half an hour she would be left entirely dry; but a grass rope held it to a wooden anchor, high on the beach.   He also perceived that he was in a sheltered bight, for though he heard the sea roar outside, only a slight rise and fall took place in that sheltered cove.   Not one of the Indians could he see from the canoe.   His first thought was to leap out and seek for a hiding place.

But this was at once abandoned.   He next thought of pushing the canoe out and proceed to sea, but he knew well that a single hand could never propel a canoe nearly forty feet long, and the wind blowing fresher and fresher and off the shore.   He then resolved to have a look whether he was on an island.   So, seizing a spear, he leaped out, and climbed up a high rock, and at once discovered that he was on a small island, about a mile from the mainland of New Zealand.   But the next thing he observed struck him with a horrible sensation.   He saw the ten savages preparing a great heap of dry drift wood, and forming a pile, no doubt to burn, roast, and then to eat him.

So struck with horror was he that for an instant he remained stationary.   One of the savages chanced to look that way, saw him, and with a frantic yell raised the alarm.

Cuthbert Gordon leaped down and rushed to the canoe, most fortunately for him, the ground sea had increased exceedingly.   He frantically struggled to launch the canoe, causing the perspiration to run from his face and hands in streams.   Already the screams and yells of the savages as they sighted the canoe and beheld him attempting to launch it sounded horribly in his ears.   His utmost efforts to float her would have failed had not a heavy ground swell came rolling into the cove, and lifted her stern.   With the last effort he was capable of, he shoved her into the water, and leaped in, bleeding profusely from his nostrils with the exertions.   On came the savages, yelling, whooping, and screaming in frantic excitement.

The desperate young man plied his paddle first one side

then the other ; fortunately the run was out of the cove. Still, he was only a few yards out when three of the Indians reached the beach, and dashed in headlong, swimming rapidly after him.   One powerful savage outstripped the other two, and was actually lifting his hand to grasp the canoe, when Gordon struck him with all his force, with his paddle, on the head.   The paddle broke, but the Indian was brained.   He had barely time to snatch up a spear, for the second Indian had seized the gunwale, and would have purposely upset him ; with a thrust of the weapon he forced the savage, desperately wounded to let go, but not till he had nearly severed his fingers with a second blow.   The bark was just then caught by the strong wind, and, despite the immense exertions of the Indians in swimming, drifted, aided by Cuthbert's wildest and most vigorous efforts, out of the cove into the open sea.   With a heavy sigh our hero fell back in the canoe, and lay still and motionless, gasping for breath, so utterly exhausted had he become by his previous fatigue, want of food, and the terrible exertions he had made to float the canoe, and urge it beyond reach of his savage enemies.

CHAPTER VI.

For nearly an hour Cuthbert Gordon lay stretched at the bottom of the canoe, with his eyes closed, motionless, and as if asleep.   The strong excitement for the last twenty-four hours had overpowered him.   The skin was torn off his wrists, and though he made light of it, he had three severe spear stabs in his breast and thigh.   The sharp rocking and rolling of the little vessel aroused him from his stupor.   The sun was shining high in a bright unclouded sky.   A strong breeze swept over the vast expanse of ocean ; but though strong, it was a fine and pleasant breeze for any craft above twenty tons to work against. But for a frail bark canoe, scarcely three feet wide, and nearly forty feet long, there was nothing a single man could do but let her drive before it. Our hero gazed upon the land he was rapidly leaving, which right and left stretched far away till it mingled in the neutral tints of sea and sky. The breeze blew direct from the land, from which he was then about five miles distant. His first care was to take two paddles and lash them to the sharp stern, so that they acted as a fixed rudder by which contrivance the canoe ran self-guided right before the breeze. He then carefully scanned the horizon all round, but not a vestige of a sail could be discerned. Over this vast expanse of water the albatross whirled with its mighty pinions ; the dolphin bared its back of gold as it dashed by and gamboled in the sparkling waters. It was a great and wonderful solitude—one man in a canoe, a speck on the face of the waters, the boundless deep, with no eye fixed upon him but the All-seeing one.

"No sail," muttered the lonely voyager. If it had been as it is at the present day, he would be sure to have seen some stately clipper ship or noble steamer directing its course for the land he was leaving. What a wonderful change two and sixty years have made in those then little known lands. One has become a mighty gold region peopled by tens of thousands; town and cities have sprung into existence, and the wild savage in his haughty nature has been humbled and driven, before the thirsty seeker of gold, to hunt the wild tracts of the interior ; sixty-two years hence, and who can say what that land may be !

"I may die of starvation," thought Cuthbert Gordon, having finished his survey of all around him. "Better so than to be mangled, burnt, and eaten by a set of fiends."

Casting his eyes about the canoe, he perceived a small heap of grass matting in the middle and several garments belonging to the crew of the Muskueto. Turning over the matting, to his intense satisfaction, he found two mat baskets, and four large gourds ; examining the gourds he discovered that they contained water. The tears rolled down his cheeks, for his lips were glued together with thirst. If ever a prayer of thankfulness issued from the human heart that of the solitary wanderer on the ocean uttered one, in deep gratitude to God.

"I must not drink too much," he said to himself, as he paused and put by the gourd. "Oh, how precious is water, what a delicious drink, more delicious than the finest and most potent juice man ever pressed from the luscious grape, but God gave that too ; it's not the use but the abuse of God's gifts that shame us."

Opening the baskets he found they contained yams and a kind of bread the savages make from the fern root —and a small stock of sweet potatoes.

Our hero seated himself in the stern of his frail bark, which, to judge by appearances, and by the brittle material with which it was built, was little calculated to drive over the storm tossed billows of the ocean, yet its very frailness and lightness was its preservation ; it merely skimmed the surface; it was like the foam of the breaker, it flew on before the destructive wash of the crested wave. No billow spent its fury upon it, or it would have crumbled into fragments, and it wafted before the gale like a straw— its fragility saved it from perishing when the stout bark oftentimes would have foundered.

Daylight vanished, not a tint from the glorious sun tinged the waves, the breeze blew fresh, and the small crested wave broke into foam, and on went the canoe ; presently vanished the short twilight, and then countless worlds appeared in the illuminated sphere above, and of which we know nothing. The silent watcher threw himself down, he felt he was alone—alone on the sea, whose waves washed the far distant shores of his native land. Could they, his loved mother and sisters, picture to themselves that he was alone on the deep boundless sea—with no hope but in God ; and the lone one had hope, for he closed his eyes in sleep ; and through the live-long night he slept ; in the morning he awoke, refreshed and hopeful still.

The next day passed, and the next, the same steady breeze, the same cloudless sky ; in vain he strained his eyes to catch a glimpse of a ship's white sail, but no, the ocean was before, behind, on every side; the frail canoe was the only thing apparent on its surface.

He looked anxiously at the sky. No angry cloud obscured its brightness; his water was out that day—he had drained the last drop. That night he felt feverish, for his hope was failing, and he felt, because he knew he had no water, more thirsty than usual. As the night set in, the breeze dropped, and some symptoms of clouds appeared in the west.

"If the wind changes," thought Cuthbert, "and blows direct on the shores of New Zealand, it would take me four days to reach it, and water and provisions are both exhausted. How long," he argued with himself, " can a man last without food or water? if he could get over the fourth day, he would go mad, so I have read."

He laid down, sleep he could not; it fell calm ; what use was the calm to him, he could do nothing. The next day was stark calm, the sky clear, and the rays of the sun scorching hot.

The fugitive had been forty-two hours without food or drink, his lips were glued together, and his forehead clammy—he felt himself raving—he lay down, he tried to pray, he strove to think, but wild visions rose before his eyes ; he beheld all those delusions men suffer under thirst, he would not let himself sleep lest he might jump overboard under some excitement. The morning of the fourth day without food or drink, he fell down in the bottom of the canoe, and pressed his hands, dipped in the sea, to his heated brain—he was still insensible. He remembered calling out aloud, " no, I will not die mad. It's God's will, I'll die, as—" he could not finish his sentence ; but just then a pleasant breeze rushed over the canoe, the first for two scorching days ; it seemed to revive him, he opened his eyes, and at that moment the loud boom of a gun pealed over the deep.

His straining senses heard the sound; he panted for breath, he called upon God to give him strength. He could not rise, but he seized a spear he put his neckhandkerchief upon it and held it up—held it up—but only for a moment, and then dropped it, and waving his hand with a faint smile he shouted, " Boarders away,—once more, and the ship's our own !" and then fell back insensible. That one moment saved his life.

Some three miles from the bark canoe coming before a steady breeze, was a stately frigate, with a cloud of snow white canvas. A crowd of men covered her decks; several officers were pacing the quarter-deck, one with a glass in his hand. The frigate was a Russian man-of-war, on a voyage round the world. The officer with a telescope saw a speck upon the calm waters, for the breeze had not at that moment reached the canoe.

He let his glass rest upon the object.

" Ha," said he to a young lieutenant near him, "there's an Indian canoe, but no one in her. Where could she have drifted from ? It's too much trouble to put a boat out, or alter our course."

" Who knows, sir," said the lieutenant, " but some nearly starved wretch may be in her, driven off some land by a gale."

" Let one of the bow guns be fired. If there is any one in the canoe they will hear the gun, and show themselves. I will keep my glass upon it."

The gun was fired, and the captain of the frigate beheld the momentary signal made by the nearly worn out tenant of the bark canoe.

"There is some one in it," said Captain Bortzoff. "Lower a boat and tow the canoe alongside."

Round went the fore yards of the Russian frigate—the Czarina. She lay to, whilst four men impelled the light boat towards the canoe. In half-an-hour the men reached the object of their mission, and looking in they beheld Cuthbert Gordon apparently dead, but taking the canoe in tow, they soon reached the side of the Czarina, and our hero was carefully taken on board and consigned to the care of the surgeon. The canoe cast adrift, the yards braced round, and again the frigate resumed its course. Fortunately for many connected with our story, the Russian frigate intended touching at several ports in New South Wales ; Port Jackson or Sydney's Cove the first. With judicious treatment, Cuthbert Gordon rapidly regained his senses, and before noon of the following day he was quite able to rise from his hammock, and tell the worthy surgeon in French, the cause of his being alone in the Indian canoe so many leagues from any land.

The next day he was kindly received by Captain Bortzoff and his officers in the cabin of the Czarina. The Russian officers spoke French fluently, and Cuthbert Gordon spoke that language well.

The captain was much interested in his narrative, and showed him every attention and kindness. The sixth day they sighted the high land over Port Jackson, and before night were at anchor in that noble bay nearly fifteen miles in length, forming one of the finest harbours in the world.

Cuthbert Gordon felt such intense anxiety that he could not close his eyes the night they anchored in the bay. In the morning the captain ordered a boat, and after bidding the commander and his officers farewell, and expressing his gratitude and thanks, Cuthbert was pulled up the bay, and entering the inner harbour, beheld, with a feeling indescribable, the Queen of the Seas at anchor in the same place in which he had left her five weeks before.

The astonishment and utter amazement of the mate and crew when they beheld Cuthbert Gordon ascend the side is difficult to describe. Mr. Thomas the first mate, could scarcely believe his senses. Captain Evans was ashore, so after shaking hands all round, and receiving a thousand welcomes, and telling them very briefly indeed what happened, he hastened ashore to find Captain Evans, for his most anxious wish was to get the captain to sail at once for New Zealand, to rescue his owner's only son from a dangerous and painful situation. When Captain Evans beheld our hero he started back, turning pale and red by turns ; but recovering himself as the young man grasped the honest skipper's hand, he threw his arms round his neck, and embracing him, wept like a child.

"I have not enjoyed a night's rest since you left," said the skipper, "no, not one ; and so my worthy generous owner's son is alive and well, thanks be to God ! In two

days I can be ready for sea. What a wonderful interpo-
sition of Providence! My dear Mr. Gordon, you look
haggard and worn, but you will soon pull up. Dear, dear
(he had told the skipper his story), and those cursed cannibals were going to roast you and eat you—and how
nearly starved you were. What escapes you have had!"

"You think you can be ready in two days."

"Yes; the third day we will sail. All the cargo is
aboard, and a very valuable one it is. I purchased two
12-pounders the other day. We have four 8-pounders,
for we may be attacked by a French privateer in the
chops of the Channel. We will now add to our store of
ammunition, and also purchase some articles to barter
with those New Zealand Indians should anything untoward have occurred since you left. Well, well, what
misery that good-natured but hot-headed Captain Hunter
has brought on himself and you all, by his mad cruise to
his island. If I had been aboard you should not have gone
with such unpromising weather as it looked that morning."

"Did you think we were lost, Captain Evans?" asked
our hero.

"Well, I was fearful you were; still, I thought it was
possible you might have made land somewhere, or, if dismasted, been picked up by some passing ship. I never
entirely abandoned hope. When the gale abated, and a
tremendous gale it was, I got the captain of the government cruiser to take a run over to Hunter's Island to see
if any trace of the cutter could be discovered; but, of
course, we came back disappointed. I did not dream you
would be driven as far as New Zealand."

It became a scene of bustle and activity on board the
Queen of the Seas. All kinds of things were purchased,
a large stock of ammunition laid in, for the war with revolutionary France was at this time hot and furious, and
the seas were overrun by her cruisers and privateers.

The Queen of the Seas was a noble ship; had one and
twenty men, for Captain Evans received for the voyage
home eight fine young men, sailors, whose ship had been
wrecked a fortnight before within five miles of its destined port, a misfortune of frequent occurrence in a sailor's

life. Thus, including our hero, there was a crew of thirty men aboard the Queen; four 8-pounders, and two handsome 12-pounders, with a couple of brass swivels on each quarter.

On the fourth day from the arrival of Cuthbert Gordon at Port Jackson, the Queen of the Seas having cleared the bay, squared away her yards, and all under sail, with a fine breeze, shaped her course for New Zealand.

Cuthbert Gordon was now nearly if not quite as well as ever he was, and burning with anxiety to reach the cove where he had left his friends.

Captain Evans and his young friend spent many hours in studying a very fine chart the skipper possessed. It struck the former that there might be some little difficulty in discovering the spot where his friends were; but Gordon said he had taken particular note of the entrance to the inlet, and that to the west of the cove there was a very remarkable island with a singular pyramid of stones, or masses of rocks built on the summit; they had remarked it on first approaching the coast, and looking away to the east they thought they perceived either a great inlet or a strait, cutting the land in two.

"Ah!" said Captain Evans, "it's all right. Here you are," putting his compass upon a channel, marked on the map as "Cook's Sound." "Here, away to the west are several islands, so when we make the Sound we must coast along till you recognize your island."

The fourth day after leaving Port Jackson, they had a heavy thunder storm, and a short gale, more resembling a hurricane, which cost them a few light spars, and the loss of a fore-top-gallant sail and yard. Contrary breezes baffled them for several days, but nevertheless they sighted New Zealand the eleventh day after leaving Port Jackson.

Fortunately the weather now became exceedingly fine and the sea smooth, so that they ran in quite close to land, and the day after made out Cook's Sound; with the wind off land they continued coasting. The next day, Cuthbert, with a shout of joy, recognised the island with the pyramid of rocks on its summit.

"I see," said Captain Evans, "this must be Dusky

Cove, though they do not give that singular pyramid on
the island. There is plenty of water inside ; but it won't
do to run in. We should never get out with a strong
head-wind."

It was early in the day, so the ship was hove to and
the long boat lowered over the side. The skipper, our
hero, and six men jumped in, well armed, and pulled away
for the island.

Our hero felt so intensely anxious, that he could scarcely
contain himself; he could almost hear his heart beat.
Rounding the island, the inlet became exposed to view.
With an exclamation of rage and vexation, he pointed out
to the skipper the charred hull of the Musketo lying on
the sands.

"By my soul !" exclaimed the captain, dismayed, "the
devils have burned the cutter ! "

"Yes," said our hero, considerably startled, " they have.
Still our friends may be all alive and well, either in the
village or with the old chief in the caverns. Let us pull
up to the creek, and land."

This they did, and landing, walked to where the hopha
was, but to Cuthbert's grief and consternation, the village
no longer existed. It had been burnt to the ground.
Captain Evans looked into his companion's anxious face
in blank dismay.

Our hero felt sick at heart, his sanguine nature was
staggered. " They may have fled to the caverns," said he.

"I'm blessed," cried one of the sailors, " if there bain't
one or two of the sooty devils a looking down at us from
yonder rocks. I'll bring down one of 'em in a shake."

"Be quiet, David," said our hero, " those are friendly
Indians ;" and he made signs to them to come down, and
raising his voice, he shouted out the name of the old chief.
The Indians uttered a cry of satisfaction, and at once
came bounding down from the rocky heights.

As they reached the level, they rushed to the side of
Cuthbert Gordon and embraced him after their fashion,
with every appearance of intense gratification. The difficulty was to procure the information required, which could
only be attained by signs. But Cuthbert Gordon, during the

short intercourse with the natives, and particularly with Matoo Patoo, could manage by signs and a few words he had picked up, to understand much of what the Indians meant, for they are extremely expressive in their gestures and pantomimic signs.

After half-an-hour's attentive conversation, Cuthbert made out, filling up gaps by his own quick imagination, that Matoo Patoo had fled from the Tolonga chief the moment she landed in Tolonga Bay. Suspecting that she would return home, the Tolonga chief, with four huge war canoes and two hundred men, came in the night and burnt the Musketo, sacked the hopha, and massacred all the women and children that were then in the village, and carried off the old chief and three women, and six men prisoners, before they could reach the caverns.

Captain Hunter and all the English, after a terrible fight, in which seven Tolonga Indians were slain, were seized and bound to long poles, and in that state carried to the canoes and taken to Tolonga Bay, to their great hopha or town which was strongly fortified by stakes, trenches, and double palisades.

This was terrible news, but still there was hope. Cuthbert made signs to enquire how far Tolonga Bay was from Dusky Cove. The Indians, by pointing to the sun's rising and setting, intimated two days.

This our hero considered must be meant for canoes paddling there, as a ship with a favourable breeze, could easily sail over two hundred miles of coast in that period.

One of the young Indians, a remarkably fine, powerful man, who called himself Outa la Poota, and was brother to poor Matoo, with his comrades had spent several days in the wood, looking for Matoo without success.

After explaining all this to Captain Evans, it was proposed with the skipper's consent, for the two Indians to accompany them on board the " Queen of the Seas," and to point out to them Tolonga Bay. After a time they understood this plan, (for not seeing the ship, they did not comprehend at first), joyfully assented, and having nothing further to detain them in Dusky Cove, they all entered the boat and pulled out to their ship.

CHAPTER VII.

IN order not to pass the bay they were in search of, Captain Evans lay-to all night. The two Indians looked at everything aboard the ship with the greatest astonishment and delight. As soon as the sun rose, they pursued their way along the shore to the westward, under very easy sail, for the breeze was fresh, and numerous islands and several shoals lying in the way, it required care and skill to keep so near the land.

The coast afforded the richest scenery; high hills, deep vales, immense forests, and beautiful sheltered coves and inlets. They saw numerous fishing canoes, but the moment the natives beheld the ship, they seized their paddles, and swiftly sought shelter in the inlets. The "Queen" was sailing under her top-sails, only about six knots an hour, so that as the sun was sinking into his ocean bed, they had sailed full eighty miles along the coast. Just then the two Indians, who were with our hero anxiously examining the land, called out with an expression of wonder, "Tolonga! Tolonga!"

Our hero gazed in the direction they pointed, and beheld a bold and exceedingly lofty headland, apparently the termination of the land, or that the coast then took a sweep to the southward. Round that headland was Tolonga Bay. Before they reached the head it was dark, and there being no moon, Captain Evans resolved to lay-to.

As they sat in the cabin that evening, Captain Evans, taking a document from his pocket and opening it, read it to his friend, who felt surprised. It was signed by Mr. Lewellen, and was to the effect that, should any illness or accident incapacitate Captain Evans from continuing his command of the ship, it was the earnest desire of the owner that Cuthbert Gordon should take the command, and act as he thought fit.

"Thank God, my good friend!" said Cuthbert, laying

5—3

his hand on the skipper's shoulder, "you are in sound health, and have no business out of your good ship. With a dozen of your crew I trust I shall be able to rescue our dear friend Lewellen and his fellow sufferers."

"Who knows what may occur?" said the captain seriously. "Our kind friend, Mr. Lewellen, had forethought. You are scarcely one and twenty, but you have had the experience of a man of forty, and are quite as capable of working this ship as I am; and as to fighting her, much more so, seeing that I never saw a gun fired in anger in my life. If we have to fight to rescue our owner's son, I must, and will lend a hand, and to-morrow I will read this document to the crew, before we enter Tolonga Bay. As well as you have been able to make out, the Tolonga tribe are a very numerous, warlike, and fierce set of savages. We are but thirty in all. Don't you remember how nearly you were all massacred aboard a fine frigate, with a splendid crew by a parcel of Malays? At all events, we are in the hands of God; but it is right to be prepared for difficulties."

As soon as the sun rose, all the hands of the "Queen of the Seas" were assembled upon her deck, and Captain Evans read Mr. Lewellen's letter to the entire crew; then sail was made, and the vessel stood in for the remarkable headland, forming the western head of Tolonga Bay.

On rounding the head they beheld a magnificent deep bay, some seven miles across and twelve miles long, protected from the fury of the sea, and from storms, by two beautiful islands stretching across its mouth, leaving three channels free from rocks or shoals. Scattered over the waters of the bay, were numerous canoes, but as usual, the moment the ship was seen they were paddled towards the shore.

Cuthbert Gordon, with his glass, was reconnoitring the shores of the bay, as the ship, under her fore and main top sails only, carefully pursued her way.

Having sailed three miles up the inlet, Captain Evans, finding the water shoal to five fathoms, brought the ship to, and furled sails. Our hero could perceive a great number of canoes drawn upon the beach, and amongst them four magnificently carved war canoes, apparently over sixty feet long. On one side of the bay, and close where the canoes were drawn up, was a very large Indian hopha, and apparently strongly fortified by palisades; the village was built on a rising ground. Our hero could see great crowds of Indians assembled upon the beach, all armed and all gazing at the ship.

Matoo Patoo's brother intimated by signs that the hopha they saw was the residence of the great chief of the Tolongas, and that it was very strong. He also said that the best plan would be to seize the war canoes; that those great canoes took years to build and carve, and that the Tolonga chiefs would rather sacrifice a hundred men and ten villages than lose these, their greatest ornaments, considered sacred by certain religious ceremonies performed over them. To lose their war canoes was the greatest disgrace a tribe could undergo.

The Indian's idea Cuthbert thought exceedingly good, and not difficult to perform. He then explained what Outa la Poota said.

"By Jove, a very good plan!" said Captain Evans. "We will get possession of the canoes, and then barter them for our friends, trusting in Providence that they are alive and well. How do you think of managing it, Mr. Gordon?"

"With one of your 8-pounders, and ten men in the launch, I will engage to bring them off," returned our hero.

"There are nearly two hundred Indians on the shore where the canoes are," said Captain Evans.

"A shot without ball will send them all scampering," said our hero, "and before they rally we will launch and get the war canoes in tow."

"Take fourteen men with you, at all events," said the captain, "and if you are pursued I can cover your retreat with a shot from a 12-pounder."

The men were all alive on board the "Queen," and eager for their work. The launch, a noble, fine boat, was soon in the water, the 8-pounder lowered and secured on the platform in the bows, and each man armed with a musket and four rounds, and a cutlass, jumped into the boat, and Cuthbert Gordon taking the tiller, they pulled away for the shore. By this time the numbers on the beach had increased, and the side of the hill on which stood the hopha was swarming with women and children. Tom Darling and Jones had charge of the gun, loaded simply with powder.

As they came within three hundred yards of the beach, a succession of terrific yells and war whoops rent the air, and showers of arrows, javelins, and stones thrown from slings were hurled at them, so that our hero thought it time to try their metal, and when within a hundred yards of the canoes "bang" went the 8-pounder, which being rammed exceedingly hard, made a stunning report. No doubt several had been present when the attack upon the Musketo in Dusky Cove was made, and beheld the havoc the small gun then caused. Before the report had died away, the beach was cleared of every Indian; they all made for the blockade round the hopha.

"Now my lads, jump in," said Cuthbert Gordon, "and launch the canoes before they have time to think and to see that no harm was done. Do you load the gun in case of need, but on no account fire unless I tell you ; we must not take life, unless driven to it in absolute self defence."

In a few minutes two of the canoes were in the water, but by this time the Indians, seeing what they were about, and also perceiving that no one was even hurt by the discharge of the gun uttered frantic yells and rushed down the hill, with a fierce determination to save their precious war vessels.

But before they reached the beach, the four splendid canoes were afloat, and the men paddling two of them off towards the " Queen," whilst Cuthbert Gordon with six of the men in the launch were preparing to tow off the other two. Spears and javelins and stones were now dangerous weapons, at such close quarters; two of the men were hit, but not severely, and Gordon received a severe blow in the side from a stone."

"Shall I give it to the beggars ?" cried Tom Darling, smarting from the blow of a bone-headed javelin.

"No, no," said our hero, "it would be a merciless slaughter. We shall be out of danger in a few strokes."

But the Indians, led on by their chief, launched a dozen of the other canoes, and numbers jumping in, they pushed off in pursuit, paddling with might and main to overtake the men in the war canoes, and to board the launch.

The canoes went through the water much faster than the launch towing the two long war vessels ; but just as our hero was in self-defence about to order Tom to fire, a gun from the "Queen" startled those in the foremost canoes, for the ball struck the water, and ricochetting, bounded over the nearest canoe, dashing the water over those in her, to their intense surprise and no little terror, for their first impulse was to paddle back to the shore with the utmost precipitation.

"That was a good and a bold shot of our worthy captain," said Cuthbert Gordon. "He evidently fired only to frighten them. We have the canoes now safe enough."

"I should just like to have given them one dose," muttered Tom ; "it would teach them manners, the sooty devils ! Who knows, sir, but that they have roasted and ate Captain Hunter or some one else by this time ?"

"God forbid !" said our hero, " I do not think that; but to-morrow we shall know, for they will now come to a parley, and try and save their war canoes. To have killed a dozen of them by firing at them so close as we were, might have exasperated them, and in revenge they might have killed their prisoners."

They were now alongside, and Captain Evans congratulated our hero on his success without loss.

" We owe our success to your shot, captain," was the rejoinder. " The Indians were astounded at a ball reaching them from the ship, and making such a splash. Had I fired I must have killed many of them, and I do not think till we know something more than we do that we are justified in slaying these Indians."

" I saw your critical situation," said the skipper, " and guessed you did not like to fire into them, so I tried my hand at a long shot, and faith I did not make a bad one."

"There's a canoe coming out from the shore, sir," exclaimed Tom Darling.

"So there is," exclaimed the skipper, taking his glass, and fixing it upon the canoe. "Four Indians paddling, and one Indian sitting in the stern."

"Come, this looks like business," said our hero. "This is no doubt an ambassador; we shall see what effect your long shot had. That and the loss of their canoes has humbled them. I trust our dear friends are unhurt and well."

As the canoe came rapidly nearer, Cuthbert examined her with the glass, and then uttered a joyful exclamation.

"The Indian sitting in the stern of the canoe," said he to Captain Evans, "is the friendly old Indian chief of Dusky Cove."

"Come, that looks as if all our friends are safe," said Captain Evans.

Outa la Poota gave a great shout of joy when he beheld his old grandfather alive and apparently well. The canoe was soon alongside, and the old chief stood up; but when our hero made signs to the Indians to paddle their canoe close alongside and come on deck, they refused, and the old chief, who looked very serious, said they were ordered by the great Chief of the Tolongas not to go on board the great ship of the white men, but to deliver the great chief's message.

"Are our friends all alive and well?" anxiously inquired Cuthbert Gordon of the old chief.

"They are alive," said the old man; "but the great chief says, if you do not bring the war canoes back before to-morrow's sun is six hours old, he will burn all the white men he holds prisoners; but if the canoes are brought back to the beach where they were taken from, uninjured, the great chief will give freedom to the white men."

Cuthbert Gordon looked at Captain Evans.

"Confound the great chief's impudence," said the skipper; "but what can we do? to attack them might destroy our friends; there is no trusting an Indian's vengeance. The old chief looks serious and disturbed, and does not even exchange words with his grandson; he seems under restraint, and yet it is not likely any of the four Indians in the canoe with him understand him."

"They may have forced him to swear by some religious ceremony of their own," said Cuthbert Gordon, "and the old chief would keep the oath."

"Then what do you think it best to do?" asked Captain Evans.

"Well, I see nothing to do, but comply," returned our hero; "I am averse to use force, for fear our friends might be treacherously slain, and the Indians fly to the woods, knowing we could never follow them there. We can go well armed—the launch, the cutter, and the jolly boat—the launch with a twelve-pounder."

"Yes, we can all go," said the skipper, "there is no fear of the ship."

"There is water," said Cuthbert Gordon, "to drop the ship up a mile nearer the hopha during the night. You, with four men, on the first appearance of treachery, could open fire upon them, and thus secure our retreat, for I am determined to force the stockade if our friends are not forthcoming."

"Well, my dear friend," said the skipper, "let us agree to take the war canoes to the beach, and say when we see our friends delivered over to us there, they shall have the canoes, and a present of various articles besides to induce them to keep their word."

Cuthbert Gordon stated their determination to the old chief. He then spoke to one of the Indians in the canoe, who nodded his head, and then without a word more they paddled back to the shore.

It was a still, calm night, and letting the ship drop up with the tide, just keeping the anchor off the sandy bottom, they came to an anchor within a mile and a half of the hopha.

In the morning all the boats were launched, and the twelve-pounder mounted in the launch. Tom Darling and Jones had charge of the gun, as they had both served four years in a man-of-war.

As soon as the sun rose the beach below the hopha was covered with Indians, and the hill-side also.

Captain Evans and four men remained on board ; they had a warp out, so that the ship could be placed with her broadside to the shore, and two twelve-pounders crammed with grape shot ready for use.

All being ready, the cutter took the war canoes in tow, and the twenty-five men were disposed, so as to act on the offensive, if necessary, and every man armed with a musket, pistol, and a good cutlass. As they neared the shore, the Indians crowded down to the edge of the water, spreading themselves in a long line. They were all armed with spears and bows ; there were neither yells, nor shouts, all were perfectly quiet ; but nowhere on the beach or anywhere could be distinguished the forms of the friends Gordon so longed to see and rescue.

Orders had been given not to approach nearer than twenty yards of the beach. Our hero fully expected to see the chief of the Tolongas and the captives ready to be exchanged for the boats ; but scarcely had they approached within twenty yards or so of the beach, than over a hundred Indians, quite naked and mixed amongst the crowd, threw themselves in the water, diving like so many ducks.

"Back the boats !" exclaimed Cuthbert Gordon, in a loud voice. "Here is treachery."

As he spoke the report of a small gun was heard from the ship, all looked round, and to their intense surprise they beheld advancing upon the ship more than forty canoes, all issuing from an inlet on the east shore. At this sight a yell of defiance was uttered by all those on the shore, and caught up by those on the hill ; and immediately a shower of arrows and spears were aimed at the boats, and simultaneously the Indian divers cut adrift the war canoes, and kept turning and pushing them towards the shore. It was now no use to think of clemency. The men shot several of the Indians towing the canoes, but others replaced them.

Our hero gave the signal, and a discharge of the 12-pounder scattered death and destruction amongst the treacherous Indians on the beach. Anxious to reinforce Captain Evans, Cuthbert Gordon selected only fifteen of the men, determined to attack the hopha and search for his friends ; the rest were sent back in the boats to help Captain Evans, and to request him to run in as close as possible, and turn his guns on the hopha, if he saw a signal hoisted.

Cuthbert Gordon and his fifteen men leaped ashore, Tom Darling having first given the retreating Indians another charge of grape, which sent them howling up the hill on which stood the hopha. Rapidly following on the steps of the retreating Indians, they soon reached the first row of palisades. Here the Tolonga chief made a stand and showed himself, but a volley from sixteen muskets slew several and wounded many before they could do more than hurl a few spears and javelins at them, wounding our hero and four of the men, but so slightly as not to hinder them in the pursuit of their object. The palisades were scaled, and with their bayonets fixed on their muskets they drove the now terrified Indians like sheep before them, wild with fury and savage determination. The Tolonga chief with a party of Indian warriors in war costume, threw themselves frantically upon Cuthbert Gordon and Tom Darling, who were scaling the second barrier, but in doing so the Tolonga chief received his death wound. Our hero's cutlass went through his throat, hurling him back a corpse, whilst the rest of his party, horrified, and finding they could make no head against the bayonet and the terrible cutlass of the white man, fled with the women and children howling in all directions. All this time the boom of the guns from the Queen of the Seas pealed through the air, but where they were they could not see her. A volume of smoke from an inner enclosure, and a bright flame shooting up in the air attracted Cuthbert Gordon, and caused him to break through a circle of huts, and dashing through a double fence of stakes, he beheld a sight that might have paralysed the stoutest heart. Four men were fastened to great stakes driven into the ground, to two other stakes two Indians were bound, their heads down and fastened to the stakes

by the heels, and round them all great piles of dry
wood were heaped, and numbers of women, after setting fire to these piles of wood were flying in all
directions.

At a glance our hero recognised his unfortunate friends
all gagged with rough pieces of wood put across the mouth
and tied round the head.

With one accord Gordon and his men rushed at the piles
of wood, and with their bayonets tossed the blazing
faggots right and left, and then our hero cut down
his friends and comrades George Lewellen and Captain Hunter, and finally the unfortunate old chief of
Dusky Cove, but he was dead—the smoke and flame
had reached him and the Indian suspended by the
heels.

George Lewellen was quite insensible. Captain Hunter,
a strong and powerful man, staggered when released, but
embracing our hero he stammered out :

" Deuced nearly roasted, by Jove."

No time was to be lost, several of the sailors were
wounded, three very severely, and Cuthbert Gordon himself had the head of a spear, the spear of the Tolonga chief
in his shoulder.

Lifting George Lewellen up, and carrying him between
two of the sailors of the Musketo, our hero aiding Captain Hunter, they all made for the beach as quickly
as possible. The firing had ceased from the ship, and
on recrossing the palisades they gave a shout of joy.
There she was, her flags flying. Not a canoe was to
be seen and the three boats pulling for the shore.

The war canoes were floating in fragments upon the
calm waters, and pieces scattered along the beach.

" Bravo, my good captain," exclaimed our hero, "you
have not been idle."

The yells and shrieks of the Indians returning to the
hopha told that they were still bent upon revenge. For
no sooner had they cleared the last stockade than they re-
appeared, shooting arrows and throwing javelins after
them, but without any serious effect.

By the time the boats reached the beach George

Lewellen began to revive, and was able to press the hand of his cherished companion.

The men in the boat looked serious. Cuthbert Gordon gazed anxiously into the first mate's countenance, saying :

" Captain Evans is not hurt I hope, Mr. Thomas ? "

" Sorry to say, sir, I fear he is mortally wounded ; he was struck in the throat by a spear ; one of our men killed, and two severely wounded."

" Good heavens ! " exclaimed our hero, as he helped George Lewellen into the cutter ; " this is terrible, and we have no surgeon."

" Ah ! " said Captain Hunter, " our liberty and life have been dearly purchased. Those cursed Indians—ten minutes more and we should have been dead men. Let us get aboard."

As they pulled to the ship Mr. Thomas, the mate, briefly stated what had occurred. It appeared that after the boats left the ship, whilst those on board were watching their proceedings, a whole swarm of canoes filled with Indians, came suddenly into view, issuing from a bight or cove on the east side of the bay, evidently taken there in the night. Captain Evans immediately prepared to receive them, firing the swivel to draw the attention of the boats.

The canoes, as they came on, divided and paddled in such a manner that they prevented more than a single canoe to be fired at at a time; but this did not alarm Captain Evans, as he saw the boats returning with some of the men, so pointing one of the guns at the largest canoe he sunk her.

The rest came shouting and yelling, and rushed alongside on the quarter, on the bows in fact, in every available part. But not a rope was left over the side, and the savages were perfectly bewildered by the height of the ship, and were shot down by the sailors as they climbed up, and the boats coming up sunk the canoes, and so terrified the Indians that they became panic-stricken, and fled. Several, however, contrived to get on deck, and Captain Evans, in driving them overboard, was struck in the throat by a huge Indian with a spear, and fell, and was

thought slain.   The Indian was killed and thrown overboard.   The two canoes that the Indians were towing
away were knocked to pieces by the guns of the "Queen
of the Seas."   Captain Evans died ere the boat reached
the ship, but not until he had heard of the deliverance of
the captives.

CHAPTER VIII.

A GLOOM was thrown over the whole ship's company
by the death of Captain Evans, so universally was he loved.
Mr. Thomas, the mate, came to solicit our hero's orders
as future captain of the ship, according to the owner's
wishes and directions.   He considered the ship was too
close in shore.

"I intended weighing our anchor, Mr. Thomas, immediately, but am so overcome by this melancholy result of
our enterprise that everything else has been unthought of.
I wish you would try if you can get the point of a spear
out of my shoulder; it's not deep, but it prevents the use
of my arm.   The wounds of the men, too, must be dressed
as well as we can manage.   I heard Captain Evans say
you had some skill in these matters."

"Well, sir," said the mate, " I passed six years of my
life as apprentice to a very clever chemist and druggist in
my native town of Swansea, and I picked up something
of his craft before I took to sea.   So, sir, if you please,
we will get that spear head out of your shoulder at once;
delays make matters worse."

Within two hours the ship was under weigh, and shortly
afterwards was brought to anchor close to one of the
islands stretching across the mouth of the bay.   On
this island it was our hero's intention to bury the dead.

And there reposed the bodies of the open-hearted and

humane Captain Evans and James Bingham, seaman.
The sad ceremony over, our hero and Captain Hunter, and
the boat's crew returned on board, and the same night
weighed anchor after landing the two Indians, as Outa la
Poota was still bent upon his search for Matoo Patoo, who
he believed to be still hidden in the woods, intending,
should he find her, to join a friendly tribe at war with the
Tolongas, and thus hoping to revenge the death of his
grandfather and many of his tribe. Cuthbert Gordon
made him and his comrade many presents—amongst them
some muskets and a good stock of ammunition. This was
the cherished object of their hearts; they knew how to
load and also to fire with tolerable accuracy.

As Port Jackson was very little out of his way, Cuthbert Gordon resolved to return there and complete the
lading of the " Queen of the Seas," and also land Captain
Hunter, whose spirits were greatly depressed by the recent
events. He gave our hero a brief account of their treatment by the savages. Several times they fully expected
to be brought out and burnt at some festival; for several
days they would fasten their hands and feet to long poles
and leave them thirty and sometimes forty hours without
food, only giving them water from a gourd. They frequently tortured the old chief and two of his tribe, and
finally killed one because he resisted and defied them.
Captain Hunter bore his sufferings much better than
George Lewellen, for he was of a very strong, robust constitution, and did all in his power to console and keep up
his young companion's spirits. But the mysterious disappearance of Cuthbert Gordon, and his fear that he had
been taken and killed by some straggling party of Indians,
nearly broke his heart; in fact, if their captivity had
lasted a few days longer, he had no doubt his young friend
Lewellen would have died.

" This has been a most disastrous party of pleasure,"
said Captain Hunter, sorrowfully; "it has cost a brave,
kind-hearted man his life. The memory of my having
proposed it will never be forgotten by me."

" My dear Captain Hunter," said our hero, soothingly,
for he saw the worthy captain was taking it to heart;

"if we we were allowed to look into the future, we could, it is true, avoid the errors and mishaps we commit ; but that wisely we are not permitted to know. You kindly offered us a day or two's pleasure, and there appeared no reason why we should not accept and anticipate much amusement from the excursion ; what ensued could not be guarded against; though misfortune has attended our expedition, we have much to thank God for."

Cuthbert Gordon was constant in his attendance upon his friend George Lewellen ; who, though of a sound constitution, was not of a temperament to undergo severe trials, or meet privation or suffering. During the entire voyage back to Port Jackson he did not quit his bed ; mind and body had suffered much ; but just before sighting the coast of New South Wales, which they did on the twelfth day, he began to recover rapidly.

The return of the Queen of the Seas to Port Jackson, Captain Hunter's reappearance, and the loss of his cutter, together with Captain Evans' death, created quite a sensation, for all who had known Captain Evans greatly lamented his melancholy fate. Cuthbert Gordon became quite a lion during his stay; but being anxious to return to his native land on George Lewellen's account, he rapidly completed his cargo, and bidding an affectionate farewell to Captain Hunter among other friends, sailed for England, taking the course round Cape Horn. George Lewellen soon regained his good looks and better spirits; the wounded men were all as active as ever, and with fine, steady weather, they made a splendid run to the Horn, but there they encountered a terrific hurricane of five days, but so ably and skilfully did the young skipper handle and manœuvre the ship, that the crew, who always obeyed him with pleasure, for his manner, though firm, was always kind and considerate, had the utmost confidence in his nautical knowledge, and would willingly, if attacked, follow wherever he led.

The Queen of the Seas was exceedingly well armed for a merchant craft of that period. She had four twelve-pounders, and the new captain before leaving Port Jackson had purchased from the government stores a twenty-four pound carronnade, which was fitted on the deck of the Queen, to work something after the fashion of a pivot gun ; a good store of ammunition was procured, our hero determining that the Queen should not fall an easy prey to any of the French privateers, then swarming on the seas, between England, Spain, and France.

After a stay of three or four days at Madeira, and brightening up the ship's sides with paint, replacing some light spars, and letting his friend Lewellen enjoy a run on shore, which gave him renewed health and spirits, they quitted their anchorage and bore away with a steady breeze for old England. In order to avoid meeting French cruisers or privateers, our hero steered a course well to the north-east, so as to make the coast of Ireland, but when within some two hundred miles of that coast, a succession of tremendous gales from the north and east defeated his purpose, and caused the ship to make great lee-way ; thus, on the 29th of September, he first made land, which proved to be in the vicinity of Mendego bay ; however, he still continued making way, till a confirmed easterly gale, promising to have its full complement of lives, caught him in the chops of the channel ; here, under reefed topsails, he kept hammering away against an amazingly heavy head sea, when one morning early, the wind strong, clear sky, and the sea breaking in on every side, two vessels were made out lying to about four miles right to windward.

Cuthbert Gordon went aloft himself, with his glass to examine them ; he could make out that one was a brigantine, the other a large three-masted schooner. They were both lying to under the smallest amount of canvas possible. When he came down, George Lewellen and the first mate anxiously asked what he thought of the strange sails.

" They are suspicious-looking craft," said the skipper, " an hermaphrodite brig, and a three-masted schooner. I fancy they are privateers."

" Rather awkward," returned his friend ; " but they may not notice us—besides, the way the wind now blows, and in this heavy sea, they would scarcely make sail to have a look at us."

6

"By edging a little more to the northward we may lose them during the night," remarked the mate.

"This is the fifth day of this easterly gale," said Cuthbert Gordon, "and no signs of slackening. We may now count upon its having the cat's allotted number nine."

There can be nothing more monotonous than an easterly gale in the chops of the channel, perpetually hammering at the head seas. It sickens and wearies the sailor, knowing that his home could be reached in forty-eight hours if it would only cease. Provisions get short, water bad, biscuit mouldy. His ship, straining, leaky, and his berth damp, and at times worse than damp—all combine to render an easterly gale at certain seasons an abomination.

But the "Queen of the Seas" was a fine well-built, new ship. She had made a quick run from the shore of New South Wales, and her provisions were good and abundant.

About half an hour after the survey of the strange sail, as the "Queen" was kept edging away to the northward, the two strange vessels were observed to be coming down dead upon them, under the easy sail they carried.

"They are privateers, George," said our hero; "but I think they will find out their mistake if they attack us; they are low in the water, and I dare say not heavily armed."

"Well, there's no help for it," said George Lewellen; "we must fight."

Every preparation was made on board the "Queen" in case the two vessels should turn out to be privateers and attack them. The 24-pounder was to be worked by Tom Darling and Jones, with two active young fellows, to assist; the rest were to work the ship and the four twelve-pounders. The men were eager for the fray. They had wonderful confidence in their skipper. The "Queen" did not alter her course, or make more sail. In half an hour the two vessels were within cannon shot. They then separated, and after skilfully steering, the brigantine took her station on the "Queen's" starboard quarter. The schooner, a remarkably beautiful craft, on the other quarter to windward; and when within musket shot hoisted the privateer flag of France.

The flag of old England soon waved in defiance; in the heavy sea then running, there was not the slightest chance of an enemy attempting to board. The privateers were evidently surprised at the "Queen's" sailing, for being kept a couple of points off the wind, the privateers were forced to make more sail to retain their positions; and the schooner watching an opportunity for drawing closer, and within hail, ordered the ship to be hove to, or they would get no quarter.

With a speaking trumpet Cuthbert Gordon replied, "that they expected none, and would give none." So the Frenchman opened the ball by a very defective broadside from his six 8-pounders, immediately followed by a similar compliment from his comrade. Owing to the agitation of the sea, these broadsides did but feeble execution, cutting a few of the ropes, and knocking a few of the splinters out of the high bulwarks of the "Queen."

"Never mind the brigantine, my men," said our hero. " Let us see what we can do with the schooner; she is full of men. So just let the brig fire away; they have only 8-pounders." Unmasking the 24-pounder himself, and watching the rise and fall of the sea, Cuthbert Gordon applied the match to the gun. Either from accuracy of aim or great good fortune, the 24-lb. ball struck the schooner's bows, tearing and smashing all before it, and as it was afterwards known, killing five men, and ripping up several planks of her deck.

"Now, my lads, with the 12-pounders." A hearty cheer from the crew of the English vessel rang cheerfully over the troubled waters, and bang went the two 12-pounders, the "Queen" receiving at the same time the fire of both vessels. The 12-pounders were loaded with grape. The crew of the schooner were evidently amazed at the weight of metal carried by the "Queen," and the damage her guns did. The three vessels now went at it in right earnest; two reefs were shook out of the "Queen's topsails; and watching his time, by a most skilful manœuvre, her skipper wore, and squaring yards,

6—2

ran full at the brigantine, her crew in the act of making more sail. The "Queen," a vessel of six hundred tons, struck the doomed brigantine amidship, and went clear over her, burying her and her illstarred crew in the depths of the ocean. George Lewellen shuddered as he heard their last cry. They had two men killed on board the "Queen," and five wounded, and the skipper himself wounded by a musket ball lodging in his left arm ; for the schooner had eighty men in her, and had poured several discharges of musketry at half pistol shot into the "Queen."

The schooner, seeing the fate of the brigantine, struck her flag and surrendered. She had lost her two topmasts and mast head ; her bulwarks were nearly shot away, and twelve of her crew were killed or wounded, and her captain carried below severely hurt.

The brigantine, before foundering, carried ten guns, four brass swivels, and had a crew of fifty men. She was called the " Etoile." The schooner was a notorious privateer, named " Le Henri Quatre."

Captain Gordon, after running over the brigantine, rounded to as soon as possible, and then came within pistol shot of the schooner.

A musket ball had grazed his forehead, and his face was covered with blood. George Lewellen was untouched, but exceedingly alarmed about his friend. But Cuthbert, after bathing his head and applying a bandage, said it was a mere scratch.

What puzzled our hero was, what he should do with his prize. True, she could not get away from him, for her mast heads were shattered to pieces. So intent were all onboard his vessel attending their killed and wounded and replacing damages to the rigging, that they were only startled into observation by the report of a very heavy gun.

All looked to windward and beheld a stately ship bearing down on them, under her fore and main topsails double reefed.

Cuthbert took his glass, and after a moment's survey, called out to George Lewellen, in a joyous tone—

"This is a British frigate, and if my eyes do not greatly deceive me, it's our old ship the 'Magician.'"

"Is it possible ? " exclaimed George. "How strange ! "

All eyes were turned upon the advancing frigate, as she gracefully drove before the huge seas, as easy and as buoyant as a cork.

The schooner, to steady herself had managed to set a reefed trysail on her main mast, and a jib forehead hauled to windward.   The Queen was lying to, with the English ensign flying.

Taking a sweep of some extent the "Magician" rounded to, and getting within speaking distance, backed her fore-topsail, and an officer, with a speaking trumpet in his hand, sprung into the mizen shrouds, and hailed the Queen.

Cuthbert Gordon with his trumpet replied, also standing on the mizzen shrouds, and exceedingly anxious to know who then commanded his old ship.

"What's your ship's name, and where from ? " demanded the officer from the frigate.

"The Queen of the Seas, from Port Jackson, to Llanelly."

"What's the schooner ? "

"A French privateer, one of two that attacked us this morning ; the schooner has surrendered, and the brigantine we sunk."

"What's your skipper's name ? " demanded the lieutenant.

Our hero's face flushed, as he replied—

"Cuthbert Gordon, formerly midshipman aboard the Magician, commanded by Captain B——."

Whether these words were heard or not our hero could not say, for the frigate forged ahead, and the officer leaped down from the rigging.

"I wonder," said George Lewellen, as our hero came down on deck, "who commands the Magician ? not our old captain, I know, for he was knighted, and afterwards commanded a two-decker."

"No ; I do not expect Captain B—— to be on board ; but it is not unlikely that our dear old friend Lieutenant Putney, her first lieutenant, may command her ; I know he expected promotion. None of our boats can be launched in this sea, but, by Jove, they are launching one from the frigate."

The crew of the Queen were all anxiously watching the frigate. A six oared gig, with six hardy seamen, were soon afloat with a young midshipman in the stern sheet, and came bounding over the crested seas like a sea bird, and in a few minutes was floating alongside the Queen, but not touching her sides. Our hero stood leaning over the bulwarks, as the young midshipman stood up, saying:

"Captain Putney would be most happy to see Mr. Gordon aboard the Magician."

"Ah! just as I imagined," said Cuthbert Gordon, joyfully to his friend Lewellen. "Just drop up as close as you conveniently can," said our hero speaking to the midshipman, "and I will swing myself aboard you."

Seizing a rope with his right hand, the boat being cautiously brought closer the next moment, our hero having lowered himself overboard, watched his opportunity, and swung himself into the stern sheets.

The midshipman, a fine young lad, of fifteen years, looked into our hero's face with great surprise—but merely observed—

"You must have fought your ship very gallantly, sir, to sink one privateer and take the other. That's a very fine schooner to leeward."

"That's what you may do, some day or other," said Cuthbert, smiling, "for, like you, I was once a midshipman aboard the Magician."

There was no time for conversation, for they were speedily alongside the frigate to leeward; and in five minutes our hero was aboard, and the next moment his hand was grasped by Captain Putney.

"I cannot tell you how rejoiced I am to see you, Gordon," said the frigate's commander, "though by Jupiter Ammon, I never expected to see you the skipper of a merchant craft; but you were just the lad to make a name, whether in the king's ship or a trader. How the deuce you took that dashing schooner, and sunk a brigantine I can't imagine."

Just then a gentleman came up from the cabin, and

hurrying over to our hero, would have seized his left hand ; his right was in Captain Putney's, saying :

" Holy Moses! do I see Cuthbert Gordon ? Be the powers of Moll Flanagan, this beats Banager ! "

" Do not make free with my left hand, Jim Murphy," said our hero, grasping the surgeon's hand with his right. " I have got an ounce of lead in my arm, which I know it will give you great pleasure to extract."

" By St. Patrick, I must have it out then at once," said the burly surgeon of the Magician. " It's not the first job you have given me, my lad ; do you remember the splinter that pinioned you to the deck like a roasted fowl ? "

" Oh, don't I, " said Cuthbert, " and the botch you made in extracting it ! "

" Ah, you were always one of the devil's darlings ! " returned the surgeon, laughing. " But come below, the sooner the job's over the better ; you were never afraid of the knife, so it will be a mere trifle to you."

" I am sorry you have so unpleasant an operation to undergo," said Captain Putney, seriously, " and I see besides you have had a sharp touch over the forehead. Any of your men killed or wounded ? but of course there must."

" Sorry to say two killed," replied our hero, " and ten or twelve more or less wounded. The schooner had a lot of men, and nothing but the height of the sea as well as the height of the ship saved us from their discharges of musketry."

Calling one of his assistant surgeons, Mr. Murphy, an extremely clever operator, stripped off our hero's coat, and in less than ten minutes he had extracted the bullet, which was fortunately near the surface, dressed his other wounds, which were slight, and putting his arm in a sling they all proceeded to the captain's cabin.

Captain Putney was extremely anxious to hear our hero's adventures. He complimented him on his achievement in taking the two privateers, and promised that the moment the gale slackened, he would send Murphy aboard to look after his wounded.

"This gale will blow out before night ; I thought so this morning when I saw the sunrise. I will tell you what I can do for you," continued Captain Putney. "You have only four or five-and-twenty men, you say, and you think there are seventy odd aboard the schooner. She may be a very valuable prize for all you know ; we will overhaul her to-morrow. I'm only cruising here in the chops of the channel. I'll put a prize crew aboard her, and send her into Plymouth, and take her crew into this ship."

"Thank you," said Cuthbert Gordon, "that will relieve my mind. I was really puzzled what to do with the crew of the schooner."

"I am only three days out," said Captain Putney, to some observations of our hero's ; "but I have a piece of good news to tell you. You have been, I think, absent nearly eighteen months from England ? "

"Yes," returned the skipper of the 'Queen'—"eighteen months and seventeen days."

"Well, you have had a lot of adventures during your absence I must say ; but as I was saying—I have some intelligence that will please you I know, and make you give up the merchant service. Some nine months ago, we had a change of ministers, a very useful thing sometimes. Admiral T——, who you remember took a great liking to you when you passed your examination, became one of the Lords of the Admiralty. He did not forget you ; and your old Captain B——, with whom you were a most especial favourite, having stated that you were treated with great injustice owing to that duel of yours at Plymouth, an inquiry was instituted. You were freed from all blame, and at once made lieutenant, and appointed to the fine dashing frigate the D——. But when they went to look for you it was discovered that you had gone on a voyage to New South Wales. Now, all you have to do after your return is to visit Admiral T——, and you will receive your appointment at once. Your old commander and mine told me this just before he sailed to join the fleet before Cadiz."

"Well, this is good news," said Cuthbert Gordon, joyfully. "The moment I bring this ship into port, and visit my family for a few days, I will start for London; nothing would delight me more than resuming my station in the service."

"And believe me, Gordon," said Captain Putney, "when you do you have friends; give them but the occasion; and depend on it your promotion will be rapid."

During the night both wind and sea went down considerably. The surgeon with his assistant visited the "Queen," and dressed the men's wounds. Cuthbert Gordon and Captain Putney went in the morning and visited the "Queen." The captain was quite pleased to see George Lewellen, saying, "your old comrade aboard the 'Magician,' has, I see, as usual, enticed you to share his adventures. You had many a scrape in old days; and upon my word, this time you have come out of your adventures with flying colours."

The schooner was next visited, and a prize crew put into her, and the men shifted into the "Magician." She turned out a valuable seizure; and some time after their arrival in Plymouth, her proceeds enriched the crew of the "Queen" far beyond their expectations.

The wind shifting into the south-west quarter brought the three vessels in less than sixty hours off the Land's-end. There they separated, the frigate and the prize proceeding to Plymouth, the "Queen" making for the Worm's Head. Taking a pilot off the bar of Llanelly, in two hours after she was at anchor off the dock, which was crowded with the many anxious friends of those on board.

CHAPTER IX.

THE arrival of the " Queen," the death of Captain Evans, and the conflict of the good ship with two French privateers created considerable agitation and excitement in the port and vicinity of Llanelly, and gained immortal renown for the skipper and crew of the " Queen."

The dock, only then completing, was, however, beginning to attract merchants and ships to the port; but sixty years has made a most wonderful change in this, even at the present day, far from agreeable town.

The great extent of swampy flat ground extending to the dock was guiltless of buildings of every kind. Neither copper works, nor works of any description existed. Neither Mechanics' Institutes nor public buildings—a wild, desert-like tract of country extended along the banks of the Lougher river for five miles. No bridge crossed the then rapid tide that flowed up the country from Lougher for miles in a broad estuary. The whole coast was the resort of daring smugglers. Especially that side of Llanelly on the sea cost, extending to the ancient borough town of Kidwelly, which, at the period of our story, far exceeded Llanelly in size and importance, though situated on a small and insignificant river.

The sands extended to Kidwelly; these sands were every winter covered with wrecks; the losses of life and valuable cargoes were awful. Carmarthen Bay, then unprotected by lights or lighthouses, was the scene of horrible suffering, for the treacherous Ceffen Cedan sands extended nearly seven miles out to sea, and at low water they appeared like an immense desert of barren sands, miles upon miles of which were to be seen, with the melancholy mementoes of wrecked ships, their bleached and rotten timbers and ribs just appearing above the sands, marking the spot where perished the unfortunate mariners.

On these wild exposed wastes of sand, bounded towards the mainland by an extent of high ridges of sand called burrows, extending in length over seven to eight miles, and in breadth two or more. In these sand hills smugglers buried their illicit goods, and wreckers hid away their plunder.

These sands and burrows are nothing altered at the present day; cultivation had advanced to the edge of the sand hills, but no further. Smuggling has certainly ceased, but every winter they are covered with wrecked materials and sometimes lifeless bodies, and noble ships are cast away upon them. Even as we write a fine three hundred ton ship, laden with silver ore lies helpless upon these sands, and some two or three years ago the Queen of the West, a ship of one thousand tons, with sixty thousand pounds worth of property aboard went ashore upon them. And yet a good and efficient lighthouse stands on Calde Island, the western head of Carmarthen Bay, and a light ship was off the Worm's Head, the eastern extremity of this dreaded and dangerous bay. Nearly all these wrecks are caused for want of sounding.

About a week after the return of the Queen of the Seas to Llanelly, it was then the month of November, the family of Cuthbert Gordon were sitting late in the evening in the elegant little drawing-room of Mrs. Gordon's cottage; George Lewellen and his sister Mary had just left to return home, for the night was a terribly wild and stormy one. The mother and son, and the two lovely girls, Amy and Lucy, Cuthbert Gordon's sisters, were seated round the fire. Mrs. Gordon might be said to be still young. She was but thirty-eight, and was still beautiful, though her beauty was of a quiet and somewhat serious cast; it had not always been so. As the wild gusts from the south-east whirled over the cottage, and roared in the great trees that skirted the little lawn, the mother shuddered, and the whole party drew close to the cheering fire.

"Ah, Cuthbert," said Mrs. Gordon, "you men may love the wild perilous life of a sailor; but how different are the feelings of the wife, the mother, and the sisters of those whom you know are exposed to the storms and hurricanes that rule with such terrible sway the wild waves which the poor frail ship drives. Every storm that raged whilst you were away made our hearts ache."

"But, dear mother," said Cuthbert, with a smile," there must be sailors. When you picture to yourself a thousand terrors, and fancying the storm raging, we are perhaps calmly gliding over a smooth sea."

" Quite the contrary, Cuth," said Amy. "" Hark to that gust, it makes the house shake. Do you know it often puzzles me how in the world a ship's sails resist such furious blasts—blasts that tear up huge oaks, and throw down houses and steeples."

"I should not wonder," said Cuthbert Gordon, " but that some unfortunate ship will leave her bows on the Ceffen Cedan this wild night," and he got up and approached the window, against which the rain now beat with terrible violence. " It is intensely dark," he continued, " but this rain will bring down the wind, or shift it into the north-west. It's very lucky that George and Mary left before the rain came."

" Ah, Lucy," continued our hero, returning to his seat, " your little image interfered sadly with George's love of the sea. See what it is to have that little urchin Cupid—"

" Oh, nonsense," interrupted Lucy, blushing, " George never was particularly fond of the sea ; he liked a cruise, but was never intended for a sailor."

" Hark ! " suddenly interrupted Mrs. Gordon, " was not that a gun ? "

" Yes," said Cuthbert, rising, " it was," and going to the window he strove to pierce the gloom that reigned without. " Ah ! " he exclaimed, " there goes a rocket in the direction of the burrows."

" Oh, dear ! " said Lucy, " perhaps it is the brig we all observed in the bay this morning."

" If she remained in the bay," said our hero, " she is assuredly ashore. I will run down to Bill Davis, the pilot, and rouse him up. We may save life ; it's the sailor's duty to assist a brother in distress."

The mother sighed, saying :

" You are right, dear Cuthbert ; but remember you will be going to London to-morrow night, and if you go out in this pitiless storm you will be all night exposed."

" Tut !   What signifies a wet jacket and buffeting with a storm on land ?" said our hero.   " What's the loss of a night's rest?   The gale is heavy, and the vessel is doubt-less ashore," so kissing his mother and sisters, he hastily put on a thick pea jacket, took a stout stick and set off for the Pembray village to rouse some of the pilots and sailors, and induce them to go with him in search of the wreck.

After his departure the mother and daughters sat some time conversing on the one engrossing subject—our hero's departure the following day to London, and the chances of his being immediately appointed to a ship.

" Mr. Lewellen is sadly vexed," said Amy, " that Cuth-bert will not be able to take the command of his splendid new ship, though he rejoices to think of his promised lieu-tenancy on board a king's ship.   He says he is sure to be a commander before he is six-and-twenty."

" Who can count, Amy," said the mother, " upon human life in a ship and in war time, and your brother is so reck-lessly daring."

" Ah," said both sisters, with enthusiasm, " do not call it reckless ; see how he fought the two privateers, and see how happy the prize money has made the men belong-ing to the Queen—how comfortable all their families have been made."

" And how wretched and heart-broken the families of those poor fellows are that perished in the brigantine. Alas ! there are two sides to the most beautiful picture ! " said the mother.

The animated sweet faces of the twins assumed a look of dejection.

" That is true, dear mother.   What gives one joy and competence often brings, as you say, misery to others ; but the storm is gone down, and the rain has ceased."

" Then call Jane, my love, and let us have prayers,

and go to bed; it will be morning before my excitable
son returns."

In less than an hour all had retired to rest in the cottage;
not a sound was to be heard. This is oftentimes the case,
when the doomed craft strikes, and the wild seas scatter
her timbers over the rocks and sands, the tempest lulls
as if satisfied with the ruin and misery it has created.
Mrs. Gordon lay awake for several hours listening, thinking she might hear her son's steps on the stairs, for his
room was next to hers; but no sound disturbed the
silence of the night. Towards morning she fell fast asleep
and did not wake till Amy entered her room about eight
o'clock.

"Has Cuthbert returned?" were the first words of the
anxious mother.

"No, indeed he has not," said Amy, drawing the cur-
tains, and disclosing a gloomy November morning, hazy
and drizzling, and blowing hard from the north.

"I am afraid," said the mother, "that there has been
a wreck, and he is as he used to be when a boy, worrying
himself to death about saving lives and property from destruction. I must not let him go to London till after to-
morrow; there is no such hurry; his arm, you can scarcely
say is quite strong yet."

By nine o'clock the family were at breakfast, and no
sign of Cuthbert Gordon's return.

"Well, I declare," said Amy, after a glance through
the window, "here's George, at this early hour; I daresay
he has some news of the wreck."

As he entered the parlour and greeted all present, with
a very loving squeeze of the hand to his affianced Lucy,
Amy said—"Have you any news of the wrecks of last
night, George?"

"Well, I hear that there is a brig ashore on Towen
Point," said George Lewellen, "where is Cuthbert? I
thought to get him to go with me to see what has
occurred."

"Why, George," said Mrs. Gordon, "he went last
night; we heard the guns and saw some rockets, and he
would run down, he said, and rouse Bill Davis, the pilot,

and others. We are high up here, and see to a much further extent than they can in the village."

"That's very odd," said George, looking surprised; "why, it was Bill Davis that brought us up word of the brig's running ashore in the night, and he wanted carts and horses to save all he could; he says he has been at the wreck all night, and brought off the captain and crew of the brig, who were all saved, up to the village."

"But," remarked the mother anxiously, "Did he say nothing of Cuthbert being there, for where else can he be if not at the wreck."

"He may not have thought of mentioning Cuthbert," said George Lewellen, jumping up. "I will take my horse and ride down to the Point at once, so farewell, till evening," and pressing Lucy's hand, he left the cottage.

Mrs. Gordon remained very thoughtful; she could scarcely say she was alarmed, for, when scarcely twelve years old, Cuthbert used frequently to go over these sands to see wrecks, and help if he could.

"Why do you look so serious, dear mother?" asked Amy, putting away various little articles from the breakfast table. "There can be no possible danger for a young man like Cuthbert traversing the sands even of a stormy night. I have often heard him say he could traverse the burrows blindfold."

"Perhaps I am wrong, my love," said the mother, "to appear uneasy; there are times when there are certain feelings gain dominion over you, let you do all you can to shake those feelings off."

"Well," said Amy, "positively, I will not wait for George's return. Come Lucy, get our bonnets, we will go down to Bill Davis's and ask his wife whether Cuthbert called there last night; perhaps we may meet him on the way."

"Well, it will be only a pleasant walk for you, the day clears a little." And the mother looked or appeared to look more cheerful.

In a few minutes the two girls were equipped, and proceeded to the village, not feeling the least apprehensive themselves, but anxious to relieve their mother's mind.

Descending the hill on which the cottage stood, they proceeded to the village of Pembray, then consisting of only a few cottages scattered over the lowlands. The cottage of Bill Davis, the pilot, was close to the sand burrows, and facing the sea. On reaching the pilot's cottage, the two sisters beheld Mrs. Davis and her eldest daughter very busy hanging up the soaked garments Bill, the pilot, had worn on the previous night.

The two girls knew Mrs. Davis very well; she was a tidy, industrious woman. She dropped a curtsey, saying: "What a night we have had of it, my dear young ladies; you must have heard it terrible on the hill—the sand hills shelter us."

"Yes, indeed," returned Amy, "we have had full evidence of its violence, and how very fortunate the crew of the brig escaped, though we heard they lost their ship, poor fellows."

"It was, my husband said, a mercy of Providence their lives were spared, it was nearly high water, and she drove high up nearly to the burrows; had it been low water they would all have been drowned."

"Did my brother call here, Mrs. Davis, last night to rouse your husband to go with him to where he supposed the wreck was?"

"Surely Miss, he did, but Bill heard the first gun, and was gone when Mr. Gordon called. Tom Wild and Morgan went with him. I begged Mr. Gordon not to go on by himself, but he laughed, saying: 'It was light enough for him,' and off he started to overtake the others, who were only gone a short time before him. Has he not come back, Miss?"

"No, indeed," said both sisters, "he has not returned, and mamma is getting uneasy."

"Law, my dears, there is no fear of Mr. Gordon; he knows the burrows as well, if not better, than any man about these parts. But, dear me, there's Morgan and Tom Thomas yonder, coming back from the wreck. Run, Eliza," she turned to her daughter, "and ask Morgan if Mr. Gordon is still at the wreck."

The girl started off, and overtaking the men, seemed to

question them, and then came running back. The girl did not speak English, but spoke rapidly in Welsh to her mother.

Amy understood the language well; she turned pale as Mrs. Davis said—looking surprised—

" Law, Miss, isn't it strange, the men do say Mr. Gordon was not at the wreck either last night or this morning."

" Good heavens ! " said Lucy, pale and frightened ; " how can that be? what can have happened ? " and she trembled so exceedingly that Mrs. Davis got frightened also.

" Do not give way to fear, dear Lucy," said Amy Gordon, who possessed considerably more firmness and decision of character ; " we are alarming ourselves perhaps needlessly. However, let us return home; George will be back directly, and bring us some intelligence. It is certainly strange; but still, his absence may be accounted for in a manner we little expect."

Thanking Mrs. Davis, and saying that they fully expected to find their brother at home before them they hastily returned to the cottage.

" My dear Amy," said Lucy, " I am horribly frightened ; only think what a dark night it was ; suppose," and she shuddered, " that he mistook the way, and got into the sea."

" You are conjuring up wild fancies," said Amy, " such an event could never occur to Cuthbert. If he did, which is exceedingly improbable, stumble or walk into the sea, he would instantly perceive his error ; besides our brother is a good swimmer, and the dash of the waves upon the sands, even if he could not see them, would be sufficient to warn him. No, whatever has caused his unaccountable absence, falling into the sea is not the cause."

Mrs. Gordon, and their attached servant girl were anxiously watching their return.

" Well, my dear children, have you heard any intelligence of your brother ? Did he call at Bill Davis's ? "

" Yes, dear mother," said Amy, speaking cheerfully, " he called, but Bill Davis was gone on. But it seems he did not go to the wreck."

" Not go to the wreck ? " said the mother, starting and looking into the expressive features of her daughters,

7

"where did he go then ?   what could have diverted his attention from the wreck, and detained him all night ? "

"Here is George Lewellen cantering up the road," said Lucy, turning back ; "God grant he brings us some good news."

George Lewellen threw himself off his horse ; he met Lucy at the gate, he looked uneasy and agitated, and his first words were—

"Has he returned, Lucy ? "

The young girl sighed, saying—

"No, I am frightened ; he has not returned—and has not been at the wreck."

"No ; he has not," returned George Lewellen, walking up the path to the cottage ; "neither is he anywhere in the burrows or in the sands—I have galloped across them several times, and I sent half-a-dozen men over them. The strong north wind has driven the sand over all foot-marks."

We cannot dwell upon this portion of our story. It will be sufficient to say that every exertion to trace Cuthbert Gordon, or account for his mysterious disappearance, failed.   Mr. Lewellen spared neither money nor assistance. Our hero was a general favourite—all the fishermen and pilots both loved and admired him.   As we said, the violent northerly gale that sprung up in the morning after the cessation of the gale, drove the sands of the burrows like a sea drift, obliterating all kinds of marks. Rewards were offered—in fact every exertion was made—and still, at the expiration of ten days, his disappearance was still a profound mystery.

The shock Mrs. Gordon received reduced her in a few days to a state of extreme weakness.   She idolized her son, without detriment to her love for her beautiful and amiable daughters.   Amy and Lucy drowned their own grief in order to soothe and console their beloved mother.

And thus we leave the families of Gordon and Lewellen, plunged in grief, and in our next chapter, follow the footsteps of Cuthbert Gordon, on the night of the wreck, and explain to our readers the cause of his mysterious disappearance.

CHAPTER X.

Cuthbert Gordon, after putting on his thick pea jacket, buttoned up to the throat, fastened on his sou'-wester, and taking a thick stick in his hand, left the cottage and proceeded down the hill towards the village. It required a very energetic and earnest temperament to induce any one to leave their snug fire side to plunge into and amidst the war of elements that raged without the cottage. The storm came in gusts, driving the cold and cutting rain in his face. The darkness was intense. Still he plodded on with bent head but firm step, groping his way sometimes, and pitching into a hedge another time, but still making headway, till he reached the flat, and shortly after, guided by a light in Bill Davis's cottage, he made towards it. Bill Davis was a rough, powerful man, not very agreeable but the best pilot on the coast. Cuthbert Gordon had often been out with this sailor, and though he did not particularly like him, still he knew he was a useful man of his class. He was Mr. Lewellen's pilot, always took his ships out and in, and his wife was once one of Mr. Lewellen's household, and a very good woman she was considered to be.

Knocking at the door, Mrs. Davis made her appearance. "Bless me," she exclaimed, starting back, rather alarmed, "is it you, Mr. Gordon? what has brought you out such a frightful night?"

"Well, Mrs. Davis, there's a wreck on the Ceffen, near Towen Point, I think; I saw rockets in that direction, so I came to rouse Davis."

"Ah, to be sure, so my husband said; he heard a gun, he is not long gone, and Tom Wild and Morgan with him."

"Oh, in that case I will hurry on," said our hero.

7—"

"Dear me, Mr. Gordon, you had better go back to your comfortable bed ; it's raining and blowing hard still."

" Ah, Mrs. Davis, you know of old I care little for either wind or rain if I can be of assistance to sufferers by wreck ; so I will overtake your husband if I can."

" Then do not go across the burrows." said Mrs. Davis very anxiously, as our hero thought, " go by the shore—it's safer ; you will lose yourself in those sand hills this dark night."

Mrs. Davis stood for a moment, looking vexed, as she beheld Cuthbert Gordon wave his hand, and hurry on, taking the way into the heart of the burrows.

" Ah," she said, as she closed the door and sighed, " This is the last, would it was over. I wish Mr. Gordon had remained at home," she then retired after bolting the door.

Cuthbert Gordon struck at once into the sand hills. These hills are some of them thirty to forty feet high, and covered with a low stunted shrub and long rush which wind closely, and keep the sand hills from drifting away altogether ; small lakes and ponds exist between these hills, so that traversing them of a dark night is anything but an agreeable occupation ; in heavy gales, the drift of the sand reminds one of the desert.

Our hero got along nevertheless, and had mounted one of those hills and paused ; he thought he heard in the lull of the gale, for the rain had evidently checked its fury, a sound of men's voices, and the next moment a flash as if from a lantern, passed across the foot of the sand hill. " Ah, no doubt Bill Davis and his comrades," thought Cuthbert Gordon, and rushing down the hill, his foot got under a tangled mass of those low knitted shrubs, and owing to the speed with which he was running, he pitched with great violence down the rest of the hill, and striking against what appeared to be some planks, down he went into a species of cave or artificial hollow under the sand hill, falling in amongst a dozen or more men busily en-gaged in stowing away kegs, boxes, &c. A volley of curses and imprecations, some in English, Welsh, and Irish, followed this intrusion.

"Curse it," exclaimed a voice. "A spy, strangle him, knock him over the head."

"Arrah, let me at him," exclaimed an Irishman, "be St. Patrick, I'll spoil his potato trap."

Cuthbert Gordon was on his legs in a minute shaking off the men, and with a tremendous blow spoiling Paddy's potato trap for a week or so at all events, but a dozen hands were upon him, when a tall man muffled in a pea jacket, and sou'-wester, and an ample wrapper round his neck and mouth, called out "Don't murder him boys, who is he ? "

"By heaven ! " exclaimed a voice, " It's Mr. Gordon."

Our hero at once recognized Bill Davis, and making a desperate effort to get free, and called on Bill Davis to aid him, but this man, furious at being discovered and re-cognised, as our hero was again attempting to force his way out, lifted his brass butted pistol, and dealt him so heavy a blow on the back of the head that it stretched him sense-less at his feet.

"Confound it, man, what have you done ? " fiercely ex-claimed the tall young man. " Smuggling is one thing, murder is a hanging matter."

"I have not murdered him," said Bill Davis, sulkily, "he has stood harder knocks than that, he's a fine young fellow I allow, but it would not do to let him get away. You must take him a trip across the Channel; before he can return, we shall be all right, and I and my family far from this."

"Well, that's not a bad idea," said the tall man. "What did you say his name was ? "

"Gordon," returned the smuggler, "he and his family came from India—his father was an officer in the army—an Irishman, like yourself."

The tall man started, and then immediately said, "Here, boys, lift him and carry him at once to the boat, I'll follow you."

"Yes, that's the plan," said Davis, "he's a better sea-man, I can tell you, than any you have aboard your cutter. He was a midshipman some years, and has passed for a lieutenant; I like him myself."

"Be the Lord Harry!" burst out laughing the tall stranger. "I trust you will never like me, if that's the method you generally use in showing your affection. Come lift him up, lads, there's no time to lose, this gale is done; we shall have the wind out from the nor'-west before morning."

"Be St. Peter! he's none of your light weights anyhow," said one of the men. "May I be blessed, if I'd ask to carry him a hundred yards on my back."

Five of the men lifted him up, and then, after a few parting directions from Davis, they proceeded to the river beach, leaving the Welsh portion of the smugglers to close up their store and efface all marks, but the storm of the next hour from the nor'-west did that effectually.

They soon reached the boat, and Cuthbert Gordon, who was rapidly recovering the stunning blow he had received, was lifted in and laid on the floor of the stern, whilst the tall smuggler drew a pistol from his pocket, and cocking it, said, as the boat shoved off, and our hero tried to sit up, "Keep quiet, young man, and no harm will happen to you; offer any resistance and the consequences be on your own head."

The prisoner was not for the moment able to reply, he felt dizzy and confused; he sat up, however, and bathed his head with water by putting his hand over the side— and felt better—he washed away the clotted blood from a severe cut, luckily not in a bad place.

"I am sorry that brute Davis hurt you so severely," said the smuggler, "there was no necessity for it."

"There is no necessity for what you are doing now," said Cuthbert Gordon, angrily. "You are making those who are dear to me miserable, and ruining my prospects in life."

The smuggler made no reply, for one of the men sung out "There she is—and blow me if there isn't the nor'-wester, too," and as he spoke a gust of northerly wind rushed sweeping over the water, and brought the light boat in a minute or two after alongside a cutter of about seventy or eighty tons burden. Some men aboard hailed.

"All right," exclaimed those in the boat, and then a rope was thrown and caught.

Cuthbert Gordon·felt bitterly vexed, his temper, too, was roused; still, situated as he was, he could do nothing but try to persuade the skipper of the cutter, whoever he might be, to put him ashore. Now in the gloom of the night, though it was clearing a little to the north, he could see at a glance that the vessel they were alongside of was no trader. She had a lofty mast, and a low long hull. However, he seized a rope and sprang on board;—as he gained the deck a man rather above the middle height, strongly built, and looking doubly so from the heavy shaggy pea coat he wore, and the sou'-wester on his head with the flaps drawn down and covering the ears and then tied under the chin, a sailor held a lanthorn, the light of which he threw upon the prisoner whilst the rest were getting on board. Our hero's face and hands were streaked with blood, but he did not know it, it was so dark.

"Why, how's this?" exclaimed the skipper of the cutter in a loud angry voice. "Who is this person, have you had a tussle with the coastguard?"

"I will answer you, if you are the owner or skipper of this craft," said our hero.

"Yes," returned the man with a laugh. "You may call me skipper if you like, and owner of the craft I am."

"Well, sir," continued our hero, in a rather angry voice, " you are committing not only a most illegal act, but a most cruel one, in seizing my person."

"Faith, I never seized your person, sir," returned the skipper, "I am sorry to see you are hurt, very sorry; but come here, Trevor, like a good fellow, and tell me how this gentleman—for such I see he is—came with you."

The tall smuggler then took the skipper by the arm led him aside and conversed with him in a low tone, whilst the rest of the crew were hoisting up the gig, reefing the sails, and setting a storm jib, for the roar of the surf on the bar and upon the Hooper Sands sounded like thunder, proving that there was a tremendous sea running outside.

After ten minutes' conversation the skipper came back

to where our hero stood leaning against the companion and thinking how bitterly and with what anguish his mother would feel at his mysterious disappearance; at one time he was half-tempted to throw off his coat and jump overboard, but he well knew, with the ebb tide then making, he would, if the best swimmer in the world, be forced out to sea to perish.

The skipper approached him, and in a quiet, gentlemanly tone said, "I am exceedingly grieved, Mr. Gordon, at this most unpleasant adventure."

"But you can easily remedy the wrong done me," said Cuthbert, "Put me ashore and I will give you the word and honour of a gentleman I will only seek my home and never by word or deed compromise a single individual concerned in this affair. My family will be distracted at my unaccountable disappearance, and I may lose my commission in his Majesty's service. Put me ashore, sir; I see you are, though a smuggler, a gentleman, though it is rather hard to reconcile the two professions, or hereafter I shall look to you, and expect a satisfaction, that will cost one or other of us our life."

"Faith, I stake my life so often," returned the smuggler, "that I think nothing of it; all I can tell you is this, we are all sworn one to the other. My comrade has sworn to take you across the channel and land you; I am bound by the same oath, and I will stand by it; when I land you, you are welcome to shoot me if you like; I shall stand before you for that purpose, and if it will enable you to take your aim better, rest satisfied, I will not seek to take your life. I have done you injury enough without intending it, but till we reach the coast of Ireland, you do not leave this craft," and turning round he called out, "Now then my lads, heave up, and be alive, the tide runs down strong, and if we delay there will be a very ugly tumble on the bar."

Cuthbert Gordon remained standing resting against the companion immersed in most painful thought. "Something," he thought to himself "everlastingly mars my advancement in the only profession that suits my views and ardent wishes; this delay may be of more consequence than may be imagined, and besides my poor mother will fret herself ill, imagining I may be drowned ; I always thought that Bill Davis was engaged in smuggling, and now I remember how his wife endeavoured to prevail on me to take the sea side instead of crossing the sand hills; he was an ungrateful brute, however, to strike me as he did."

He was disturbed in his thoughts by the crew of the cutter hoisting the close reefed mainsail, and heaving up the anchor. It was blowing half a gale from the nor'-west and dark and thick. The crew appeared to consist of eight men, a boy, and the skipper and his companion. She was a fine buoyant craft with great beam, and as her anchor was stowed and she got a way upon her, she soon convinced our hero that she was able to bear a great deal of bad weather. It was still intensely dark, and to one unacquainted with the channel, it would be a fearful risk to attempt the passage over the bar.

The binnacle was lighted, and the man at the helm steered by compass, the skipper of the cutter standing beside him watching.

The roar of the surf on the Hooper was tremendous, and again on the bar, and less on the Pembrey sands ; on all sides the thunder of the breakers was enough to distract a helmsman ; indeed, none but a smuggler, and a daring one too, would ever have dreamt to attempt the passage out on such a night, and after so fierce a gale from the south-west.

Cuthbert Gordon drew near the binnacle and looked at the compass. It was six miles to the bar, and they had to pass the dangerous coast, upon whose reckless sands numbers of vessels perished yearly.

The cutter was lying as close to the wind as she could, and no doubt had the tide been at flood or full, she might have weathered the western end of the Hooper, but the ebb tide had a powerful tendency to suck vessels on to those dangerous sands.

Gordon did not care a straw for the safety of the cutter, but he very well knew that if she touched on the edge of the Hooper, with the heavy ground swell running on it, she would go to pieces in five minutes, and every soul perish. He kept looking at the compass and listening to the hammering of the surf on the sands, when the tall smuggler, approaching the skipper, who stood close to the man at the helm, said, "Shall we clear all on this tack, Herbert ? "

" So Maguire says," returned the skipper ; "are you all right, Maguire ? " he demanded of the helmsman.

"All right, sir," returned the man, "Im steering a point more to the windward than would be required in broad daylight."

"Then I tell you, man," said Cuthbert Gordon, in his clear convincing tones, "that if you keep steering as you now do, south-west by west, in ten minutes you will be on the spit of the Hooper."

The tall smuggler started, and said something to the skipper.

"Well, blow me ! " said the helmsman, "may be you had better take the helm ; do you think, be gor, that this is the first time I ever handled a craft in this channel ? "

"First or last," said our hero, "you are risking all our lives," and pushing the man from the helm, he called out in his trumpet voice, " stand by the fore sheet there forward," and instantly put the helm down. It was time ; they had not six feet of water to spare, and already they were within the influence of the ground sea ; two minutes later, and they would have been in broken water. As it was, two heavy seas broke against the cutter's bows as she went in stays, and nearly threw her back on the previous tack. There was a dead silence for five minutes.

" You have saved the cutter and all our lives, Mr. Gordon," said the skipper, with much feeling in his tone and manner and catching our hero by the hand as he relinquished the tiller to the terrified Maguire, who clearly saw the fearful peril they had escaped.

" The man was steering right enough," said Cuthbert Gordon, quietly, "provided it was young flood or high water ; but to have cleared the spit with this wind and sea, and an ebb tide, it was necessary to steer west nor'-

west, and that you cannot do. You are safe enough now, if you do not run on shore on the opposite sands; not that I object to your doing that, for I could save my life and regain my freedom."

"I will not detain you an hour, Mr. Gordon," said the skipper, "on reaching the other side. I have sworn to land you on the Irish coast, which I trust we shall make by to-morrow night. In forty-eight hours you can get back to Milford Haven from Waterford, so that the grief of your friends and relatives will be short lived, and little detriment can ensue to your own prospects. Pray, Mr. Gordon, I beseech you, pardon me this untoward event. I have never asked any man's pardon, whether I was right or wrong; but, I cannot tell why, I wish to obtain yours," and the skipper frankly held out his hand.

Cuthbert Gordon's nature was a kind and loving one. He was hot-tempered, and at times excitable; but even a great wrong he could forgive if he beheld the offender repent his offence. He took the hand offered, saying—

"I bear no resentment; another time this adventure would make me laugh; now it is serious. But I respect an oath, though that oath is given in a bad cause. So let the matter rest."

The skipper wrung the young man's hand earnestly, saying—

"You will know me better by-and-bye. Now pray come below and change your soaked garments, and take a glass of wine or grog, and let me dress the hurt you received from that rascal Davis's pistol."

"Let us pass the bar first," said our hero. "It's an ugly place; we shall then have the open sea before us— your pilot may make another mistake."

"You are right," returned the skipper, and calling the boy, he told him to go into the cabin, light the lamp, and get ready some wines and spirits. Cuthbert Gordon remarked that the skipper's friend or comrade stood aloof and did not make any remark, but kept pacing the deck. After a short run to the north-east, the cutter was again put about, and this time she fairly ran over the bar through a tremendous breaking sea, which washed her deck from stem to stern, knocking her gig to pieces, and very nearly washing two of her crew over the side.

"What a sea you have on this bar," said the skipper; "but she's a gallant little craft, is she not, Mr. Gordon?"

"She's a good sea boat, evidently, but overmasted," returned our hero. "I once made, not long ago, either, the run from New South Wales to New Zealand, in a cutter not more than thirty tons, and in as heavy a gale as ever I saw. It's the ebb tide against the recent sea raised by the late south-east gale that raises this tumble of a sea."

"So I supposed," said the skipper; "it's an ugly sea and no mistake. Now, come below; we have a fair way before us, and it will be daylight in three hours more."

The cabin of the cutter was a very handsome and commodious one, with six berth places and sofas; in fact, she was a yacht, and considered at that day a remarkably handsome and fast one. How and why she became a smuggling cutter our readers will learn as we proceed. On the table was one of those contrivances called fiddles, to prevent bottles, &c., from being capsized in a heavy sea. A good fire was blazing in the handsome brass stove, and a large lamp, with bright burners, hung from the ceiling. The sides of the cabin were ornamented with pistols, carbines, and short pikes, placed in fanciful shapes.

"Now put off your wet pea-coat, Mr. Gordon, I can supply you with a dry one, and take a glass of hot spirits and water; you will find it beneficial after so many hours' buffeting and the bad usage you have received." Whilst speaking the skipper began stripping off his sou'-wester, pea-coat, and shawl round the neck, and then Cuthbert Gordon beheld an exceedingly handsome, gentlemanly man, about six or eight and thirty years old, attired in a sailor's costume of blue cloth. Calling the boy, a basin, water, and towels were brought, and our hero was enabled to divest his face and hands of the stains upon them. The skipper insisted on washing off the clotted blood from the deep cut on the back of the head. "That rascal hit hard, by Jove," he muttered, as he dried the wound and placed a large piece of sticking plaster he took from a medicine chest, having cut away the hair, and then Cuthbert Gordon very willingly mixed himself a tumbler of hot grog.

"I say, boy," said Cuthbert's companion, "just go on deck, and tell Mr. Trevor to come down; he likes a glass of grog and a pipe as well as most people."

Our hero put on a dry pilot coat and sat down, determined to take things as they came. There was no such thing in those days as teetotalism. All men drank to a certain extent, not perhaps a great deal more than they do now; there was moderation then as well as now. Our hero was, however, extremely moderate in general; he could enjoy himself like his messmates aboard ship, but was temperate and rarely exceeded or unnerved himself. Presently the person called Mr. Trevor entered the cabin, and threw off his muffler, and then our hero perceived a remarkably fine young man, not more than thirty, his features were good, and his manner perfectly gentlemanly; still he had not, in Cuthbert Gordon's opinion, the open, cheerful, frank, prepossessing countenance of the skipper. He also was attired under his muffler in a simple sailor's dress of fine blue cloth.

"You look comfortable, gentlemen," said Mr. Trevor, mixing himself a strong tumbler of punch; "faith! one requires something of this sort after the buffeting we got on that confounded bar. It is blowing hard still, but we are lying too till daylight; the men say that we shall find a tremendous sea in the Channel."

"That's likely," said Cuthbert Gordon, "a south-east gale makes a heavy sea in the Channel, and it has blown very hard this week past."

"Well, I think Mr. Gordon, if you will take a turn in and rest for a few hours you will feel all the better; I'm inclined for a snooze myself, not having had one these two nights."

"Well, as I slept well last night whilst you kept watch," said Mr. Trevor, "I will take my turn on deck."

"Very good," said the skipper, "let you and I turn in, Mr. Gordon."

Our hero feeling some ill effects from the blow he had received, willingly accepted the offer of a berth, and he and the skipper turned in; Mr. Trevor lighted a pipe and went on deck.

CHAPTER XI.

IT was about ten o'clock on the following day when Cuthbert Gordon awoke; he knew by the decreased motion of the cutter that the sea had gone down considerably. He jumped up, and finding himself not much the worse for the blow on the head, he dressed himself, and entered the cabin. The fire was lighted, and preparation for breakfast going on. On ascending to the deck, he perceived the skipper and Mr. Trevor, as he was called, pacing the deck.

"Ah, I am glad to see you, hearty and well," said the owner of the cutter, holding out his hand, with a good-humoured smile; "nothing the worse I trust for that unlucky knock on the head."

"Well, nothing to signify," returned our hero.

Mr. Trevor merely said "Good morning," and then added, "now, let us go down to breakfast, and then I'll turn in."

"You know where you are, I suppose," said the skipper, pointing to the land some four miles distant.

"Yes," returned Cuthbert Gordon, looking round, "yonder is Milford Haven; I see the wind has veered round to its old point, south-east, looking, in my opinion, for another gale. I have little faith at this time of the year in those sudden shifts of wind into the northward."

"The old gale holds its own outside," returned the skipper, "but if this breeze continues, we shall make the Irish coast to-night, though it does look very greasy and thick to windward."

When they entered the cabin, Darby, the steward's boy, had placed a very substantial breakfast on the table, so well secured that the plunges of the cutter did not disturb them. The conversation turned upon various subjects. Cuthbert Gordon, however, did not exactly like the tone of levity and derision with which Mr. Trevor treated most subjects of conversation.

" By the way, Mr Gordon, I have not told you my name ; you will, I dare say, be suprised when I tell you I am a namesake of yours, and perhaps a relative."

" Tut ! " exclaimed Mr. Trevor, "there are a thousand Gordons in Great Britain. If you claim relationship with them all, Herbert, you will form a very redoubtable clan."

" I have no doubt," returned Herbert Gordon (the skipper's name), " but were it possible to trace pedigrees you would find all the Gordons spring from the same original stock. May I ask you where you were born, Mr. Gordon ?"

" In a very far off land," returned our hero. " I was born at Curache, in India."

" Your father was probably an officer in the Indian Army."

" Yes," returned Cuthbert, " he unfortunately fell in battle there. There was another officer of our name in Calcutta, who afterwards became Lord Dunskelling."

Had Cuthbert Gordon looked at Mr. Trevor he would have perceived that he changed colour, and cast a strange enquiring look at our hero.

" Did you ever hear from any of your family—pardon me for asking those questions," added Mr. Herbert Gordon, " but perhaps you might have heard it spoken of. Was your father a relative of the Mr. Gordon you mentioned as being in India at the same time ? "

" Well, I have heard it said," returned our hero, "that the Honourable Alfred Gordon held certain rights that in justice belonged to my father ; that was all I ever heard. I suppose there was a family connection of some kind between them."

Mr. Trevor stood up, saying ; " I shall take a pipe and go on deck," and he did so.

"You, perhaps," said Mr. Herbert Gordon, after a pause of a few moments, " think I was joking when I claimed relationship ; but strange as it may appear, it's a fact.

Your father, William Cuthbert Gordon, and I were cousins by the female side. You appear to know but little of your father's family."

" I confess," said our hero, rather surprised at the turn the conversation had taken, but at the same time inter-ested," I know exceedingly little, if anything, of his early life."

" Ah, so I thought. Now I will tell you some things that may surprise you now I know that you are William Cuthbert Gordon's son, who married the only daughter of Colonel Ludlow. Am I not right ? "

" You certainly are."

" Well, then, though you see me in the somewhat disre-putable character of a smuggler, nevertheless, your father and I were at school together, and if he lived and had his just rights, he would be Lord Dunskelling instead of the present strange eccentric man who bears that title, and has the estates. You look astonished, but I tell you facts. The present Lord Dunskelling resides in Dunskelling Castle, a very fine old pile of building, which stands within pistol shot of the creek I intend running this cutter into to-night or to-morrow night, as the case may be. Now, do you not think it exceedingly singular that you and I should meet in this strange way."

"Very," replied our hero, "but may I ask you how is it that you a gentleman born, bearing a good name, with education and intellect, can possibly follow the unlawful occupation of a smuggler ? "

" A very just question, which I will answer by-and-bye. Just now my mind is bent upon another subject, and it's one that interests me. Lord Dunskelling, it seems, shortly after leaving India, married ; his wife, whom she was I do not know, died giving birth to a little girl. This child, being a girl, has nearly driven him mad, for he would give half his wealth for an heir. It has been reported that he married again, but finding his second wife bring him no heir he cast her off. Now, I know that you, the son of William Cuthbert Gordon, in default of male issue, are the next heir to the title and estates of Dunskelling. You look incredulous, Mr. Gordon; but I am not, I assure you, spinning a fabulous yarn. Your claims are far stronger than Mr.—— " The skipper paused. " Your claims are infinitely stronger than mine. Mine is the female branch."

" All this appears very unaccountable to me," remarked our hero. " It is true I have heard my mother say that my father was very cruelly treated in his youth ; but she never mentioned his possessing any claim to a title or to any estate."

" That is very possible," returned Herbert Gordon. " Your mother very wisely considered it useless to unsettle you, by infusing ideas of title and wealth into your brain that might never be realised."

" Then why," returned Cuthbert Gordon, with a smile, ' do you impart such information, and fill my brain with chimeras? though I candidly tell you it will scarcely disturb or distract my thoughts, or lead me to indulge in vain views or projects. If my father, knowing he possessed certain rights, abandoned them, it would be worse than folly for the son, who knows nothing of those rights, to bother his brains about them."

"But mark my words," returned Herbert Gordon emphatically, "the time will come when you will assert your claims. Your great grandfather Gordon was a Roman Catholic and a partisan of James the Second ; he was of the elder branch of the Gordons, the present Lord Dunskelling the younger. A most iniquitous will threw the estates and title into the possession of the younger branch. It was a period of trial and suffering in Ireland; the laws were harshly administered, your great grandfather a suspected man ; therefore afterwards no stir or effort was made to cast aside the will. But I maintain that even now the present lord would lose the title and estates, if a claimant having large funds at his disposal disputed his right."

" Well," said our hero, " two things are wanting—ambition, and a long purse. I have neither."

8

"The ambition will come; but now I will tell you something more. I have deceived you as to my name. My mother was a Gordon, but my own name is Herbert O'Dowd. And that gentleman pacing the deck overhead, you have heard me name as Trevor, is called Hugh Trevor Fitzpatrick; he is a nephew of Lord Dunskelling—but the uncle and nephew hate each other. Like myself, Fitzpatrick has run through a fine property. A wild, reckless life, extravagant love of pleasure, has stripped me of nearly all.

Passionately fond of the sea, and delighting in adventure, careless of repute or reputation, unable with my reduced means to support the luxury of a yacht, which I always had, I found some wild excitement in smuggling transactions—and thus Fitzpatrick and myself became smugglers."

"It's to be deplored," said Cuthbert Gordon, seriously, and—looking into the handsome open countenance of O'Dowd, "You are still young, and—"

"May do better," added O'Dowd, with a laugh; "but," he added seriously, "perhaps I may; I have a deep purpose at heart; but of that I will not speak. I am alone in the world, I may say; an only sister I have, but she is married to an English officer of property and high family."

"Now, may I ask you," said Cuthbert Gordon, "why, knowing nothing of me, and becoming acquainted in so strange a manner, that you make these revelations, which, to a certain extent, weakens the chances of your friend Fitzpatrick succeeding to the estates and title of Dunskelling."

"I will tell you. In the first place, we cannot account for those sudden and singular prepossessions we imbibe for persons seen only once. Take for example that often abused feeling called 'Love at first sight,' and which feeling has led to the most romantic and heartfelt devotion and passionate attachment. I dearly loved your father; you strongly resemble him. When Fitzpatrick told me your name was Gordon, and that he believed you were the son of the disinherited William Cuthbert Gordon, I became interested; when I saw you clearly and heard your voice, I became convinced, your own narrative, of course, settled the matter. I told Fitzpatrick that I considered you the real heir to the title, if not the estates. He laughed at me, and said ' the d—— may take the title, and the old lord with it, so that I gain the estates. It would take a long purse to unseat me.' "

"' But,' said I, ' you would not act unjustly.'

" ' Well, upon my soul, O'Dowd, your ideas of justice for a smuggler are rather unique,' and there the conversation ended."

A sudden violent heel of the cutter, and the roar of a heavy squall passing over the little vessel, caused the inmates of the cabin to jump up and hurry upon deck.

The crew of the ' Wave,' the name of the cutter, were busy close reefing the mainsail, and shifting the gib. The wind came in squalls, and more to the southward.

"Well, Mr. Gordon," said Mr. Fitzpatrick, and he spoke in rather a sneering tone, " has our friend O'Dowd, for I know he has dropped our nom de guerre, as you are a relative of ours—has he been explaining to you our relative claims to the peerage of Dunskelling ? "

"He has made me acquainted with many things I certainly did not know previously," returned Cuthbert Gordon, coldly, for he did not like Mr. Fitzpatrick's tone or look."

"Ah, well," said Mr. Fitzpatrick, " you will be nothing the better for the knowledge you have gained."

"Perhaps not ; but you need not trouble yourself with my thoughts or ideas."

Mr. O'Dowd joined the two young men, who were beginning to get into a conversation not very likely to lead to a friendship between them.

"We shall not make our port this night, Mr. Gordon," said Mr. O'Dowd, " the wind is scant, the sea heavy, and the look of the sky portends much bad weather."

"I should say it does," returned our hero ; " but your vessel is an exceedingly easy and weatherly boat, and looks up to the wind wonderfully well, and in such a sea."

"There was never a better craft built," remarked the Wave's owner ; "as you remarked, she is rather overmasted for winter work, when our channel is almost always in an uneasy state, the gales are so frequent and so changeable. Nevertheless, if the wind holds as it is, and no worse, we shall make the Irish coast in the morning."

And such was the case, for when Cuthbert Gordon came upon deck the next day, the coast of Ireland was in sight, but with every appearance of a heavy gale of wind before many hours were over.

"Yonder," said Mr. O'Dowd, pointing to a bluff headland, "is the Seven Heads. In four hours at most, we shall make Castle Townsend;" but as they made the land the gale increased so rapidly, and the sea so heavy, that the boom was stowed and the trysail hoisted.

"There is a sail coming out from the land, sir," exclaimed one of the crew from the cross trees, where he had mounted to fasten a rope.

"The deuce there is," exclaimed Herbert O'Dowd, taking his glass and ascending the rigging, and securing himself, he took a look at the sail just sighted.

"By St. Patrick, it's the 'Fox,' revenue cutter, and no other;" and he looked rather serious.

"Confound it," exclaimed Mr. Fitzpatrick; "how is that? I thought that you had certain intelligence that the 'Fox' was laid up for repairs in Plymouth?"

"So the letter I received stated," said O'Dowd; "nevertheless, that's the 'Fox,' the fastest revenue cutter on the Irish station. In moderate and light winds we always have the best of it," continued Herbert O'Dowd, to an observation of our hero's, who was now able with the glass to make out the cutter from the deck. "But I have never tried her in heavy weather like this."

"What do you intend doing, Herbert," questioned Fitzpatrick! "it will not do to be overhauled here, with our hold partly stowed with contraband goods."

"No; that it certainly will not. She is standing out. No doubt makes us out; we must try a race with her."

All the crew of the "Wave" were on deck anxiously watching the approaching cutter. As the wind was, both cutters were close hauled—one standing in, the other out.

"Now, my lads," said O'Dowd to his crew, "stand by, and be lively; have everything in readiness. If she puts about and follows us I shall stand on. Down with our trysail, and up with our double-reefed mainsail, and we shall soon see which has the best legs."

"Aye, aye, sir;" and at once the boom was placed in its place, and the mainsail reefed and ready to hoist.

Cuthbert Gordon was anxiously watching the cutter. Should she overhaul the "Wave," what would be the consequence? He felt a great regret that Mr. O'Dowd should become subject to the law, and be tried as a smuggler. For Mr. Fitzpatrick he felt very little, if any interest. As for himself he would on an explanation, no doubt receive his liberty, which was dear to him. Still, he unaccountably wished that the "Wave" would outsail the "Fox."

"What do you intend doing, Mr. O'Dowd," said our hero, as the cutter rapidly drew near. "The 'Fox' is a much larger craft than this cutter."

"Yes; she is 120 tons, and a very fine, fast vessel. I will stand on unconcerned. I know I am suspected—but that's nothing. He cannot put out a boat in this sea. So if he puts about and follows me, I must try our sailing qualities."

As the revenue cutter drew near, Cuthbert Gordon had a clear view of her. She was a fine looking craft, not exactly like the vessels of her class of the present day. She had neither their wedge-like bow, nor their long counter and fine quarter. Still, she had a look of speed, and also a warlike appearance about her. Her long pennant blew out, stiff and straight as a staff; and a number of men were clustered on her bows gazing at the "Wave." Instead of continuing her course, she ran up as close to the "Wave" as to permit words to be heard, and immediately an officer hailed the "Wave," and desired her to heave to, the "Fox" going in stays at the same moment.

"Now, my lads," said Herbert O'Dowd, "up with the mainsail the moment she fills on the other tack." The "Wave" was then put about, and as she filled on the other tack, up went the mainsail, and the jib shifted at the same time. The moment the " Fox " beheld this manœuvre she put her helm down, and at the same time fired her bow gun into the " Wave," cutting away a back stay, which was quickly repaired.

"Fire away, my darlings," said one of the men, " may you never want saltpetre."

At this moment a sudden and violent squall passed over both vessels, covering them with the spray torn from the tops of the seas.   When the spray passed on, the crew of the " Wave " gave a cheer, for the mainsail of the " Fox " was dashing wildly about; the gaff had snapped.

" Come," said Herbert O'Dowd to our hero, " this will give us an advantage, at all events."

" Yes," returned Cuthbert Gordon, " if your mast stands this heavy strain ; you are carrying a press of sail for this rapidly increasing gale; the 'Wave ' is burying herself."

All aboard were forced to reeve ropes to hold on by, and it took two men to the helm.

" It's getting very thick," returned O'Dowd, " so that shortly we may expect to lose sight of each other; we can then alter our course.   As it is, if I get rid of her I must make the coast near Dunskelling Castle, and land what cargo I have in one of the numerous creeks this side of Cape Clear."

The " Fox " very rapidly repaired her mishap.   Still twenty minutes to a craft, if equal in speed, is a serious advantage ; but it was very apparent to our hero, that the " Fox " in the heavy sea then increasing, must have the advantage from tonnage.   He also expected every plunge the " Wave " made into the breaking surges, she would carry away her mast or· boom.   She was a noble sea boat, but racing in such a gale was perilous work.   Every sea washed her decks, and a tremendous one curling over her larboard bows, swept the boat from its fastenings and carried it clean overboard, and very nearly took two of the men with it. Mr. Fitzpatrick was knocked down, and only that he was secured by a rope, it would have ended his career.

Mr. O'Dowd and our hero shook some of the moisture from their pea coats, and then cast a look at their pursuer.

"Holy Moses, hurrah!" exclaimed one of the crew, "something has happened to the 'Fox.'"

Mr. O'Dowd seized his glass, and almost immediately shouted out joyfully—"Her main-sail is split, and her mast-head gone; there's an end of the chase. Now, my lads, down with the mainsail and secure the boom. By St. Peter, she's a beauty; I thought every moment the mast would go over the side."

"It is high time," thought our hero, as the huge sail was with difficulty gathered in, and then having secured the boom, a storm jib was set. Taking the glass, he perceived that the, 'Fox" cutter had abandoned the chase, heaving her head for the land.

"Well, how is she now Mr. Gordon?" said O'Dowd, coming up.

"Fortune favours you this time, she is making the best of her way for the land."

"Ah!" returned Herbert O'Dowd, "that indeed is a bit of luck, for we could never have carried on as we did much longer for the poor little 'Wave' was burying herself. So far we are clear of the 'Fox,' but it has the appearance of being an awful night."

As the sun set, and as the shades of night fell over the terribly agitated sea, the gale became a hurricane, shifting a point or two more to the southward and westward. Before midnight so furious was the war of elements, with extremely vivid lightning and heavy peals of thunder, and blinding showers of snow and sleet, that the crew were bewildered, when a blast more furious than the rest tore the trysail in ribbons, and then another squall and a tremendous sea nearly swamped the "Wave," knocking over the two men at the helm, and had not Cuthbert Gordon seized the tiller, for every soul on board was on deck, and got her round before the tempest, the next sea would have overwhelmed her.

Herbert O'Dowd was evidently exceedingly anxious.

"We are driving in at a desperate rate for the coast," he remarked to our hero, who relinquished the tiller to two of the crew. "We shall be amongst the Islands of Cape Clear in two hours, and we cannot carry a stitch—

it is a perfect tempest and as dark as pitch. If we could only catch a glimpse of the land there are plenty of fine creeks where shelter could be had."

"Suppose you try and heave her to under close reefed foresail and a small portion of your mainsail hoisted; hoist the peak against the mast, and firmly lash the sail by the reef earrings."

"We can try," said O'Dowd ; "but there's a fearful sea."

With careful management and skill this was done, and for half an hour all hoped she would lie to till daylight, but a monstrous sea broke over her bows, tore the boom from her fastenings, and split the sail, blowing it into ribbons ; though they saved the boom, the cutter was swept round and dashed madly before the unpitying blast. The darkness was intense, and the roar of the tempest was like thunder.

Cuthbert Gordon, not acquainted with the part of the coast they were running down upon, could give no advice; he saw plainly enough that their fate would be very shortly decided, for the instant the cutter struck she would go to pieces. In battle or in tempest he scarcely knew what fear was ; he did not think much of himself, but he thought of his fond devoted mother and loving sisters, and the thoughts of their agony at his loss saddened him.

"Have you no canvas ? " asked our hero of O'Dowd, who was striving to pierce the gloom standing on the bows of the cutter, but the showers of sleet added to the fearful gloom of the night.

"It would be better to try again to arrest our course, for if we could manage to delay till daylight, which will be in two hours at most, you might save life."

"No canvas will stand this furious tempest," said O'Dowd ; "believe me, Mr. Gordon," and he pressed our hero's hand, "the drawing you into this terrible peril crushes me."

Cuthbert Gordon returned the pressure, saying :

"Hope the best, we may drive upon a sandy beach up one of those creeks or inlets you mentioned. It is possible;

all we have to trust to now is providence, for I see your crew are paralysed or something might be done."

"I fear not, Mr. Gordon; no seamanship could make this cutter face these breaking seas, or make canvas stand against such gusts. We are, I fear closer to the coast than we think ; had the lightning lasted we might have got a glimpse of the land, but with this snowdrift we shall not see it before we strike." Suddenly the cutter was lifted on a tremendous sea and then hurled down it with terrible velocity, and then was felt a shock that rent the vessel asunder. A wild shriek of despair mingled with the roar of the tempest and the thunder of the surf, and the days of the " Wave " were numbered—she was split to atoms, and her shattered timbers scattered over the ruthless breakers that thundered over the frightful reef on which she struck, and which lay between her and a place of perfect security.

CHAPTER XIII.

JUST before the unfortunate " Wave " struck upon the reef, Cuthbert Gordon had made his way aft, but the tremendous shock threw every one on the deck prostrate, and as the cutter divided, the next sea swept every soul into the raging breakers that surrounded the reef.

When our hero felt himself hurled from the deck, he uttered a short prayer and closed his eyes, for he expected to be dashed to pieces on the reef ; but the reef was some feet below the tide at low water, and a cross sea caught him and swept him, as he supposed, clear. He came against something hard, and he grasped it, and being a good swimmer and naturally cool and collected, he held on, through a succession of surges, whilst the furious blasts of wind drove him on ; he was quite sensible, but so boiling was the sea, and so heavy the breakers rolling in, he could not prevent himself from being buried in the sea, and at last torn from the boom of the cutter, which he had seized. It was intensely cold, still he struggled for that life which God gave him, and which it was his duty to preserve by every exertion in his power. His limbs were getting numbed, when a huge breaker seized him, and hurled him with terrible violence amongst a reef of rocks. Though frozen and almost exhausted, he strove to resist the receding wave, but another mountainous sea seized him, and threw him, totally exhausted, bleeding, and senseless, high upon the sandy beach ; and there he lay, apparently dead, the dull dreary light of a November morning just tinging the storm-tossed clouds to the east-ward.

How long Cuthbert Gordon remained insensible he could not say, but when he did open his eyes, it was with a vacant dreamy look ; he saw nothing—a kind of mist was before him ; but gradually his recollection returned, and then the haze cleared from his eyes, and he began to distinguish objects.

He perceived that he was in bed and in a large and lofty chamber, and after a time as his sight became clearer, he saw, seated near the fire, by a table covered with various articles—phials, bottles, tea cups—an elderly dame, dressed in black silk, and a peculiar cap on her head. She had spectacles on, and was diligently regarding the progress of a piece of knitting upon which she was employed ; her side face was towards him. It was broad daylight, but the blinds at the windows were drawn down. As yet the invalid had not attempted to move ; he lay perfectly still ; but as he gradually recovered power and recollection, he endeavoured to turn into another position and the attempt caused him to utter a cry of pain, for every limb seemed powerless. The exclamation, however, roused the elderly dame, for she looked up and seeing our hero's eye open, she arose, and with a smile said, as she approach'd the bed—

"The blessed saints be praised, you have opened your eyes at last—this is the third day. Can you speak, my dear?"

"Yes," replied Cuthbert, "thank God I am able to do that; but what do you mean by the third day?"

"Why, my dear, this is the third day since you were brought here, bleeding, shockingly bruised, and quite insensible; but does not talking hurt you?"

"Well, no dame, it does not; but I am very weak, and can only move my right hand a little."

"You cannot be otherwise than weak, my dear sir," said the old dame, "for excepting some drink and a little beef tea I gave you, you have had nothing. But Dr. Burke said you must not be allowed to talk when you come to yourself; so be silent, and thank the saints in glory that you are saved."

"Oh—one question, my good dame, and I will obey you—was any one saved from the wreck beside myself?"

"As yet my dear, we have not heard; five poor bodies were washed ashore about a mile from here—all torn and mangled by the rocks, but they were—the saints be glorified and forgive them—they were all poor mariners. We heard that the vessel lost was Mr. O'Dowd's yacht, but nothing has been heard of him, or of our master's nephew, who was thought to be with him. Oh, dear! to think of born gentlemen, of good means and families, turning wicked smugglers. There, now, my dear, be quiet; you are, I see, agitated, and that is bad."

"Ah!" sighed Gordon, a racking pain shooting through his head, which was bandaged all round, "Ah! poor O'Dowd. But, dame—am I in Dunskelling Castle?" he asked anxiously.

"To be sure you are—there now do be quiet—I will answer no more questions; take this composing drink." The patient obeyed the order, and shortly after dropped off into an uneasy slumber.

Three more days passed, and then Cuthbert Gordon's strong constitution rallied. Move out of bed he could not, for his limbs, though no bones were broken, were sadly bruised, and the flesh in places lacerated. His head had escaped the rocks wonderfully, or he must have perished. During those three days the old dame, and a tidy, comely girl, were constant in their attendance on him. Dr. Burke had paid one visit, said he was going on well, and all he required was quiet, and nourishing food and simple fluids; his attendance was no longer necessary.

The eighth day of his residence in Dunskelling Castle he was lying quietly in his bed, the old dame sitting by the fire, the blinds were up, and a cheerful glimpse of sunshine flooded the chamber with its enlivening power. The invalid felt wonderfully better, he could move his limbs and his hands without pain, the bandages were taken off his head, and he felt a most decided inclination to get up and sit in the nice easy chair by the side of the fire, and write to his dear mother and relieve her terrible anxiety. He was about to call dame Brennen to his bedside, to ask a hundred questions, when the chamber door opened, and a head and face appeared at the opening. Cuthbert Gordon gazed spell-bound, speechless; in his unsettled imagination he thought he beheld a vision; it was, however, no vision, but the face he saw was one of the loveliest the imagination of a poet could picture for the theme of his pen. It was that of a young girl scarcely sixteen, certainly not more, with a profusion of the richest auburn hair, hanging in clusters of ringlets over neck and shoulders; an exquisitely fair, oval countenance, with the bright colour of health and youth in her rounded cheek. As her eyes met those of our hero a bright sweet smile parted the small, beautiful lips, and with, " Ah, I see you are better, cousin, I am so glad," the head was withdrawn, and the door cloed.

The sick man' head fell back upon the pillow; he closed his eyes, for he wished to keep the lovely youthful face before him in his imagination. "So," said he to himself, "that beautiful girl is Lord Dunskelling's daughter ? She called me cousin." After a moment he summoned dame Brennen, who came to is bedside, bringing her chair, and taking off her spectacles, with a smile said :

"I see, m' dear sir, that you are well enough to talk, and are longing to ask questions."

"I am longing to get up, Mrs. Brennen," replied our hero; "and I think I could do so very well."

"Well, I think you may," observed the housekeeper, "I expect your clothes will be here to-day from Cork."

The young man looked surprised, saying : "Where are my own ?"

"Oh, my dear soul, there was scarcely a rag left on you, they were so torn in shreds by the rocks. Luckily in your jacket, much as it was torn, your pocket book, and some letters, and a ring were found safe, or you would not probably be here."

"Then how did it all happen, Mrs. Brennen ? I am sure I ought to be deeply grateful for all the kindness and attention that I have received at yours and his lordship's hands."

"Oh, I assure you his lordship is very anxious about you ; he saw you when you were brought here by his orders, and took charge of your pocket book, and letters, and purse, and watched anxiously for your recovery the first three days ; but most important business called him to Cork, and then to Dublin, but we expect him next week ; and I am sure that dear angel of a girl, his daughter, was as anxious about you as if you had been her own brother ; many a time when you slept she came in and watched you while I went for something."

"Ah, that accounts for those strange visions I thought I had, which I attributed to fever. But it was no vision I saw awhile ago, at all events."

"No, my dear, that was her dear sweet face you beheld, I saw her peep in, but seeing you awake, she went away."

"It is a face I shall never forget," said Cuthbert Gordon, thoughtfully.

"No, it's not likely you will," said Dame Brennen, seriously, "it's like is not often seen in this world, the blessed saints watch over her," and tears stood in the old dame's eyes.

"Have you had any tidings of Mr. O'Dowd or Mr. Fitzpatrick ? Were their bodies found ?"

"No my dear sir, they were not found ; it is, however, said they were saved, washed upon the little Island of

Chickens—or Chick Rock, as it is called—but nothing positive is known. One of the men was saved on the mast, but frightfully hurt; he is in the village. It's from him, the priest, Father Boyle, got all the intelligence of the wreck; he told the priest that there was a gentleman in the cutter called Gordon, who was carried off from the Welsh coast by force, and feared he was drowned. Miss Dunskelling and her governess go to Cork to-day, but they will be back in three or four days."

"But who found me and thus saved my life?" questioned our hero.

"Tom MacGrath the gamekeeper, found you in the early morning. He saw something dark on the sands, close by a terrible range of rocks, which the great waves were tumbling and foaming over, and as the tide was coming in would soon carry off the dark object, which, though the light was only breaking, he thought was likely to be a body cast ashore from some wreck. So he went down to see, and there you were all in rags, and, as he thought dead; he dragged you further up, but could not lift you, so he ran for help, and with the two fishermen they carried you to the lodge. When they perceived that you were not dead, the keeper came to the castle and told me all about finding you, and gave me your pocket book and the other things, and when I saw your name in gold letters on the pocket book I took it to my lord; he opened it, read some of the contents, and seemed greatly agitated, and at once ordered that you should be brought here on a sofa, and sent for Doctor Burke—so now you know all."

Cuthbert Gordon remained for several moments immersed in thought. Dame Brennen saw he was preoccupied, so she left the room to look after her household affairs. He knew, for his mother had often spoke of her early life, that Lord Dunskelling had once been a suitor for her hand when in India; and also that her father and Lord Dunskelling were cousins. The character given of his lordship by Mr. O'Dowd and Mr. Fitzpatrick was anything but pre-possessing, and yet by the housekeeper's account and the kind treatment he had received under his lordship's roof, such a description of character did not quite assimilate.

Feeling a great inclination to get up, he looked round the room, but saw no garments of any kind that he could put on. However, the next day, two suits of clothes arrived from Cork, and the housekeeper handed him a letter which he at once guessed was from Lord Dunskelling. Opening it, he read the contents with considerable surprise, they were as follows :—

"Cork, November 28th, 179—.

"Lord Dunskelling's compliments to Mr. Gordon, is happy to hear that he is rapidly recovering health and strength, and begs he will make himself at home in Dunskelling Castle. Mr. Gordon need not be uneasy respecting his family, as a letter has been forwarded to Mrs. Gordon, stating his safety, and also where he was. In six or eight days Lord Dunskelling expects to arrive at the Castle, till then he requests Mr. Gordon not to leave, as he most particularly wishes to see him before his return to England."

"His lordship is very kind, indeed," said our hero, greatly moved by the contents of the letter. "One great anxiety is off my mind. My dear mother, by this time, knows I am alive and where I am."

That evening he dressed himself, sat up, and felt wonderfully better. The day after, Mrs. Brennen, seeing him so very much stronger and walking about, asked him if he would like to take a ramble over the house and see the family pictures and other very valuable curiosities the present lord had collected abroad.

To this proposal our hero willingly assented, he had exceedingly admired the view from his chamber window, and the building seemed to him to stand on a slight elevation, commanding most varied views over sea and land, with extensive shrubberies, noble oak and elm trees surrounded a lawn of thirty or forty acres.

"I should so like to breathe the fresh air, Mrs. Brennen ; indeed I think it would make me soon quite well, and enable me to start for England."

"You would not go, surely, without seeing his lordship," said the old dame.

"Certainly not," returned Cuthbert Gordon, "that would be exceedingly ungrateful. He says in his letter he will be here in a few days."

Our hero followed Mrs. Brennen from the chamber, proceeding through a long corridor having many chambers leading off it ; they descended a flight of stairs, and Mrs. Brennen opening a door, they came out on a spacious gallery running round three sides of a large lofty hall. Cuthbert Gordon paused, and leaning on the rails, gazed down into the hall with a strange feeling pervading his brain. He now beheld what ought to have been, he was told, his father's residence, the birthplace of many of his race, original settlers in the time of Elizabeth, the lands won by the sword.

"What a noble hall!" said our hero to Mrs. Brennen who stood by his side.

"Yes," said the old dame, with a sigh, " it is a grand hall ; and forty-five years ago that hall echoed again with the voices and laughter, and boisterous merriment of the dependants of the old lord, who always kept up great state. There were harpers and bagpipers, and huntsmen and hounds at the house, always full of gaiety, and other such feastings and junketings ; but I shall never see the like again—those days are passed away for me."

"You must have been very young, Mrs. Brennen, to remember those times ? "

"Not so young, Mr. Gordon, for I was then sixteen ; but that was quite old enough to remember the doings of those days. My mother was housekeeper, and my father chief huntsman to the old lord—a situation much thought of in those days. The present lord keeps neither horses nor hounds—I mean hunters. Four or five in-door male domestics, and the same number of females constitute the present in-door establishment.. Ah, my dear sir, times are changed, and men too. Let us go into the great drawing room, where you will see the portraits of Lord and Lady Dunskelling, and their daughter, the Lady Dora"

Opening a door, the housekeeper ushered our hero into

really magnificent saloon, lofty, and handsomely furnished. Over the white marble chimney piece hung three
small but beautifully executed portraits.

"Whilst you are looking at these," said Mrs. Brennen,
"I will go and open the windows of the picture gallery."

Cuthbert Gordon approached the portraits, and certainly Dora Dunskelling was the first that attracted his
attention. "Oh, how like, and how exquisitely lovely."
As he said the words he was startled by a sweet voice
behind him, saying, "Oh, it's Mr. Gordon," and turning
round, to his surprise he beheld two ladies—they had
entered the room whilst he was occupied gazing at the
portraits. They had both their bonnets and travelling
mantles on, and fur tippets round the neck.

"I beg pardon, ladies," said our hero with a low bow,
and his eyes fixed upon the charming face of Lord Dun-
kelling's daughter; "Mrs. Brennen was so kind as to
permit me to wander over the house."

"Make no apologies, Mr. Gordon, I beg," said Miss
MacCormack, the governess; "we are, I assure you, ex-
ceedingly glad to see you are so rapidly improving in health.
Let me introduce to you Lady Dora Dunskelling."

Dora, with a sweet, playful smile, said, as she held out
a hand fair and small enough to captivate a saint, and our
hero was no saint, "Oh, you know we are cousins, my
papa says, so there ought to be no formality between us;
besides you have seen me before, for I often peeped
in to see how you were getting on after your terrible
shipwreck."

Cuthbert Gordon took the hand and very gallantly
kissed it, saying, "I really believe, Lady Dora, that your
kind visits acted like fairy spells, and drove away all my
pains and aches."

The young girl laughed, and looking into Miss Mac-
Cormack's face, said, "Now do not you think it is extremely formal for a cousin to call me Lady Dora? I do
so dislike it."

"Fortunately, Dora," replied the governess, laughing,
"the remedy is remarkably easy."

"Bless me!" exclaimed Mrs. Brennen, entering the

9

room, and starting back, "when did you arrive, Miss MacCormack ? "

Dora had thrown her arm round the old dame's neck and kissed her, saying, "why you are not vexed, nurse, are you, at my coming back a day or two sooner than we intended ? "

" No, bless your dear, sweet face, no ; you are the light of my eyes, my darling, and the sun never shines so bright when you are away.   Has his lordship arrived ? "

" No," said Miss MacCormack, "he is in Dublin; the reason we came back to-day was that we had an escort of dragoons as far as Glandore.   The people are hostile and troublesome there, and bent upon plundering a revenue cutter that went ashore in the late heavy gale."

Mr. Gordon remarked, " I suppose, Miss MacCormack, the cutter you mention was the ' Fox ? ' "

" Yes," returned the governess, " that is her name; she is not much injured, having run into the outward harbour on the soft mud. If you will excuse us, Mr. Gordon, we will go and take off our things, and if you feel well enough, we shall be glad of your company to tea."

" I shall be too happy," returned our hero, with a look at Dora.

The young girl was as innocent as a child, and what was she but a child, reared in seclusion ? she wanted a month of being sixteen, but she was tall and exceedingly graceful, and more fully formed than most girls are at that age.

" Well, good-bye, cousin Gordon, for the present; if you will wait till to-morrow I will show you my gardens and green-houses and my pond of gold fishes, and I dare say the fresh air will do you a world of good."

" Your company, cousin," said our hero quite delighted with his new found relative, "will drive away all the sad fancies that have beset my sick couch, these many days back."

" Oh, dear me, you must not be sad with me," said Dora, "I am sometimes inclined that way myself, so two sad people would be terrible company for each other."

Dora and her governess retired, and then Mrs. Brennen

observed with a smile, "I think, Mr. Gordon, you had better wait till to-morrow, when lady Dora will show you the pictures in the gallery, and explain them better than I can. Don't you think she is beautiful?"

"She has the most fascinating face I ever beheld," said Cuthbert Gordon, "it is almost too lovely."

"Ah! in a year or so more," said Mrs. Brennen, thoughtfully, and then looking up into our hero's pale but hand-

" You 'wou... she added :—

The person addressed started, and couple."
Brennen, but the old lady was exceedingly serious, so he made no reply, but retired to his chamber, deeply immersed in thought, and remained gazing out of the window upon the distant sea, seen through a vista of noble oaks that bounded and encircled the lawn or rather park, till daylight faded away, and then Dame Brennen came to tell him the ladies were in the red drawing room, and that tea was ready.

Cuthbert Gordon was the last man in the world to be accused of vanity; his tall and graceful figure looked well in any costume, nevertheless he did give a look into his mirror before quitting the chamber; he was pale, it was true, but his fine open manly countenance, so prepossessing in strong health, was more interesting from recent illness. The garments sent him fitted him well, they were after the fashion of private gentlemen of that period.

The red drawing room into which he was ushered, was very handsome, but not near so large as the one adjoining; a bright fire blazed on the hearth, and everything looked so comfortable and homely that it recalled his own home to his memory.

Miss MacCormack was a lady of some six and thirty years, she was handsome, very lady-like, and exceedingly agreeable. Dora welcomed her cousin in the same kind sisterly manner, called him frequently Cuthbert, without the slightest feeling that she was acting familiarly in any way unbecoming her age or station. Her father said to her at parting :—

"My dear child, you have my consent to treat Mr.

9—2

Gordon, not only as a cousin which he is, but as a brother; there need be no formality between you, make him happy and comfortable till I join you again, and if I am detained, do not on any account let him depart before I reach home."

Dora kissed her father's serious brow; she loved him dearly and he idolised his child. What his views were, or what his thoughts, we cannot say; at all events he threw the young couple into close intimacy after lives. that was most li

CHAPTER XIII.

DAYS passed over, and, must we say it? Cuthbert Gordon evinced no desire to set out for England. Lord Dunskelling was still in Dublin, the times were terrible, rebellion filled the land, outrages were rife through all the counties, but at Dunskelling all was quietness and peace.

The young cousins rambled together through the old mansion, and out into the shrubberies. Dora shewed her hot-house plants, her pet fish, and her favourite pony. In the evening she played and sung, and every word, every tone, sank deep into her hearer's heart. To him, Dora Dunskelling was all the world; he told her of his early life, related his adventures, to which the young girl listened with breathless attention, with her large blue eyes fixed upon his dark ones, scarcely breathing, when, listening to the scenes of peril he had passed through. No word of love passed, not for worlds would our hero have spoken of what he felt. She appeared the personification of truth and innocence, but he could not help loving her with a profound devotion. One evening, just two days before Lord Dunskelling's intended return, Dora invited Cuthbert Gordon, as Miss MacCormack was not very well, to accompany her to the hamlet of Dunskelling, and to some cottages where she had many pensioners. The day was unusually fine for a December day. In four days they would have Christmas, and Dora was anxious that none of her pensioners, and their name was legion, should want any little comfort during that festive season. Having performed her happy task and received the blessings of the poor, many an encomium was passed upon the handsome couple, with remarks that for the first time made Dora's heart beat faster, for she could not but understand the kind words and wishes of the many that expressed their feelings ; for Cuthbert Gordon's manner was always kind an winning, and his fine figure and prepossessing countenance attracted general attention. The colour was rich in Dora's cheek as they left the last cottage where her favourite pensioner lived with an only daughter, a comely girl, who supported her mother and young brother by her own industry aided by Dora's donations ; for the mother, a widow, could not use her limbs, being afflicted with rheumatism.

"May the saints in glory bless you, Alanna," said the widow, clasping her hands. "You are as fair a pair of creatures as ever God made and blessed. May ye never be separated, for he made ye one for another, and the love that is in your hearts. Acushla ma chree is in your eyes, and may it flourish for ever in this life !"

Dora's cheek burned, but she merrily said : "Good bye, Mrs. Kyle, I hope the spring and summer will restore you the use of your limbs. Now be sure, Mary," she added, turning to the daughter, " to give the medicine regularly, and rub the lotion on the limbs well and carefully," and they left the cottage.

"How very much the fishing population suffer from rheumatism," said Cuthbert, as they walked on quickly, for it was nearly sunset.

"They do, indeed, poor things," said Dora, "but see what a life they lead, perpetually in wet garments, and they are besides so careless."

They had, on their way back, to pass along the skirts of the park, a high fence on one side and the open sands on the other, and through which ran a small creek, navigable for some two or three miles inland for boats.

They had just reached the gate, or rather stile, leading into the park, when six men, habited as sailors, with heavy bludgeons in their hands, sprang from behind a fence, and rushed upon Cuthbert Gordon. The foremost of the men, presenting a pistol, cried out, " A shout or a stir, or resistance of any kind, and I'll blow your brains out! "

This man Cuthbert Gordon struck to the ground, as Dora uttered a cry of agony and despair. As Cuthbert stooped to seize the man's bludgeon, the five others threw themselves upon him, and despite his furious struggles, bore him to the earth, and at once secured his hands with cords. Two of the men seized the distracted Dora, and deaf to her shrieks, carried her inside the park gate, and told her to go to the house, no one would hurt a hair of her head; but if she screamed any more it would only cause the death of her lover.

Dora, at once, knowing she could do nothing to help her unfortunate cousin, rushed wildly across the park to get assistance. The butler beheld her, and so did Miss MacCormack from the drawing-room window, and bewildered rushed out of the hall door, but before they reached her the young girl fairly fainted from terror and the wild beating of her heart.

She was carried into the house, and quickly recovered; still valuable time had been lost, for when the whole household and the gamekeeper rushed down the park, having learned what had occurred, nothing was to be seen except some blood on the ground, and the marks of a terribly severe struggle, but the actors in it were all gone.

It was then dusk, but light enough for them to perceive a boat pulled by six oars leaving the mouth of the creek, and standing out to sea. On returning to the castle, Miss MacCormack, who was sitting beside Dora's couch, for the terrible fright she had endured and the over-exertion of running, and her own internal feelings, quite overpowered her, and feverish and ill, she had retired to her chamber. She said :—

" This is a sad affair, Julia, and a most incomprehensible one.   For what purpose could this outrage be committed ? "

Miss MacCormack looked exceedingly thoughtful. There appeared to be something on her own mind relative to this outrage that disturbed her, but she evidently did not wish Dora to observe that, so she roused herself from her thoughts. She saw very plainly that Dora regarded Cuthbert Gordon with a feeling far stronger than that of cousinship and was also aware that Lord Dunskeling wished a union between his daughter and her cousin, and from some reasons of her own she also wished to encourage Dora's incipient love. Mrs. Brennen just then entered the room—"Oh dear me," she exclaimed, " what times we do live in. They have carried off Mr. Gordon in a boat, and gone to sea ! "

" Well, thank God," said Dora, " they have not killed him ! What horrified me, was hearing one of the men say he would blow his brains out if he attempted to move."

"What ought to be done, my dear child ?"

" Send a messenger on horseback," she said, recovering her energy and thought, "to Skibouge Cove—there's always a revenue vessel there—mention my father's name, and say that a gentleman residing in Dunskelling Castle has been forcibly carried off to sea in a rowing boat. I am sure the cutter will put to sea in pursuit, and endeavour to track those who have committed this outrage, and any of the fishing hookers at Skibouge will willingly go also and endeavour to discover those who carried Mr. Gordon off."

" I will do so," said Miss MacCormack ; " I am bewildered, for I cannot imagine why and for what purpose this outrage was committed."

" They were all sailors," said Dora to Mrs. Brennen, " and strangers to me. I could see them plainly enough ; they were not disguised, neither were they ruffianly-looking men—all young, and just like the sailors in ships—they were gentle to me in their manner, though they did threaten me if I screamed. Alas ! my screams could reach no one from that lonely spot."

Whilst every exertion possible was making to trace and overtake the abductors of Cuthbert Gordon, our unlucky hero was lying bound at the bottom of the boat that six stout young seamen impelled seaward. He felt amazed at his situation, and could not imagine why this fresh outrage had been committed, and by whose command. He saw that the men pulling the boat were sailors; it was dusk as they rounded the island and reef upon which perished the " Wave."

" Well, now sir," said the man pulling the stroke oar, " if you'll only be easy I'll untie your hands, for be gor, it's not pleasant anyhow to be pinioned like a fat capon."

" If you mean that I will not try to escape," said our hero indignantly, "you are mistaken; I will pass no word of that kind."

" Oh, my lad, escape if you can, it's only natural; I threatened to shoot you, and you knocked me down, and be gor, your fist is like a sledge hammer, but I bear you no malice; I didn't intend to shoot you, though I said it; no one will hurt you ; but if you follow my advice, take it easy ;" and drawing his knife, he cut the cords that bound our hero's hands, and which had been drawn so tight as to rub off the skin.

The captive rose and sat down in the stern sheets, and then looked about him ; they were two or three miles from the shore ; it was getting very dark, the wind was off the land, and the water smooth.

His thoughts were centred upon Dora, and the agonised look of her beautiful features, when she beheld him overpowered, was more heartbreaking to him than all else.

" There she is ! " exclaimed one of the men in the forepart of the boat; " all right."

Cuthbert Gordon looked seaward, and beheld what appeared a fishing hooker, lying to. In less than ten minutes the boat was alongside.

" Here we are, Mullins, all right. Now sir, jump up," continued the man, turning to our hero, " there's no use moping like a sick cat. You can't help it, so grin and bear it."

" I know it is useless complaining," replied Cuthbert,

almost staggered by the singularity and strangeness of the outrage committed upon him ; " but it strikes me that you will pay dearly, some day, for this monstrous outrage upon a person who never injured you."

"Well, I can't say you have injured me ; but just go aboard, you will find old Jack Mullins, the skipper of this here hooker, a regular sea lawyer, and he thinks himself a sea cook besides."

Knowing how utterly useless it was to complain, or argue matters with ten or twelve determined men, well paid to act as they were doing, the young man seized the shroud and sprang on board the hooker. The skipper, a wild-looking, hairy individual, so enveloped in pea-jacket, handkerchiefs, and a sou-wester, as to be almost imperceptible, as far as his features were concerned, looked at our hero from head to foot in the dim light.

" Well, Denis," he sung out, addressing the man who had hitherto spoken to our hero. "Blow me, if I can make out nohow why you have brought this here young man in the togs of a shore-going gent."

"Come here, Jack, and I'll soon put you up to the matter," said Denis, " but let the hooker go ahead, and keep well to the eastward."

A man went to the tiller, another let draw the fore-sheet, and the third slacked the main-sheet, and the hooker gathered away.

Now, what to do sorely puzzled our hero, his fate appeared to him a very strange one; twice carried away by main force, once from his home, and again, from one he loved with all the strong passion of his nature. His first abduction he could easily comprehend ; he was wanted out of the way for a short time, so he was carried across the channel, and at the time he considered it most lamentable, but he deemed it the most fortunate event of his life, for his thoughts were all centred upon Dora Dunskelling.

He felt quite satisfied that he was not carried off by these men in the hooker, for their own projects. There was some one able and willing to pay for the outrage committed upon him—who could it be ?

Assured that O'Dowd, if saved from the wreck, was

incapable of the act, his thoughts turned upon Mr. Fitz-patrick; had he been saved, might it not be possible he was at the bottom of the plot, and no doubt the instigator. Cuthbert was, according to Mr. O'Dowd, the nearest in succession to the Dunskelling title. Might not Mr. Fitz-patrick have an idea that he should secure the hand of Lord Dunskelling's daughter, who, let the title and estates go where they might, would still be a great heiress ? He remembered to have once asked Dora, if she had ever met Mr. Fitzpatrick.

"Oh, yes," she replied, " he has resided at Dunskelling Castle for months. I could not bear him, his presence and his conversation made me uncomfortable ; and finally, my father, disgusted at his extravagance and pride, quarrelled with him and requested him to leave the castle, making him a handsome allowance. I was not more than fourteen at that time," continued Dora, " but I know I hoped I should never see him again; but if he is unhappily drowned, his faults and his errors must be forgotten, in commiseration of his miserable end."

From these thoughts the young man was roused by the skipper of the hooker coming up to him. There was very little light, for the night was a dark one, so much so that features could not be distinguished.

"I am very sorry, young man," said the skipper, " that I am to have a share in this here affair of yours, I'm blowed if I ain't."

" Well, I am glad to hear you say so, skipper," said our hero, for the act is one, that some day or other, will have to be severely atoned for."

" As to that, I can't say, but I don't think so. You will never find any of us again when we part."

" But if you are sorry at being mixed up in this outrage," said Cuthbert Gordon, " surely you can easily get rid of the responsibility. Put me ashore."

" Shiver my timbers, I can't do that. I'm only one out of eight hardy determined fellows bound together by oaths. No, no ; you must lump it, till you can get a chance of escape. Now just come down into my cuddy, I will have a yarn with you, for blow me if I don't think it's a cursed hard case to send a fine young fellow like you to——hem," coughed the skipper, after seeing one of the crew coming aft. "Come below, I'm going to supper, and dash it, a man must eat and drink, though he may know that the next day it's all up with him."

Our hero thought the skipper a very strange mortal, but anxious to know where he was to go, and also to find out perhaps who was the contriver and instigator of his abduction, he followed the skipper into the miserably small cabin of the hooker.

"This here cuddy ain't very big," said the skipper, "and it's not over lofty, seeing you are a head too tall for standing in it, but we get use to these here inconveniences at sea."

A small candle was stuck in the neck of a bottle which just rendered things visible ; there was a small cabin, with a fire in it, and on the fire a large iron pot in which something was boiling ; but the smell of the cabin was indescribable ; it was a compound of stale fish, bilge water, coal tar, tarred rope, and sails and wet garments ; it had four berths, or rather four shelves, about eighteen inches broad, and eight of these cribs, intended for sleeping in, had about fourteen inches to spare from the deck. It would require a very composed sleeper to lie in one of these wooden boxes, or otherwise a remarkably hard head. Cuthbert could and had borne a great deal of suffering one way or another during his one and twenty years of life ; but the smell of the hooker's cuddy he considered the worst of his trials. He sat down with an air of resignation watching the operations of his companion, who opened a locker and pulled out two wooden plates, a loaf of bread, two or three rusty knives and forks, and a jar, which he placed on the locker. He then divested himself of his immense pilot coat, his wrappers, and his huge sou'-wester, and, looking at him more carefully, our hero perceived that he was a youngish man when divested of his beard and moustache, certainly not more than eight and thirty or forty.

"Now, Mister," cried the skipper, lifting the cover of the pot, and sticking an iron fork into it. "Let us have supper," and he pulled out a piece of salt junk, and put it on a trencher. "Hollo, boy," he shouted out through the hatchway, "take this here pot and bring the kettle with some clean water in it."

A boy of some twelve or fourteen years came and seized the pot, intending to consume the soup for his own individual use. It was impossible to envy him. The skipper cut off slices of the junk, and placed them on a trencher, saying :—"I fear, Mister, it's rather hard, but I've eat harder."

"Thank you," said Cuthbert Gordon. "I am not the least hungry."

"Ah !" said the skipper, shaking his head, and making vigorous efforts to masticate a piece of beef that would have choked any ordinary mortal. "Ah! you were not born to be a sailor."

"You are mistaken, skipper, for I was a midshipman seven years, and would shortly be a lieutenant aboard a frigate, but for this affair. However it's no use talking of what I should be ; the fact is I am unlawfully a prisoner aboard this craft."

"Well, I am vexed—I'm blowed if I ain't ; and I ax your pardon, sir, for the part I am acting. I knows really nothing of this affair. I am made a tool of, and unless I sacrifice myself I can't help you, sir ; and even if I kicked against it, there are eight stout fellows who are bound by oaths, and according as their project is carried out so they will be paid, and no offer of greater pay will make them break their oath, you see, sir. I'll tell you how I stand. I served on board a man-of-war nine years —but the kettle boils ; if your honour won't eat, maybe as how this cold night you'll take a drop of hot grog,"— and taking out two horn mugs, he as he spoke, opened the jar, and put a bowl of sugar on the locker beside our hero.

Anxious to gather all the information he possibly could, as to his situation, from Jack Mullins, who appeared inclined to be very communicative, Gordon mixed himself a horn of whisky—and whisky of a very superior kind.

Pleased to see his guest help himself, the skipper did

the same, but like Father Murphy, he was exceedingly sparing of the water.

"Well, what made you leave the service?" questioned Cuthbert Gordon.

"The cat, sir—the cursed cat with the nine tails. I was a wild youth, sir, and no mistake! My parents were very respectable people, and had a good and likely trade, and had money, and gave me a fair education; but I made bad use of both the money and the learning. I got into scrapes went to England, and when drunk was pressed. Well, I did not dislike the service for all that; but after nine years and rising to be a petty officer, I fell under the claws of a tyrant. I struck a master's mate, and kicked him. I was not drunk. No matter what I kicked him for, he deserved it. I was to have two hundred lashes and be kicked out of the service, just escaping swinging to the yard arm by a miracle. Well, Sir, I took my punishment and was turned adrift. I got well, and watching an opportunity, I met the cause of my mishap at Portsmouth, and gave him a crack over the skull, that though he got quit for his life forced him to quit the service. I got away to Ireland, despite the hue and cry after me, found both my parents dead, and my brother John gone off to America with all they left behind them. I was a marked man, so I became a smuggler. In one of our affrays with the Coastguard, I shot the chief officer. Luckily he did not die. I was caught, imprisoned, and condemned to death —but I had friends. Four of the men now aboard this hooker here—tried with me for smuggling and assaulting the Coastguard, and killing one of them—were sentenced to fifteen years' transportation—but we managed to break out of jail, having had assistance to enable us to do so; and my comrades bound themselves by terrible oaths to the man who assisted them. We are now waiting for a schooner from a port to the northward, bound for the Gambia river, on the coast of Africa. This schooner is to be employed in the slave trade, and we are bound to serve in her, and I daresay none of us will ever return to this country again. Now, that's my yarn, your honour; I have told you my bad qualities and bad deeds; and, bad as they were, blow me if I would hurt the hair on a child's head ; but I respect an oath. This hooker will be left to the care of the real owner, and the boy you saw a while ago, when we all join the schooner."

" So," said Cuthbert Gordon, bitterly, " I am to be conveyed to the coast of Africa—and what then ? "

" Well, your honour, that I can't say ; but this I will say—I am only bound to my comrades till we reach the Gambia river, I may then either continue aboard the slaver or shift for myself. You may manage to escape, and I will aid you all in my power. From what I can make out, you are wanted out of the way for a year or so, and they make sure of your not getting back for many a long day. I am not in the secret, neither am I bound not to speak of what I do know. Having said so much, I'll mix another horn and tell you all about this slave schooner."

This relation convinced the listener that Lord Dunskelling's nephew, Fitzpatrick, was the contriver of this plot for carrying him off, in order to continue his projects against the peace and happiness of Dora, and to seize the estates should anything happen to Lord Dunskelling, who, suffering under a terrible disease of the heart, might at any moment, if excited, be carried off.

He could not, let his life be what it might—and it was bad enough by his own showing—he could not but feel grateful to Jack Mullins ; he could see into the character of the man, otherwise with his daring spirit he would have proposed to attack the other men, and attempt to take possession of the hooker, but he clearly perceived that Mullins would never turn against his comrades ; besides, after the acts he had committed, he could never show himself again in either England or Ireland without a certainty of hanging if caught.

It was a terrible misfortune to have to sail in a slave schooner, the crews of such vessels being always composed of the most reckless and lawless men to be found, to whom suffering and death were as nought—men who could laugh and exult over the tortures of wretched slaves and treat them worse than dogs.

"You must not give way to moping, sir," said Jack Mullins, as he replenished his horn, "it's no manner of use."

"I never do," replied Gordon. "I have had my trials young as I am; I am thinking of others, not of myself. I am strong and not easily put down ; if I had had any serviceable weapon those six men would never have taken me alive."

"So Dennis Malloy said," returned the skipper ; "he feared at one time you would have forced them to extremity."

"That is to say," said our hero, "if there was no other alternative, those men would have taken my life."

Jack Mullins rubbed his head and looked mystified.

"Now tell me," said Cuthbert Gordon, "what you know of this slave schooner."

"Faith, your honour, I know no good of her captain, anyhow, they say he's a born devil, is drunk ten hours out of the twenty-four, and cursing and swearing the other fourteen, for they say he never sleeps—but that's fudge."

"Then how comes it that you and others ship with such a ruffian ? "

"Because, sir, we're all marked men, and one voyage, if successful, will make us, and then we shall get away to America."

"In what character do you suppose I am to ship aboard this slaver," asked Cuthbert Gordon, almost fiercely.

"Well, sir," returned Jack Mullins, looking up into the flushed features of our hero, " Dennis Malloy, who undertook the job of entrapping you aboard, says he has received orders to supply you with clothes and whatever you may want from the stores of the schooner, which carries out a large quantity of sailor's apparel and a thousand other things to barter with the African. slaveholders."

Nearly suffocated with the smell and fumes of the hooker's cuddy, Cuthbert got up, saying he would go on deck.

" Well, sir—one word more, please not to be offended ; take the skipper of the schooner quietly, it's no use teasing the tiger till he shows his claws, bear up till we reach the Gambia, and I swear I will do all I can to lend you a hand to escape out of the slaver."

"I thank you for your good intentions, Mullins, and will try and follow your advice, which to certain tempers might be valuable. I value life, but I value it ten times more for the sake of others that are dear to me than for myself. I am passionate and hasty, and cannot answer for what I may do or bring on myself, if irritated by brutal treatment."

Cuthbert Gordon then went on deck. It was a fine moonlight night, with a cold, keen wind off the land. The hooker was under her full sail standing to the eastward; there were ten men and a boy aboard her, besides Jack Mullins. As he came up from the cuddy, Denis Malloy and three others went down, but Mullins approached and offered our hero a heavy new pilot coat, saying the night was exceedingly cold; he had never used the coat, and he had several others.

The young man thanked him, and as he was thinly clad and intending staying on deck all night he was glad of the comfort the coat afforded him.

CHAPTER XIV

As soon as the sun rose the hooker was hove to, some four or five miles off the coast, and a flag with three stripes—red, white, and blue—hoisted at her mast head.

The captive had remained all night upon deck, though Jack Mullins, the only one who spoke a word to him, pressed him to lie down in one of the berths in the cuddy, but our hero much preferred the fresh air, and towards morning, stretching himself under the weather bulwarks, slept for an hour or two. This was no hardship to him, he had done so many and many a time,

Jack Mullins proffered him some hot coffee and biscuit for breakfast, and a piece of his salt junk. The coffee and the biscuit satisfied our hero, whose thoughts and reflections left him listless. The sweet, youthful face of Dora haunted his mind ; when this dear image faded away there came one of his mother and his sisters, fretting and pining at their loss. Altogether for one of his hopeful and energetic temper, he was much cast down.

Mullins appeared on deck the next morning divested of every particle of beard and moustache, and dressed in jacket and trousers of pilot cloth; looking far from an ill-favoured man when shaved and dressed ; on the contrary, he appeared a smart, active seaman. He had a telescope in his hand, and was anxiously watching every sail that appeared in the eastern horizon. About mid-day he called out, " Blow me, here she is." All were on deck in a moment, and our hero, taking the glass from Mullins, fixed it on the approaching schooner. She was miles more to the southward than they expected ; but she had evidently made out the hooker's flag, and altered her course, the hooker at the same time slacked her fore-sheet, and stood away for her.

Cuthbert Gordon perceived that the intended slaver was a remarkably long, low craft, with lofty masts raking aft in a remarkable manner; she looked above two hundred tons, and was to the eye a singularly handsome vessel, and evidently built for speed. In half an hour they were close alongside, and the schooner, backing her topsails, remained stationary, and as the sea was very smooth, with a gentle swell from the southward, the hooker ran alongside, and fenders being put overboard the schooner, she lay without injury. Aboard the schooner there appeared fourteen men and two boys; a man walking backwards and forwards with a glass under his arm, Cuthbert Gordon judged was her skipper.

" Now, my lads," exclaimed the man walking the schooner's deck, " be sharp, pitch your kit aboard, and lose no time. How many are you ? "

" Ten, in all," returned Jack Mullins, whilst the man

10

named Denis Malloy jumped on board the schooner, and aproaching the skipper, gave him a letter and said something to him at the same time that caused him to look round and fix as fierce and scowling a pair of dark eyes upon Cuthbert Gordon as man need see.

Our hero was scanning the skipper's person at the same time, and their eyes met. There is a wonderful power in the human eye. That one glance made those two men bitter enemies.

As the skipper knitted his thick, shaggy brows, he broke the seal of the letter, and reading it through, gave a short, snorting laugh, saying :—" Aye, aye, I understand ; get him aboard at once, and cast off the hooker."

The skipper of the schooner was a man rather above the middle height, with immense breadth of chest and shoulders, short massive limbs, and long arms, his face was bloated, and a kind of crimson purple ; he wore neither beard nor whiskers, but his eyebrows were a mass of dark, tangled hair, more like bristles than aught else ; his lips were thick, and almost as protruding as a negro's.

" Now, sir," said Jack Mullins to our hero, " better step aboard ; I will see, as I now become first mate of this schooner, what I can do with our skipper for your comfort."

Stepping on to the deck of the schooner, our hero walked calmly and quietly up to where Captain Bruton stood, watching his approach.

" Are you the skipper of this craft ? " asked Cuthbert Gordon, fixing his eyes upon him.

" I am the captain of this schooner," fiercely returned the skipper, his fiery red face becoming a deeper crimson. " Why do you ask me? What the devil is it to you ? "

" Because," returned our hero, " I wish to warn you that you are committing an illegal act."

" Illegal, be d——," roared the skipper, stepping forward. " Cast off that hooker, and brace round the fore topsail, and take this mad fool out of my way. Curse me, if he annoys me with any more of his palaver and law, I'll clap a stopper on his jaw and put him in irons, and not take them off till we make the mouth of the Gambia."

Cuthbert's proud spirit was chafed. We by no means intend portraying a perfect hero; he had one great fault, and that was, he had small command over a fiery temper. Before the skipper had well-finished his speech, Gordon's hands grasped his collar, saying:

"If I am to be treated like a dog, better perish now than suffer further indignity."

The astounded skipper grasped Cuthbert Gordon also by the collar, and as the men rushed forward to separate them, the skipper roared out furiously:

"Stand back there, fools; do you think I want help to crush this viper?" and exerting his great strength, he thought to lift our hero from the deck, and then dash him down again. Captain Bruton was, we may say, in his prime—just forty—and proud of his strength. Cuthbert Gordon was a much taller man, but scarcely one-and-twenty; still he possessed what was always considered by his comrades aboard ship, a most extraordinary strength joined to great activity. Exasperated, almost maddened, he brought his whole power and energy into play, and a fearful struggle took place; but at length, grasping the skipper by the shoulder and the waist, he raised him up, and the next moment dashed him with terrible violence upon the deck, leaving him stunned and bleeding from the mouth and nostrils. The entire crew stood perfectly confounded and bewildered, several, however, raised the captain and carried him below.

Cuthbert Gordon considered his days were numbered. The perspiration poured down his face in a stream, and he panted for breath. Nevertheless, he had seized a heavy handspike lying on the deck, and stood resolved not to yield life without a terrible struggle. Recovering from their intense astonishment, the crew of the schooner prepared to revenge their captain's disaster, each seized a weapon, and all were preparing to make a rush upon our hero, when Jack Mullins came hastily up from the cabin :

"Avast, there, my mates, avast, it's your captain's orders that the young man is not to be touched; he's not much hurt—and it was a fair trial of strength."

The men looked amazed, but obeyed.

"Now cast off the hooker and make sail."

The hooker was cast off, and left to the management of one man and a boy ; the fore topsail was braced round and filled, and the schooner resumed her course.

Captain Bruton possessed but one solitary virtue, if we can call the feeling he experienced a virtue. He respected strength, being himself a very powerful man, and had he not weakened his constitution by continued intoxication, few men would have had a chance with him.

In a fair trial of strength, if defeated, he bore no malice ; on the contrary, he respected the man that could overcome him. Instead of getting into a furious passion and seeking vengeance upon our hero, the very moment he recovered breath, and the blood was washed from his mouth and nostrils, he said :—

"Go, Mullins, go up. Don't let the men injure that young man. By —— he will kill half a dozen of them before they could secure him, without fire-arms."

"That's very likely," said Mullins, running up upon deck, and preventing any further scrimmage; he then without a word to Cuthbert Gordon, returned to the captain, who was exceedingly shaken, and was lying on a cushioned locker, bathing his face and nostrils with vinegar, and, strange to say, remedying the bruises and hurts he had received by swallowing glass after glass of pure brandy.

He looked up at Mullins at intervals and questioned him.

"Now tell me who the devil is this young man. I would as leave have a bear's hug as a grip of his on my throat. I thought all my ribs were cracked."

"He's an officer in the navy," said Mullins, "and of high family. There will be a row about this affair."

"Why curse it, why didn't they say he was an officer in

the navy. All they said in the letter Denis Malloy gave me was, ' that he was a sad scamp, and half-cracked, and had done no end of mischief, and had committed a forgery; that his family wanted him out of the way till they hushed the forgery up; that I was to take him with me to the the coast of Africa, and also wherever I went with my cargo of slaves, and there let him loose to find his way home."

" And what do you get for this job, Captain Bruton ? " asked Mullins.

" What do I get," said the skipper. " Why curse it; don't you see what I have got ? I shan't be well of the bruises for a week; however, I don't want to hurt him. Let him have a berth here, and grub with you; let him have some clothes from the stock aboard. But this I can tell you, I'm —— if he shall quit this craft till we get to Cuba, so he must grin and bear it."

Satisfied that he had succeeded so far, Jack Mullins, who, with all his faults and errors, was a good-hearted man, proceeded to join our hero upon deck.

By this time Cuthbert Gordon's temper was cooled down, though he felt not the slightest regret for having acted as he had done. There was a most lawless set of men aboard the " Wave," to judge by their looks, and they eyed our hero as he paced the deck with rather a savage scowl. He, however, paid no attention to their looks or mutterings.

When Jack Mullins joined him and told him that the captain bore no resentment for the severe fall he had given him, he was certainly suprised. He thanked Mullins for his kind feelings towards him, and only wished it might be in his power to show his gratitude.

" Well, sir, I thank you for your kind wishes; but it's not likely I shall ever see the old country again. If we live and get a full cargo of slaves to Cuba, I shall settle there; it's a hanging matter for me to be caught; still, from old recollections, I love his Majesty's service. If I met one tyrant I had many a kind-hearted commander, and I don't forget the five happy years I spent aboard the old ' Magician.'"

"What! the 'Magician,' commanded by Captain Granby?"

"The same, sir, God bless him; as brave and kind a man that ever trod a quarter deck, or led a ship into action."

"You are right, Mullins," returned our hero, "I was for five years or so midshipman aboard the 'Magician.'"

"Well, your honour, isn't that strange; blow me, but the very first look I had of you I liked you, though in course I left the old ship long before you had a berth in her, sir, but it was easy to see you were every inch a seaman."

"What does your skipper intend doing with me—taking me to the African coast?"

"Why, sir, he does say he will do so; I can't make out altogether. They must have paid a pretty sum to bribe all hands. Howsomever, you will be sure to get away when we gets to the Gambia, and make for some British settlement or outpost.

It was four or five days before Captain Bruton was able to leave his cabin, and then he took to a bout of drinking with the second mate, a brutal drunken rascal. Mullins could drink, and did drink at times, but he rarely got drunk and never so drunk as not to attend to his duty. All the crew drank, and strange to say, they were supplied with an unusual quantity of spirits even for a slaver.

The tenth day after leaving the coast of Ireland, a heavy gale of wind right in their teeth brought the captain on deck for the first time after his fall. Our hero occupied the half of Mullins's cabin, they had it to themselves, and he also was supplied with garments fit for the voyage.

A thorough seaman and loving the sea in all its moods our hero could not abide a life of idleness. Books there were none, and no one to converse with except Mullins, who often amused an hour spinning him some yarns of his strange life.

Captain Bruton, when he came upon deck, limped a little, his leg was a good deal hurt, he looked round and perceived that Cuthbert Gordon was steering.

The schooner was a dangerous craft from the weight

and height of her spars, but a most splendid sailer, and worked as near the wind as a cutter. He looked aloft, and saw that the fore-topsail was furled and the top-gallant-mast struck. Cuthbert Gordon gave the tiller to one of the crew, and leaning upon the bulwarks, watched the heavy seas as they came rolling in and deluging the decks with a copious flood.

There were three reefs in the mainsail and also in the foresail, and a second jib set, and no other sail. The skipper was half drunk, and as he steadied himself against the companion, he said :—

" Who the devil ordered the fore-topsail to be furled ? "

Mullins said he did, for the schooner buried herself more with the topsail set.

" Who told you that ? " said he, savagely. " That's some man-of-war crankism. I know my craft better than any of your men-of-war's men. Steady, you beggar at the helm ! " he sung out to the man at the helm, who handled the schooner very differently to our hero. She had just shipped a very heavy sea.

" Now go aloft there," he shouted, " and set the fore-topsail with two reefs in it. I suppose you men-of-war's men," (suddenly turning round and facing our hero), " fancy these here sharp crafts can't carry sail, and that they are overmasted, and all that there kind of stuff."

" I never saw one of them in really very heavy weather that could carry their masts easily," returned Cuthbert.

" Then, —— me, I'll show you what the ' Wave ' can do, and how she will carry her masts through this petty tumble of a sea."

The men went very reluctantly to set the fore-topsail, for which—as if the schooner could keep her course—there was not the slightest necessity. With her sharp bows she went, as it were, right through the seas, scarcely lifting to them, and when badly steered, her plunges through the breaking seas threatened to pitch her masts out. Seamen soon discover if an officer is a thorough seaman or not. The crew of the " Wave," by many apparently small things, easily perceived that their prisoner was a first-rate seaman, and knew well how to manage a craft in bad weather.

It was by his advice that the foretop was taken off the schooner, and very soon after it was set, being a broad heavy sail for the size of the schooner, she buried herself tremendously, and not skillfully managed in a very heavy head sea, the topmast gave way in the cap, and masts and yards went over the sides. The fury of Captain Bruton was excessive; he blew his crew up in the foulest and most aggravating manner, so much so, that the men looked threatening, and finally he went below, and for the next three days was dead drunk.

At length, to the intense relief of our hero, on the thirty-sixth day, they came within sight of the African coast, near Mogador. He was firmly resolved to seize the very first opportunity to escape from the ship. Latterly, when drunk, the captain seemed inclined to seize upon every opportunity to provoke a quarrel. He came upon deck with loaded pistols in his belt. He had also become odious to the best portion of his crew. He swore fearfully, whilst his threats were continual. He frequently, when exceedingly drunk, fired across the deck, at the masts, to the risk of the crew, but harmlessly to the masts, for he never even hit them; and one day he fired as our hero was coming up from his berth, and the ball passed close to his cheek. Altogether it was very evident he was, from intoxication and wickedness, fast losing the little command he ever had over himself. Having made the mouth of the Gambia, the schooner passed the bar safely, and running up the river came to an anchor, opposite a town, on its northern bank, called Jellefree. There was not a single European vessel to be seen. Immediately after anchoring, the schooner was surrounded by canoes full of natives.

Gordon perceived that the captain had armed the second mate, and four of the very worst men—these five men were particularly devoted to the captain; and Mullins gave our hero a hint to be cautious, as he was certain those five were spies upon his motions. The King of Barra, the potentate that ruled this portion of the coast, was considercd a powerful chief. He imposed with impunity a heavy tax on all ships trading to his dominions, and the next day two of the king's large canoes eame and drove away all the other canoes, and his principal custom-house officer boarded the "Wavc" and levied the large sum of £20. This tax was paid by every vessel, no matter from what country. The person who levied this sum was the Alkaul himself. He was also governor of Jellefree. Some of the blacks spoke English. Cuthbert Gordon thought they were the most troublcsome, exacting lot, that ever boarded a ship.

The next day, with a strong favourable breeze, the schooner was got under weigh, and proceeded much higher up the river, which was deep and muddy, the banks covered with impenctrable thickets of mangoes, and the country they got glimpses of was flat and swampy. The two negro pilots said there were no sharks so high up, but numbers of huge hippopotami, which the negroes at-attack and kill for the sake of their teeth. Captain Bruton intended proceeding up the river as far as Jonkakende, where several European traders rcsidcd, and there he intended purchasing his cargo of slaves. These wretched, unfortunate, and cruclly treated human beings, are brought to the river's bank, and if therc should be a slaver there, they are quickly disposed of; but should there be no vessels the slaves are fettered and turned out to work, two ehained together, and thus, wretchedly fed, and fear-fully over-workcd, hundreds die before an opportunity oceurs for selling them.

Owing to some reasons of the captain, the ship was brought to an anehor several leagues before reaching Jonkakende; the slaves werc to be brought to him where he lay. Our hero picked up from the pilot negroes all the information he could concerning Jonkakende. He learned that there were several English residents there, and therefore he rcsolved to make an attempt at escape, though four armed sailors kept watch all night.

About this time sickness began to show amongst the crew. It had taken them seven days to reach their then anchorage. The mcn got heated towing the schooner;

they showed the first symptoms of fever. Two days after casting anchor, four of the crew were down with fever; Mullins far from well. Captain Bruton drank harder than ever; swore Cuthbert Gordon should take his share of work, for he was not going to feed idle hands. Having a project in his head, Cuthbert Gordon merely replied that he was willing to do a sailor's duty, and would; and he did so, for he was a strong man and had a fine constitution, and touched no spirits.

Denis Malloy was next struck with the fever, and became delirious, and before morning one of the sick men died; the season had become fearfully unhealthy.

"If I linger in this doomed ship," thought our hero, "I shall probably be attacked, and if attacked no doubt be left to perish."

The only chance he had of making his escape was by silently dropping overboard, and swimming ashore. The sickness had struck a terror into the men's minds. Jack Mullins, to whom our hero paid every attention, unfortunately became delirious, and the skipper, instead of making some effort in running his vessel out of the pestilential part of the river where he had persisted in anchoring, only drank the harder, to drive away the fever, as he said; how he escaped it was marvellous. Notwith-standing the sickness, two men, relieved every two hours paced the deck well armed, with orders to shoot any man who attempted to leave the ship, and the boats were hoisted aboard every evening.

From the vessel to the shore was nearly half-a-mile, and the tide, ebb or flow, amazingly swift. On one side of the ship lay a dreary swamp, on the other, impenetrable jungle and thickets, for nearly two leagues. Still Gordon argued with himself, if I could only reach Jonkakende, the English residents would, he felt quite satisfied, defend him against any attempt of Captain Bruton to recover him. All night long those on board the schooner could hear the howlings of wild beasts, and the shrill cry of the jackals. The first batch of slaves was expected down by raft the next day, so he resolved that night to attempt to recover his freedom.

A bold and determined swimmer, our hero thought little of the swim across the tide. For the last two nights he had slept on deck. Denis Malloy had so far recovered from the fever that he insisted on coming on deck; he was fearfully low in spirits, exceedingly superstitious, and from the first attack of the illness, though a very strong man, exceedingly desponding. Denis and a comrade were keeping watch; it was a very dark night, and a thin unwholesome mist covered the swampy ground, and spread over the river. Our hero did not wish to make his attempt to escape till near morning; he heard Denis Malloy's voice, and he wondered at his being on deck; he walked forward and found Denis sitting on a windlass, shivering as if in an ague. This was the man who had the command of the party that carried him off from Dunskelling; latterly he had evinced a wish to converse with Cuthbert Gordon, but the attack of fever prevented him.

Approaching Denis, our hero said, kindly—"You are wrong, my man, to come up on deck during the night; your attack is still lingering about you."

"Yes, sir, it is, bad luck to it for a fever; but it's little odds, I shall never see the ould country again; this will be an unlucky voyage to all concerned in entrapping you aboard this vile ship."

"It was a cruel wrong, certainly, Denis," said Cuthbert Gordon, surprised; "but why do you say that now?"

"Because," returned the sailor, shaking in the kind of ague that overpowered him, "don't you see the first five men attacked, were my five comrades in that ere business, and one's dead, and dickens a long I'll be, before my chalk's rubbed out."

"This weakening fever depresses you," said our hero. "I assure you, much as I have suffered by it, and shall no doubt suffer, I bear you no malice in thought or deed for the act."

"Well, thank your honour for that," said the sailor; "God bless you; you have a noble kind heart. I was not always bad, but drink and bad company made me what I am. I'll tell you what I'll do, sir; I'll make a clean breast of it, and tell you how it all happened."

"You will—curse you both; but I'll clap a stopper on both your tongues," exclaimed the captain, who had approached them unheard, and then he stamped upon the deck, to arouse the crew; at the same time making a grasp at our hero's neck, for seeing escape would now be frustrated, he was going to leap overboard. Thus, again these two powerful men held each other.

But, resolved to escape or perish, just as the crew came rushing upon deck, Gordon, calling all his power into the one effort, threw himself and the skipper over the low bulwark of the schooner. A frightful imprecation escaped the captain's lips as they struck the water, and his grasp relaxed as our hero shook him off and dived. As he came up some way across the river, he could see lights on board the schooner, and the shouts of the men as they lowered the boat, and again the shouts of the skipper, who was an excellent swimmer, directing them to where he was; but the tide was sweeping their boats down the river. Cuthbert Gordon made way for the right bank of the river; there was so thick a mist on the water that he lost sight of the schooner altogether, but the night was so still, that the sound of men's voices reached him, and the noise of oars in the rullocks was distinctly heard.

Suddenly he came against a large mass of something; a loud frightened snort ensued, and then a huge hippopotamus plunged madly through the water, nearly smothering Cuthbert Gordon in the commotion he raised. The heat was intense; he could still hear the boat, but further down the river, for being a good swimmer he crossed the stream rapidly, and in a few minutes more he touched the muddy bottom. Scrambling up a bank, he sat down, thanking Providence that he had succeeded so far, and very little troubling himself as to how Captain Bruton prospered.

CHAPTER XV

AFTER resting for a short time, the fugitive resolved to push on a few hundred yards and then climb up a tree and wait for daylight, for the howling of wild beasts and the cries of the jackals, intimated that the inhabitants of the forest were abroad, and as he thought they might have no objection to him for a meal, he very soon selected a tree, and got up into it ; he had neither shoes nor covering for the head, the shoes he had lost whilst swimming and the straw hat also. The loss of both these articles would be severely felt, when he should commence his journey by daylight.

He calculated he was about three leagues from Jonkolengo, and possessed not an article of any value, save a silver pencil case, and a penknife.

As he sat on his perch in that dismal jungle, listening to the various calls and growls, and cries of the various animals prowling through the intricacies, his thoughts naturally reverted to his dear relatives and to the young and beautiful girl, whose sweet face he beheld in imagination. Would she forget him if it pleased Providence that he should survive the perils he had yet to undergo before he reached his native land? Would she still feel the same interest and affection, he often pictured to himself she did? There was no fear of his going to sleep on his perch, in the midst of his thoughts, for every now and then, some wild animal came below the tree, snuffed the ground and uttered a hideous cry.

As the day dawned, in looking down, he beheld two hideous hyænas very composedly seated beneath the tree looking up at him. As soon as they clearly beheld him, they set up a horrid howl, and one, with every hair on his back bristling like the quills of a porcupine, glared at him savagely, for he was only a few feet above them ; breaking off a branch, he struck one of the beasts a smart blow on the nose, which made the brute show his teeth like an angry dog; but as the daylight increased and the sun rose, they disappeared into the depths of the forest.

Descending from his perch, he beheld a hippopotamus crashing through the branches, making his way towards the river; innumerable birds hovered about, uttering the most singular cries; the whole forest seemed alive.

Pushing his way through the entangled masses of underwood, and carefully looking out for wild beasts, after an hour's hard labour, tearing his ankles and legs, and lacerating his feet, he freed himself from the thicket and jungle lining the banks of the river.

At this time he felt a chill come over him, which he imputed to his having passed the night in wet garments. As he gained the open ground, he observed numerous cattle feeding on the plain, as well as several antelopes. As he proceeded he noticed a great number of asses, grazing on the briars and leaves of plants; they seemed so docile and accustomed to be handled that he thought the best thing he could do was to catch one of them and save his feet, and this he did; first making a kind of covering for his head out of platted flags, which in a great measure protected him from the scorching rays of the sun. As he rode on, following the mouth of the Gambia, he felt exceedingly unwell, but he tried to shake the sensation off, when two natives came out of the thicket and joined him.

Gordon was aware that the Mandingos are a harmless and kind race of Africans, although their countenances are far from pleasing,—having the flat nose and great protruding lips of the negro race.

The two blacks looked up into Cuthbert Gordon's face. They were clad in cotton dresses, had sandals on their feet, and each carried a bow and arrows and a long spear, and a cane basket strapped to the back.

"Massa white man English?"

"Yes," returned our hero, knowing that many of the slave drivers could speak a little English, he then said—"Jonkakende!"

"Yah, yah!" returned the negroes, pointing before them in a southerly direction, and repeating "Judun yat!" What that was our hero could not say. He felt at this

time a great faintness coming over him, so much so that
he could scarcely sit the animal he rode, and the next
moment would have fallen had not the kind negroes supported him. They were approaching a hamlet. He tried
to rouse himself, and one of the Mandingos gave him to
drink of some not unpleasant liquor from a gourd. This
revived him a little, but he felt satisfied that the fever was
upon him, and no wonder. The village consisted of sixty
or seventy huts—each of tho huts formed by a circular
mud wall about four feet high, covered over with bamboo
canes, and thatched with grass. Before one of these huts
his conductors stopped, and, lifting him off the ass,
carried him into the interior, and laid him on a bullock's
hide stretched upon a frame of canes, whilst two women
—the wives of one of the Mandingos—attended to him,
using many strange words and stranger gesticulations.
Here our hero lay three days, most kindly treated by them
—their simple remedies and his own powerful constitution
completed his cure. The people who had so kindly assisted him were slaves employed by the aristocratie portion
of the Mandingo race in cultivating the land, and in taking
care of their cattle, having a person like an overseer over
them to see that they did their work.

As he got the better of the fever, he felt a longing to
breathe the fresh air—for he had to share the hut with
the two young wives of the Mandingos and their four
children. Nothing could be kinder than the women, and
for Mandingos, they were rather agreeable looking.

The fifth day the overseer entered the hut. He was a
frightful negro, but, as he himself stated, he spoke English
like a white man, and had twice been to America, and
once to the West Indies.

"Hi, massa," said the negro ; ' you berry well soon.
Where you come from and where you go ? "

"Well," returned our hero, "I wish to go to Jonkakende."

"Berry good ; dere is one good white man dere. But
hi, massa, where you come from ? "

"From a slave schooner in the river."

"De slave schooner," repeated tho negro slowly ; "do

schooner ab sickness aboard, de ship drop further up the river yesterday to Jonkakende. De captain near drown —why you go from ship ? "

" Because I wish to go to Jonkakende."

" Bery good, hi massa, liky no stay in ship, but hi, me show you the way to-morrow."

Our hero thanked the overseer, and said he should be well enough to go. It vexed him to think he had nothing to give the two young wives, when he recollected the silver pencil case and the knife with mother of pearl case. The next day he was much better. He gave the pencil-case to one wife and the knife to the other. They seemed highly pleased with the bright silver and the shining mother of pearl.

As he took a short walk he began to think he might have some trouble at Jonkakende with the captain of the schooner. Quite unsupported as he was and unknown, his testimony might not be believed; and yet what was he to do without any resources whatever ?

In the evening the overseer came.

" Hi, massa, me tink bad you go to Jonkakende. White man no dere now. De slave ship dere and de captain, I hear, hunt de country for you. What you do, massa? "

To explain matters to the overseer appeared useless; he, however, said—" Captain slave ship bad man—he take me away by force from my country."

" Hi, massa, dey all bad men in de slavers. Dere be no English ships in de Gambia for months. Two English ships at Sierra Leone—dey stay more den one month for slaves—better go dere."

To cross the country to Sierra Leone appeared to our hero scarcely possible, till the overseer told him he could get him a guide, a young negro who had escaped from King Barra, and was going to his own home below Sierra Leone.

" But," said our hero, " how shall we live ? "

" Oh, holly golly massa, you live well. Demba good shot with bow, he kill game, de people good dey feed you."

As there were no ships at Jonkakende our hero deter-mined upon the adventure of crossing the country with a negro youth for a guide ; consoled with the idea that his companion spoke good English, he having been servant from a little boy with a Doctor Leadly, at Pisanco, but was carried off and made a slave, and was very likely to be one of a batch destined to be killed for a feast in memory of a dead king of Barra.

The Mandingo wives gave him sandals and a good covering for his head, and a bow and arrows and a spear ; the next day Demba arrived ; he was hiding.

Cuthbert Gordon was surprised to see a remarkably fine young negro with pleasing features, who spoke English as well as a negro can speak the language.

Demba, having caught a couple of asses, and the worthy Mandingos having supplied them with three days' provisions, they set out at once.

Gordon expressed his gratitude by all the signs in his power to the Mandingo and his two wives, and told the overseer to tell him he felt that they had saved his life.

We must touch briefly on our hero's journey over a vast tract of country, driven out of their course by great rivers and hostile tribes, till meeting a party of slaves coming from the interior, Cuthbert Gordon learned that there were some white men in the town of Jarra, four leagues off. Demba, to whom our hero had become greatly attached for his fidelity and courage, proposed going there.

To this he willingly assented, and the following day set out, travelling all night, except for two hours' halt, when they lighted fires to keep off wild beasts. They reached Jarra, the largest town they had yet entered ; the houses were built of clay and stone ; this town was situated in the Moorish kingdom, Sudiner. Still all its inhabitants were negroes, paying tribute to their detestable and cruel oppressors the Moors.

On making enquiries at a negro hut, our hero learned that there was only one white man in the town, all the others had departed. On requesting to be conducted to the house where the white man lodged, the negro of whom they enquired led them to a hut, and as they reached the entrance the white man came forth, but as soon as he

11

saw Cuthbert Gordon, ho eagerly held out his hand, exclaiming in a joyful tone, "God bless me! how rejoiced I
am to see a white face again. An Englishman I suppose."

"Yes," returned our hero, "and I assure you it gives
me equal pleasure."

The Englishman then invited our hero and Demba into
his hut, to share it with him.

"I fear," said Cuthbert Gordon, much interested by the
thoughtful, serious countenance of the stranger, "that we
shall be a burden to you, for, to tell you the truth, I possess
not a single fraction of any kind of money; we have sub-
sisted for three weeks by the charity of hospitable tribes,
and our own shooting with the bow."

"That need not hinder you from sharing my hut and my
fare," said the stranger; "though all my attendants have
deserted me from fear of the Moors, I still possess concealed about my person some gold dust and coins; but
what can bring so young a man as you are into this wild
part of Africa; not exploring, surely?"

"No," returned our hero, "I never intended getting
into this country, I wanted to reach Sierra Leone or Cape
Coast to find a ship to return into Europe, but great rivers
and a fierce savage race we fell in with, forced us away
from the coast, and hearing of white men being in these
parts I pushed on here."

"I am still puzzled," said the stranger, "but we shall
understand one another better by-and-bye; now let me
introduce myself, and then offer you some refreshment.
My name you may have heard, as this is my second
visit to this country, to discover the source of the
Niger."

"What!" exclaimed Cuthbert, looking eagerly up, "you
are Mr. Mungo Park! how rejoiced I am that I came
here; yes, I have often heard and read of all you have
suffered in your first attempt to discover that famous
river."

"Well," returned Mr. Park with great animation, and
much pleased, "when deserted by all, Providence sends
me a companion. Before we come to mutual explanations
let me offer you a share of my provisions,"

"You will find this young negro," said our hero, "very useful if we proceed together any distance, he speaks English, and was even a servant to Dr. Leadly."

"What my good friend Leadly, of Jonkakende, and Pisanco."

"Yes, massa," put in Demba, "Dr. Leadly good man, true good, massa."

"Then why in the name of fate did you leave him," said Mr. Park.

"Some bad men steal me," said Demba," and carry me to bad king and sell me; I escape and got nearly to Jonkakende, and then I think I like go to my own country, and my peoples, and dis massa want go look for ship, and we go, but no possible go coast-ways, and le Moors, fright me, and we no pass rivers, and now me ink take massa to Benin, sure find English ship here."

"My dear sir," said Mr. Park, turning to our hero, if you had gone to Jonkakende, you would have received very attention and assistance from the kindest hearted man breathing—Dr. Leadly."

"You will understand how it all happened," said Cuthbert Gordon, "when you hear my somewhat strange tory."

Demba was sent out to procure several articles Mr. Park wanted for their mutual comfort, and before night our hero acquainted the renowned traveller with his history—but in very brief terms.

Mr. Park was extremely interested and surprised.

"I see," he remarked, "that you are anxious to return o your own country; you will find it a toilsome, dangerous ourney to reach the coast, you have got so far inland. Though deserted by all my comrades and mere paid attendants, I am still resolved to prosecute my search. I may perish—but the darling object of my life I must and will try o accomplish." He then related to Cuthbert Gordon all his adventures and terrible disasters from the period of his anding, to his desertion by all who followed him from Pisanco.

"How you, Mr. Gordon, a total stranger to this country,

11—-

without arms or means, penetrated so far, amazes me; it only shews me what fortitude and indomitable courage will do. I must rest for a few days, for I have endured great hardships, and a slight attack of fever has left me weak."

Cuthbert Gordon became so deeply interested in this daring and enterprising traveller, and so won by his courage, simplicity, and enthusiasm, that he agreed to accompany him in his enterprise, on his promising afterwards to seek a port from whence they might embark for Europe.

"We shall be able to make the Bight of Benin," said Mr. Park, overjoyed at having such a companion; and Demba, who had become so deeply attached to our hero, vowed he would accompany his massa all over the world.

After a rest of three days, Mr. Park procured a protection from the Moorish chief Ali, who ruled Ladamai, and then they set out, Mr. Park furnishing our hero with an excellent double barrel gun, and some garments and shoes, out of the store left with him when deserted by his attendants. After a toilsome journey they reached Dena and after a few days' rest, they arrived at a village within a league of Goomba.

"Now," said Mr. Park, "my dear young friend, we approach the object of my search, in three days we shall reach the banks of the Niger." They were received by the Dooty of the village, a negro, with the greatest kindness, who ordered a sheep to be killed to entertain them.

Our hero observed to Mr. Park how in general the nature of the negro was simple and kind, offering a strange contrast to the ferocious Moors who delighted in cruelty and blood.

"Quite true," said Mungo Park, "were it not for the predatory bands of Moors roving the country, my object would have been attained on my first journey."

A large party of negro men and women sat down with our travellers in the open air to enjoy the feast of the sheep and other dainties. In the midst of the merry-making, a trampling of horses was heard, and the next instant a large party of Moors spurred furiously in amongst them, but the negroes fled. A Moor, with a drawn sabre, made a furious cut at our hero, as Mr. Park strove to drag him into a hut, for he had seized his gun and stood on the defensive. Though the blow took effect, Gordon had fired at the moment he received it, and the Moor fell dead. A scene of frightful confusion ensued; Mr. Park and the distracted Demba were seized, tied, and put upon horses, and carried off prisoners to Dalte. Mr. Park's sufferings, and his after fate, are to be found in his own history. Cuthbert Gordon and he never met again.

CHAPTER XVI.

TIME rolled on with Mrs. Gordon and her charming daughters. After the mysterious disappearance of her son, Mrs. Gordon had resumed her usual mode of life, but the colour on her cheek had faded, her spirit was broken, the hope of her life was crushed in the bud. Still, she had children to love and cherish, and she strove all in her power to bear up against the terrible blow she had received in the loss of her son, for almost every one firmly believed that in some unaccountable way Cuthbert Gordon had been swept away by the tide and carried out to sea. To this public opinion neither Amy nor Lucy would give the least credit. They said it was almost impossible that a strong man and an excellent swimmer, like their brother, could meet such a fate. Still they could advance no argument to show how else he could have been lost.

Shortly after Cuthbert Gordon disappeared, Bill Davis and his family quitted Pembray, and several other resident fishermen changed their quarters for some distant seaport town. Mr. Lewellen and his son were indefatigable in endeavouring to trace or gain some clue to our hero's disappearance. George Lewellen, like Amy and Lucy, scouted the idea of his having been drowned; he insisted, strange as it might be, that he was still alive, and had been carried off by smugglers; but what smugglers, or where carried to, he could gain no clue further than that a suspicious-looking cutter had been seen in Caermarthen Bay the day before the storm, and that the same cutter was seen rounding Caldy Island by the Tenby fishing boats. Even this vague rumour kept hope alive with the young people, and they did all they could to cheer and encourage Mrs. Gordon—but hope deferred maketh the heart grow sick. George Lewellen and his father had proceeded to London on mercantile business, when, one morning, some three months after the disappearance of Cuthbert Gordon, as mother and daughters were returning from visiting Mrs. Lewellen and her daughter, they met a man in the garb of a seaman coming from Pembray. As soon as he came up with Mrs. Gordon and her daughters, he looked at them very earnestly, and then doffing his tarpaulin hat and smoothing down the hair over his temples, he said, addressing Mrs. Gordon, "I axes your pardon, ma'am! be you the ladies as lives in the cottage yonder?" pointing to their cottage.

"Yes," said Mrs. Gordon, anxiously, her heart beating with an unaccountable feeling, "we are."

"Well, ma'am, so I thought, and I'm blessed if I ain't glad as we touched at this here port, for I have some news you may like to hear."

"Oh! dear mother," exclaimed both daughters, catching her hands, their faces flushing with joy, this good man, I feel certain, brings us news of dear Cuthbert!"

"Bless your two beautiful faces," said the sailor, "that's the name, sure as a gun—Cuthbert Gordon, that's it. I'm blowed if I had not forgot the name altogether."

Mrs. Gordon trembled so that she could scarcely stand; the tears ran down her cheeks, and her lips moved in a prayer of thanksgiving to Providence. Her son lived. What a balm to her fond and aching heart!

Catching the rough hand of the old salt, Amy said, her cheeks glowing and her eyes sparkling—"Ah! you are come to tell us that our dear lost brother lives. Is it not so? But come, here is our home; come in, we can hear, and speak to you of him who is dear to us all," and they entered the little gate, and proceeding to the house, made the surprised sailor sit down in their little back parlour, and then Lucy procured a jug of ale, and put it with a glass before him, whilst the mother, quite overpowered, sat down with her eyes fixed upon the bewildered seaman.

"Now tell us all you know, like a dear good man—we are dying to hear all you have to say."

"Why, bless your dear little hearts, you make me feel like a craft in the wind's eye, all shaky. But here's all your good healths, ma'am," the old salt bobbed his head, took a long pull at the jug, not troubling the tumbler, and then wiping his mouth with the back of his horny hand, he began :—

"You see, ma'am, I must spin my yarn my own way. If I goes boxing the compass, and yawing here and there, I shall get in irons and never get out of them, no how. You see, some months ago, I was a seaman aboard the 'Sarah Ann,' a fine ship of 400 tons, bound for Quebec. We left Liverpool with a full cargo and five-and-twenty steerage passengers. After seven days' run, we fell in with strong head winds, cross seas, and then stormy weather. The steerage passengers all got knocked here and there and were sadly put about, except a regular seafaring man and his family—this man called himself Bill Davis."

'Bill Davis!" repeated mother and daughters, looking at each other, and then Mrs. Gordon said—"We had a pilot here of that name, who had a family, and who went, it was said, to Liverpool."

"That's the man, ma'am; he hailed from these here parts. You see, ma'am, Bill Davis, being a regular salt,

soon made himself useful aboard, and he and I became
very thick, and after a time, for we had a precious long
voyage, we both on us spoke of our past life. He told me
he had made a pretty penny by smuggling in these here
parts.   Well, ma'am, many of our men were knocked up
by fever, and Bill Davis willingly did duty as a seaman, our captain saying he would make him a handsome
present when he reached Quebec.   One day in a heavy
gale we carried away one of our spars, and a heavy
piece struck Bill Davis on the head, and nearly killed him.
He had his wife and eldest daughter to nurse him ; but he
got very low, and said he would be sure to die.   Howsomever, we made Quebec, and he was carried to lodgings,
still very low and desponding.   I had shipped in a bark
bound for Swansea, and I went to see Bill before I sailed.
I told Bill where I was bound to, and says he, taking my
hand, 'Jem,' says he, 'will you do me a good turn ? '

"'Never say die ! ' says I, ' if I don't—only say what it
is; it will ease your mind, for I see you have some'at
heavy on your conscience.'

" ' You're right, Jem,' says he, ' I have something on my
conscience, and I'm justly punished for it,' and then,
ma'am, he told me how your son surprised him and some
comrades stowing away smuggled goods, and that they
wished to secure him, and get him taken across channel, till
they had time to clear off their goods and get away themselves; but Mr. Gordon was so mortal strong that he
capsized two or three of them, and would have got away,
when Bill Davis knocked him senseless with a blow of a
brass-mounted pistol.' "

" Oh, Heavens ! " exclaimed the mother, " and he had
saved Bill Davis's wife, and helped him, and his family in
their distress ! "

" Yes.   Bless your heart, ma'am, so he told me, and he
said he never was happy from the thoughts of his ingratitude, and now he was punished by being struck down by a
blow on the head the same as he gave Mr. Gordon. ' And,'
says Bill Davis, ' I cannot rest until I have Mrs. Gordon's
pardon, and she knows that her son is not drowned, but
only taken across the channel in a smuggling cutter that

belongs to a gentleman named O'Dowd, living at Castle Townsend, in Ireland. Now, Jem, if you are going to Swansea, you will ease my mind by promising to go over to Llanelly and enquire for Mrs. Gordon, at Mr. Lewellen's cottage, Pembray, and tell her all I have told you, it will ease my mind, and I may get well. So I promised to do so, and as luck would have it, we were discharged at Llanelly, and were consigned to Mr. Lewellen ; so I came here at once, ma'am.' "

" And we are deeply grateful to you for doing so," said Mrs. Gordon, " but is it not strange that if my son was only carried across the channel, he has not returned ere this, as sufficient time has been surely given to those men to secure their contraband goods from being seized."

Jem Baines rubbed his head.

" This does appear strange, and I cannot make it out, nohow. But you can write ma'am, to Mr. O'Dowd, at Castle Townsend."

" Very true," said Mrs. Gordon, " so I can, and I most sincerely trust I may gain good intelligence. At all events I am greatly indebted to you for your kindness in bringing me this good news, and I willingly pardon Bill Davis for his share in the transaction." Then pressing a small recompense upon the reluctant seaman, he took his departure.

" Well, dear mother," said Amy, " you see George's idea that our dear Cuthbert was carried off by smugglers was quite correct; but is it not strange that a gentleman, as the sailor described this Mr. O'Dowd, should be a smuggler ? "

" Yes; most strange," said the mother. " I cannot understand it, but will write at once. What discourages me much, is the fearfully disturbed state of Ireland; the rebellion has broken out, and horrible crimes are committed. It is very doubtful whether any letter to any country town in Ireland would reach its destination."

Such indeed was the case, for Lord Dunskelling and Cuthbert's letters to Mrs. Gordon never reached their destination, nor did Mrs. Gordon's letter to Mr. O'Dowd.

Weeks passed over, and Cuthbert's fate continued a

mystery to mother and daughters, leaving them hoping, but fearful that some mishap must have occurred to prevent our hero's return.

We must cross the Channel to Dunskelling, and see how fared our young heroine, and how affairs went on in the castle after the abduction of her cousin. Dora Dunskelling could no longer remain ignorant of her real feelings for her cousin Cuthbert. The scene she had witnessed, and the fright and agony she had experienced on beholding the frightful struggle between her cousin and the six men who carried him off, quite overpowered her and made her nervous and ill for several days. Messengers were sent off to her father with intelligence of the outrage. Every means were tried to discover the authors of the abduction, but quite in vain. The desperate state of public affairs put it out of the question to trace or punish any crime; bands of armed men roamed the country, ostensibly calling themselves patriots, but too often they were merely gangs of lawless plunderers. Miss MacCormack and our heroine became alarmed at their situation in Dunskelling Castle, with only five or six male domestics; till they received a letter from Lord Dunskelling, stating that he would soon return, and in the meantime that an officer, Captain Dunlop, and a party of Dragoons, would be quartered for their protection in the castle. His lordship also stated that he was suffering from his old complaint—disease of the heart—which prevented his moving for a few days; but his physician said the attack was not a severe one.

This letter made Dora sad.

"I do fear my beloved father suffers more than he will allow; this heart disease is a terrible one, is it not, Julia?"

"It is severe, my love," returned the governess, whilst the attack lasts, "but I believe not dangerous." They knew but little of diseases of the heart in those days.

"I will keep quite secluded in the west wing," said Dora, "whilst these soldiers remain in the castle; it is consoling to be able to sleep free from fear of an attack, still it is very unpleasant to have a party of rollicking, reckless dragoons about the house and grounds."

"Oh, my dear, their officer will keep them in order; the men will be entirely in the east wing; their captain only need be an inmate of the front parlours."

The following day, Captain Dunlop and twenty dragoons arrived, and took possession of the quarters prepared for them. The captain was assigned one of the parlours for his sitting-room, and a bed-room in the eastern gallery. Dora, Miss MacCormack, Mrs. Brennen, and the five female domestics occupied the west wing. Both wings led into the body of the mansion by a spacious gallery.

Captain Dunlop was a very gentlemanly-looking young man, but exceedingly foppish, both in dress and manner. He had heard it said in Cork that Lord Dunskelling's daughter was one of the most beautiful maidens in the south of Ireland or elsewhere, and a great heiress. The captain felt monstrously delighted when he heard he was to be quartered in Dunskelling Castle for several weeks, and his appointment to that post created quite a sensation amongst the military in Cork city. The captain was greatly disappointed when several days passed and not even a glimpse of the beautiful lady's drapery was to be had. He saw Miss MacCormack frequently, but that was no compensation to the worthy captain, though she was still young, handsome, and agreeable. Speaking to the governess one day, he said :—

"I trust his lordship's daughter is not unwell. I have not yet had the honour of seeing her."

"She is very young and very retiring, Captain Dunlop," said the governess. "No doubt when his lordship returns she will be less reserved."

The captain felt chagrined; he came to Dunskelling prepared to fall in love, but he could not make love to Miss MacCormack, nor to Mrs. Brennen, the housekeeper; and though he perceived that there were two or three of the female attendants exceedingly pretty, it would not do, according to the worthy captain's intenions to be caught larking with Lady Dora's personal attendants.

"Well," thought the captain, "I shall surely see her in church."

Accordingly the gallant captain, on the ensuing Sunday, marched his men, himself on horseback, to Dunskelling church, distant about a quarter of a mile from the castle; his men were all English and Protestants, there were not five of that persuasion in the vicinity of Dunskelling, and the gentry in the neighbourhood had quitted their mansions and proceeded to Cork or Dublin, being too much afraid to remain in so disturbed a district.

Dora Dunskelling, wrapped in her fur mantle, and accompanied by Miss MacCormack and one female attendant proceeded on foot to the church; for the day, though cold, was fine and dry, and Dora by no means loved display.

Captain Dunlop, in his splendid uniform, had his men drawn up at the church door, and through the double row of fierce, moustached dragoons, the fair heiress of Dunskelling passed, creating intense admiration, and at the church door stood the bold captain, hat in hand, and bowing low, he let his eyes rest for a moment on the pale but very lovely features of Dora—with a gentle inclination of her head she returned the captain's salute, and passed on to her own seat.

We greatly fear the captain's devotions were sadly deranged by the glance he had caught of that fair face—so youthful, so thoughtful, and so deeply interesting. The sermon over, the captain dismissed his troop, and hastened to accompany the ladies back to the mansion.

Miss MacCormack could not do otherwise than introduce the captain; and Dora politely, but coldly, hoped he found his quarters in her father's mansion comfortable.

The captain tried to bring in some high-flown compliment in his answer; but Dora cut it very short by simply saying, she trusted the necessity for his visit would soon end, as for herself she was not at all afraid.

"Surely, Miss Dunskelling," said the dragoon, "you would never trust yourself to the tender mercies of a race of uncivilised barbarians as all the Irish are."

"You forget, Captain Dunlop," returned Dora, " that

we are Irish, and do not look upon our poor misguided countrymen as savages; were they as bad as you represent and think them, your little troop of soldiers would be a poor protection to Dunskelling Castle and its vicinity."

"I should not fear an attack from three hundred of those miserable rebels, Miss Dunskelling," returned the captain, a little piqued, and speaking rather loud.

"Be dad then, my bould captain," said a bold manly voice close to them, "you'd have a sorry chance of it wid all your fine gould lace, and hat and feathers ; be gorra it makes me laugh to hear you talk."

All paused surprised, and looked up at the speaker. Standing on the brow of a bank some six yards above, was a tall, powerful young man, dressed in the green uniform of the rebel bands ; he had a belt round his waist and stood leaning on a short pike.

Such an apparition in broad daylight, in so dangerous a costume, and almost within call of a troop of dragoons, completely astounded Dora and Miss MacCormack ; as to Captain Dunlop, who, with all his foppishness, was a truly courageous man, he flushed with passion, and willing to show his gallantry before our heroine, said, drawing his sword—"Audacious rebel, you shall pay dearly for this insolence; if I catch you, I'll shoot you as I would a dog," and he made a rush to ascend the bank.

"Shall I lend you a hand, Captain Avick ? be gorra, you don't want pluck anyhow," and actually stooping over the bank, the rebel held the staff of his pike to the ascending dragoon to help him.

"Pray let the man go, Captain Dunlop," said Dora, "he must be mad to shew himself thus boldly."

"Bless your beautiful face !" exclaimed the rebel, "not a hair of your pretty head will ever be hurt by one of us ; let the soldier be, he'll larn wisdom, and keep his tongue quiet another time."

But Captain Dunlop was a brave and active man, and steep as was the bank, he was on the point of reaching the top, when the treacherous soil gave way, and he rolled to the bottom, soiled, but not hurt ; there was a shrill whistle heard, and the rebel, looking over the bank, laughed heartily, saying—"Good-bye, captain dear, we shall meet again; be gorra, I'm sorry you slipped; I hoped to try a fall wid you meself."

"Don't be afeared, Miss Dora," he added, "the saints in glory bless you; sleep quiet acushla, for no one shall hurt you," and then the rebel disappeared.

"I trust you are not hurt, Captain Dunlop," said our heroine, with much kindness of tone, "though at the same time I rejoice you did not reach the top of the bank, for there was evidently more than one man up there."

"Thank you," said the dragoon, "I am not in the least hurt, but regret I did not get within arm's reach of the impudent scoundrel; I will send out half a dozen men and a sergeant to scour the vicinity. Do you recognise the rascal as one of the peasantry about these parts, Lady Dora?"

"No!" returned our heroine, "I certainly did not; it was a most strange act of rashness and folly on the part of that misguided man, for your men must have passed the spot only a few minutes ago."

They had now reached the lawn, and shortly after entered the mansion; when the captain hastened to send out a dozen of his troop with the sergeant, desiring them to make a circuit of several miles, and not to return till morning and endeavour to find out if any number of the rebels were lurking in the vicinity of Dunskelling.

Dora, whatever the gallant Captain Dunlop thought of her, did not bestow one single thought upon the bold dragoon. Her thoughts were always fixed upon her absent lover; though the last few days' anxiety concerning her father had displaced Cuthbert from the entire occupation of her mind. That night she retired late to rest.

Captain Dunlop was sitting in one of the front parlours; he had just finished his supper, having previously visited his men's quarters, and had one of the troop with his loaded carbine stationed in the hall, pacing backwards and forwards. The captain kept reading and thinking of Lady Dora, and how blessed the man would be that could call her his. He was getting wonderfully sentimental, when suddenly a tremendous crash took place

in the hall, followed by a cry of alarm from the sentinel.
As soon as the captain heard the crash he rushed out into
the hall; all was darkness; he called out, "are you
hurt, Harrison?"

"I'm most brained," moaned out the unfortunate
dragoon, "the lantern has fallen."

The captain ran back into the parlour for a candle, but
the room was in darkness, and at the same moment he
felt himself seized by two powerful men, who pinioned his
arms, and one of them, placing the cold barrel of a pistol
in his mouth, said :—

"Take it easy, Captain dear, be gorra, or I'll be forced
to give you a leaden pill."

Captain Dunlop, had, however, a distaste to pills of any
kind, and he struggled fiercely, and shouted boldly. The
consequence was, he was gagged, his feet and hands tied,
and then he was left to his own reflections. By this time
the whole house was roused. Dora and Miss MacCormack,
who slept in the same room, heard the tremendous crash
of the lantern, and started up in their beds.

"Good heavens! what is that?" exclaimed Miss Mac-
Cormack, trembling with agitation, "and no light in the
room."

"I think it's the hall lantern," said Dora, springing out
of bed. "I will procure a light."

Not such an easy thing in those days of no lucifers.
Dora had plenty of courage, and whilst Miss MacCormack
was trembling in bed, (for she was exceedingly timid),
Dora had lighted a candle. We may say or think what
we please, but light gives courage, and when the darkness
was dispelled, the governess got out of bed, and both began
dressing in haste.

But the silence was now broken by loud shouts, musket
shots, and screams from the adjoining room.

"Ah, my God!" exclaimed Miss MacCormack, "the
house is beset with rebels," and she buried her head in
the clothes.

Dora ran to the door and began bolting and securing
it. A man's voice and a knock startled her.

"Don't be afraid, Lady Dora; they won't harm

any of your household. I'll shoot the first man that comes near your chamber. We shall be gone in an hour."

"Dear me!" that is the voice of the man in the rebel uniform whom we saw this morning. What can he be about? I trust in God that no lives have been sacrificed."

"It was a very short struggle," said the governess; "they must have surprised the dragoons in their quarters. You do not hear a sound now."

"No doubt," said Dora, "they have locked in all the servants."

In this uncertain state they remained, without any sound disturbing the silence of the night, till the early dawn gave courage to some of the domestics, who broke open their doors, and finding the coast clear, men and women rushed to see what amount of plunder had been carried away; Mrs. Brennen and Lady Dora's two attendants to see how their young mistress and the governess had fared during the attack upon the mansion.

The butler and the two indoor male domestics found the hall door wide open, and in the parlour the unfortunate Captain Dunlop tied hand and foot, and gagged, and the dragoons all confined in their barrack room, deprived of all their arms.

In the meantime the young mistress, the governess, and the housekeeper, proceeded to inspect the rooms, for they were now satisfied that the party were a gang of robbers, and not rebels. It was a well planned affair, but without an agent in the house to assist their plans, it would have been impossible to have so completely succeeded. It was soon discovered that a domestic named Doran was missing. They could not perceive that any of the rooms or the furniture in them had been either injured or disturbed, till they came to his lordship's library. The door of this room, always locked in his lordship's absence, was smashed, and the great chests containing plate burst open and their contents gone. Desks were broken open, and the papers they contained scattered over the room in every direction.

Dora and the governess stood amazed and bewildered.

To restore order was a difficult thing; what papers wero taken or destroyed they could not say. All they could do was to gather up those scattered about, and put them into the chests. Every drawer and cabinet in the library had been smashed in opening them, and every species of valuable property stolen.

As all were engaged in their examination of the mansion, the troopers sent out with Sergeant Hopkins returned, without having succeeded in tracing any kind of rebel force in the vicinity. The men were perfectly savage when they heard how their captain and comrades had been treated. Captain Dunlop, besides the mortification he endured at being so roughly treated, was very much hurt by the gags and the cords used to secure his hands and legs. Nevertheless, in two hours he had mounted his horse, and followed by a dozen of his men, left the mansion, trying to get some trace of the robbers before night. The rest of the men employed themselves catching the horses turned out of the stable by the robbers. A mounted messenger was at once dispatched to Cork with a letter from Dora to her father. Alas! poor girl, long before the messenger reached Cork, Lord Dunskelling had ceased to exist. A sudden attack of apoplexy had caused death.

About four o'clock in the day, as Dora and Miss MacCormack were gazing out of the drawing-room window, they beheld a man in the Dunskelling livery, spurring a jaded horse up the avenue. Dora turned pale, and an unaccountable feeling of alarm caused her to tremble so that she could scarcely answer the governess, who saw her sudden change of colour.

"That is a messenger from his lordship," cried Miss MacCormack, "let us go down into the hall."

"God grant that my beloved father is not taken ill," said Dora; "I feel a strange oppression, a foreboding of calamity weighing me down."

"The effect of our terror last night," replied the governess.

Mrs. Brennen was in the hall, and one of the servants, seeing the messenger, through the side window, dis-mount from his foaming horse, hastily threw open the door.

"Ah," exclaimed Dora in an agitated voice, "it is Burke, my father's own groom."

The governess and Mrs. Brennen became alarmed as the man, hat in hand, and his cheek pale, and himself looking much fatigued, entered the hall. He gazed at Lady Dora Dunskelling in a hesitating manner as she advanced, and in a trembling voice, said :—

"You bring me evil tidings, William Burke, I fear."

"Alas! my lady," said the man, casting his eyes upon the floor, "alas! I do."

"My God," exclaimed the heiress of Dunskelling, clasping her hands, "my father no longer exists." A faintness came over her, and the next moment she foll back senseless into Miss MacCormack's arms.

As Miss MacCormack and two of the females carriod our heroine to her chamber, Mrs. Brennen, shaking with torror, said :—

"Do you mean, Burke, that his lordship is dead ? "

"It is true, ma'am, too true, the Lord save us! He had orderod his carriage, and all was prepared for our return to Dunskolling, and his lordship was just loaving his room when he staggered, reeled and fell. A doctor was sent for on the instant, for we could only imagine that he had a fit; but the Lord save us! before tho doctor arrivod he was dead. It's now eight days ago."

"Eight days ago!" exclaimed Mrs. Brennen, and all prosent; "how is this, and no intelligence to reach us ? "

"It was not my fault," said the man; for I was despatchod on the instant for Dunskelling, but aftor passing through Kellecn I was met by a party of armed men, knocked off my horse, my hands bound, and then I was thrown across a horse and taken to a place where thore was a party of rcbcls, more than three hundred strong, encamped. I was left for hours lying bound on tho ground. I was untied, howcvor, at night, and given some food, but told if I attempted to move five yards from where I was I should be shot down without mercy. In this way I was kept for six days, and then they told me if I did not join the band it would go hard with me. 'Why the dickens,' said I, 'did you not ask me before to do so—to be sure I'll join;' but the next day a tall man with a mask over his face, came to where I was, and says he to the men, 'give that fellow his horse and at sunset let him be off, and make the best of his way to Cork, where he came from, and if ho comes this road again shoot him.' 'Be gor, your honour, you may depend I won't,' I replied. So, as soon as it was dusk they gave me my horse, and told me to be off, and you may be sure I did not want to be told so twice; but after riding towards Kelleen I turned into a cross road, came over the hills, riding hard all night, and as you see, only got here now with the sad news."

CHAPTER XVII.

MORE than a fortnight passed over before the orphan girl was able to leave her sick couch, the several sad events occurring so rapidly the one after the other, unnerved her gentle spirit; but the shock of her father's sudden death completely overpowered her.

Let his love, and temper, and disposition, be considered by those who knew him little or well, to be harsh and tyrannical, he had been a fond father to her, and she had loved him well and tenderly. Besides this irreparable loss, Dora had much to grieve and distract her mind,

12—2

She knew that Gorman Trevor Fitzpatrick claimed the title and estates; but she always understood from her father that he had made his will and carefully provided for her welfare and happiness. During her severe illness, partly delirious at times, she knew nothing of what had taken place after her father's death. When able to sit up, her governess and constant attendant, Miss MacCormack, made her acquainted with all that had occurred in that short interval. Her lamented sire, of course, was laid in the last resting-place of his race, Gorman Fitzpatrick attending as chief mourner and assuming the title of Lord Dunskelling. On hearing of Dora's illness, he had despatched messengers from Cork almost daily, with inquiries after her health, and stating that he every day expected to be able to leave for Dunskelling Castle; and he also intimated that every possible attention should be bestowed upon her welfare and happiness.

Dora sighed, saying :—

"Ah! God forbid that my happiness or my welfare should depend upon his care. He is not the next in succession, if my cousin, Cuthbert Gordon, lives—so my dear father said in his last letter to me."

"You are yet too weak and ill, my dear girl, to talk upon such matters," said Miss MacCormack. "You will retard your convalescence by tormenting your mind. Depend on it your lamented father has left you carefully provided for."

Dora then inquired if the dragoons were still in the castle.

"No, my love; Captain Dunlop and his troop left for Kerry; the country is still in open rebellion. Gorman Fitzpatrick—or Lord Dunskelling as he is now called—has filled the house with his own servants, and the stables with his horses. He you know, is a Roman Catholic, and it is said he is but a lukewarm upholder of the Protestant cause; but still, not inclined to embroil himself with either parties in this unhappy strife."

"In the frightful state the country is in," remarked our heroine, "any act may be committed with impunity; the more I think of it, the more I am persuaded that the attack upon this mansion was no act for mere depredation and robbery—though all the plate and valuables were stolen, papers, deeds, and parchments would have been left. But they are all gone—no doubt my dear father's will with them.

"If this be the case, I am in Gorman Fitzpatrick's power; if he chooses to style himself my guardian, who will, or can, gainsay it?"

"If the country remains unsettled," said Miss MacCormack, "it may be difficult to dispute his power, but, in settled times, you would, I think, become a ward of Chancery, and could withdraw from his protection and power."

Dora, though weak and languid from the fever and anxiety, resolved in her own mind neither to be frightened nor cajoled into any measure by Lord Dunskelling. How bitterly the young girl bewailed the disappearance of Cuthbert Gordon; he would have been her protector, and his strong arm and noble spirit would have made an oppressor quail. Young as Dora was when Gorman Fitzpatrick resided at Dunskelling Castle—who was at that time looked upon by the late lord with a tolerably favourable opinion—young as she was, the angry flush would come to her young cheek when he attempted to smooth her silken curls and call her his little wife. "No," she would exclaim, indignantly, "that I will never be."

But now, with such power in his hands, what might not his scheming nature attempt or dare?

At length, one morning, about the sixth week after Dora's bereavement, a carriage, with four reeking horses, and followed by half-a-dozen well-mounted and armed domestics, drove up the avenue and halted at the portals of Dunskelling Castle. Its lord had at length arrived. Dora returned to her own suite of rooms, and left Miss Mac-Cormack and the housekeeper to receive his lordship. Miss MacCormack, shortly after his arrival, rejoined her.

"Well," said Dora, nervously, "he has arrived?"

"Yes," returned the governess; "and a couple of

friends with him ; and he says he expects half-a-dozen more in a day or two. Nevertheless, he asked most anxiously after your health, and hoped, as your future guardian, you would——"

"Ha !" interrupted Dora, "just as I thought—he has already constituted himself my guardian—a plain confession that he considers my dear father to have died without a will. God forgive me if I wrong him, but I fully believe he not only had a hand in the carrying off of my poor cousin Gordon, but in the attack and robbery of the castle."

"Nay," said Miss MacCormack, with a change of colour her pupil did not perceive, "you are too severe upon his lordship; wild and extravagant he always was, but of deeds, such as abduction and robbery, you surely cannot dream of accusing him. He said, very considerately, I forgot to mention, that if you would be in the least inconvenienced, he would prevent his expected guests from coming."

"Well, it's the least he could do," said Dora ; "there is little respect shown to the dead in filling the mansion with revellers; it is scarcely two months since the grave closed over the mortal remains of my beloved and lamented father."

Miss MacCormack made no reply.

Mrs. Brennen, the following day, came to say his lordship was very desirous that she should select whatever apartment she pleased for her own individual use, and for her female attendants.

"Where we are now, in the west wing," said Dora, "will suit me best ; it is more remote from the principal chambers in the interior of the mansion. They are moderately-sized rooms, but they suit me the better in that respect."

Lord Dunskelling's two guests remained, but no others arrived, the rebellion was nearly crushed, though the country was terribly unsettled ; still the Royal troops had completely the mastery everywhere, and the Government was getting firmly secured again.

After little more than a week Dora could not well

refuse to see Lord Dunskelling. Miss MacCormack had considerably changed her opinion of his lordship, and frequently remarked that he was a very handsome man, and much changed in manners and appearance for the better.

"There was great room for improvement," returned Dora, quietly, as she proceeded to the red drawing-room, where she expected to see his lordship.

He was there, awaiting her arrival.

Dora was just seventeen; she was tall and fully formed; graceful, and perfectly easy in her manner, and self-possessed. Though her cheek was pale from her recent sufferings, she still was most exquisitely lovely. Lord Dunskelling, as well as herself, was, of course, in deep mourning. We have said he was a very handsome man—tall and well-formed—but the general expression of his features somehow failed to attract or to please after the first introduction. He came forward eagerly to receive Dora, and appeared amazingly struck by her beauty and altered appearance since the period of his residence in Dunskelling Castle. He held out his hand to her frankly, and in a subdued, softened manner, said he hoped his presence in Dunskelling had not put her to any inconvenience, as he was most anxious to arrange matters so that her will and hers only should be consulted.

"I thank you, my lord," returned Dora, very quietly, just touching his lordship's hand, and then taking a seat, "for your anxiety on my account."

"Pardon me, Dora," interrupted Lord Dunskelling, "you seem to forget we are cousins. Why such exceeding formality? Though the law of the land gives the title and estates to the nearest male descendant, still there is no necessity that such a state of things should cause cousins—and cousins partly brought up together under the same roof—to regard each other as strangers."

"You quite mistake me, my lord," returned Dora, "if you imagine I envy you either the title or estates of Dunskelling, you sadly mistake my feelings. I have always been aware that the title and estates of Dunskelling would go to the next heir; but my lamented father himself informed me that the heir to the estates was a gentleman named Cuthbert Gordon."

"Your father was perfectly correct," returned Lord Dunskelling, very calmly and quietly, "and I believe, were that gentleman living, he might dispute my claim, with some chance of success."

"Living!" repeated Dora, her heart beating painfully, fixing her large and most expressive eyes upon her companion. "You do not mean to assert that you consider Mr. Cuthbert Gordon, who was carried off in my presence by a party of men in sailors' attire, to be"—she hesitated, but added firmly—"to be no longer living?"

Lord Dunskelling felt a malignant satisfaction, though he strove to diguise it, in witnessing the emotion felt by Dora, he however said—"I do not positively assert that this young man is dead; nevertheless, he has not been heard of since his affray with a desperate gang of smugglers, who, somehow, were informed that he was an officer in the navy, and secretly a spy upon this coast."

"You can scarcely hope, my lord," said Dora Dunskelling, with a most peculiar expression of countenance as she regarded him, "to make me believe so ridiculous a report, when you with a Mr. O'Dowd and Mr. Cuthbert Gordon were all three wrecked in a smuggling cutter on this coast, and it was well known that several bodies of unfortunate, misguided men were cast ashore along with my cousin, Mr. Gordon, who was cruelly seized and overpowered on the Welsh coast, and forced on board Mr. O'Dowd's vessel, which he called a yacht, but which you know was a smuggling cutter."

"Those were sad days, Dora," returned his lordship, quite coolly; "days I bitterly repent; but, you see, I was neither drowned nor a sharer in these smuggling exploits of O'Dowd's—poor fellow, he paid with his life the penalty he so rashly incurred. We were both cast upon a small island close to the reef on which the cutter struck. He was alive when picked up, but he only lived a few hours. I was more fortunate, though I was a long time recovering."

Dora regarded her cousin with a most incredulous look ; the fact was, she disbelieved all he said; she however remarked, " Well, my lord, let us change the subject, I have my own thoughts respecting the carrying off Mr. Gordon ; and I scarcely think that those who committed that outrage would exactly like to burden their consciences with the crime of murder."

There was an almost imperceptible quivering of Lord Dunskelling's lip, and a very angry flash from his dark eyes, but he conquered the emotion, as Lady Dora continued, "I should like to know, my lord, how I am situated, whether my father left a will, and under whose control I am to consider myself."

" God forbid, you should be under any person's control, Dora," returned Lord Dunskelling, "of course the law makes me your guardian till of age, but my guardianship will be merely assumed, to obey your wishes."

"Then I should like," said our heroine, firmly, " to at once leave this house to be placed under the care and protection of the Rev. Archibald Carew, rector of Ardmore. It was my father's wish, alas ! he knew his life hung of late years by a thread, and he himself said he would appoint that kind-hearted and good man my guardian, and that his wife would be as a mother to me, and his daughters be as sisters."

" Your father could not have selected a more upright, and honourable guardian ; unfortunately I can find no papers or document of any kind tending to prove that my uncle made a will or executed any legal document to that purpose. Nevertheless, that shall be no hindrance to your wish being complied with. The frightful state of the country has forced Mr. Carew to leave Ardmore with his family, but no doubt he will return in a few days, that part of the country being now perfectly tranquil and the rebels dispersed and driven as fugitives into Galway.

" I will send a messenger to Ardmore, and if you will write to Mr. Carew and state your wishes, you may at the same time tell him that the moment he pleases, he may employ his legal adviser to see into your rights; for though no will has been found, your just claims on your father's estates will be considerable, and no kind of difficulty will occur in your getting possession of them."

All this was said with so much apparent frankness and kindness of tone and manner, that Dora was, in spite of herself, surprised and softened.

Lord Dunskelling saw right well he had in a measure mollified Dora's opinion of him, it was what he aimed at, for he had already settled his plan of action.

"I thank you, my lord," said Dora, rising, "for acceding to my desires. Mr. Carew, some time ago, expressed a wish that should Miss MacCormack be at liberty, she would be most welcome to reside with him as governess to his two youngest daughters. Had my dear father lived, she need never have required another home."

"Neither need she now, Dora," returned his lordship. "Your means will be most ample, and no doubt you would wish to retain as your companion the instructress of your early girlhood."

"We shall see how things will be when the country becomes settled, but I will go and write to Mr. Carew."

"Now I hope, Dora, though you still persist in styling me my lord, as if I were neither your cousin nor guardian, nor former associate for several years, and in which formality you see I do not imitate you, but as I was about to say, I hope whilst you do remain in Dunskelling that you will not confine yourself to your own suite of rooms, but make me happy by seeing you and Miss Mac-Cormack join our dinner table. The gentleman who remains is a quiet, inoffensive person, and incapable of intruding his conversation upon you."

"As you please, I can have no objection."

Lord Dunskelling thanked her for feeling no longer afraid of him, saying :—

"Indeed, Dora, my past life was enough to prejudice most people against me, but I trust, the future will in a measure undo or obliterate the past."

"Well," thought Dora, as she retired along the corridor, "he is either very much changed or he is assuming a character of amiability to carry out some deep laid scheme what I think, I will keep to myself, for I cannot bring myself to believe in those very sudden transformations."

"Well, my love," said Miss MacCormack, as Dora entered their private sitting-room, "was his lordship very amiable?"

"I have no complaint to make against him," replied Dora, sitting down before her desk, intending to write to the Rev. Archibald Carew, "one of his friends has departed and he requests our company at meals, as formerly."

"And you refused, of course," said Miss MacCormack, pausing in her embroidery.

"No, indeed, I did not, I think it would have been ungracious to have done so, and give unnecessary trouble to the servants ; so, till I get an answer from Mr. Carew, we shall not require separate establishments under the same roof."

Miss MacCormack looked at Dora, whose calm, sweet features betrayed no unusual emotion ; Dora's side face was turned towards the governess and her thoughts were fixed on the subject she had so much at heart—a residence under the roof of Mr. Carew—she, therefore, did not perceive the strange expression of Miss MacCormack's countenance.

After a moment's pause the governess said :—

"Then Mr. Carew has returned to Ardmore."

"So Lord Dunskelling says," returned Dora ; "I am so glad. Ardmore is such a charming, quiet place, and the family so amiable, pious, and kind-hearted, they are dearly loved in the vicinity."

"Nevertheless, they had to take refuge in Cork or Dublin ; their kind-heartedness would not have saved them during the troubles of the last few months."

"That was not owing to the ingratitude of their own parishioners, or their neighbours ; but to the lawless bands that traversed the country, and who respected neither creed nor character."

Dora finished her letter and sealed it, ready to be despatched to Ardmore in the morning, a distance of fourteen miles from the castle.

The dinner and evening passed over without anything occurring to disturb the tranquillity of the three persons concerned. Lord Dunskelling did all he could to make himself agreeable to the ladies. He was, when he pleased, a perfect gentleman, had abundance of conversation at command, and was well read, and had travelled.

Dora's manner never changed ; calm, quiet, and unexcited, she listened without any emotion to his lordship's recital of perils he had undergone in a yacht voyage to the coast of Africa and various other parts. The next day a mounted messenger was despatched to Ardmore with our heroine's letter, with one from Lord Dunskelling.

During the day, Dora visited the library for the first time since the death of her father. She was aware that the new lord had been there, and carefully collected all the papers and documents that were scattered about the chamber after the robbery, for when picked up by the domestics they were thrust into all manner of places, temporarily.

But his lordship had been exceedingly careful in the re-collecting, had them consigned to an iron chest, and the chest placed in a closet in his own room. The library in Dunskelling Castle had been a favourite room of the late lord's. The windows commanded exceedingly fine views over the park and the boundless sea beyond, as well as a great extent of coast. Dora loved the room also ; here she had often sat reading to her dear father, and here for hours, when she was a mere child, she was placed on a stool at his feet whilst he told her tales of Indian life, and read instructive works to her. Let the man have been what the world pleased to think him, there was at least one kindly, loving feeling left in his heart, and that was doting love for his only child.

CHAPTER XVIII.

Miss MacCormack accompanied Lady Dora to the library, who, when she entered, looked round the room with a feeling of sad oppression.

With all Lord Dunskelling's suavity of manner, and apparent attention to her slightest wishes, she could not mistake the looks she at times caught fixed upon her. She was afraid of him, and a suspicion entered her heart that created a pang there. She thought Miss MacCormack's conduct also strange, if no worse. She was always, when she could, talking of what a wonderful change had come over Lord Dunskelling—"his whole nature," she said, "seemed altered—he certainly was always handsome, but the former reckless daring look, has been replaced by a calm, thoughtful expression, which becomes him much, and I feel perfectly satisfied that whoever becomes Lady Dunskelling will have no reason to regret her situation."

"Perhaps not," returned Dora, quite calmly, "whether a man is eminently handsome or otherwise, matters little if his other qualifications do not come up to the same standard. His lordship may feel remorse or regret for the past, and I sincerely trust he does; for you yourself, Julia, have often admitted that he led a terrible life."

Julia MacCormack coloured, but with a light laugh, said :—

"Ah, my dear, I fear if the lives of all young men of fashion and wealth were critically looked into, you would find it difficult to meet with the model of perfection you hope to discover."

"You quite mistake, Julia, if you imagine I seek perfection; I am neither thinking of men, their perfections, or their imperfections. My thoughts are occupied upon my unprotected situation, and the fearful loss I have experienced. The only man I ever experienced a feeling of friendship or affection for is my cousin, Mr. Cuthbert Gordon, and that feeling is not likely ever to be obliterated," and so the conversation ended, Lady Dora rather chagrined at seeing such a change taking place in the mind and opinions of her once attached governess.

Before we return to our heroine in the library, we will give a very brief outline of Miss MacCormack's history, her feelings, wishes, and projects. She was the only child of a country gentleman, of small fortune, but very extravagant ideas ; with scarcely five hundred a year his expenditure exceeded a thousand.

Mr. MacCormack clung to his system of making £500 do duty for a thousand, and his wife, to do her justice, helped him. She declared, though the estate was only £500 a year, it ought to be more than a thousand; the consequence was, that before their daughter Julia, a very pretty and accomplished girl, reached her 17th year—the estate had to be sold, and two years afterwards Julia became an orphan.

Clever, observing, and keen-sighted, Julia MacCormack, with a good name, a good figure, and handsome face, but without a shilling, began the world with the full determination of making herself independent, and, like the old gentleman, who dying told his son to " make money, honestly, John, if you can ; but make money at all events." Miss MacCormack promised in her own thoughts to do as the old gentleman wished his son to do.

She became a governess, and by great good fortune the lady she first lived with was a distant relative of the late Lord Dunskelling, and she recommended Miss MacCormack to his lordship, to superintend the education of his only daughter.

This was a grand opening for the young governess, and she entered upon her duties at Dunskelling Castle with hopes revived ; she was but doomed to disappointment in certain wild hopes and projects. His lordship was still young enough to take another wife. He would not be the first lord who had married the governess of his only child. She was really very handsome, very accomplished, and exceedingly agreeable, and displayed the fondest love for the little girl—who loved her in return, thinking her love purely unselfish. But Lord Dunskelling had become gloomy, reserved, and quite averse to society of any kind; the only pleasure he appeared to experience was the child-like love of his beautiful daughter. Miss MacCormack, with a large salary to compensate for the gloom of Dunskelling Castle, still began to find the solitude almost too much for her. Her marrying schemes were fast vanishing when Gorman Trevor Fitzpatrick came to reside at the castle, and to be looked upon as his uncle's heir.

Here was a prospect for Miss MacCormack; she was only eight and twenty, looked younger. At this time Dora Dunskelling was scarcely thirteen.

A wild, reckless spendthrift, was Gorman Fitzpatrick, with neither principle nor religion, though, as his father had been a Catholic, he called himself one. However, he promised his uncle to seriously consider the matter, and study the differences between the two creeds, and he made no doubt as he was a bad Roman Catholic he would in time make a good Protestant.

This his uncle insisted on if he made him his heir. Whilst residing in Dunskelling Castle, Gorman Fitzpatrick was forced to give up his reckless habits, having dissipated all he inherited.

Miss MacCormack was handsome, about his own age, perhaps a year older, and very lively and agreeable. He first made love to her to wile away the time, and then he felt a kind of fancy for her, and Julia, in time, really loved him; but having nothing very bad in her disposition beyond the desire to become independent by any means, she resisted all his overtures and endeavours to destroy her virtue.

"I tell you what, Julia," said Fitzpatrick to her, as they were one day alone in the saloon, "just put it out of your head that you will ever be my wife, and I'll let you into a secret, and in the end, if we succeed, I promise you a fair share of the spoils."

This was very plain speaking to a lady, to whom he was continually acting the lover, and who had resisted

with great determination all his most passionate appeals
to give him her love in return without the priest's sanction.

This bare-faced proposal neither shocked Miss Mac-
Cormack, nor took her by surprise, for she latterly very
clearly saw that a union with Gorman Fitzpatrick was
not a thing to be accomplished. She therefore said very
quietly :

"Well, Gorman Fitzpatrick, you certainly speak plainly.
However, what is your secret, and what are your projects,
and how am I to benefit by them ?"

"Upon my soul, Julia, you are a clever girl, and just
the wife I should like; but you see you have not a
hundred thousand pounds' fortune. If you had half that
sum I would marry you to-morrow."

"I dare say you would, Gorman ; that is, you would
marry the fifty thousand pounds, and take me into the
bargain as a make-weight !"

"No, faith, you wrong me there, Julia. I do love you;
but I am frightfully in debt !"

"But will you not succeed to the Dunskelling estates ?"

"No; there's the rub ! The present lord has no just
title to them, and he knows it, and that fact is distracting
his mind ; besides his conscience is probing him; he has
not been a good boy all his life, and I firmly believe in
the end—that is, when he is near his end—that he will
restore the title and the estates to the rightful owner."

Julia MacCormack was astonished, but she said :

"And who is the rightful owner ?"

"Ah ! A person you never saw or heard of, nor I
either. A Mr. Cuthbert Gordon, a son of a Captain
Gordon, who was killed in India. You see, Lord Dunskelling, when in India, (he was then the Honourable ——
Gordon,) fell distractedly in love with the beautiful and only
daughter of a Colonel Ludlow, and proposed for her with
her father's consent, for they were great friends. But Miss
Ludlow was already in love with a poor subaltern, Lieut.
Gordon, who had come out to India with her in the same
packet. Therefore she refused the Nabob. In revenge,
he and the colonel had the lieutenant sent into the most
unhealthy station in India."

"In the meantime Colonel Ludlow suddenly died, and the Honourable —— Gordon had the settlement of his affairs. To suit his own views he managed to make it appear that his friend, the colonel, had died enormously in his debt, so much so that his daughter was left nearly a pauper. He then offered to cancel all her father's debts, thinking this generosity would work in his favour—but not a bit of it. Cupid had too strong a hold for Miss Ludlow, she insisted upon paying every fraction of her sire's encumbrances; refused a second time the hand of a Nabob worth £150,000, married Captain Gordon, and was a happy wife till he was killed in some engagement or other with the native princes. The widow and her children are now somewhere in England, where I cannot say, but I shall find out. On becoming Lord Dunskelling the Nabob returned to England, full of hatred to the Gordons; married, and his young wife died in giving birth to Dora. Of late he has become morose, at times tyrannical and unsocial, caring for nothing but his daughter; he is stung with remorse for the past, and I do not know the moment when he may cast me out and reinstate the rightful heir."

"But how on earth, Gorman, did you learn all this?" asked Miss MacCormack.

"Well, I confess, Julia, I am not very scrupulous; besides, a cousin of mine, O'Dowd, knows the whole family history. He it was who told me that if the present lord died I could never inherit either the title or the estates. So I set to work to find out what was preying on Lord Dunskelling's mind, and getting possession of the keys belonging to the two chests in the library, I found out, from private letters and other documents, what I have now told you."

"And what do you propose to do?" returned Julia MacCormack, not evincing any degree of shame at Gorman Fitzpatrick's delinquency.

"Stand my ground as long as I can; his lordship may live a few years or die any moment, for he has a frightful disease of the heart, and any agitation half kills him. My object is to marry the heiress. Dora will inherit, no

13

matter who takes the title and estates, the whole of her father's personal property, a sum not less than £150,000."

" Well, in truth," replied the governess with a slight increase of colour, " you are building castles in the air. You make love to one woman with the intention of marrying another, and candidly tell her so. You must form a very strange opinion of me. However, your intended wife is a mere child of thirteen, and already with a very considerable appearance of great dislike to your company. In fact, as she has told me herself, she would feel quite happy if you were gone from Dunskelling, for she can't bear being teased and tormented by you."

Gorman Fitzpatrick laughed.

" But do not you see, Julia, I only want Dora's gold and you to enjoy it with me? the world is wide and I do not care a fig where we dwell, so the means of enjoying life are to be had."

The lady shook her head, saying :

" Your projects are wild and fanciful, and to my mind quite chimerical. Whilst the old lord lives you are powerless, and three or four years must elapse before you could dream of asking for Dora's hand; and depend upon it she will never consent, and her father will never force her, against her inclination, to become any man's wife."

" But," said Fitzpatrick, " the old lord will not live four years, his physician says it's impossible. When he dies he will die suddenly. I must so manage as to become Dora's guardian."

" What part are you expecting me to play in these wild projects of yours, all depending upon the most improbable chances ? You do not suppose for a moment that his lordship will die without making a will and appointing a proper guardian for his child, if he has not done so already. Really, Gorman, I can have no hand in such out-of-the-way schemes."

" But listen, Julia; if I can manage to get that £150,000 without marrying Dora, what do you say then ? Will you be my wife and cross the seas with me, and share the fruits of my bold attempt ? "

" Make me your wife, and you may depend I will not

shrink from any peril or risk you may incur," was the answer.

"Agreed," said Gorman Fitzpatrick, taking Julia's hand, "agreed; another time, I will make you better acquainted with my plans, for I have several," and they separated.

Gorman's conduct and frightful dissipation very speedily disgusted Lord Dunskelling, and after a violent altercation, during which Fitzpatrick unguardedly let out some of the information he had gleaned of his lordship's early life, they parted in violent recrimination, Lord Dunskelling desiring him to quit Dunskelling for ever, declaring that he should neither succeed to the title or estates.

Gorman Fitzpatrick left Dunskelling after a rather unpleasant interview with Miss MacCormack, in which she steadily refused to share his fortunes otherwise than his wife, and to take a wife on his uncertain means he said would be ridiculous.

"I shall return here, depend on it," he remarked, "and return as Lord Dunskelling; we are living in troubled times. Who knows what may turn up? I like a wild devil-may-care life, and will now join O'Dowd and become a smuggler, *par excellence*," and thus they parted.

Miss MacCormack mused over this episode in her life. Her marriage projects appeared hopeless; but she was not of a nature to be deeply or devotedly attached, so she bore the absence of Fitzpatrick extremely well, and began to think, after all, that her chance of independence hereafter lay in attention and affection to the young heiress of Dunskelling, and from that hour she really devoted herself to her, and her education. Nearly four years passed in peace and quietness, and Miss MacCormack, now thirty, and no longer as attractive as formerly, was settling down into a matronly staid woman, having completely banished Gorman Fitzpatrick from her heart and mind. When the shipwreck of O'Dowd's cutter caused Cuthbert Gordon to become an inmate of Dunskelling Castle, Miss MacCormack was astounded. Here was the very heir Gorman Fitzpatrick had spoken to her about.

13—2

When she first heard that it was O'Dowd's yacht that was lost, she experienced a pang of regret for the fate of her quondam lover; but she discovered that he was saved and that O'Dowd had perished. Then came the abduction of Cuthbert Gordon, the plundering of the castle, and finally the death of Lord Dunskelling, and the assumption of the title by Gorman Fitzpatrick.

"Did I not tell you," said Fitzpatrick, in their first interview in private, "that I would return as Lord Dunskelling? and you see I have kept my word."

"Yes," said Miss MacCormack, thoughtfully; "but how long will you keep the title and estates?"

"Till one with a better claim takes them from me," returned his lordship, "and I think when that does take place, if it ever does, I shall be in a position to make a hard fight of it; if I lose, I may still defy Dame Fortune; but Julia, have you any portion of your former love left for me?"

"Well, that greatly depends upon yourself, we are not so young as we were."

"I still think you are a very charming woman, Julia, and I assure you I feel just the same for you as ever."

"But not sufficient love to make me Lady Dunskelling."

"Not exactly yet," returned the new lord, with a laugh. "You still keep on that tack, Julia."

"Most decidedly," returned the lady; having kept my reputation intact to thirty-two, you do not often find women cast it away from them for idle chimeras; indeed, after thirty, women are not easily misled. Do you know that we have had the heir of Dunskelling here under this roof, and that the late lord intended to unite him to his daughter?"

"Of course I knew all about it, for we were shipwrecked together. Ah! there was a chance lost. If Davis had only held him fast, my rights could never be disputed."

"But you had him carried off," said Miss MacCormack, fixing her dark and very meaning eyes upon her companion.

"Oh, of course I had. I do not want to have any mystery about the affair with you, and I think those to whose tender mercies I confided him will take very great care of him, so that he will not, even if he survives the climate, be very likely to return to this country for some time."

"But surely, Gorman," said Miss MacCormack with a shudder, and looking this time really shocked, "you have not conspired against the really noble-hearted young man's life."

Lord Dunskelling frowned, as he somewhat fiercely said—"If I desired his life, I could have had him knocked on the head as easily as have had him carried off."

"Then why say if he survives the climate—he, a powerful, healthy youth, accustomed to various climates and hardships?"

"Tut, how you run on," interrupted Lord Dunskelling; "I only sent him a voyage to Africa in a slaver. Every one visiting the slave coast of Africa runs a slight chance of his life, yet you see thousands frequent that coast, seeking fortune—he stands the same chance as another, no more. I wanted him out of the way; for, by all accounts, he was making love to Dora Dunskelling, now, I suppose, rather a handsome girl."

"I should rather think," said Julia MacCormack, "that their love is mutual."

"Pooh!" muttered Lord Dunskelling, angrily, "the love of a school-girl," and he laughed scornfully.

"School-girl!" repeated Miss MacCormack, "you are very much mistaken in imagining Dora Dunskelling a school-girl, and if you dream of gaining her hand in marriage, the sooner you abandon that project the better. She detests you!"

"I care very little about her love or hate," returned Lord Dunskelling, "my wife she shall be, willing or unwilling. And now, to be plain with you, Julia, and put all love out of the question, give me your word to assist me in carrying out my plans, and the day I make Dora Dunskelling my wife, I will make you mistress of £10,000."

How Miss MacCormack acted our story will unfold.

We now return to our heroine in the library of Dunskelling Castle.

Having regarded many an object in the room that recalled recollections, some pleasing and some painful, the orphan went to the book-case, to take down a book to pass an hour in reading. As she took the volume from the shelf a folded paper fell upon the floor. It was a letter, and on taking it up she perceived it was directed to her father.

"No doubt," thought Dora, "one picked up on the morning after the plunder of the chests and other effects." She opened the letter, scarcely conscious of what she was doing, for it recalled her father so forcibly to her thoughts, and mechanically she let her eyes rest on the contents, but after reading the first few lines she started, and became riveted into earnest attention, as she perused the following carefully, and with deep emotion :—

"My Dear Lord,

"Your letter of the 25th took me by surprise. I did not reply at once, for I anxiously waited for the important deed you stated you would send by private messenger. I received it on the 30th, and sat down at once to carefully peruse it. I read it twice, taking notes each time, and now I give you the result. It is perfectly clear and undisputable, that the title and estates of Dunskelling, unquestionably, by this deed, belong, by right of succession, to the son of Captain Gordon, who was, as you state, killed at Alumdabad. If this son did not exist the title and estates would be yours; but you have inherited them, thinking no such deed had been ever executed by the late Lord Dunskelling. The fact is, this paper clearly, and in truth, justly, upsets and nullifies every deed or document previously executed by the late lord, for it was drawn up, executed, and properly witnessed only three days before his death, purposely to cancel all other deeds or settlements made by him. It appears a deed of atonement in repentance for a most unjust act of disinheriting.

"You say you now wish the title and estates to revert

to the rightful heir, but not till after your death ;—you
say the exposure would be worse than death, but you are
too sensitive, for you were not cognizant that this deed was
in existence till lately. Your large personal property will,
of course, go to your daughter. Without this important
paper your nephew, Fitzpatrick, would succeed to the
title and estates, and from the account you give me of his
mode of life and of his being a Roman Catholic, such a
succession would be far from desirable. You declare
yourself favourable to the succession of Mr. Cuthbert
Gordon, who is in the naval service of the king, and also
that you ardently desire a union between Mr. Gordon and
your daughter; such a union, in my opinion, would be
most desirable. I would, therefore, at once communicate
with Mr. Gordon, whom you describe as most amiable. I
think I have said enough till we meet next month in
Dublin. As to the doctors' opinion on your life, remember
that their verdicts are far from infallible.

    " I remain, my dear Lord,

        " Your obedient and attached friend,

                " J. P. STURGEON."

Dora read this letter with astonishment, and no little
perplexity of mind. "So, then," thought the young heiress,
"my dear father had no right to the title or estates from
the beginning ! Poor Captain Gordon, who lost his life
fighting the battles of his country in India, was the real
heir. Where was this deed, and where is it now ? and
where is the real Lord Dunskelling ? "

Looking at the date of the letter she perceived it was
written not more than a month before the wreck of Herbert O'Dowd's cutter. She determined not to show the
letter to Miss MacCormack, but to keep it and its contents
to herself; searching amongst several of the books, she
found other papers thrust into them; several letters also
to her father, but none of any consequence that she could
perceive—no doubt picked from the floor and put in the
books by the servants, who forgot all about them. She
collected them all together, and placed them in a
drawer.

About four o'clock in the day the messenger returned from Ardmore, and to her intense vexation, with her letter unopened. None of the family had arrived. The housekeeper stated that Mrs. Carew was ill in Dublin, and that the family would not return till her health was perfectly re-established.

Lord Dunskelling saw that Dora looked chagrined, and he observed :—

"This little delay, cousin, I trust does not distress you. Your letter can be forwarded to Dublin by to-morrow's mail, and no doubt Mr. Carew will offer you the accomodation of his house till he and his family return, since you seem to consider a residence under this roof so disagreeable."

Dora made no reply; she could not bring herself to state one thing, and wish another, for she was above duplicity in any form.

We must now leave our fair young heroine to fight her way against two united powers, for before three days had passed over she became perfectly convinced that Lord Dunskelling and Julia MacCormack were acting in concert to bring about some project in which she was unfortunately destined to be a principal performer.

CHAPTER XIX.

WE left Cuthbert Gordon struck to the earth by a blow from a Moorish sabre, after having shot one of the marauders, as they made a furious onslaught on the unoffending negroes.

Fortunately the sabre turned in the Moorish hand, so

that only the flat struck him, but so severe was the blow, that he lay as if dead, with the insensible negro stretched right across his body. The Moors pursued the fugitive negroes only to the extremity of the village, then pillaged the houses, bound Mr. Park's hands and feet, and threw him across a horse, serving Demba in a similar manner, and having completed their savage foray to their satisfaction, mounted their horses, and galloped off.

Our hero, recovering from the blow, soon became conscious of a heavy weight nearly suffocating him, for the dead negro's arm lay across his face and mouth. Making an effort, as he recovered recollection, he shook away the body and after a time sat up, and looked around ; as he did so, several negroes came cautiously creeping back into the place where the feast was held and which had terminated so fatally.

Seeing our hero alive, they ran eagerly to him, helped him up, and showed, by every kind of gesture, and abundance of chattering, that they were highly pleased at his being still alive. The negroes then sat down to bewail their losses and some to carry away the dead. The dead body of the Moor had been removed by his companions.

Our hero bitterly bewailed the captivity of his kind friend Mr. Park and also grieved for the loss of the faithful Demba. He felt an intense desire to follow on the track of the Moors, hoping some chance circumstance might enable him to aid in rescuing his friend and Demba from the cruel and perfidious Moors. But after a time he made out that they were sure to cross the desert with their captives, for they had carried off several of the young negroes belonging to the village. The Dooty advised his going back to the Gambia river before the rains set in and to return by Kameaba as the Mansa (governor of that place) was friendy, and he would be well treated. There he could stay out the rainy season and then traverse the country with the Slatees and their coffle of slaves proceeding to the Gambia river.

This advice Gordon acknowledged was good. But his high spirit and kindly nature tempted him to persist in following in the track of the Moors. He had about his own person some gold dust; with this resource he could make his way through the country for some time. The loss of Demba greatly distressed him, for he was a most faithful, intelligent youth, and the tribe he came from possessed none of the generally repulsive features of the negro, neither was their colour the same. He resolved to stain his skin and attire himself like Demba; some of the natives whom he made acquainted with his design, assisted him; they stained his face, arms, and legs, to the colour of the Toulah tribe; this tribe resides near the Gambia, have soft silky hair, and, like Demba, pleasing features.

The weight of one black bean of gold dust would purchase provisions for three days, and with a little persuasion and the offer of half his gold dust he engaged three negroes to accompany him, promising if the track of the Moors led across the desert to give up the pursuit.

All our hero now possessed was a pistol, ten charges of powder and ball, and eleven quills of gold dust, and two strings of beads.

For nine days Gordon coaxed his guides to persevere, suffering great fear at times from straggling parties of Moors, but still gaining intelligence of the track the band, that had Mr. Park and Demba in their power, pursued. At last, however, they discovered that the Moors had crossed the desert, and in the night our hero's guides decamped, having heard during the day that a body of cavalry, all Moors, swept the adjacent country, plundering and killing and carrying off the inhabitants.

Our hero was now alone, hundreds of miles from the sea-coast, in the midst of a wild, forest-covered tract, infested by wild beasts, and the open part of the country traversed by ferocious Moors. He was convinced that to persist in his object in following Mr Park, would be to perish, and to retrace his way would be no easy task without a guide. He was sitting at the foot of a tree, finishing a very frugal meal, and debating with himself what was best to be done; he had but one day's provision, and his pistol was a poor weapon to hunt down eatable food with. The two days previously, they had not passed a single village. Just below where he sat was a considerable open space, surrounded by thick jungle; whilst gazing listlessly across this space, he perceived a figure come out from the jungle, and stand gazing earnestly on every side. By the attire our hero knew that he beheld a native, but he was too far to distinguish features, and yet it struck him the figure and dress resembled Demba's. Starting up, he shouted loudly; the figure turned round, and gazed up at our hero; and then, after another scrutinizing glance all round, came towards him, and as he approached, and he could see the features, he recognised, to his intense satisfaction, Demba himself. The negro did not recognise our hero, for his attire and stained skin made him imagine he saw a native; but as soon as they were nearly face to face, Cuthbert held out his hand, saying in English, "My poor Demba, how rejoiced I am to see you."

With a cry of wild joy, the negro seized the hand offered him, and kissed it repeatedly. "Oh, massa, massa, me die for joy; me tink you killed by the cussed Moors. How you here? Oh, golly; dis bery good luck for Demba."

"But how did you escape from the Moors, Demba, and where is Mr. Park—is he still their prisoner? But you look worn and jaded. Have you had any food to-day?"

"No, massa; me no eat food two days, hiding in de jungle from de Moors; dey hunt me with dogs; but I swim de river and escape."

Cuthbert Gordon took off his bag and displayed his little store of food, happy that he had it to share. The negro ate ravenously.

"Oh, massa, nebber fear, now; I find plenty of food; de cussed Moor not come in forest."

It was in truth a simple repast, consisting of a little meal mixed with water, and some nuts.

"We must now," said our hero, "endeavour to reach

some village, or else we shall have to pass the night in this forest, which is infested with lions; I saw three yesterday."

Demba knew nothing of the country, but he said they would surely fall in with a village. He then told our hero how cruelly the Moors had treated Mr. Park. They went towards the desert; Demba watched an opportunity the first night before entering upon the desert to get the fastening on his leg loose, and fled in the night. The next day, four Moors pursued him with dogs. But he crossed a river, and crept into a tangled jungle and lay a day and a night without food or drink, every instant expecting he would be devoured by wild beasts. Cuthbert Gordon felt exceedingly for the cruel captivity of Mungo Park, but trusted when the Moors should reach their destination, he would be able to procure his release, from some one in authority.

Demba told his master, as he always called him, that they must proceed fast to reach a good village before the rains fell, for during that time it would be impossible to travel, and he heard the Moors say that there was a great war up the country with King Daisy, therefore they had better try to get into the Mandingo country, and stay at Jalinkadoo or Boor, where there was plenty of gold to be had by washing the sand, and when the rains were over, they could easily travel with the Slatees, and make for the Gambia.

"The people in Mandingo," said Demba, "good people. Dey steal to be sure, but den dey don't rob and illuse you."

Cuthbert Gordon smiled at Demba's ideas of thieving and robbery, but the fact is, the Mandingos like to steal anything in a quiet, easy way, and they are adepts at that kind of work; but they will not openly rob and insult you, like very many of the other tribes. Their chiefs require to be paid for their protection, and he remembered the king of Bondi taking an amazing liking to a blue coat with brass buttons, that Mr. Park put on in honour of the interview. He was obliged to take it off and present it, and his majesty, who happened to have on only a very short cotton shirt, immediatcly dressed himself, to thc intense admiration of his wives and attendants.

The whole of that day our travellers kept to thc forest, and at night collected a great quantity of fire-wood, and igniting it, by flashing a pistol in some dry grass, they agrecd to keep watch by turns, for the cries of the jackals, and the roar of the African lion, as soon as the sun set, made the forest resound again.

They saw several hyenas approach the fire during the night, and one lion, but they were easily frightened by throwing a flaming brand at them.

Demba advised our hero to wash off his colour before reaching the Mandingo people; they liked the white man but hated the dark-skinned tawny Moor and Arab. The meal and nuts were all eaten for breakfast, but after three hours' travelling over an extensive plain, they with joy perceived a woman and a boy driving an ass before them.

On overtaking them, the woman regarded them suspiciously, at least she did our hero, but Demba told her his comrade was a white man—and pulling back the cotton vest he wore, he exposed his chest, which was not stained; this seemed to please her. She told Demba she was carrying salt to Nemassa, but if they went away to the left they would soon see the village of Burnaw, where the Dooty would furnish them with food and lodging if they had anything to give for it. This intelligence gave the travellers good spirits, and pushing on, in less than an hour they reached the village.

Here they were very well treated, but our hero's little stock of gold dust was diminishing, and seeing a very excellent carbine with the Dooty, he gave up nearly all he had, with some of his amber beads in the bargain, for the carbine and twelve charges of powder and shot. Demba got a present of a bow and a sheaf of arrows, with which he was very expert, and after a day's rest, and being well instructed as to the road, they pushed on for Siboododoo, which they were told was the healthiest place they could pass the rainy season in.

After three days' hard travelling and meeting many

mishaps and escapes from rapid rivers and wild beasts, they reached their destined village, by which time Cuthbert Gordon had scrubbed himself, with Demba's assistance, nearly as white as was nature. The people of the village seemed to regard a white man with great curiosity. Here they were visited by a tremendous thunderstorm, which they thought predicted the approach of the rains. The people of Siboododoo were very short of provisions and said they could not keep the travellers, and advised their pushing on to Kameaba.

This our hero saw he would be obliged to do, for the villagers had barely food enough to last out the rains; so, without delay, they again went on, and after a great deal of suffering and nearly exhausted, living only on what they killed in the woods, they reached Kameaba. The rains having already set in, further they could not go, for the streams had become furious torrents.

Pretty well accustomed to the manners of the negro villagers by this time, and by constantly conversing with Demba, our hero could make himself understood by the natives in their own tongue helped out by Demba when in difficulty. Having reached Kameaba he proceeded to visit the Mansa of the village.

It was then the mouth of July, and Cuthbert Gordon knew he would not be able to leave Kameaba for more than two months, and he also knew that the Mansa would not support him and Demba for nothing; for food at this period was extremely scarce all over the country.

On entering the Mansa's hut he found himself and Demba surrounded by a crowd of men and women, all being very anxious about what brought the white man to Kameaba.

The Mansa was a stern, fierce, repulsive looking old negro, with two wives and a daughter. The daughter was a very fine, tall, well-shaped negress, very unlike her sire; but her mother, he afterwards understood, was a Joulah, and very handsome according to their notions of beauty. At all events even the Englishman thought Oroonotoo, the daughter, a very interesting looking damsel, who was scarcely sixteen, and attired somewhat coquettishly and with several ornaments about her person.

"Well, white man, what has brought you here in the rainy season? Have you the means to pay for your keep?" said the Mansa.

"Well," returned our hero, "I will pay as long as I can, for a hut and some meal. We shall be able to find food for ourselves."

"I can't give you a hut," said the old man, gruffly.

"Yes, father, you can," said the daughter, quite calmly; "and he can share our food too."

"Not without paying for it," he returned, muttering something.

"Well, I will pay for the hut, and for what you will give me. When my stock is out we will talk further."

"Don't be afraid," said Oroonotoo, looking kindly at our hero; "we won't let you starve till the rains are over."

"Yes, yes," growled the old negro; "but pay now for what you get."

The daughter cast a contemptuous look at her sire, as Cuthbert pulled out two quills of gold dust and some amber beads, and placed them before the Mansa. The old man's eyes glistened as he clutched the quills.

"Very well," said he, "you shall have as much as this is worth. When it is out you will have to pay more."

Disgusted with the old miser, but pleased with the sympathy of Oroonotoo, Cuthbert followed the negro, who was to show him the hut they were to live in, and a miserable place it was, but it afforded shelter from the rains which fell the next day with great violence. During the weary rainy days, Cuthbert Gordon exerted himself to make Demba a Christian. The young man had become so attached to his master that he declared he would give up his country and follow our hero to England. He listened with praiseworthy attention to all the explanations given, and very soon began to comprehend how simple and few are the requirements to make a man a Christian; and he also saw how humane and charitable were the precepts Christ taught, in comparison with the benighted and cruel creed of the negro.

Demba caught the fever, and Cuthbert untiringly watched him through it. The Indian girl frequently visited them, and brought presents. Shortly after Demba began to get well, Cuthbert was attacked severely. Oroonotoo was unceasing in her kindness, and profuse in sharing her own food with the invalid, and to her care and one of her women he owed his recovery. The old Mansa was furious, but he idolized his daughter, and one word from her checked his most furious moods. He insisted, however, on having Cuthbert Gordon's gun, pistol, and, in fact, all he possessed of value.

"Let him have them," said his daughter; "you shall have them again."

Our hero could not but be grateful to the African maiden, and he told her he was so, and regretted he could never show how much he was so.

"Oh!" returned Oroonotoo, "you get well and able to travel, and I am pleased."

The rains were tremendous; there would be no possibility of stirring till November, till the east wind set in, and dried up the ground; whilst the old Mansa still hankered after gain, and positively refused more food till our hero and Demba promised to pay him in gold dust for the food furnished them.

"But what is to be done?" asked Cuthbert of Oroonotoo. "I have no more gold dust."

"I will tell you," said the girl. "Every year after the rains a party from this village goes to collect the sanno berroo (gold stones). You can come with us; in a very short time you will collect enough gold, by washing sand, to enable you to pay my greedy father. I will show you how to work. If you resist I fear my father's avarice is so great that he would cause you to be stopped, and perhaps deliver you over to the Moors."

The young man was too honourable to wish to deprive the Mansa of his dues; and talking the matter over with Demba, he agreed it would just be as well to go to the gold-diggings. He knew there was abundance of gold dust to be had where the expedition was to go. It would not be very much out of their way, and perhaps they might hear of a vessel on the gold coast. At all events they could collect gold dust enough to carry them all the way to the Gambia river, and there purchase a canoe and descend to Kacalonga, where they would surely find a vessel at that time of the year. Our hero therefore told the Mansa's daughter to tell her father that he and Demba would go.

When the rainy season had ceased and the dry parching east wind set in, and they considered the time fit to travel, those forming the expedition prepared for departure. But first the negroes fired the dry grass ; which process afforded our hero a grand spectacle. In the middle of the night the sight was magnificent, vast volumes of flames shooting up to the sky, and rushing over plain and mountain far as the eye could trace ; in the day vast pillars of smoke were to be seen rising up and obscuring the sky. Hundreds of wild animals, snakes, lizards, and birds fell victims to this proceeding, but after this yearly burning the grass springs up fresh and sweet, and shortly after the whole country puts on a smiling aspect.

CHAPTER XX.

EIGHT-AND-TWENTY persons formed the gold-washing party of the Mansa of Kameaba ; who nearly all performed the journey on foot, driving before them a dozen asses laden with utensils, provisions, and the materials for erecting two large tents.

The coverings of the tents were made from plaited
14

grass, for as no rain had to be guarded against, all the travellers required was to be sheltered from the sun and the night dews.

Oroonotoo provided them with the simple utensils for gold-washing, which consisted of a hoe for digging up the sand, some calabashes for washing it, and a bundle of quills for holding the particles of gold when washed.

In three days the party reached the gold region without accident. Our hero was deeply immersed in thought during the journey, in truth, he had much to think of. It was twelve months since he had been carried off from the coast of Ireland; what would his poor mother think of his strange disappearance? His prospects in the navy would be injured. As to asserting any claim to the Dunskelling property or title, he never dreamed of it, ignorant as he was of the old lord's death.

At times he often imagined Fitzpatrick was the author of his abduction, then again he thought it was not exactly right to charge him with so cruel and outrageous an act. Of Dora Dunskelling he thought unceasingly; she was in truth dear to his heart, and many a time a vision of her sweet lovely face cheered him in the privations and sufferings he had gone through.

"Tell you what, massa," said Demba, the evening before reaching the gold regions, "me no like dat debil de Mansa; he looked wicked at us."

"What for, Demba? We are going to work for him to pay for our food and lodging. Were you ever at a gold-washing, Demba?"

"No, massa; but me heard great talk about it; women soon show us what do. But me watch this cussed Mansa; praps he sell us to de Moors."

"He could scarcely do that, Demba. There are no Moors near here; besides, if the Moors came, they would be sure to plunder him of all his gold dust."

The following day, after arriving at the gold region, various forms and ceremonies were gone through by the seekers, and then they all set out for a very rapid stream where the gold was to be found. What surprised our hero was, that year after year they all frequented the same place, never seeking elsewhere. Gordon, with his hoe on his shoulder, and Demba carrying the calabashes, approached Oroonotoo, who was a few yards before him, with two negro women, carrying calabashes.

"You promised to show me," said he to the young Mandingo maiden, "how to sift the sand for gold. I fear I shall do but little without an instructor."

Oroonotoo looked up into the speaker's face with a troubled expression; but she bade him come with them. "We can only sift the sand. The men search amongst the stones; they will make your fingers bleed."

"But the white man will bring us no luck," said one of the women, spitefully. "Let him go to the men."

"No," said the Mansa's daughter, angrily; "come with me, my father said I was to show the white man how to sift or he would not get sufficient to pay him."

"That's no reason," said the woman, "that I should throw away my luck, and my omen was good," and she walked away. The other woman remained, but she walked on before them.

Oroonotoo said in a low voice:—

"Do not stay here after the third day; go away up yonder hills," pointing to a steep range that bounded the plain they were on. "Go south always, and you will reach Pala or Manbaro—the people there like white men."

"Why," began our hero.

Oroonotoo made an impatient gesture and repeated "Go—gather all the gold you can. Keep it; but go" —and then she joined the other woman, who now looked back.

"Humph," muttered our hero; "there must be evil intended us. Demba was right; that old villain has some project in his head."

"I said he debil, massa," put in Demba. "Ah, if massa had de gun."

"I wish I had, my good fellow; you see this rapid stream comes no doubt from yonder hills away to the south. When we do go we will follow this stream."

Cuthbert and Demba then watched the women; they observed that each took a portion of sand into their cala-

14—2

bashes, and then began slowly at first to whirl it round; a portion of sand, as they increased the rotary motion, being thrown out. This was to get rid of the coarse sand; changing the water several times till it came off quite clear—the sand left, they sift from one calabash to the other, till finally they seek in the residue for the particles of gold. If they collect two or three grains in each washing, they consider their labour remunerated.

"Ah," said our hero to Demba, "this is slow work, but nevertheless we must try," and to work they went. The young man could not resist a smile, as he looked at his attire and his occupation; and the women knee deep in the stream; the wild river in some places a torrent, with huge boulders and fantastic-shaped rocks, rising from its bed. Overhead a blazing sun; but a strong breeze swept over the barren plain, rendering the heat bear-able."

"If ever I live to reach dear old England," said our hero, as he strove to turn his calabash scientifically, and spilling half the sand, "I will remember this scene, and sketch it."

Oroonotoo was singularly expert. She contrived to pass our hero, and watching an opportunity, dropped several grains of gold into his calabash, and passed on. Cuthbert looked into the girl's face, but it was very serious. In this manner the day passed, and he found with Oroonotoo's gift, that he had twelve grains; Demba fifteen—these they put into a quill, and stopped it with a bit of cotton.

That night our hero and Demba felt very fatigued in the arms, so after cooking their frugal supper, they gladly retired to rest. The next day, the same work; this day's toil produced forty grains between them. Having retired to a kind of cavern in a huge mass of rock a short distance from the tents, they lit a fire, ate their supper, and lay down to sleep upon a heap of withered grass and leaves.

Despite his anxious thoughts, and the unusual toil, Cuthbert Gordon slept soundly.

In the middle of the night he was awoke by a hand grasping his arm. Opening his eyes, by the faint embers of the expiring fire, he beheld a figure standing beside him ; it was Oroonotoo.

He started to his feet, but the Mandingo girl said, "Hush ! hear me. You are betrayed, and by my miserly, hard-hearted father. Another day and you would be lost and delivered over as a slave. There is your carbine, and powder, shot, and ball," and she showed him his gun and a canvas bag. " Follow the stream up the hills ; horsemen cannot follow that track. Now wake Demba and go."

Cuthbert caught the maiden by the hand, saying earnestly, " And you, Oroonotoo, to bo left to meet the rage of your father."

" I have nothing to fear ; Oroonotoo is to be a king's wife," and kissing the hand that held hers, she let it go, and darted out of the cavern, quick as light, and became lost in the gloom of the night.

" Holly golly, massa, let us go. Dis no joke ; de cussed Moors come to-morrow. Oroonotoo a good girl ; ja, ja. I thought that debil Mansa, he worse than debil. De Mandingo say debil white ; ja, ja. De debil sure to be black."

" Well," said our hero, thoughtfully, " pack up the bag of powder and shot, give me the meal bag, and let us be off. We must get out of sight before day-break."

" This is very strange," thought our hero to himself, as he gladly grasped his carbine. " This is a second time that I owe my life to the noble kindness of a race called savage and uncivilised. Poor Matoo Patoo and Oroonotoo—two names I shall long remember. Who is to be Oroonotoo's husband ? " questioned Cuthbert Gordon of Demba.

" King Bambarro's son," said Demba. " Her father dare not hurt her, no fear ; dat why he let her do what she please."

It was a very dark night, with scarcely a breath of wind ; not a sound disturbed the stillness save the roar and rush of the rapid river as it foamed over the rocky impediments in its course.

Keeping as near the stream as possible, and encountering many obstacles in their course, they managed to reach the foot of the steep rocky heights, just as a faint gleam in the eastern sky warned them that day was breaking. To ascend the heights required considerable activity and strength, but by the time the sun rose they had gained a considerable elevation, and then they paused to rest, heated and somewhat fatigued.

"Golly, massa, dis bery nice place; no cussed Moor come here; dey fear de spirit of de mountains, and so do de niggers."

"But you are not afraid, Demba?"

"No, massa, now you teach me dat dare be no spirit, and dat Goramighty be ebberywhere."

"Then you think, Demba, that the rascally Mansa will not send his people here to look for us."

"Sartan sure, massa, dey no come here; dey tink de gold spirit lib in de bowels of de mountains, and keep watch over de gold."

As the light increased, Cuthbert began a survey of the country, from the height on which they stood, and a wild and savage scene presented itself to his gaze. The river, whose wild erratic course they had followed, he could now perceive, pouring its volume of water through a narrow gullet or ravine, and, foaming over abrupt ledges of rock, gained the plain, in a splendid cascade. Though it had taken them three hours to gain their elevation, so circuitous was the course of the river, that the two tents of the gold washers were distinctly visible, at a distance of scarcely three miles. Whilst gazing out over the plain, he suddenly perceived a party of horsemen emerge round a projecting head formed of masses of rock, and ride on slowly towards the tents, passing actually beneath the precipice on which they stood—they were ten in number.

"Ah, cuss dem, dere they are," exclaimed Demba, exultingly, "dem Moors."

Gordon recognised the group also as Moors, who rode completely armed, with carbine, sword, and long spear, and pistols in their girdles; they were about two hundred feet below them.

"No doubt," said our hero to Demba, "that is the party that rascal, the Mansa, wished to betray, or sell us to."

Just as our hero spoke, one of the Moors, looking up, beheld them, and instantly the troop halted, and all looked up the precipitous face of the mountain. They seemed puzzled. Our hero did not move, he well knew the Moors seldom or ever quit their horses ; the negroes, when pursued, usually make for the mountains. One of the Moors, however, evidently made out that our hero was a white man, for he unslung his carbine and took deliberate aim at him.

" Holly golly, massa, come down," said Demba, eagerly.

"There is little risk," returned our hero, as the ball struck the rock below him; "those short carbines of the Moors shoot wild and are of poor range."

"Give dem a shot, massa ; cuss dem debils."

"I will give them one in return," said Cuthbert Gordon, loading, as a volley of balls rattled against the face of the cliff ; two or three struck close to his feet, knocking splinters out of the rock.

Resting his long carbine, Cuthbert Gordon took deliberate aim at a Moor mounted on a very splendid horse, feeling some compunction lest he should hit the nobler animal of the two ; he was always accounted a very clever shot, and this time he did not belie his character, for the Moor rolled from his horse, struck by the ball, whilst the horse started off wildly across the plain. Demba danced about like a man in a frenzy with delight. Several of the Moors threw themselves from their horses, to lift the fallen man, whilst five of the number rode after the horse ; but the wounded man was on his feet in a moment, which somehow or other pleased our hero, for notwithstanding all he had suffered from the Moors, and the cruel captivity of Mr. Park still rankling in his mind, he felt loth to slay even an enemy, when no good result could ensue.

"Now then, Demba, let us go, the rascal is not much hurt, for he mounts another horse and they are getting out of shot; they would be mad to attempt to scale this precipice in the face of even one armed man, who would pick them off one by one; they are only now going to the tents." This our hero thought a very fortunate escape, thanks to Oroonotoo's having discovered her father's intentions and defeated them.

They had now to make their way across a vast extent of mountains without any knowledge whatever of their difficulties or their means of affording them food; to descend into the plain without crossing the range would lead to captivity. So all our hero could determine upon was to keep to the south as much as possible.

Here scarcely a sign of vegetation appeared; neither did they, after a walk of a league, perceive either animal or bird; the mountains rose to a considerable height above them, which convinced our hero that there must be a lake on the hills to supply so vast a body of water as flowed through the plain and formed the rapid rivers below; following as close as possible they came to a long almost level run of fine sands here and there. Cuthbert Gordon turned to Demba, who carried five calabashes full of water, which were now a useless encumbrance.

"By the look of those sands I think it is likely there is more gold here than below; see how some parts of the sands sparkle."

Demba ran eagerly down to the stream, and filled his calabash with the glittering sand, and sifted it, displaying with intense delight nearly half an ounce of pure gold.

"Holly golly, massa, dis here place all gold! we find one pound in de day."

"But the worst of it is, Demba, we cannot eat it, and I see no signs of vegetation or animals; however, we will camp here to night in yonder cavern, pick up enough gold to answer our purposes, and then push on."

The next day, as they had meal and nuts sufficient, they remained collecting gold, finding grains of pure metal as large as a small pea. Quite conscious that it would be a folly to load themselves with gold, Cuthbert Gordon and Demba, with a couple of pounds of the precious metal, concealed within the lining of their garments, and two or three dozen of quills, full of the smaller particles, recommenced their journey without an ounce of food. This was not a very pleasing prospect; but our hero felt certain, gazing at the immense range of mountains, that there must be small valleys with vegetation and animals to be found as they proceeded. It was quite impossible to follow the stream, for it sometimes fell from between masses of rock impossible to ascend. However, after encountering considerable difficulties, they suddenly, towards sunset, just as they were beginning to feel exceedingly hungry, came upon a scene that amazed and delighted them. After struggling through a wild and narrow defile, they beheld beneath them a singularly lovely valley, rich in vegetation, and in the middle a beautiful lake, nearly two miles in circumference.

"Ja, massa, dat fine view," exclaimed Demba, smacking his lips. "Look dere; plenty of ducks."

Cuthbert saw the lake was swarming with them; and close by the water's edge were two antelopes browsing on the short, sweet, green herbage which grew in luxuriance along the side of the water. The lake was surrounded with high hills, and apparently impassable. However, as food was absolutely necessary, our hero put a ball in his carbine, and stealing round some high rocks, brought down one of the antelopes. Clouds of ducks, and several strange aquatic birds rose from the surface of the lake, astounded at the report of a weapon they probably now heard for the first time; but after whirling in circles for a few minutes they settled again, within easy shooting distance.

"We can stop here for two or three days," said our hero to Demba, who was busy collecting firewood from a patch of trees that skirted one entire side of the lake, which it was very evident during the rainy season rose very many feet higher than it was then. From this source flowed the river, whilst numerous mountain streams and torrents supplied the lake with water.

Having collected wood, a fire was made, and Demba cut steaks from the antelope; the want of meal was much felt. However, our adventurers were by no means fastidious; indeed, antelope steaks were considered by the negroes and the Moors choice food, and so it was.

The next day they killed some ducks, and Demba found some underground roots, that he said were good, and which when roasted had a pleasant sweet taste.

Still anxious to get on, and longing to behold the sea, our hero and his faithful attendant proceeded on their way, carrying a supply of roots, antelope meat, and two or three brace of ducks.

After four days' toil, and considerable peril from the wild nature of the hills, and the sudden and dangerous precipices, they succeeded in passing the ridge of mountains, and beheld at length a vast extent of level country, some five thousand feet below them.

Our hero had kept as closely to the south as the nature of the country permitted. They had spent seven days in crossing the ridge of mountains. It took them the whole day to descend, and just as it was getting dusk they reached a negro village.

The inhabitants looked at them with intense surprise, and asked them where they came from. Our hero's beard, whiskers, and moustauche were in a wild, tangled state; his linen garments all in rags, and the shoes on his feet with scarcely a morsel of sole left. Demba was in a worse plight—he was altogether in rags, and no covering for his head but a piece of platted grass.

Demba stated they had crossed the mountains, but the negroes, a remarkably hideous race, shook their woolly heads in evident disbelief. They said no one could go across the mountains; the spirits would kill them and bury them in the bowels of the earth. Cuthbert let them think what they pleased. There was very little to be had in this village except some yams which they purchased, and a few pounds of meal. They could gain but little information from the villagers, who appeared of the lowest class of negroes. But they were far from unkind, and for two quills of gold dust the negroes offered to conduct them to a considerable village called Kalakalamba, governed by a Dooty, and subject to the King of Bambara. It would take two days to reach it; but there they would be able to purchase clothes, and anything they might want. They started for this place, and reached it in two days, after a severe and most tiresome walk.

Kalakalamba was a town, and surrounded by a wall made of mud.

Here, again, our hero was an object of great curiosity. However, as he stated to the Dooty he was able to pay, he was given a good hut to live in, and using only the gold dust in the quills, he got Demba to purchase all they required, and on his return, closing the door of their hut, they cooked their supper, and, quite worn out, threw themselves upon the heaps of dried grass in the corner of the hut, and were soon in a profound sleep.

CHAPTER XXI.

THE next day, refreshed by a long sleep, Cuthbert Gordon awoke, with fresh spirit and energy. The inhabitants of Kalakalamba traded with the peope of Wolli, who had many slave dealers amongst them.

Here our hero contrived to get rid of his superabundant beard, and to purchase some cotton garments for himself and Demba, and also sandals. Shoes were out of the question, but a very sagacious old negro, who had seen Europeans at Wolli, and understood what shoes were, after looking at our hero's, undertook to make soles for them, and this he actually did, not certainly after the manner of the European craftsmen, but so well as to be of great service to our hero, who rewarded the negro cobbler with two black beans weight of gold dust.

One evening, whilst our hero and Demba were eating

their supper in their hut, the door opened, and a negro, habited like a Slatee, or a slave driver, entered. He was a large man, but even for a low caste negro was frightfully ugly, his enormous lips projecting a couple of inches beyond his nose, and his forehead so low and flat as scarcely to leave room for his eyes. Without any salutation he squatted down beside our hero, and after looking at him and Demba with great scrutiny, he said, in the Mandingo tongue :—

"White man want to go to the Gambia ?"

"Yes," said Cuthbert Gordon, "I do."

"Ja," said the slave driver, "I am going with a coffle of slaves to Pisanca, and I will guide you to the Gambia river—journey five days. Have you gold dust enough to pay for my services ?"

Cuthbert Gordon very well knew that to travel with a slave driver was his safest plan, but he did not much admire the appearance of the fellow. Still, if he waited till he found a good looking Slatee, he might wait till the intense heat set in.

"Well," said our hero, "when do you set out, and what shall I pay you ?"

"If you will give me one hundred bars I will provide you with two asses, and see you safe to the Gambia river, where you can hire or buy a canoe, and descend the stream to where the ships lie to take in slaves."

Cuthbert Gordon was willing to hire the humble animals proposed to him, but one hundred bars was an imposition; a bar was worth two shillings—one hundred bars, Demba said, would purchase two stout horses, and Cuthbert Gordon resolved to do so. He told the Slatee he intended purchasing two horses, and when they reached the Gambia he would sell them for half price.

"Ja ! ja ! that will do well," said the Slatee. "I can sell you two small horses, and will buy them back, if not injured, when we reach the Gambia."

"Very well," returned our hero ; "show me them tomorrow, and if I like them I will buy them, and pay you handsomely for guiding us."

"Ja ! ja ! that will do; " so, getting up, he left them.

"Dat big old thief," said Demba, "better find our own way."

"I think not, Demba; we have a very dangerous country to travel through, and infested by Moors."

The next day the Slatee showed his horses; they were not bad ones, though their condition was indifferent. Our hero not wishing to appear too flush with gold, bargained hard with the slave driver, and at last he got the beasts for little more than half price. Having paid for them, he agreed for the remuneration he was to pay for the Slatee's protection and guidance, for the Slatees were nearly as much afraid of the Moors as the negroes themselves. A miserable substitute for a saddle and two straps of hide formed the equipment of the horses, our hero manufacturing his own stirrups and bridle. Thus equipped, they prepared to start the next day at daylight.

Forty-two unfortunate captives, taken in war, formed the slave coffle, with nine women, some young, and with no other covering save the hip cloth. The women and some of the men were quite different from the negro race, —having soft silky hair, skin scarcely a shade darker than the Moors, and with well-formed pleasing features. Five tall, strong, muscular negroes formed the guard along with the Slatee. The slaves were all hand-cuffed one to the other, and a strong rope passed from end to end of the line. If slaves show a disposition to be troublesome, they are fastened five or more in a row, and a strong pole fastened along the back of their necks. On the fourth day they were to be joined by a very large coffle.

Our hero felt sick at heart as he looked upon those wretched beings, thus heartlessly condemned to a cruel slavery; three of the women were scarcely seventeen years old. Before they had proceeded four leagues, Cuthbert Gordon quarrelled with his guide, and angrily denounced the Slatee's barbarous treatment of the women slaves; there was one with a very sore foot, and she carried, like the rest, bundles of food, &c., on her head; she could not keep the pace required, and one of the brutal drivers severely flogged her on the second day's march, for which act, our hero took his whip from him, and broke it over his head, knocking the negro down.

This led to a fierce and furious altercation. Cuthbert very coolly told the Slatee if he laid a hand upon him, he would shoot him through the head, and if he continued to savagely beat the slaves, he would quit him; but if he behaved humanely, he would give him fifty bars over at the end of the journey.

This appeased or appeared to satisfy the Slatee; but the other drivers seemed as if they would revenge the blow. However, they sulkily retired and drove on the slaves, who looked on with that silent apathy so often remarkable in slaves; not so the women; they seemed greatly excited, and clasped their hands, and seemed as if they blessed their protector. All that day and the next a sulky savage silence prevailed; the drivers struck several of the men, and cursed and abused the women, but the melancholy coffle proceeded, though the women's feet bled, and they could scarcely keep up with the forced speed of the men. The following night a halt was made in a thick wood called the wilderness; the women were unable to keep up, the Slatees driving them at an unusual rate, anxious to join the other coffle, the guards of which were well armed, whilst they had only knives and bows.

Demba looked very uneasy, and kept a watchful eye upon the five negro drivers. Great fires were lighted; the slaves chained, and a stout rope placed round all their necks; they were then put in irons, and food and water given them.

Cuthbert Gordon had got heartily sick of the slave coffle, and made up his mind to depend upon himself and Demba to find their way. They went a short distance from the Slatee's quarters, lit their own fire and cooked their provisions. Having laid in a store of wood, and tethered the horses where they could procure good grazing near a clear running brook; they could perceive the fires of the Slatees, and the dark forms of the negroes as they passed to and fro watching the slaves.

Cuthbert Gordon was to take the first rest, and Demba

watch. He laid himself down on the withered grass they had gathered ; he was tired, and at the same time more depressed than usual, feeling anxious about those who were dear to him. Many months must elapse, perhaps, before he could once more put his foot upon English soil, for few British vessels, at this period, touched at the Gambia river on their return voyage ; he would therefore probably be forced to embark in a slaver for the coast of America or Cuba. In the midst of his perplexed thoughts he fell fast asleep, with his right hand resting on his loaded carbine.

Demba replenished the fire, took a look at his master, shook his head, and muttered, " Dat bery bad man, Karata, the Slatee; me go hear what dey say."

He then crept carefully and silently on his hands and knees into the thick brushwood, and then rising, made a circuit till he perceived the Slatee's fire and the six negroes sitting round it drinking a strong liquor from some calabashes. Again creeping on all fours, and as silently and cautiously as an Indian on a trail, he came within hearing of the group, hid by the thick low shrubs, through which he thrust his head. The Slatees were conversing earnestly, with the long rope attached to the slaves fastened to a stake beside them.

" But we can change our road," said one of the negroes. These were the first words Demba heard.

" Yes," returned Karata, the Slatee, " and strike for the Senegal river ; whatever we do must be done before morning. We can chain that watching rascal Demba with the other slaves."

" But he will betray us to the captain of the ship if we kill a white man."

" You are a fool," said the Slatee ; " there's no one fool enough to kill a white man in this quarter of the moon, it's not likely ; take all the gold he has, for I saw, when he paid me, that he had another bag of gold, which he took out by mistake, and all the grains were as big as small beans."

" Let us tie him to a tree, and the wild beasts will do the rest," said the others with a savage laugh.

"But you forget," returned Karata, "that he has a gun, and is a mortal strong man, and ready with his blows; if we don't master him whilst asleep, he is sure to kill one or two of us."

"Then the sooner we set about the job, the better," said the others.

"To my mind," said one, "the best way is to stick a knife in that fellow Demba."

"Well, be it so," returned the Karata; "I think, after all, it's the safest plan. Whilst the white man sleeps you can steal upon that spy, who is sure to be dozing, and stick your knife in him."

"Tank you for nothing," thought Demba to himself, as he stole back to his master, his heart beating somewhat faster, but with full confidence in his master's courage and wisdom.

On reaching their resting-place he threw on some wood, and woke up his master.

Cuthbert Gordon sprang to his feet, grasping his gun. "What's the matter, Demba? alarmed by wild beasts, eh?"

"Worse, a great deal, massa, dan wild beasts;" and then he told him what he had heard, and the plot the Slatees and the negro drivers had to kill and plunder them.

"Ah, now we know what they intend to do, there is little danger. Where are the horses?"

"Dat is de bad ting," said Demba; "de horses by de stream close to de slaves, and in sight of dem villains."

"It will be dawn in a few minutes," said our hero, "take your bow and follow me; they will never attempt to attack us openly; we will get our horses and leave them."

"Holly, golly, my master great heart," said Demba; and then they began moving towards the Slatee's resting-place. It was nearer dawn than they thought, for a faint light was visible through the trees. As they approached they were heard treading on the branches lying scattered about. The negroes sprang to their feet and gazed towards them, when, to the amazement of our hero and

Demba, a volley of musketry flashed from the bush on the other side of the stream, and two of the negroes fell mortally wounded beside their fires. A wild yell then pealed through the still air, and a party of men, full twenty in number, rushed across the stream, and, with frightful imprecations, attacked the Slatee Karata, and the other three negroes. The slaves, roused by the firing, sprung up, uttering frantic yells of delight when they beheld the murder of the Slatee and the negro drivers.

Amazement for a moment held our hero and Demba inactive : the men attacking were Africans, wearing turbans, and a kind of tunic, and all armed with cutlass and musket.

"They are Fouta Terra robbers," said Demba, fairly frightened. "Let us catch our horses and be off."

Our hero saw it was time, in truth, and made a rush to where their horses were, daylight rapidly increasing ; but with a wild shout a dozen of the robbers pursued. Cuthbert Gordon had his hand on his horse, when one of the men aimed a blow at him with his musket clubbed, for as Demba had heard, the Africans consider it a fearful omen to kill a white man during the first quarter of the new moon.

Our hero turned the blow aside and shot the man dead. He now succeeded, and so did Demba, in mounting their horses, but the brute our hero bestrode seemed paralysed with fright, for he instantly lay down ; Demba's, on the contrary, took to flight with exceeding good will, half-a-dozen muskets being discharged after him without effect, the fugitive wisely dodging in amongst the trees. In the meantime Cuthbert Gordon, after a furious struggle, was borne to the ground, and struck savage blows with the butts of the muskets, the Fouta Terra robbers only refraining from killing him from superstition. They then stripped him of everything, except his cotton trousers and shoes, and taking leather thongs, bound his hands fearfully tight, and after spitting in his face and reviling him as a Christian, they fastened him to a tree, and left him nearly insensible.

The slaves during this scene, did all they could

15

to free themselves, shouting with joy at the death of the Slatee Karata, and imagining that they would recover their liberty, though two of the women, who were but slightly bound, got away and fled to the woods; the rest remained too securely chained.

The robbers, having scraped together all the booty they could, and literally stripped the Slatee and the five negroes naked, and also their own comrade, killed by the shot from our hero's carbine, began beating the slaves for daring to attempt to escape. They tightened their ropes, and with blows and kicks, and a torrent of savage abuse, they forced them across the stream and, entering the wilderness on the opposite side, disappeared from our hero's view.

Cuthbert Gordon, in his terrible situation, stripped and exposed to the scorching rays of an African sun, did not despair of release.

He felt quite satisfied Demba would not go far from the spot, but hide till he thought the robbers had departed. When travelling with Mungo Park they were always in dread of the Fouta Terra banditti ruffians, even more cruel than the Moors. These men were disbanded and fugitive soldiers of King Abdaran. Friends to no tribe, they wandered the country in bands, killing, plundering, and carrying off the natives and selling them for slaves. They were supposed to be Mahomedans, but uniting the grossest superstitions of the negroes with the abominations of Mahomedanism.

As the sun rose above the trees, and its rays spread through the branches, our hero suffered terribly from the scorching heat on his chest and shoulders, and even more from the stings of innumerable insects which settled on him; he strove, by rubbing his hands against the tree, to break the cord by friction, but in vain. Right before was the horrible sight of the dead negroes, and, no doubt, in a very short time, birds of prey and wild beasts would be attracted by the smell to the spot. Altogether, his situation in tho heart of a wilderness, fast bound to a tree, was appalling enough to make the stoutest heart quail.

It mostly happens in this world, bad as it is generally accounted, that an act of mercy meets its reward. As Cuthbert Gordon, rendered nearly furious by the stings and bites of greedy ravenous insects, was making tremendous efforts to burst his bonds, he perceived some one creeping along the side of the rivulet. Looking eagerly at this figure he perceived it was a female, and on a nearer approach he recognised her to be the female slave with the sore foot, and the one the negro driver so cruelly beat, and who for that act was chastised on the spot by our hero. She evidently did not see him, for the trunk of the tree hid his body ; it was by twisting his head round that he saw her ; he called out in the Mandingo tongue to the girl ; she looked up and saw his eyes fixed upon her ; she uttered a cry of joy, jumped up, and eagerly ran towards him. She was from a far-off tribe and scarcely understood him, but she at once tried to undo the thongs, but his struggles had so tightened them that her efforts were in vain. She wrung her hands with vexation, but Cuthbert Gordon directed her attention to the river, and told her to get two sharp stones and hammer the thongs against the tree. She understood him, and ran eagerly to the river and selected the stones, and after some hard pounding she cut the main rope across ; this freed him from the tree, his hands still, however, bound ; but getting the sharpest stone he could, the African girl held it firmly while he sawed away at it till he freed himself, and then sat down exhausted, but first taking a drink from the stream and thanking Providence for his singular escape from a horrid death ; for so few natives crossed the wilderness that his chance of rescue was small indeed.

Whilst he was resting himself, the African girl had disappeared, but in less than half an hour she returned with a collection of herbs, with which she commenced anointing his bleeding and smarting skin ; the soothing effect was wonderful ; he felt instant ease, and sitting under the shelter of a noble, thick branched tree, he was protected from the heat of the sun. He expressed his gratitude to the young girl in the Mandingo tongue. She understood his signs and some of the words, and seemed quite pleased. She went away again to look for the plant well known in that part of Africa as the negro's umbrella, the leaf of the liboa. The singular and immense leaf of this plant, when placed on the head, not only protects the wearer from the heat, but completely shelters the negro from the rain, which he detests. Having succeeded in finding the plant she returned, and showed our hero how to use it. Notwithstanding his bruises, and cuts, and lacerations, Cuthbert Gordon could not but smile, as he gazed at his companion and himself in their very primitive costume. The young girl, accustomed by nature and habit, thought nothing about it. She appeared so happy at being free, and of being of service to the white man who befriended her when cruelly treated, that she seemed to wish for nothing more; she was scarcely seventeen, and a tall and exceedingly well-formed maiden, with bright eyes, pearly teeth, and a skin very little darker than a Creole. Whilst our hero was recovering from the terrible usage he had received, the young girl was hunting for ground nuts, the only food they could expect to get in the wilderness without a gun or bow; he had moved from the vicinity of the dead negroes, when suddenly the unmistakable roar of the African lion caused the girl to quit her search for nuts, and rush back terrified to where Cuthbert Gordon stood, for the roar of the lord of the woods roused him into energy.

Whilst looking in the direction of the sound he heard the galloping of a horse, and in a few minutes he beheld his own horse flying, evidently terrified, along the border of the stream. He called out at the top of his voice to the horse, and ran as well as he could to cross his path. The sagacious animal neighed, and of his own accord ran to him ; his saddle and bridle were gone, but the horse did not offer to stir. The African girl trembled all over, as a second roar almost caused the horse to dart off again.

Cuthbert Gordon made the girl stand behind the horse which he firmly held by the neck. The next instant a magnificent lion, with enormous mane and tail, stalked majestically through the brushwood, and when within twenty yards of them paused, and gazed fixedly at them. The African girl sunk at Cuthbert Gordon's feet perfectly paralysed, whilst the horse trembled in every limb, the prespiration covering every part of his body.

Cuthbert gazed at the magnificent beast before him, so grand and defying in his strength, with admiration not unmixed with awe, knowing how utterly impossible it would be without arms of any kind to resist an attack. After looking at them for a few moments, and lashing his sides with his bushy tail, he uttered a long ominous howl, and then, to Cuthbert Gordon's surprise, he lay down with his eyes steadily fixed upon them. Making signs to the young girl to move back, slowly and quietly, our hero did the same with the horse; in this manner they reached the place where the dead bodies of the negroes lay. But the lion immediately got up and uttered a roar so terrible that the ground seemed to vibrate beneath their feet.

Our hero now expected an attack. One must instantly fall a victim; but the African girl told him with a shudder to move back and leave the dead bodies of the negroes between them and the lion. This they did, and had not proceeded twenty yards from the bodies before the lion made a terrible spring forward, but instantly stopped on seeing the bodies; with a fearful growl he struck his paw into the chest of a dead negro, and stood thus in an attitude of defiance, gazing at our hero, as he still continued hastily to retreat. Just then he heard a loud shout from the other side of the stream, and looking in that direction, to his intense gratification he beheld Demba leading his horse, pushing his way through the thicket, and making signs to him to cross the stream. This he did, still holding the horse by its long mane—the young girl following.

They soon joined Demba, who showed the most lively satisfaction and joy in finding his master alive, and not seriously hurt; he recognised the African slave girl at once; he said he had lost himself in the wilderness, and until he came upon the track of the Fouta Terra robbers he was unable to get back. He heard, and then saw the lion, and was awfully alarmed; but he felt satisfied when he saw the lion stop by the dead bodies, for though it was a rare thing for a lion to prey on dead carcases, still, he would stay by them on the principle of the dog in the manger. They were now in the heart of the wilderness, without provisions, or arms to procure them; it would take two days to cross it—so our hero remembered Karata, the Slatee, saying—and that it was full of wild beasts. All they could expect to get for food was ground nuts; but Demba and the African girl were good foragers, and after an hour's search brought in a good supply. Demba's escape was most fortunate; to have remained, he said, would only have made matters worse—for the Fouta Terra robbers would have slain him without mercy; but he knew they would not on any account kill a white man at that time; but he guessed that they would leave his master to be devoured by wild beasts. So as soon as he thought he was safe, he stopped his horse; but, as stated, lost his way getting back; he had all his gold safe, so if they could extricate themselves from the wilderness, they would soon reach a village. That night they supped on the ground nuts, and made an immense fire, and watched by turns, for an incessant roar and cries of wild beasts continued through the night. Demba, who understood the young African girl's language, learned her brief history. She belonged to a tribe called Faradoo, who were attacked by the soldiers of the king of Manbarra, and made slaves of. She was sold to the Slatee Karata, together with her brother, mother, and sister.

They were all carried off by the Fouta Terra robbers. She had escaped by being left, with another sick slave, only slightly bound, so she managed to escape. Where her companion went to, she could not say. She herself crawled into a mass of bushes close to the place where the robbers attacked the Slatee. She crept out after she thought they were all gone, to see what they had done with the white man who had protected her from the slave driver.

What the poor girl could do now she was free, puzzled our hero ; her family in slavery, and she herself full a hundred miles from her own tribe.

CHAPTER XXII.

THE next day, Cuthbert Gordon made the young girl sit upon one of the horses, for her feet were so cut that she could scarcely move. In this manner, always keeping as much south as possible, they passed through the wilderness in two days, and at the close of the third, they reached a walled town, the walls pierced for musketry, and governed by a Negro Dooty. Their appearance created great surprise and curiosity ; but when Demba explained that they were attacked and plundered by Fouta Terra robbers, they were treated most kindly by the simple inhabitants, who gave them a hut; and Demba stated that though his master was plundered and ill-treated, he had got away on his horse, and so saved some of his master's property, and that they could pay for what they got.

The Dooty, a kind, elderly negro, with a wife and several children, when he heard the girl's story, offered to take her into his household and treat her well. The young girl was pleased at this offer, and gladly accepted it, thanking our hero with the tears in her eyes, for his kindness to her. Cuthbert Gordon remained here five days to recruit his strength, and recover from the bruises and lacerations he had received, in his encounter with the banditti.

Having purchased clothing and various other small matters, and a good bow and arrows for Demba, and having received careful instructions how to proceed, they left the town of Sunbani, and after a three days' journey through a very well cultivated tract of country, came upon the Gambia river, at a small village opposite the strong walled town called Neobe. Heartily sick of the privations and sufferings he had endured for several months, Cuthbert Gordon resolved to sell the horses, purchase a canoe, and descend the Gambia river till he came to the English settlements on its banks; most earnestly hoping he should find some European ship, if even a slaver, on board of which he could take his passage with Demba, whom he resolved, at the young African's most urgent entreaties, to take with him to England.

They found no difficulty in disposing of their horses and purchasing a good canoe, and stocking it with provisions. They also purchased a musket and powder and shot; the negroes of the village were accustomed to see white men, for they trafficked with the different settlements on the river. They told our intended voyagers, that they could reach Pisanco easily in three days, and there they would find white men, and perhaps a ship waiting for slaves.

The voyage down the Gambia was easy and pleasant. Numerous boats were both ascending and descending; those descending being laden with elephants' teeth and tusks, cotton cloths, Indian corn, &c.

The third day they reached Pisanco, but being told that there was a fine American schooner lying below Jonka-kende, taking in slaves, and about to sail for an American port, our hero only stopped at the factory established there long enough to purchase proper garments for himself and Demba, and to barter whatever gold grains and dust they had for dollars. Two fine brigs had sailed, one for England, the other for Holland, only five days before his arrival.

Pulling down the river the following day, they found the American schooner at anchor close to the western shore, very busy shipping slaves.

Cuthbert Gordon pulled alongside; his first sight of what was going on on deck was certainly not very encouraging. The schooner was a handsome vessel of about two hundred and sixty tons. Walking the deck was a tall wiry-looking man, in cotton garments and broad brimmed hat; his countenance betokened a confirmed drunkard, and greatly reminded him of the captain of the "Wave;" he was, however, a younger man, perhaps two-and-thirty; he had a thong whip in his hand, and as the wretched slaves came up the side from the raft, he applied his whip savagely to the backs of any of the slaves who loitered or looked stupefied. In this brutality his crew eagerly imitated him, kicking the poor wretches about the shins and shaking them, apparently for mere pastime, as they passed them down into the hold; there were men, women, and mere boys, and a few girls of thirteen and fourteen years of age. The Slatees, who owned them or sold them, were quite as great brutes as those who bought them.

This state of affairs aboard the "Pelican," the name of the schooner, disgusted our hero, and nearly induced him to abandon the voyage in such a craft; but recollecting he might have to wait months for a ship, and burning with anxiety to return to his native land, he smothered his disgust and walked along the deck to where the captain stood gazing over the side at the raft, on which were some twenty or thirty slaves.

The skipper turned round and looked at our hero with some surprise, and at Demba with greater.

"Well, stranger," said he, "Where the —— do you come from? how did you and that sooty rascal get aboard?" For so busy were all aboard, that our hero and his companion were scarcely noticed. Before our hero could well reply, the skipper added, "Want to sell that feller, eh?"

"No," returned our hero, quietly, "he is not a slave; I came to know if you can give us a passage to whatever port you are bound to."

"Guess I'm bound to South Carolina. Can you pay your way?"

"Yes," returned our hero.

"Ha! cuss that black rascal," exclaimed the skipper, dashing forward and laying on with all his force the whip he held on the brawny shoulders of a negro, who looked savagely at the men who were dragging him towards the hold. He was an immense negro, a match, if his hands were unchained, for half a dozen of the crew. After belabouring this negro till his face was purple, the skipper paused, and the negro shook his clenched hands in the captain's face, and uttered some terrible threat in his own language, and which Demba told his master meant, he would have his heart out of his body yet. With repeated blows and kicks and lashes, this gigantic negro was actually thrown into the hold, and afterwards chained so that he could not even move.

"Oh," thought our hero, sick at the sight, "the day will come when this horrid traffic of human flesh and blood, black it is true, but which God made, as well as he made the white, will cease."

"Well, stranger," the skipper began again, recovering his breath, "it's hard work those black beggars make for us."

"Did you ever try gentle treatment and kindness with these miserable creatures?"

The skipper burst into a hoarse laugh "What, you're one of the missionary tribe are you? then blow me, but you've come to the wrong box. Just top your boom. Curse me, if it ain't droll, gentle treatment. Ha, ha, ha, with a cursed nigger."

Mastering his indignation, our hero said, "You are mistaken; I am not a missionary. I am a seaman, and have served several years in the British navy—but ——"

"Oh, you have, have you? what brought you here, then?" interrupted the skipper.

"Well, I can tell you that another time. What will be your charge for this youth and myself for our passage?"

"I'll give you your passage and grub for that nigger; stranger, is it a bargain?"

"Certainly not; he will never be a slave whilst I can help it. I am ready to pay you any reasonable sum for our passage and food, in dollars."

"What do you say to one hundred dollars—I guess it's not out of the way, is it?"

"You shall have that amount," returned Cuthbert Gordon. "When do you sail?"

"This tide; this is the last batch. You can see the hold is full."

"And yet," returned our hero, "you are putting more in."

"Oh, cuss the black rascals," returned the skipper, biting off a piece of tobacco and chewing it, "some of them will die to spite me, so there will be room enough in a few days."

"Yes; and have those remaining alive eat up by disease, and worth nothing."

"Guess you are a cussed bad calculator; you don't know how we manage the thing. If we bring half our cargo to port we are well paid. You don't want to go ashore any more, do you?"

"No," returned our hero; " I have no business ashore. All I have is in the canoe."

Whilst this conversation was going on, the first and second mate, both to all appearance as rough and reckless as their skipper, with the assistance of the crew, having finally stowed away the last negro, after an infinitude of oaths, imprecations, and blows, cast off the rafts just as the tide turned. When this was done all hands had a can of spirits served to them ; some drank it with water, some without. If they were hot before what must they have been after such a dose, in such a climate? and yet most of the slavers from America and Cuba drank to excess. There were five of the crew below sick, and three had died; so the skipper, who was awfully afraid of fever, and who kept his courage up by constant intoxication, was extremely anxious to get to sea.

The anchor was soon up, and the schooner, with a light breeze and an ebb tide, dropped down the river.

Cuthbert Gordon beheld the entire proceedings of the skipper and his crew with intense disgust, and had half a mind before she got under weigh to enter his canoe and return ashore; but once dropping down the river he made up his mind to endure anything to get once more to a Christian country. He proceeded with the captain to have a look at the accomodation. The cabin was not a bad one; it was small for the size of the vessel, as much was sacrificed for the sake of the stowage. It was dirty and uncared for. However, Cuthbert said :—

"You have no objection to let my servant put my things to rights here and to attend upon us; you are short of hands, I see—so he may save you a hand."

"I guess you may do that. My cussed boy took ill the first week we were here, and is down a shark's maw long ago. Guess two or three of the others sick in the forecastle will go the same way. Have a glass of liquor, stranger," and he opened a locker, and took out a jar of brandy and two glasses.

"No, thank you," returned our hero. "You are taking poison in such a climate as this—drinking brandy. I do not dislike it in moderation, but never touch it in hot climates."

The skipper burst into a hoarse laugh. "Poison do you call it ?" and he held half a tumbler up to the skylight; "well, cuss me, but I guess it's palatable poison. Here's you're health, Mr.——, what am I to call you ? "

"My name is Gordon," returned our hero.

The captain nodded his head, and down went the brandy unmixed, his face resembling the setting sun.

The skipper, the first mate, and our hero slept in the chief cabin; Demba and the second mate, and a kind of steward, accepted a space boarded off from the forecastle. The crew consisted of fourteen hands, six of them sick.

Before they passed the bar at the river's mouth, the slaves had become amazingly troublesome. Demba told his master that there were men of two hostile tribes aboard, and that he heard the huge negro say in his native tongue, that they would yet master the crew of the slaver, and cut the throats of every soul on board, and then fight the King of Bamra's men.

"They will, poor wretches," said our hero, "have to fight a worse enemy—the fever. It is impossible, if the captain persists in keeping them below, without telling off a party at a time on deck to breathe the fresh air, but that disease will carry off half."

Cuthbert Gordon spoke to the first mate on the subject, but he was a pig-headed, brutal fellow, an awful drunkard, and cruel from liking.

The second day at sea tight-bound, and scorching hot, a fierce fight took place in the hold between the two tribes of negroes ; yells and screams, mingled with the frantic cries of women came from the hold. Cuthbert Gordon begged the captain to take off the hatches and let a party up, and endeavour to pacify the miserable slaves. But the skipper and first mate were drunk, and walked the deck armed with cutlass and pistol, and swore the first man that let a nigger on deck they would shoot. The second mate, though a rough, silent kind of man, was yet reasonable, and drank the least of any on board. He admitted to our hero that they ought to be let on deck in gangs. But none of the seamen joined him. though the smell from the hold was already almost unbearable.

They had scarcely lost sight of the land, when thick, sultry oppressive weather set in, and no wind. The captain now said he would be short of water, and refused the slaves half their allowance. This roused them to fury. The captain had up the negro who he said was the cause of the tumult ; he had him chained and savagely beaten, and then thrown back into the hold. This led to a dangerous outbreak between our hero, the skipper, and the first mate ; the latter in his fury snapped a pistol at

Cuthbert Gordon's head, who, with a blow of his clenched hand, felled him senseless upon the deck. Four more of the crew sickened, and still not a breath of wind. The schooner was a doomed craft. Cuthbert Gordon, with Demba, did all they could to alleviate the misery of the slaves below. The captain, between intoxication and fear of infection, would only allow one hatch at a time to be off. This our hero insisted upon. The skipper had become afraid of the determined spirit of his passenger, for his crew were diminishing daily, and he himself was mostly in his cabin. If the first mate had anything human in him, the craft might have been saved; but he nourished a terrible hatred to Cuthbert Gordon, and only watched for an opportunity to gratify his vile nature in revenge. Demba carried water to the women, and our hero willingly assisted with his share; they seemed grateful to him; but they said they would murder the captain yet; and they also said that there were twenty dead in the hold. Not one of the crew would go below; but Cuthbert Gordon so worked on the fears of the captain, that he permitted the irons of four slaves to be taken off; and they brought the dead to the open hold, and the crew twisted them up with ropes and cast them into the sea.

The first mate then swore at the four men to come up to be ironed again, but they mocked him, and cursed him and told him to come down and do it. None would go down; ho then had the hatch put on, and swore not a drop of drink should they have till the four negroes were handcuffed. But the climax came at last. Four of the crew died that evening, and the first mate sickened, and during the night a tremendous gale set in; the captain was dead drunk; our hero resolutely took the command, and the crew and the second mate obeyed him like men doomed. Before morning, a tremendous sea swept the deck, hurried two men into eternity, burst the hatches, and carried away and smashed all the boats. Just as the dawn made, a ferocious yell resounded from the hold, and above one hundred and sixty negroes, freed from their fetters, scrambled upon deck, uttering the most frantic imprecations. Cuthbert Gordon was at the wheel, and Demba close beside him; the schooner was under a treble-reefed topsail, main trysail, and storm jib. Unaccustomed to the deck of a vessel in a gale of wind, the infuriated negroes were tumbled one over the other into the flooded lee-side of the deck, so that a few resolute men might easily have mastered the miserable wretches, but the men were appalled and terrified, and fled below.

Luckily it was sufficiently light for several of them to recognise our hero, and Demba. As the gale lulled with the rising sun, nearly all the slaves had freed themselves from their irons; the women and sick remained below. The captain and mate barricaded themselves in the cabin, and kept firing through the skylight at the negroes, killing two or three, which so infuriated the others, that led on by the gigantic negro, Mahado, they burst the cabin doors, and smashed the skylight to atoms; others rushed forward, burst up the fore-hatch, and, armed with hatchets, marlinspikes, and staves, in fact every available weapon for murder, the work of death commenced. In vain Cuthbert, through Demba and his own knowledge of the Mandingo tongue, attempted to arrest their ferocious anxiety for revenge. Mahado threatened our hero with a hatchet, and said if he did not steer the schooner to land, he would torture him to death. He placed ten of his party with knives and hatchets to guard our hero and Demba, and then the miserable captain and mate were dragged on deck. Cuthbert Gordon sickened at the sight. The negroes had to throw themselves upon him, and hold him down on the deck, whilst the wretch Mahado brutally hacked the captain and the sick mate with the hatchets picked from the schooner's stores, and finally pitched them, still living, into the storm-tossed sea.

In less than an hour not a white man remained aboard the schooner, save Cuthbert Gordon. All the sick were mercilessly butchered and cast into the sea, and not till then was he released, and threatened if he did not steer for the land they would torture and kill him. Demba was horrified, he risked his life several times to save his master from his countrymen, and the savage Mahado

knocked him over twice with a blow from the handle of
his hatchet.   Before midday the wind and sea fell, and
then the negroes of the two tribes, who differed in their
religious creed, and were mortal enemies beside, began a
furious contest, in which four negroes were slain, and
many cut and slashed by the sailor's knives they had
seized, till finally one party with Mahado kept the after
deck, the others clustered forward.

None of the negroes knew anything of navigation or of
a ship's manœuvres—they looked around eagerly for
land, and not seeing any signs, they told Demba if they
did not see it the next day they would kill him and his
master.   Demba knew very well that was an impos-
sibility, and he trembled to think what might be their
fate.

Every part of the vessel was ransacked, food, wine and
spirits dragged up on deck—all the women were got up,
and so horrible was the nature of these negroes that they
threw their own sick overboard.

The Englishman felt sick at heart at witnessing such
atrocities.   The fate of the captain and crew was
terrible to think of, but they brought it on themselves,
for he was satisfied had they acted with gentleness
and humanity from the beginning, the fatal catastrophe
would have been avoided.   The negroes were worked up
to a pitch of frenzy from suffering, and a negro roused to
fury is no better than a wild beast, whereas they may be
induced to suffer much privation by kindness and gentle
treatment.

CHAPTER XXIII.

WIND and sea went down rapidly, and before night the sky cleared and a dead calm came on again. Mahado and his tribe made several onslaughts upon those in the fore-part of the schooner; and so furious became their hatred to each other that it appeared very evident they would, if infuriated from drink, surely fight till one or other was exterminated. As the sea calmed down the negroes commenced hunting out everything in the vessel. From the small hold under the steward's cabin they pulled out an eighteen gallon cask full of some liquor, and staving in the head, a frantic exultation took place; the cask contained rum. Mahado's party intended to retain this prize for themselves, but the temptation became so great that those in the bows made a furious rush to fill some buckets they carried, and then a horrible strife ensued; with the ferocity of savages they used their knives and hatchets, cutting fearful wounds in each other's bodies.

Disgusted at their ferocity, and seeing that if they drank more they would become mad, for even whilst fighting, all that could, dipped something into the cask and drank the rum like water, our hero watching his opportunity, secured a hatchet, and then turned the cask over and spilt its contents over the deck. But Mahado, the gigantic negro, perceived the act, and with a howl of frantic rage he called some of his comrades, and rushed towards Gordon.

"Get up the mast, massa, or he kill you," shouted Demba.

To attempt to resist was madness, so, making a spring through the crowd, he and Demba reached the rigging of the mainmast and sprang up; but Mahado, with his hatchet, springing after, and poor Demba's foot slipping, he fell within his reach; the next instant he was brained

16

by the hatchet of Mahado—his hands relaxed their grasp, and without a groan the faithful, kind-hearted Demba was hurled into the sea and immediately sunk. But his death was instantly avenged, for the hatchet of Cuthbert Gordon fell with a terrific force upon the skull of the negro, inflicting a horrible wound, and dashing him violently on deck, where he lay writhing in frantic agony. Several of his comrades attempted to follow our hero up the rigging, but gaining the mainmast, Cuthbert with his hatchet cut away the shrouds and left the mainmast standing without support, tumbling the exasperated natives over one another on the deck. He then sat down, burying his face in his hands, and fairly wept, grieved and struck to the heart by his faithful follower's death.

The deck swarmed with swarthy negroes, thirsting for his blood. Mahado was dead, and pitched into the sea, but his comrades vowed to put his slayer to a torturing death.

Our hero felt that he had never in his life been placed in so fearful a position; turn which way he would not the faintest gleam of hope appeared. The only solitary exception to absolute despair was the chance of a vessel coming up with them in the next twenty-four hours. He knew there were fire-arms in the schooner, but it was not likely that any of the slaves knew how to use them.

How the night passed he scarcely knew; sleep he did not, and yet visions of horror rose up before him. Demba's fate haunted him; not a breath of wind was stirring during the night; a long heave of the sea alone gave motion to the schooner. During the dark hours much commotion existed upon deck. The two opposed tribes still carried on a vain and useless contest. More spirits were got at, and when daylight came our hero could perceive many of the negroes stretched out, some dead from stabs, some from illness, and many from intoxication. As the light increased, and the rising sun dispersed the light mist that lay upon the heaving ocean, our hero gazed eagerly towards the horizon. With a cry of joy he perceived the topsails of three large ships away to the westward. He could not say whether they had a breeze or not for some time; but after anxiously watching he perceived that they gradually rose to view, and after an hour their lower yards were visible, which proved that they were advancing with a light breeze.

The negroes on deck now turned their attention to the ship. Some of them, probably accustomed to river navigation, were endeavouring to set the sail on the foremast; but the negroes having possession of the forecastle, now that they were deprived of their leader, the gigantic Mahado, attacked them with savage ferocity, and again blood was spilt, and fearful gashes inflicted with knives and boarding pikes. The women were huddled together in groups, seemingly terrified at the fierce contests between the men.

Before noon the vessels were distinctly visible from the deck of the schooner. When the negroes saw them they appeared terrified, and at once looked up at Cuthbert Gordon on the cross-trees, and then a consultation took place. Our hero could very well imagine what they were consulting about, as the ships were evidently steering in their direction, and one considerably in advance of the others appeared to be a large frigate.

No doubt the negro thought that our hero, if released by the crew of the ship coming up, would make known their murdering the captain and crew of the schooner. He was the only witness against them; if they could kill him they would consider that their crime would be undiscovered.

Gordon watched their proceedings rather anxiously, for he knew one thing they could do to destroy him, and it seems the negroes thought of that themselves, for two powerful fellows seized the ship's axes and commenced vigourously cutting away the mast. With eagerness Gordon watched the advancing ship, which he clearly made out to be a fine frigate, and by the cut of her sails he judged her to be French.

Every blow at the mast made it quiver as the huge splinters flew from it; and as blow after blow was struck, and the heave of the sea came, it began to totter. He would have crossed to the foremast but the ropes were cut,

He, however, prepared to spring into the sea as the mast fell, and then get upon it, and trusted to be picked up by the frigate's boats. At length, with a wild yell, the negroes perceived the mast to totter, and then with the heave of the sea, to fall. Cuthbert Gordon, as it fell hanging over the water, leapt into the sea, and dived, and then coming up, he saw the mast floating within a few yards of him, and with very slight exertion he soon got upon it, and then looked toward the frigate. She was now coming rapidly up with an increased breeze, and fired a gun. The schooner's sails also filled with the breeze, and the negroes managed to steer right before it.

The slaver was a very fast schooner, and though only her fore-topsail and square sail were set, she went rapidly through the water. The escaped man feared that the frigate would pass without seeing him; but fortunately for him, those on the quarter deck had for some time been watching the schooner with their glasses. They had beheld the fall of the mainmast and were greatly surprised, there being neither wind or sea to cause such an accident. They could perceive that the deck of the slaver was crowded with negroes, and as the frigate was kept away so as to follow right in the wake of the schooner, the consequence was, that Cuthbert Gordon, waving his arm, was noticed.

The frigate was then hove to, and a boat lowered, and four men and a midshipman pulled up to the mast.

"Eh bien, mon ami," said the youth, steering the boat as it ran alongside the mast, "how is this? how was your mast carried away? is yonder schooner a slaver?"

"I will tell you all about it," said Cuthbert Gordon, as he got into the boat, in such good French, that the midshipman exclaimed :—

"Diable! are you Français?"

"No," returned our hero, "I am Anglais."

"Give way, my men," said the middy to the crew; and then looking keenly into our hero's face he said, "Are you the captain of yonder schooner?"

"No, monsieur, I do not belong to her. I was a passenger only."

"Diable, c'est drôle," returned the middy. "What brought you on the mast?"

Cuthbert Gordon smiled, but made no reply, for they were alongside the frigate.

The sides of the frigate were crowded with men, gazing with considerable surprise at our hero. On reaching the deck an officer came forward, and looking at Cuthbert Gordon, whom, notwithstanding his dripping condition and simple attire, could not be well taken for aught but a gentleman, he said :—

"Are you the captain of yonder slaver?"

"No," replied Cuthbert Gordon ; "I was, as I informed this young gentleman, only a passenger. The cruelty of the skipper worked upon the tempers of the slaves; they contrived to rise *en masse* during a gale, and massacred all the whites aboard. I managed to get up the mainmast after killing the ringleader, and it was to destroy me they cut away the mast. The vessel is American. I am English, and my name is Gordon. I was an officer in the English naval service."

The lieutenant of the French frigate looked surprised at the name of Gordon, repeating it, saying :—

"These murderous black rascals must be punished, Monsieur Gordon. I will state what you have now told me to my commander, Captain François Beranger. This frigate is the 'Vengeur.' Those vessels astern are two British merchant ships with prize crews aboard. However, while I speak to Captain Beranger, you had better go below with the young mid who took you off the mast, and as I think I am the tallest man aboard, and of your height, I will send you a change of garments. You must have spent some time in France to speak the language so fluently.

Our hero said—no ; he had not ; but he had served several years at different stations where French was much spoken, and he had lost no opportunity of gaining a knowledge of a most useful language.

Lieutenant Jaques Poulton then retired, and our hero

descended into the midshipman's berth. The midshipman who had taken him off the mast was nearly as old as Cuthbert Gordon, and had seen a good deal of service. His name was Augustus Armand.

There were several other young midshipmen below, who looked with surprise at the tall, powerful figure of our hero, as he entered their domicile; a marine shortly made his appearance with a complete change of garments, and a request that as soon as our hero could equip himself that he would be pleased to come to Captain Beranger in his cabin.

"I shall be at his command in a few minutes," replied Gordon; and then entering a small cabin he changed his soaked scanty clothing for the undress suit of a French lieutenant.

Though happily rescued from a terrible fate, Cuthbert still lamented and deplored the loss of his humble, faithful attendant, Demba, and bitterly regretted having ever entered as a passenger aboard the slaver.

He had also a depressed feeling at his own situation. He might remain a prisoner of war for many months, if not years. Where he would be taken to he had not the most remote idea. His present treatment was, however, most kind. So, having changed his clothes, he left the cabin, and told young Armand that he was ready to wait upon the commander.

On ascending the deck he looked round and perceived that the frigate was not more than one hundred yards from the schooner. The frigate's sails were hauled up except her three topsails, and they were braced round so as to check the frigate's progress. On the quarter-deck he met Lieutenant Poulton.

"I am greatly obliged to you, Monsieur," said Cuthbert Gordon to the lieutenant; "I trust I am not putting you to an inconvenience, supplying me with these garments, for I know at sea we are not in general overburdened with clothes."

"Parbleu! No; you are right, monsieur," returned the lieutenant, laughing, and looking pleased at his companion; "but, you see, we are not long out—we are just come from Sierra Leone. We formed part of the squadron sent to bombard and destroy your settlement there. Our flags are hostile, you know; but brave men are always friends. Do you know, I have discovered who you are."

Cuthbert Gordon looked surprised.

The Frenchman laughed. "We have not seen one another before; but if I am not mistaken, you were a midshipman aboard the 'Magicienne,' when she so bravely fought the French frigate, 'Madaline,' and the corvette, 'Le Fondre;' that's four years ago, is it not?"

"Yes," returned Cuthbert Gordon, immersed in thought, "I have marks of that fiercely contested fight upon my person yet."

"Ah! Parbleu, I thought I was right," returned Lieutenant Poulton. "You were scarcely more than a boy in years; but, by St. Peter, neither your blows nor your skill belonged to your years. You boarded twice, the second time your leader, the third lieutenant, was killed, and the 'Madaline's' crew were driving your men back, when you sprang in amongst them cheering and urging back your men with such vigour, that you drove them to the quarter deck. Do you remember wounding and disarming a young officer who opposed you?"

"I do very well," said our hero, interested, "but you were not that officer."

"No," returned the lieutenant, "but I am his brother. A sailor, thinking you were wounded severely, for you fell with the force of the thrust, put a pistol to my brother's head, and would have blown his brains out, but you knocked the pistol up, and saved his life; ten minutes after, the 'Madaline's' flag was struck, for the corvette 'Le Fondre,' seeing the crippled condition of the 'Magicienne' made sail and escaped."

"All this is quite true; but, Monsieur, where were you? you must know we were not able to hold our prize beyond the following day. A French line of battle ship, two frigates and a corvette, giving us chase.

The 'Madaline' was so cut to pieces in rigging and sails, that we had no chance of getting her away. So taking the prize crew out of her, we abandoned her; and after a short but sharp brush with the leading frigate we escaped."

"Well," returned Lieutenant Poulton, "I was second lieutenant of that leading frigate, and in the exchange of shots, I was the only officer wounded, though two men were killed and several wounded ; that 'Magicienne' was a wonderfully fast ship."

"We had no officer hurt by your fire," said Cuthbert Gordon, "but one man killed and seven wounded."

"My brother," continued Lieutenant Poulton, "afterwards told me how you had saved his life, and that you visited him when lying ill in his berth the very night the French squadron hove in sight. So you see, when I heard your name first, a kind of vague remembrance came over me; a few minutes reflection brought back the associations belonging to it, therefore it gives me great pleasure to show kindness to one who saved my brother's life. I spoke to our commander, as kind and brave a man as any in the service, and he now wishes to see you, and begs me to tell you that you must not for a moment consider yourself a prisoner aboard the 'Vengeur,' but a guest ; so now come below. Captain Beranger has sprained his ankle, so he is confined for a few days in his cabin."

The French lieutenant led the way into the cabin of the "Vengeur." Captain Beranger was seated on a sofa, with a table before him covered with papers, which he was examining ; he was a fine-looking man about fifty, with a very pleasing and agreeable countenance.

Saluting our hero with great politeness and kindness of manner, he begged him to be seated, and let him know the full particulars relating to the slave schooner, and also how he came to be a passenger in such a craft.

Captain Beranger listened, greatly surprised, and evidently interested ; for Cuthbert Gordon, without entering into details respecting his abduction, merely said he had been seized and put on board a schooner bound for the Gambia river, stated how he escaped, and that finally, after considerable suffering, in traversing the interior of Africa, he had engaged a passage in the American slaver.

"Yours has been an exceedingly distressing case," said Captain Beranger, "for you would now be holding a lieutenancy in your navy, and time to a high-spirited young man is everything. I really am puzzled what to do with those murderous rascals, the slaves aboard the American schooner. I have half a mind to sink her and them together, but you say there are many women amongst them, and many who did not join in the murder of the captain and crew, besides which they were goaded to the act by cruelty and ill-usage. No doubt you are most anxious to return to Europe. We are bound to the Isle of France, the two prizes we took off Sierra Leone will make a run if they can to Bordeaux. Now if I give you eight or ten hands out of the British prisoners aboard the two ships, will you venture to run the schooner to her destination and deliver her to her owners. We are not at war with the Americans, and I should like to save the schooner—I don't care about the negroes—what do you say ? "

" I am exceedingly grateful," returned our hero, surprised at Captain Beranger's generosity, in not only releasing himself but some of his countrymen also. " As to venturing, I care nothing of the risk, and could, I think, easily manage the slaves ; but they have broken into all the stores of the ship, and wantonly destroyed and wasted them ; there are still above two hundred negroes aboard, besides the women—to re-provision the schooner I should have to run up the Gambia, and the cost would be considerable. Our boats are all destroyed, and as you know, our mainmast has been cut away."

"Confound the black rascals!" said Beranger, " I think now the easiest way would be to sink her or leave her to her fate."

" Suppose," said Lieutenant Poulton, " Mr. Gordon were to run the schooner into the Gambia, and put the negroes ashore, and let them shift for themselves ; with six good hands he could then take the vessel to New York. You, Monsieur, could furnish him with a paper which would secure him from capture by French cruisers, and English ships of war would not of course molest him."

"Parbleu! that's the best plan," said Captain Beranger. "Get out the boat at once, and put the carpenter and his gang in. You can rig her a jury mainmast in a few hours, and we can spare her ten days' provisions; I dare say some of the schooner's provisions are yet to the fore."

After some further conversation, our hero and Lieutenant Poulton proceeded on deck; at this time it was quite calm, and the four vessels within a very short distance of each other. A boat with a young midshipman was despatched aboard the prizes to pick out eight able hands out of the English prisoners, whilst Lieutenant Poulton and Cuthbert Gordon proceeded on board the schooner with an armed crew, the Launch with the carpenter and his gang, and some niggers following, to carry a spar for a main-mast.

The negroes were in a state of fearful panic, and as the boats reached the side they threw themselves into the hold pell mell, leaving the deck quite clear.

Before sunset a mast was supplied, and before noon the following day the schooner was ready to make sail for the African coast. Eight sturdy English tars, frantic with joy at their escape from a long captivity, were working with might and main to get the vessel in the best possible trim. The negroes were had up and examined, the hold cleared out, and the slaves told if they behaved properly they would be restored to liberty. They threw themselves on their faces, kissed the feet of the white men, and by every abject gesture and exclamation testified their gratitude, stating that it was Mahado that encouraged them to act as they did, maddened as they were by their sufferings.

It happened that no time was lost by the "Vengeur," for the weather continued a perfect calm for nearly three whole days; by that time Cuthbert Gordon had got his crew in order, and his vessel in exceedingly good trim;

there was a fair store of provisions still in the schooner but very little water, the negroes having wantonly stove in the casks. The cabin was uninjured, and amongst the late unfortunate captain's stores, a considerable sum of money was found.

The evening of the third day, a breeze sprung up from the westward, and Cuthbert Gordon, taking a grateful leave of Captain Beranger, and a most brotherly one of Lieutenant Poulton, hastened on board the schooner in the good serviceable boat provided him from one of the English merchant ships. The "Vengeur," after firing a gun as a farewell salute, braced round her yards, and stood away on her course, followed by her two valuable prizes, whilst the schooner, close-hauled, stood in for the African shore.

CHAPTER XXIV.

FIFTEEN months have elapsed since we left our heroine, Dora Dunskelling, under the care of her assumed guardian, and in companionship with her treacherous governess.

The rebellion of 1798 was crushed, and its leaders, for the most part, executed or annihilated ; tranquillity was restored to most parts of the country, though in the hills and wild tracts of the mountains small bands of rebels still existed. But though crushed and overpowered, bitter rancour and hatred was still nourished by the vanquished, and the wounds which had been inflicted, were destined to rankle and fester for half a century after.

During the struggle, law, especially in the remote districts, was set at defiance, and many acts committed which remain unpunished and unredressed to the present day.

Dora anxiously awaited for the arrival of the Carews at their rectory; but days and weeks passed, and she neither received letters nor news of them. Lord Dunskelling was frequently absent; all the old domestics had been replaced by new; only Mrs. Brennen and Miss MacCormack remained of the former inmates. Dora was not at all blind to the deception the latter was practising. She appeared as if she felt a great deal for the unprotected situation of her *ci-devant* pupil, but she constantly kept repeating how anxious Lord Dunskelling was to secure her happiness and independence. The loss of her father's will, she said, caused his lordship great trouble, as it left him quite unable to judge what her father's wishes were respecting her. It was doubtful how the law would settle matters, when complete tranquillity was established. His lordship appeared greatly changed.

Dora quietly said it was high time, and she was glad to hear he was altered in his mode of life. She felt unhappy where she was, and would, the moment his lordship returned, insist on being placed under the care of some lady of respectability, until she was of age and could take care of herself. When in her power, she intended providing handsomely for Miss MacCormack, but she certainly wished to be no longer under her care.

Miss MacCormack felt this, and knew it. She sometimes repented the part she was acting, for though she had experienced some attachment for Lord Dunskelling, that had passed away; and mercenary motives now principally swayed her actions and thoughts. To get Dora to become Lord Dunskelling's wife was her object. She knew right well he would not be able to retain the title or estate should Cuthbert Gordon survive the voyage he had been sent; though Lord Dunskelling told her that, once in possession, the real heir would find it next to impossible to unseat him, as the costs would be ruinous to a small income.

After six or seven months' trial, Miss MacCormack came to the conviction that Dora nourished a profound attachment for Cuthbert Gordon, and a confirmed dislike, if not hatred, to Lord Dunskelling. By fair means it was very evident to her she would never become his wife. She knew Dora's disposition too well to think that fear or threats would conquer her repugnance to an union where her heart was not concerned. What to do, greatly puzzled this heartless, scheming, and by no means clever woman, for with good principles, and a firm determination to aid and assist the young girl she had reared, her prospects for the future would, in the end, have been much brighter.

Lord Dunskelling, after three months absence, returned to the castle. He appeared moody and unsettled.

"Well," said he to Miss MacCormack, on the first opportunity, "have you been able to work upon the mind of Dora? Do you think she would now be inclined to listen with a favourable ear to my proposals?"

"I have done all I could," returned Miss MacCormack, "and I candidly tell you I do not think her in the least changed. She has bestowed her affections on Mr. Gordon, and I am sure she is not one to be turned."

"Pooh," interrupted Lord Dunskelling, contemptuously, "don't tell me about women not to be turned. Half your sex are as easily turned as a weather-cock—the other half, like the wind, as changeable. To-morrow I will have an hour's conversation with her. I shall then make up my mind what to do; but mine she shall be."

The following day, as Dora was leaving the breakfast-room, and just as she was thinking of requesting his lordship to order a carriage to be got ready, that she might proceed to visit Mr. Carew's residence, and learn when she might expect the family home, he said,

"Dora, I wish to speak with you in the library in half an hour, if that time suits you."

"I was just wishing to drive over to Mr. Carew's," said our heroine, quietly. "You must feel and perceive that my residence here cannot be pleasing to me. I do not object to the treatment I receive, but I wish to be amongst my own sex and acquaintances. I am no longer to be considered the pupil of Miss Mac-Cormack."

Lord Dunskelling replied, "Certainly not, Dora; you greatly misunderstand your situation, if you think that there is any restraint put upon your freedom of action. Order the carriage when you please, and drive over to the rectory; you may learn more recent tidings than I have heard. It is too late in the day to drive there and back; but to-morrow, by leaving early, you can do so. Will you, then, favour me with an interview in the library? in an hour say."

"As you please, my lord. I can have no objection."

"Lord Dunskelling looked after her youthful, graceful form, with an expression of countenance not easily defined. There was no pity expressed for his intended victim, but a fiendish determination to carry out his projects to their full extent.

Dora retired to her own private sitting room in a very thoughtful mood. She very well imagined what would be the subject of her conference with her self-styled guardian. She rather wished the subject broached, and thus the matter be ended for ever, for Miss MacCormack had long led her to believe that Lord Dunskelling intended to offer her his hand. She had merely replied that he ought long ago to have known that such proposals could never be accepted by her. Dora Dunskelling possessed a surprising degree of firmness and decision in her character, and the conviction that she was betrayed by one who ought to have cherished and protected her, gave her infinitely more courage and nerve to meet the trials before her.

Her attachment, if not love, for Cuthbert Gordon, strengthened and increased her resolution; for though he had never informed her that he loved her—her woman's heart too well told her he did, fondly and devotedly, and she still trusted in the mercy of Providence in preserving him and restoring him to his country. She never doubted, from the first, but that Gorman Fitzpatrick was the author, or the instigator of his abduction ; where he was taken to, and for how long a period he would be detained, she could form no idea, but not for a moment would she allow herself to think his life was in danger. After this interview, she was firmly resolved not to remain under the same roof with Lord Dunskelling. She would insist upon being placed under the protection of some lady of respectability, in either Cork or Dublin, till her father's affairs and her own position were finally settled.

Lord Dunskelling was gazing out from the library window, as Dora entered the room. She was somewhat paler than usual, for she felt satisfied this was a crisis in her young life. It was impossible to imagine exactly what might occur from the interview. She knew that Gorman Fitzpatrick was a man whose passions were violent and unchecked, and in his usurped position as Lord Dunskelling, she had no reason to flatter herself that he would be restrained by any feeling for her happiness and welfare.

Turning round and perceiving Dora, his lordship presented her with a chair, and taking one himself, said, after a moment's pause :—

"You expressed a wish yesterday, Dora, to leave Dunskelling. Such a desire betokens a dislike to the home of your fathers, or to me, the possessor."

Dora uttered not a word.

"And yet," he continued, "you must be aware that from your early girlhood I have cherished an affection for you, which with the increase of years has become a consuming passion."

"My lord," interrupted Dora, quite calmly, though a flush came over her cheek for a moment, not certainly caused by any feeling of interest in the person addressing her, but of maidenly dislike to the subject from a man she could not but look upon with aversion and a certain dread. "My lord, the less said on that subject the better ; I can understand perfectly our relative positions. You are holding and claiming a title to which you well know you have no right."

"You are in error, Dora," interrupted Lord Dunskelling, quite calmly. "I hold the title and estates of your late father, till a stronger claimant proves my right to be illegal. You cannot blame me for that."

"Certainly not, if you had not taken cruel and unjustifiable means of removing the real heir to the title and estates of my lamented father."

"Do you really suppose, Dora, that Mr. Cuthbert Gordon, who you imagine to be next in succession, was carried off by persons employed by me. Really, cousin, I do not see what part of my conduct hitherto could lead you to such a supposition. You positively have a very bad opinion of me."

"I should not have made such an assertion, Gorman Fitzpatrick," said Dora, firmly, "had I not convincing proofs of the part you played in that outrage"—and taking from her pocket-book a folded paper she handed it to Lord Dunskelling, who, however, betrayed not the slightest agitation or excitement, as he read the short letter through, and having finished it, he very coolly re-folded and politely returned it to the surprised maiden —for surprised she was at the little indifference he appeared to feel.

"That letter is in my handwriting, certainly, Dora, though how you got it I cannot say. However, it has served a turn, and therefore I will come to the point at once, for now, I may say, we thoroughly understand our position. I did get Mr. Gordon out of the way, for two reasons. One, that he might not win your love, which I coveted; and the next, I had a vague idea, which I got from my cousin O'Dowd, that he was a nearer claimant to the title and estate than myself. In love and war, artifice often wins the day. I have only done what many a crowned head has done before me—removed a barrier to success. Do not be impatient, my fair cousin," continued Lord Dunskelling, seeing a flush on Dora's cheek, and that she was about to rise from her chair. "I will speak plainly, and this much in praise of myself I will state, that when I determine upon a project, I carry it out or perish. To be plain, then, you must either accept my hand and become Lady Dunskelling—and my life will be devoted to ensure your felicity—or enter a convent."

"A convent !" repeated Dora Dunskelling, rising up as she spoke, and gazing into her cousin's face with a look of incredulity. "You surely cannot imagine, Gorman Fitzpatrick, that I can listen to such a threat, with any other feeling than that of contempt. I am a Protestant born and bred, and strong, thank God, in my faith. The day is gone by for such outrages to be committed with impunity."

"Nevertheless," interrupted Lord Dunskelling, "such is my determination. I do not mean that you are intended to become a nun. But in a convent you will stay, till you consent to become my wife, or till—but no matter what my other project may be, you now understand me. You know that my aunt is Abbess of the Ursaline convent in Galway, and there I will take you to-morrow, unless on a night's reflection you change your mind."

"That will never be," replied Dora, indignantly. "I have listened too long to your unmanly threats, which have no effect upon me. I am in your power, to a certain extent, but when you least expect it your iniquitous schemes will be defeated, and your projects recoil upon yourself. If your aunt attempts to retain me against my will, within the walls of the convent, she will become amenable to the law, and bring ruin and disgrace upon herself, and the community she presides over."

"We shall see, cousin, we shall see," returned Lord Dunskelling, with a bitter smile, as Dora, with an indignant flush upon her cheek and brow, left the room.

She at once retired to her own chamber, locked herself in, and throwing herself into a chair gave way to a burst of grief, as she thought upon her orphan state and her truly unprotected situation.

Some one trying to open the door startled her, and with an effort she roused herself from the feeling of despair

17

she was giving way to. She enquired who was there, and was answered by Miss MacCormack. At first she felt inclined to refuse seeing her *ci-devant* governess, but a sudden thought struck her, and rising she admitted her.

Miss MacCormack was looking exceedingly pale, and was evidently much agitated. Dora made no observation, but closed the door and sat down.

Miss MacCormack stood for a moment irresolute, then, with a sudden impulse, she threw herself on her knees beside her former pupil, and taking her hands in hers, said, passionately :—

"Oh! Dora! Dora! can you forgive me?" and letting her head drop on the young girl's lap, she burst into tears.

"I have been a weak, selfish woman, Dora, but not the guilty one you imagine," said Miss MacCormack, between an hysterical sobbing she could not check. "You think me worse than I am, but as I hope for mercy hereafter, I am only guilty of endeavouring to induce you to think well of Gorman Fitzpatrick, and persuade you to become his wife, and all this for selfish motives. I do not deny but that at one time I did feel an affection for him, but that has long passed away. My sole motive for my un-principled conduct was a mercenary one. I wished to secure a certain independence."

"How could you, then," said Dora Dunskelling, making her take a seat beside her, "expect to enjoy an independence, purchased at the expense of your conscience? Had you no trust in me?   Did you imagine I had neither heart nor generosity; that one, whom I formerly loved and esteemed, would be left to battle with the world, after spending her youth in training my childhood and girlhood, in fact, a mother to an orphan girl? Ah! Julia, you judged but lightly of me."

"No, Dora, no," returned Miss MacCormack, passion-ately, "I never misjudged your generous, noble nature; but it is useless my attempting to offer any vindication for my selfish, weak, infamous conduct. All I can say is, that I deserve your utmost contempt. I have destroyed my own happiness, and forfeited for ever your esteem and love. You may forgive me, but you can no longer love me."

"I do forgive you, Julia, most sincerely forgive you. My affection for you has certainly received a rude shock. Still, sensible that you have erred, you may endeavour to repair that error, by aiding me to defeat the bold projects of my self-constituted guardian. He has, I suppose, told you I had this letter," showing Miss MacCormack the paper she had given to Lord Dunskelling.

"In this letter, intended for you, he boasts of the successful way in which he succeeded in entrapping Mr. Cuthbert Gordon, and in putting him on board a vessel bound for the coast of Africa, to be engaged in the slave trade—and he adds, with cold-blooded brutality, that it was not very likely his right to succeed Lord Dunskelling in the title and estates would be disputed by Mr. Gordon, as there were a hundred chances to one of his ever returning to England."

" But," eagerly interrupted Miss MacCormack, "that letter I never received or read. " I knew not of it, till this very day—nay, not till an hour ago, when Gorman Fitzpatrick, fiercely, almost savagely, upbraided me with betraying him, by letting you have that letter. I stated that I had never received it, never had seen it, and knew nothing of its contents. He called me a liar and a deceiver. Then it was that my conscience smote me ; and I rushed from his presence, vowing to redeem the past by aiding you to escape from the snares he is laying to poison your young life. But how, Dora, did this letter get into your possession ? say, and believe me, I deeply repent my past conduct, and would now willingly lay down my life to save you."

"The letter was given me by that kind and excellent woman, Mrs. Brennen. It was enclosed in a letter directed to her."

Miss MacCormack looked amazed.

" I can only account for so strange a circumstance, by supposing that Lord Dunskelling had written two or more letters, and in absence of mind, put the one intended

17—9

for you into a cover, directed to his housekeeper, and the one for Mrs. Brennen went to some one else. I think this likely, because Mrs. Brennen told me, when Lord Dunskelling arrived here after my dear father's death, he found certain chambers he expected altered, left in the same state, and I remembered his saying to Mrs. Brennen, 'How is this? Did I not tell you in my letter, to make several alterations in the arrangements of these chambers?'

"'I never received any such letter, my lord,' said the housekeeper.

"'Well then, it was lost, I suppose,' replied his lordship; 'the times are troubled, and post office arrangements remarkably uncertain.'"

"Ah!" said Miss MacCormack, "I have thought there was something in your mind for a long time, that has rendered your manner towards me cold and distant; but how strange that Lord Dunskelling, when he did converse with me, never made any allusion to that letter; neither did he ever touch upon the subject of Mr. Gordon's disappearance. I certainly suspected he had something to do with the affair; but I only imagined he had him carried over to England, to put him out of the way, that he might not create an interest in your breast."

"Has Gorman Fitzpatrick told you, that he intends placing me in the convent of Ursaline Nuns, in Galway, with the Abbess, his aunt?"

"Yes," returned Miss MacCormack, "and if he once gets you within those walls, your fate will be in his hands. In the troubled state of the country, and the secluded way your lamented father brought you up, and shunning all society of late years himself, no enquiry would most likely take place respecting you, which would not be answered by saying you had selected the convent in Galway as a residence, having a tendency to become a Catholic, and finally, to become a nun."

"Then what is to be done," said Dora, now really alarmed, "depend on it we shall not be permitted to leave the house; all the old domestics are dismissed, except Mrs. Brennen, and no doubt we are watched."

"Nevertheless," observed Miss MacCormack, "we must get out of this mansion to-night. All we have to do, is to reach the village. You know Mrs. Drogan's farm; Drogan himself is one of the kindest hearted men in the parish. Claim shelter from Mrs. Drogan for a few hours. Drogan will gather together in less than an hour fifty of your father's tenantry, all devotedly attached to you. Gorman Fitzpatrick will not dare to force you from them, and then a messenger can be sent to the Rev. Mr. Carew."

"But he is in Dublin," interrupted Dora, eagerly catching at her governess's project of escape.

"No," exclaimed Miss MacCormack, "he returned to his rectory a fortnight ago. Your letter never was sent to him. Thus you will be able to put yourself under his protection; he will take care to see you placed in your proper station, and secure your rights to your lamented father's property."

"Your plan is seemingly a good one, and if accomplished successfully, I should feel happy and secure under the protection of my kind friends the Carews; but do you believe we can succeed in leaving the house? Gorman Fitzpatrick, the concoctor of so many schemes, is not likely to let us escape from his hands; all the doors will be carefully guarded, and more especially as he now knows you will no longer seek to deceive me; he will equally think it necessary to secure you from betraying him."

"Still," said Miss MacCormack, anxiously, "I am satisfied I shall be able to outwit even Gorman Fitzpatrick. As soon as all is still in the mansion, I will come for you; muffle yourself in your large mantle, and once outside the house, the walk of two miles to Drogan's farm will be nothing; you will not be missed till after breakfast and before that time Darby Drogan will have driven you in his spring cart to the rectory."

"Mrs. Brennen, of course," said our heroine, "must be aware of our intentions, for she will have to bear the brunt of Gorman Fitzpatrick's rage."

"Mrs. Brennen would sacrifice her life to release you

from the grasp of your would-be guardian. It will be through her interference that we get clear of the house. So now, adieu, dear Dora, and trust to me, though in truth you have little right to do so."

CHAPTER XXV.

IT was quite one o'clock in the morning before the inmates of Dunskelling Castle were buried in repose—at all events, not a sound was heard along the galleries and corridors, and no light was to be observed in any of the windows. It was a still, quiet night—no breeze was to be heard rustling in the great oaks that stretched their giant branches, so as almost to touch the west wing of the mansion. There was no moon; but bright stars spangled the heavenly vault; the only sound that disturbed the stillness, was the not distant murmur of the Atlantic swell as it rolled in upon the shingle beach.

Dora and Miss MacCormack had left Dunskelling Castle without any difficulty by the private entrance into the park, the key of the door being simply turned in the lock on the inside. This surprised Dora, who knew that the doors were locked nightly, and the keys deposited on a table in Lord Dunskelling's chamber. They passed out from the mansion into a kind of shrubbery, and then into the gravel walk leading to the lodge, where dwelt the new keeper and his family.

"We must get out of the park," observed Miss Mac-Cormack, "without disturbing them at the lodge; the new keeper is a surly fellow, and would betray us in a moment—in fact, all the new domestics are a strange set."

"We can get out," replied Dora, "by the swing gate which opens on the Tarbet road ; it's a long way, but unless we scramble over the high fences, we cannot get out of the park."

"True," said Miss MacCormack, who carried a bundle of clothes.

"Where was Mrs. Brennen; and how was the key of the door procured?" questioned Dora.

Either Miss MacCormack did not hear the question, or did not think it necessary to reply, for no answer was returned, and she quickened her steps. They crossed the park, and reached the spring gate. Miss MacCormack held the gate for Dora to pass through ; there was a thick hedge on each side of the gate, and just as Dora passed out, a thick mantle was thrown over her head, and pulled so tight she could scarcely breathe, much less cry out, and at the same moment, she felt herself lifted into the strong arms of a man, and carried swiftly along the road for five minutes ; she was then, she judged, lifted into a carriage of some kind, and the man who held her, remained in it with her, still firmly pressing the mantle over her face and head. Miss MacCormack beheld this act with perfect unconcern ; she quietly closed the gate, and began retracing her steps to the castle.

"So," said she to herself, "my acting must have been excellent, and yet she was very innocent to be so deceived. However, I think she ought to have known my disposition better, than to think I would humble myself to her, or to anyone else, for the matter of that." Having reached the private door, she paused and listened, pushed it open, and then in the indistinct light, she perceived the figure of a man.

"All has gone well?" said Lord Dunskelling, for he it was.

"Yes, capitally ; she thought me a penitent, and fell easily into the suare ; it was so well managed she did not utter a cry."

"Good," returned his lordship. "Now, give me the key ; just lock the door."

"No," returned Miss MacCormack, "leave the key in

the door ; how else will you get people to believe she left the house of her own accord ? "

"Well, so far, this scheme prospers, if our man carries it well out. If all fails, we will start for America, with one hundred thousand pounds—not a bad capital for beginning life in a strange land. And now, Julia, let us retire to our rooms; act your part well to-morrow, and the game and the spoil is ours. As to the title, I cannot, I know, hold it a twelvemonth."

So saying, they retired to their respective chambers.

In the mean time, Dora Dunskelling, held firmly in the grasp of her abductor, could scarcely breathe ; but even in that painful situation her thoughts were busy. She was again betrayed, and by the instructor of her girlhood, and one whom she had truly loved in her early years. How such base deception could exist in the female breast, astonished her ; she was new to the world and its false-ness ; true hearts there are, especially amongst the softer sex ; but, alas ! the dominion of the demon of gold has a wide sway, and even women fall, at times, a prey to its lust.

For two hours the vehicle that carried Dora proceeded over exceedingly rough roads. The man who held the mantle round her, at length relaxed his hold, saying, in a calm, conciliatory voice :—

"Keep quiet, and do not utter a cry, and you will not receive any ill-treatment."

"I will promise nothing," said Dora, as soon as she regained breath. "The first opportunity I get, I will cry aloud for help."

"I am sorry you make that resolution, Miss Dunskelling," said the same voice, and it was a very gentlemanly, quiet voice, "because I must convey you to the convent in Galway. I wish to do so without further violence ; but if you persist in your determination, I must use other means."

"If," said Dora, surprised at the tone and language of the speaker, "you are committing this cruel act for gold ——"

"Nay," interrupted the man somewhat eagerly, "you

mistake. I act from an oath, and an oath sacred to me; I will carry it out. Nevertheless, in my heart I pity you; you are young and lovely, and a man must be swayed by stern motives, that would injure or distress you."

Dora was silent; and, five minutes after, the vehicle, whatever it was, suddenly stopped, and then a voice said, in Irish, which Dora thoroughly understood, "The chaise is on the road, but you must cross a field to it; there is no lane from this cross road on to the main road."

"Cannot you lead your horse through the field," asked the man beside Dora.

"Faix, it would take a fox-hunter to cross the dyke, and the dickens a gate is there for a mile."

"Well, never mind," said Dora's conductor, "the driver ought to have known better than to come so far down the main road."

"If you will walk across the field, Miss Dunskelling," said the same voice, "I will remove this mantle, if not, I must contrive to carry you."

Dora thought for a moment, and then said:—

"I will walk."

The mantle over her head was removed, and Dora could look about her. In the dim light she regarded her conductor and her own situation. She was in a farmer's spring cart. The man had got out, and was standing by the side of the vehicle ready to help her to descend. He was a tall man, habited in a common frieze coat, reaching to his heels, and his features, all but the eyes, were hid in an ample red handkerchief, and his hat pulled well over his brows. Dora cast a look round her; but excepting a countryman, the driver of the cart, she did not perceive any one.

The man in the grey frieze offered her his arm, to assist her over the stone stile leading into a fallow field. She, however, got over herself, and he then led the way across a ten or twelve acre field. At the further end of the field was a gate, and by the gate a post-chaise and pair, and a postillion. It was a common posting carriage. Closing the gate, Dora's conductor opened the door of the chaise and put down the steps. For an instant she hesitated, but feeling all remonstrance would be fruitless, and only lead, perhaps, to rougher treatment, she entered the chaise, thinking her conductor would also enter ; but he did not. He closed the door and got on the seat in front. The postillion mounted, and instantly drove off. By the look and breadth of the road, Dora judged they were on the mail-coach road, but leading to what place she knew not.

"They will surely have to pass through some large town," thought our heroine, " and stop at several places before they can reach Galway. If so, I am determined to make an effort to attract attention, and get rescued from my abductor, whose appearance and manner surprise me." She could very well imagine she had been thus spirited away through the deceitful artifice and treachery of Miss MacCormack. To take her away openly from Duns-skelling would undoubtedly have led to inquiry. What would be said, or thought, or invented, to account for her strange disappearance in the morning, she could not imagine. But something, she felt confident, would be devised, detrimental to her in some way.

The chaise drove on till daylight, and just as the field-labourers were turning out of their cottages, it stopped before the door of a small, mean, two-storied house, with a sign over the door, betokening it to be a Shebeen House, where the stray traveller or day labourer may get bread and cheese and a glass of fiery whiskey. Not a soul appeared on the premises but a very old woman, and a girl of some ten or twelve years old. The man got down from the seat in front, and opened the door, requesting Dora to alight. The old woman and the girl looked with great surprise at our heroine, who, jaded and weary, gazed round her with an anxious look. Just then a horn rung in the still air, and the rattling sound and tramp of horses announced the approach of a carriage. Dora hesitated ; the horn probably belonged to the guard of a mail-coach. She would claim assistance, but the moment the man, who was leading her into the house, heard it, he passed his arm round her waist, and, despite her struggles and cries, bore her up a flight of stairs, and into a back room, and laying her down, drew a pistol from his breast, and said, in a low tone :—

"Another cry or shriek for help, and it will be your last."

"Coward !" exclaimed Dora, "that will not stop me ;" and making a sudden rush to the window, which was open, she called out in a loud voice for help. The mail coach for Tralee had just passed the house, the horses in a canter. Apparently the sound of Dora's voice reached the guard's ear, for as she was dragged from the window she saw him stand up and look back, but the next instant the vehicle whirled out of sight.

Her persecutor let go his hold, and with a muttered imprecation on himself, thrust his pistol into his breast, and stood gazing on the beautiful form and flushed check of his victim. He threw off his hat and handkerchief, cast his great frieze wrapping-coat aside, and Dora at once recognised her abductor to be the gentleman who first accompanied Lord Dunskelling to Dunskelling Castle, some little time after her father's death, and who he introduced to her as Mr. Maxwell ; though she never exchanged a dozen words with him after the introduction, she remembered him instantly. He was a young man, some seven or eight and twenty. Handsome he certainly was, and gentlemanly in manners, but there was a remarkable wildness and fierceness in his dark eyes that had almost startled Dora on her introduction to him. Divested of his frieze coat and wrapper, he appeared in the ordinary dress of the country gentleman of that period.

Dora sank into a chair with her eyes fixed upon Mr. Maxwell. A variety of passions were struggling for mastery in George Maxwell's features as he stood before her.

"You called me a coward, Lady Dora. Do you imagine, for a moment, that I meant what I threatened ?" exclaimed George Maxwell, almost passionately. "My life would have been at stake if your cries had brought in the guard of the mail, and I tried to frighten you."

"Nevertheless," returned Dora Dunskelling, calmly,

"it was a coward's act, and the crime you are now committing is equally so ; and as I told you before, no threat shall hinder me from procuring assistance if I can."

"Your are a bold and brave girl," said George Maxwell, "and I abhor the oath that has bound me to aid the plans and projects of a greater scoundrel than myself—that is the man calling himself Lord Dunskelling. You need fear no insult from me. I have a young wife and child whom I dearly love. To save them from destitution and misery, I bound myself to a ——. But I am wrong, and infringing my oath. I wish to relieve your mind from fear of personal insult, and if possible induce you to permit me to conduct you to your destination, without forcing me to adopt measures I detest. As it appears to me, I do not see that your situation in a convent will be worse, or indeed half as bad, as remaining under the roof and in the power of a man so reckless and unprincipled as Gorman Fitzpatrick."

Dora Dunskelling was surprised ; but her dread of her persecutor was considerably lessened by his statement. Still, to permit herself to be shut up in a convent, and completely in the power of an aunt of Gorman Fitzpatrick, had something terrible in the prospect. She had an idea that any act might be committed in a convent with impunity. No one would be able to tell where she was concealed; as to Lord Dunskelling forcing her to marry him, she had no fear of that. He had some other object in view she felt sure, and which was to be gained by shutting her out of the world for some time.

These ideas take a little time to state, but they passed through her brain in a few seconds.

George Maxwell stood waiting for Dora's answer, calmly and patiently.

"It appears to me, Mr. Maxwell," said Dora, ".a very cruel alternative you offer me. I should not be forced into a convent, being of a different persuasion to those within its walls, were it not for the purpose of concealing me from the world. How do I know but I may be immured for life ? "

"God forbid, Miss Dunskelling, God forbid; if I

thought that, I would violate my oath, and blow my employer's brains out afterwards, which would free you."

Dora shuddered at the vehemence and strange and terrible resolution of her persecutor. However, after a few moments' thought, she said :—

"I can never consent, Mr. Maxwell, to go quietly to my doom, if an opportunity offers of freeing myself from such a fate. I regret seeing a gentleman in the situation you are, bound by such unholy oaths. You appear to regret it yourself, and for your own peace of mind hereafter, and the happiness of your wife, I wish you had not been placed in such a position as to require to be the handle of another man's bad passions."

George Maxwell seemed to feel Dora's words. He was not, however, at all shaken in his determination ; he paused, seemingly in thought, and then said :

" I regret, Lady Dora, your determination, though I applaud your spirit and resolution; but it will avail you nought ; the consequence will be that we shall travel all night. I will bring you up such refreshments as I can procure in this place. I am not now alone ; two confederates, well armed, and determined, meet me here. I would therefore entreat you, after partaking of some refreshment, to seek repose ; there is a bed in the adjoining room," and pointing to an open door he retired, after locking the door, and putting the key in his pocket.

" Surely," thought Dora, rising and going to the window (it was a side window overlooking a small yard, and had a side view over the mail coach road) "surely I can attract some persons passing along this road who will afford me assistance." Whilst gazing out from the window the key in the door turned, and being opened, George Maxwell re-entered, with a little girl carrying a tray with a coffee pot, a cup, and some bread, butter, and cream, which she placed on the table. She observed that George Maxwell carried in his hand a hammer and some nails.

When the girl retired, he said, " You must excuse me,

Lady Dora, for taking these precautions ; you declare you will use every effort to escape ; now as my life depends on frustrating such an event, I must use precautionary measures. To-morrow, by eight o'clock in the morning, we shall reach our destination ; till then I must leave nothing to chance." So saying, he proceeded to the window and closed the two lower shutters, and nailed them firmly.

"In the next room," said he, "such precaution is not necessary ; the window looks into the garden where one of my confederates will keep constant watch till evening."

"You take great care," said Dora, indignantly and bitterly, " to secure the misery of an unprotected orphan girl—God forgive you, but the day will come when you will repent all this."

"I do repent it, and my blood boils with rage," returned Maxwell, passionately. "But there is no help for it ; do you imagine that all the risk I run is in guarding you ? No, no ; I am, or rather was, a rebel leader, and a thousand pounds would reward any man who could lay his hands upon me. But they shall never take me alive, to exhibit me as a traitor and a rebel ; once having placed you in a convent, I cross the seas."

So saying, he quitted the room ; leaving our heroine much matter for reflection.

Wearied and fretted, and a little exhausted by want of sleep, after partaking of a cup of coffee, Dora went into the adjoining chamber, which contained a small, but clean bed, and two chairs, and a basin and jug of cold water, and fastening the door she threw herself on the bed, where, notwithstanding her vexed thoughts, she shortly fell asleep, and slept several hours.

It was dusk, as our heroine was again placed in the chaise ; George Maxwell took the seat in front, muffled in his frieze coat, and without Dora seeing a soul in the house, save the little girl, the chaise drove off.

"They will have to pass through some town, surely," thought Dora, as she frequently gazed out from the window, but somehow it was so managed that the pair of horses for change were always ready on the road side, and no house of any kind near.

In the dead of the night, they passed rapidly through a large town, but not a soul was stirring in the silent streets. Several villages were passed in the same way. Whilst changing horses, George Maxwell invariably stood at the chaise door, and thus the night passed. Just as the dawn was breaking, after the last change of horses, she could perceive a large town before her, but the postillion turned into a by-road, and passed round the town, which was Galway, and after an hour's drive, they arrived before the great gate of the convent of Ursaline.

Dora felt her heart beat faster and painfully, as she beheld the large and somewhat gloomy pile of building, surrounded by a high stone wall, enclosing the convent. The postillion dismounting, pulled a huge ring, in the great closed wooden gate, framed with iron, and the solemn toll of a large bell fell upon the ear.

George Maxwell approached the chaise door and threw it open, at the same time that a small door opened in the convent gate, and a female appeared at the entrance.

Dora, fatigued, and for the first time a little alarmed, gazed about her; the convent appeared to be situated in a dreary, treeless country; over the high upper windows could be seen only the wall.

"Do not give way to fear, Lady," said Maxwell, in a low voice; "when you have passed through yonder gate, I am absolved from my oath, and if my life is spared, it's but a very short time before ample justice shall be rendered you; I have risked life to place you within these walls; I would risk a dozen lives to free you from your bondage."

Dora made no reply, there was no use hesitating; there was not a human being in sight save the postillion, the porteress, and her conductor. With a sigh she passed through the door, the porteress evidently expecting her; the door closed and was locked; and thus Dora Dunskelling was shut from the outer world, within the walls of one of the strictest convents then existing in Ireland,

CHAPTER XXVI.

GALWAY, of all the towns in the south and west of
Ireland, has the most striking remnants of its Spanish
settlers remaining even to the present day   At the time
of our story much more so ; many of its houses were then
built after the Spanish fashion ; it abounded in convents,
its streets were crowded with priests and monks, besides
many other particularities very striking to the visitor to
that ancient town.

About three miles to the west of the town, and within
a musket shot of the wild sea-beach, stood the convent
into which our unfortunate heroine was introduced. It
had large gardens within its massive, high, stone walls,
but no labour of culture could induce the trees to flourish ;
the moment they overlooked the walls, the strong blast
from the ocean, highly impregnated with saline particles,
withered and dried them up ; for the furious gales
sweeping over the mighty Atlantic first strike the sea-
coast of Galway, stunting the trees, and where very much
exposed, burning up the herbage, giving a dried, parched,
barren look to the land bordering the sea-coast.

A very short time indeed does nature look smiling and
green in what may be called the far west of Ireland.   The
storms of the early part of September break the branches
of the trees, scatter their leaves, leaving those that contrive to cling to the parent branches looking as if they
had endured a scorching fire.

The convent wall was so high that only the upper
room windows looked over it, and they were not inhabited
by the nuns, being used as store rooms.

Though only three miles from the gay town of Galway,
the aspect of the country immediately surrounding the
convent was wild and deserted, with very little sign of

vegetation.   This aspect of savage wildness did not extend
to Galway itself; to the east and north lay a beautiful
smiling country, rich in vegetation, sheltered from Atlantic storms, whilst the town itself was in many respects
picturesque, and romantically situated.

Our poor heroine was ushered by a cold, formal, middle-
aged nun, into a sombre, gloomy parlour ; and the next
moment the lady Superior of the convent made her
appearance.   Our heroine regarded this lady with
attention ; she wished to see if her countenance bore any
trace of a kindly heart.

But a very cursory glance satisfied her that, if
kindly and charitable feelings did exist in her heart, her
countenance strangely belied them.   The Abbess was in
years about fifty, tall, spare in form, with a long face,
thin nose and lips, and small, piercing, grey eyes ; whilst
the expression of the features betokened a cold, calculating,
selfish disposition.   After looking keenly and fixedly into
the open, beautiful features of our young heroine, she
said, casting a glance over a letter she held in her
hand :

" Lady Dora Dunskelling, I presume ? "

" Yes, madam," returned Dora ; " I am the daughter
of the late Lord Dunskelling."

" And the ward of the present Lord Dunskelling ? "

" No, madam," returned our heroine, firmly ; " I am
not the ward of Mr. Gorman Fitzpatrick, or he would
never have dared to have me forcibly taken from my
home, and confined in a convent.   I am not a Roman
Catholic ; by immuring me in this place, Gorman Fitzpatrick has outraged the law, and debarred me from the
privilege of attending a Protestant place of worship ; and
I protest plainly and strongly against so cruel and illegal
a wrong."

The Superior, whilst Dora spoke, never took her cold,
piercing glance from her flushing features ; the slightest
possible colour tinged her high cheek bones, and a com-
pression of the thin lips was perceptible.

" You make use of very strange language, Lady Dora
Dunskelling," said the Superior, after a slight pause ;

18

" besides, your accusation againt Lord Dunskelling, whom you somewhat strangely style Gorman Fitzpatrick, does not, by any means, correspond with the statement in this letter. You declare that you were forcibly torn from your home by your guardian and conveyed here. Now, this letter," and the Abbess held up a paper, " this letter from Lord Dunskelling arrived here yesterday evening. Instead of being forcibly torn from your home, you actually contrived to gain possession of a key that opened one of the doors of the mansion, and secretly fled in the dead of the night, and to aid and assist your flight met a Mr. Maxwell, to whom you had been introduced by your guardian."

" Madam," exclaimed Dora, rising to her feet, her face and neck burning with shame and indignation, " what monstrous fabrication has this cowardly man, falsely calling himself Lord Dunskelling, stated? Surely, madam, you cannot for a moment believe such a detestable falsehood ? "

" The simple question is—did you, or did you not, Lady Dora, quit your guardian's mansion, in the dead of the night, without his knowledge ? "

" Oh, villain ! how easily now I see through your plans and projects," exclaimed Dora, passionately clasping her hands, and with difficulty restraining her tears. " I see, madam," she added, and with a bitter feeling at her heart, " that it is quite useless my appealing to you, or protesting against the vile, slanderous falsehoods contained in that letter, purposely to shield himself from—"

" I am not going, young lady," harshly interrupted the Abbess, rising and waving her hand with an angry motion, " to stay here and listen to such language. You are confided to my care, by your proper guardian, to keep you from indiscretion till of a mature age, and by proper instruction to instil more virtuous ideas, and a stronger sense of decorum, into your mind. You are very young, too young to be left either to your own guidance or the worldly and seductive persuasions of the other sex. I will send Sister Martha to show you your chamber, your guardian will forward your trunks and wearing apparel in a day or two ; till then you will be supplied with whatever you may require." So saying, with a stately air she left the chamber.

Dora stood, her eyes suffused with tears, though her high spirit struggled to conquer her emotion, prompting her to defy the machinations of her detestable cousin ; but she well knew how futile would be her efforts, how little her high spirit would serve her, within the dreary walls that now enclosed her.

It was quite evident that the Superior of the convent was in league with Gorman Fitzpatrick. What her motives could be for running so great a risk as immuring a Protestant maiden within her walls against her will, she could not say or imagine. Could she hope to make her a Catholic and take the vows, and thus gain a large portion of her wealth for her poor convent, for poor of late years it had become ?

Many a victim had in earlier times been worked upon by priestcraft ; they might think they could influence her mind, and bend her to their will. With an inward prayer to Heaven, to give her strength and power to resist the arts of those in whose power she was, Dora became calmer. Just then Sister Martha entered the parlour.

CHAPTER XXVII.

LEAVING our heroine to contend against the machinations of her persecutors, we return to Cuthbert Gordon, on board the slaver.

After parting from the frigate, which stood away with her prizes to the eastward, our hero steered for the coast of Africa. Amongst the eight British seamen selected from the two merchant ships captured was an old man-of-war's man of the name of James Perkins. He was not more than forty-five, and had served twenty years in the British navy. He was a man of the middle height, strongly built, well featured, with a pleasing countenance. Why he quitted the service none of his companions knew. The other seven were mostly young men and ordinary seamen.

Cuthbert Gordon was anxious to make the African coast as soon as possible; the weather being hot, and the stock of provisions not abundant. The following morning after leaving the frigate the coast was sighted. Our hero was determined in his own mind not to run for the Gambia river, but anchor off the shore, and land the slaves in the large "Launch" left them by the frigate. He named his intentions to James Perkins, who was a thorough seaman, and he agreed that it was a much better plan. The men were all anxious to get rid of the blacks, many being still unruly, and showing signs of a mutinous spirit. The next day they made the coast, and anchored in a small cove, not more than half a mile from where the schooner lay at anchor in ten fathoms' water.

The "Launch" would carry twenty negroes and four men rowing; but the fierce state of excitement the negroes were in, and their bitter, ferocious animosity to each other, renewed as soon as they knew that they were clear of the French frigate, rendered the taking them ashore in any numbers dangerous.

The young commander could understand the Mandingo men pretty well ; and when the moment came for landing them, several of them, in the most excited manner, told him that they would rather die on board, or be made slaves of in America, than go ashore where they would be sure to be murdered by the other blacks ; or, if they did escape them, they were certain to fall into a worse slavery from their own kings. So they begged him to put the others ashore, and carry them to their destination in America; but leave the ship to be landed with the ferocious negroes they would not.

Their entreaties, on consulting Perkins, were granted. It was determined to land the worst lot of negroes, and keep the rest ; for to compel them to leave might lead to bloodshed, and perhaps the loss off some of his crew. On searching the schooner, to their surprise, they found plenty of provisions for all, and an abundant supply of water could be had on shore close to the beach. Accordingly, the negroes were selected and landed ; and when all that chose to go were got rid of, nearly one hundred remained; but as they evinced great joy, and promised to be well conducted, and as they were of the same tribe, all looked well. Water was laid in, the hold well cleaned and ventilated, and the negroes allowed to come ten at a time on deck. The second day they were able to set sail and bid adieu to the African coast.

The third day the guns were got up and placed in position, and ammunition put ready at hand, as it was quite possible that they might be chased by some French privateer, who might not be very scrupulous, and who might disregard the protection papers of the commander of the " Vengeur."

Cuthbert Gordon's crew consisted of his mate, and eight fine, active young seamen, all extremely willing and eager to obey him, and also very grateful for their liberation from a French prison.

The schooner was a remarkably fast vessel even with a jury-mast. After seven days' run before a moderate, but favourable breeze, just off Newfoundland they encountered some heavy breezes, and finally calms and dense fogs. On the ninth day an easterly breeze cleared away the fog. It was ten o'clock in the morning when Cuthbert Gordon came on deck, having been up most of the night. Just then, as the fog cleared off, they perceived within less than a mile of them, a long, rakish, threemasted schooner. She was under jury-masts, no doubt dismasted in a gale, and had rigged herself out as well as she could.

"That's a privateer, Sir," said the mate, joining our hero, and handing him the glass. "She's full of men." As he spoke a wreath of smoke curled out of her side, and the report of a heavy gun pealed over the quiet sea, and up went the privateer flag of the French Republic.

"Run up the stars and stripes," said Cuthbert Gordon; "ten to one, if this calm continues, but she will board us. As you say, she is full of men, and that gun was a 12-pounder. She is full three hundred tons."

"It's to be hoped," said the mate, "that they will respect our flag, 'cause we are all English, and our papers American. Those *parler vous* and privateers are devilish like pirates."

"I have a protection from the commander of the French frigate," said our hero. "They will surely respect that; if not, we must fight them;" and he looked into the mate's face. Perkins rubbed his hands, swore an oath, and said :

"All right, Sir, that's your sort. We won't skulk, depend on it; anything but a French prison, especially to any one as has tasted one."

Cuthbert Gordon looked aloft, then along the horizon, but saw no signs of a breeze. His men were not idle; the mate was a thorough man-of-war's man, and the sailors were full of spirit. They never bestowed a thought upon the fact that they were but ten men in all, and that the privateer had fifty or sixty at the very least, judging from the number they saw on her deck, and that she carried 12-pounders.

Closely watching the privateer, Perkins saw a boat launched and several men jump into it, push off and row towards the English vessel.

The mate and crew armed themselves with pistols and cutlasses, and waited quietly the result. As the boat approached Gordon had a clear view of her crew.

There were four men pulling, four more were in the stern sheets and two in the bows, and he could easily see that they were all armed; they were a rough, fierce-looking crew, all beard and moustache, dressed in woollen shirts and duck trousers, with a broad belt, with a brace of pistols stuck in it. The man steering the boat was a tall, strong man, with a red beard and head, with a scar across his cheek and nose of a livid crimson; judging by his dress and weapons, he was a superior officer. They pulled rapidly alongside, and were all scrambling on deck, making fast the boat; but Gordon and the mate resolutely repulsed them; our hero saying :

"Your officer can come on board, and see our papers; but I will not submit to be boarded as if you were boarding a prize."

"Sacré Diable! what do you mean?" exclaimed the tall man, drawing a pistol from his belt. "Do you question my right to board your craft? *Sacré Dieu*! don't you know we can sink you in ten minutes if you are insolent?"

"No," returned our hero, still quite quietly. "I do not know, neither do I hinder you from coming on board and looking over our papers. Our flag is not at enmity with yours; are you privateers or pirates?"

"Curse your insolence!" said the privateer captain, for such he was. "What are you? You are not an American, you speak our language too well for that. But I will come and see what you are," and he jumped on deck, saying, "Now show your papers."

Perkins, with a look of defiance, handed the papers. The Frenchman ran his eyes over them.

"Sacré, how is this? This is a slave schooner. I ask you again; what countryman are you?"

"An Englishman," said Cuthbert Gordon.

"Ha! Parbleu, I thought as much; and your crew Englishmen—"

"Yes."

"Bon, by —— you are a set of pirates, you are not the original crew of this craft. How do you account for having possession of her?"

Cuthbert Gordon handed to him the commander of the "Vengeur's" protection.

The privateer's man looked at it, and then, with an oath, tore it in bits, swearing it was a forgery, and that they were a set of bloody pirates, who had murdered the American crew, and seized the ship and cargo of slaves.

He had scarcely uttered the words before he was in the grasp of Cuthbert Gordon, and the next instant, to the dismay of his men, he was hurled over the side sprawling into his boat.

A volley of furious maledictions ensued, pistols were levelled and fired, but our hero's crew were not to be frightened, for an attempt to board was gallantly repulsed; one of the privateer's men wounded, and another pitched into the sea.

The captain of the privateer was frantic with passion; he discharged his pistol at his assailant, inflicting a very slight scratch on the left shoulder; our hero could have killed him, but felt satisfied at having pitched him into his boat. Furious and thirsting for revenge, the privateer's boat pulled away for their vessel, the crew uttering imprecations and vowing a terrible revenge.

"I wish, Sir," said the mate, "we had sunk the boat. We are within range of their 12-pounders now, and there's no wind."

"There's a dark line along the horizon to the eastward," replied Cuthbert Gordon. "We shall have a breeze in a short time, and I think we can outsail the privateer under her present canvas."

In the meantime the boat reached the side of the Frenchman, and all getting on deck except six, they made fast a warp, and commenced towing her head round, which having accomplished, they at once opened fire with their 12-pounders, but they were mistaken in the range, for no harm was done to the schooner. They then put out immense sweeps, and commenced sweeping her, with the boat still ahead, towards their intended prize; but the dark line to the eastward rapidly advanced, and before the privateer had gained two hundred yards, the breeze filled the schooner's sails and the privateer's nearly at the same moment, the sweeps were taken in, the boat hoisted on deck, and all sail made.

The privateer, named the "Sans Culotte," was accounted one of the fastest vessels of her class afloat. She had taken and plundered many vessels off the coast of America, and was commanded by Captain Henri Maria Carobert, a man of the most ferocious temper and cruelty of disposition. He had been dismissed the French navy for brutally shooting his second lieutenant, but from some flaw in the evidence, he escaped conviction for that crime, but was dismissed the service for cruelty to his seamen.

Having funds of his own, and the revolution breaking out, he built and fitted out a privateer, and selected a crew of one hundred and twenty men, from various parts; men chosen from the most furious "Sans Culottes," steeped in crime, and revelling in the shedding of blood; and yet, when pressed in any hostile encounter, and the enemy not greatly inferior in guns and men, abandoning the conflict in a most cowardly manner. Carobert's first exploits were against British vessels in the channel, but being severely handled by a British privateer of much inferior force, but quite superior in sailing qualities, he changed his cruising ground to the American coast. The "Sans Culotte" could scarcely be called a privateer, being more of a pirate; for when an opportunity offered the sailors plundered neutral vessels and murdered the crews.

Such was the intention with regard to the schooner "Breeze," which some ten days previously had been dismasted, and nearly sunk by coming in contact, during the night, with an enormous iceberg. She speedily repaired her injuries, and got up jury-masts, being well provided with spars. Even under this rig she was more than a match for most vessels of her tonnage afloat. She had light sails, purposely for spreading in fine weather; so that even under jury-masts she had a great breadth of canvas.

Having the advantage of the wind, she at once bore down on the "Breeze." But the schooner was well under weigh, Cuthbert Gordon taking the helm, so that the mate and his little crew might all be in readiness to work the guns, should the privateer commence the contest, which soon took place. Luffing up in the wind, she fired a broadside of round shot into the schooner, which whistled almost harmlessly through the sails and rigging.

Besides the mate, Perkins, there were three of the seamen well able to handle the guns, having served for short periods in the navy. Determined not to run without firing a shot, Gordon manœuvred the "Breeze" in such a manner that he baffled the privateer in her intention of running him aboard; and passing across her stern, with his four guns loaded with grape, he completely raked her deck, then crowded with men, killing several, wounding a number, and throwing them into great confusion. A cheer from his little crew leaped over the waters, and trimming their sails, they passed on, receiving another discharge, wounding one man, but not severely, and knocking the starboard bulwarks to splinters.

"We will now try how we are as to speed," said our hero to his mate Perkins, "they work the privateer very badly; still, we can never attempt to board her, and therefore it will not do to sacrifice life uselessly."

"But if she outsails us," observed the mate, "and she looks a clipper, we must fight her, for depend on it, there will be no quarter given us."

"They are bad gunners, that's one consolation," replied Gordon. "I will be guided by circumstances; get all our guns double shotted; I will watch an opportunity, and see if we cannot bring down one of her masts."

The two vessels, on a trial of speed, proved very closely matched, the "Breeze" just keeping out of range of the "Sans Culotte's" guns. However, when the wind fell, the privateer, to our hero's surprise, gained rapidly on him, and towards sunset, was sufficiently near to open fire upon the "Breeze."

~~~~~~~~~~~~~~~~~~~~~

CHAPTER XXVIII.

THE commander of the schooner gazed anxiously round the horizon ; the breeze was evidently slackening, and yet the sky looked squally and wild. Still, the privateer came up. He very well knew what their fate would be, should the exasperated crew of the "Sans Culotte" board them ; that they would give them no quarter, was very certain.

"We have nothing for it," said our hero, turning to Perkins, the mate, and his little crew, who were looking serious, but determined. "Let the blacks up, and arm them with all the weapons you can find."

"They will cut our throats the first thing," said Perkins, with an oath ; "they are desperate now."

"So much the better," returned our hero ; "they will fight when I tell them that the crew of the privateer will massacre them all as well as ourselves. Our case is desperate ; we can't outsail them, and they will shew us no mercy. Ram the guns with grape, and I'll run them aboard, instead of their running us."

"Hurrah !" said the crew, "let the niggers up ; they'll fight like devils."

"The hatches were taken off, and the excited negroes,
~~~~~~~~~~~~~~~~~~~~~

alarmed by the firing, scrambled upon deck, just as a shot from the privateer crossed the deck, knocking over some three or four of them, who gave a shout of rage.

Gordon, with some difficulty, got them to listen to him; they soon understood him; the fact of the shot killing two of them and wounding several, was convincing, and in their language they swore that they would kill every man in the "Sans Culotte," if they were put aboard.

In a very short time most of the negroes were armed with pikes, hatchets, knives, bars, in fact, anything that came to hand. Suddenly tacking, the schooner, receiving at the time the privateer's fire, Cuthbert Gordon put the helm up, and the next moment ran right aboard the astonished Frenchman, firing his two heavily loaded guns into his crowded deck.

The vessels became entangled; then the negroes, headed by Gordon and Perkins, and followed by the crew of the "Breeze," leaped on to the deck of the privateer, the negroes uttering the most frightful yells.

Perfectly astounded, the privateer's men fell back before the boarders, and then a most extraordinary and frightful hand-to-hand contest took place. Once they tasted bood, the ferocity of the negroes redoubled, and the crew of the "Breeze" fighting heartily, the crew of the "Sans Culotte" took a panic, just as Cuthbert Gordon cut his way aft and engaged the captain.

"Ah, sacré! pirate!" shouted the privateer's captain. "Take that," and he raised a pistol and fired, but the ball only grazed our hero's forehead, grazing the skin. With a blow of his cutlass he felled the captain to the deck, and before he could prevent it several negroes drove their knives into him, and raising his body pitched it overboard.

"Kill all, kill the murderous whites to a man," was now shouted by the infuriated negroes, who pursued the privateer's men through all parts of the vessel. All that could fled into the schooner, fighting desperately. Some ran up the rigging of the "Breeze." Cuthbert

Gordon now saw that it was all over with them. Eighty or ninety armed blacks thirsted for the blood of all the whites. Two of his men fell slain, the rest fled into the schooner. He himself with Perkins fought desperately. Several negroes fell by the cutlasses, but, frantic with excitement and eager to shed blood, they fought regardless of life, hacking their victims with hatchets and knives. A blow from behind with a hatchet dashed our hero senseless upon the skylight, which was smashed to pieces, letting him fall through to the floor of the cabin, where he lay stunned and perfectly unconscious.

When he recovered his senses, he raised himself up. It was pitch dark. Leaning on his elbow, he wiped the blood from his eyes and face and listened. A faint, very faint light came through the broken skylight, but something had evidently been thrown over it. He heard the flapping of sails, the knocking about of blocks, and the whistling of wind through the rigging, but no sound of a human voice or foot could he hear above.

"This is very extraordinary," thought our hero, making an effort to rise, which he found he could do, as he was only stunned; but a gash at the back of his head still bled, and his face and neck he felt were covered with blood. He suspected that the negroes in their fury had pursued the whites aboard the schooner, and that a sudden squall had separated the two vessels. Returning thanks to Providence for his singular escape, and fully convinced that not a soul remained on board the privateer but himself, he tied his handkerchief round his head to stop the bleeding, and groped amongst the broken furniture of the cabin to try and find the door, which having discovered, he put his foot upon the stairs, and felt a human body, which groping over, he ascertained to be that of a white man. As he pulled it aside, a low moan came from the lips, and then a heavy sigh.

"Poor fellow ! he is alive," thought Cuthbert Gordon, as he stooped and partly lifted and carried the body into the cabin.

He then commenced groping in the lockers and cupboards, and at length got hold of what he found was a tinder box, and hanging over it a large tin candle case.

This was fortunate, for immediately he struck a light and lighted a candle, and as the light fell on the body, he recognised Perkins, the mate. His eyes were open, and in a faint voice he said, " Water." The mate had a great cut across the left cheek from a knife, and his forehead was streaming blood from a gash from a cutlass.

Taking a cushion from one of the lockers, our hero placed it under the mate's head, and was proceeding to look through the cabin for water or wine, when a creaking noise behind him caused him to turn round, and the light of the candle fell upon the pale face of a man protruding through a large sliding panel in the back part of the cabin.

" Who are you ? " asked our hero, in French. " Come out, for you must belong to this vessel."

" Eh ! mon Dieu ! oui," said the head. " Je suis Français."

" What are you ? Where are those black devils ? Where are the crew of this ship ? "

" I am the steward and cook."

" Good," said our hero, " you are the very man I want. Come out. There are no blacks or any of the privateer's crew here. We are English."

" Eh, mon Dieu ! I am glad," said the Frenchman. " Mademoiselle, mademoiselle," cried the steward, looking back into the large bread closet where he had concealed himself. " Don't cry. We are safe. Les Anglais have taken the ship, and killed all those sacré negroes."

Perfectly astonished, our hero approached the immense bread locker into which the little French steward had got, and beheld a female rising up from a mass of biscuit. He raised the light, and as the female looked up she uttered a piercing cry, clasping her hands, and exclaiming :—

" Oh, my God ! is it possible ? Cuthbert Gordon, can it be you indeed ? "

The light fell full upon the pale, terrified face of the

young girl, and with an exclamation of astonishment he drew from the locker the companion of his youth, one whom he loved as a sister, poor Mary Lewellen. Neither could speak from deep emotion, whilst the little Frenchman stared at them both perfectly bewildered.

Placing Mary on the cushioned locker, he desired the Frenchman to get some water or wine at once, and give the wounded man some. The steward ran to do so.

The tears were streaming down Mary Lewellen's cheeks. Whilst looking up into Cuthbert's face she shuddered, saying :—

" Oh, Heavens ! your face and neck are streaming with blood ; alas, the horrors I have undergone. But God be praised ! you have saved me from a terrible doom. But I tremble to think of the fate of those so dear to me."

" I am so bewildered," said Cuthbert Gordon, " that I scarcely know what to say. Compose your mind, dear Mary ; you shall tell me all by-and-bye. I will wash away this blood, and see how fares my poor comrade. Get the steward, who seems a kind creature, to get you anything you may want, whilst I go on deck. Perhaps I may find another of my crew alive."

Mary Lewellen lay back upon the locker pale as death. She saw her early friend proceed on deck, and she called Dubois the Frenchman, and begged him to give her also some water. She felt quite faint. Perfectly bewildered by the strange event of Mary Lewellen being on board a privateer, Gordon, who was wishing to ask a thousand questions, hurried on deck, for the vessel heeled over at times as if pressed by a strong breeze.

The dawn was making as he gained the deck. A gloomy, stormy sky was overhead, and a thick mist lay over the troubled waters. A horrid sight met his gaze, for the deck was strewed with the dead bodies of negroes, Frenchmen, and, to his deep grief, three of his own crew.

The planks were clotted with blood ; the ropes, and blocks, and sheets were flapping wildly about, and the sails one moment filled, and then, as the schooner shot up in the wind, they shook and shivered in the breeze with a loud report. Though clear of fog overhead, he could not see twice the length of the vessel ahead. Finding a bucket, he dipped it overboard, and washed his face and head, feeling better even from that simple remedy. He knew he had several flesh wounds, but not, he thought, serious. As the light increased, he began to examine the dead.

There lay eleven negroes, nineteen Frenchmen, and the three Englishmen, a ghastly sight, for all showed signs of the ferocity of the contest by their frightful wounds; for no sooner were they knocked down, or wounded, than the negroes stabbed them with their knives, or brained them with their handspikes.

Whilst gazing at the blood-stained deck, he was, to his infinite surprise, joined by Perkins, the mate, who came up, unassisted, from the cabin. He was ghastly pale, and disfigured by the gash across his cheek; but otherwise, he had received no severe wound. He had, like our hero, been knocked senseless, and had fallen down the companion stairs, which had saved his life, for had he fallen on the deck they would have killed him.

"We have had a bout of it," observed the mate, plunging his head into a bucket of water. "Those cursed beggars, as I said, when once set on would cut all our throats."

"True," returned Cuthbert Gordon, "so would the privateer's men. I cannot imagine how they all came to leave this vessel; but how do you feel?"

"Oh, I'm all right, Sir. A black villain gave me a knock over with a crow bar, just after I got this slit in my cheek, from the cutlass of one of those pirates of Frenchmen; but, Lord help us, they have killed all our poor fellows; here's three of them," and he looked sadly at the three young men who, the day before, were full of life and vigour.

"We had better try and trim the sails, Sir," continued the mate, "and get the craft to lie to, while we pitch these bodies overboard. Please, Sir, call up the Frenchman, and we shall be able to manage it. I can't go aloft for awhile; so if it does blow, it will only rid us of our topsails."

The Frenchman, Dubois, was called, and with his assistance, though no seaman, they secured the loose ropes and blocks, tightened the sheets, and bracing round the topsails, got the schooner to lie to, and then fastened the tiller. They next opened the ports, and committed the dead to the great deep. Weak from their loss of blood, and recent exertions, our hero and Perkins lay down on the deck quite exhausted, whilst the good-natured Frenchman ran down to his pantry, and brought up some wine and brandy, and a sheet of sticking plaister from the medicine chest. The wine greatly restored them, and pieces of sticking plaister to their cuts stopped the bleeding.

Anxious beyond measure to learn how Miss Lewellen had fallen into so extraordinary a situation, Gordon hurried below, whilst Perkins and Dubois went into the fore cabin to see if any bodies remained there.

Mary Lewellen, though in deep affliction, strove to rouse herself from her painful thoughts, and receive her old and esteemed friend and playmate with affection.

"You are anxious, dear Cuthbert, I know, to ask me many questions, and I have much to say, which, however, in our present strange situation, must be said in few words. I may, however, tell you at once, that your dear mother and sisters were quite well in health a month ago, though fearfully distressed at your mysterious absence. They heard about your being in Lord Dunskelling's mansion, and of your being carried off from there by some unknown persons. Since then they have waited in intense anxiety to hear more tidings of you. Your mother would have gone over to Ireland, but the distracted state of the country prevented her, and they now remain patient and hopeful in the house where you left them."

"Thanks, dear Mary," said Cuthbert Gordon, "for thus relieving my mind. Nearly two years have passed since I was forced from my home, on the night of the shipwreck. I had gone through much, suffered a good

19

deal, but always trusted in the goodness of Providence as a safeguard. But now tell me, Mary, of yourself, of your family, for it appears incredible to me to see you aboard this vessel."

"Alas! Cuthbert, you can scarcely imagine the agony of mind I endure, torn from my beloved parents by the brutal captain of this ship, leaving my beloved father and brother, if not killed, at all events desperately wounded, for I saw them both struck down, and rushed to save their lives, when the privateer captain seized me, swearing I was his prize, and that I should be his wife. Ah! my God, what agony I endured as he forced me on board this vessel. It is now four days ago; I have been from one swoon to another, sick and faint, so that the wretch left me to the care of Dubois, who, when the vessel was taken by the blacks, hid me, and then himself, in the bread locker, hoping to save our lives. Alas! what would have been our fate had the negroes gained possession of the ship?"

"But how, dear Mary, came you and your family on the seas, in this part of the world, and exposed to such dangers?"

"Ah! Cuthbert, it's too long a tale to tell you now. My dear father suffered great reverses of fortune most suddenly, lost immensely by the failure of foreign banks, his large estates in Jamaica becoming almost worthless, from the bad management and heartless conduct of his agents; so that in order to retrieve his fortunes and look after his West India estates, he resolved to proceed to Jamaica and stay there till he set things to rights. My mother would not stay behind, and we all wished to accompany him; for a separation of three or more years distracted us. My father willingly yielded. The 'Queen of the Seas' was accordingly fitted out, freighted, and, with a large sum of money to pay off certain encumbrances, we embarked, taking leave of your dear mother and sisters with feelings of deep regret.

"The 'Queen of the Seas' carried four guns, and we had a crew of eighteen men, and a brave skipper. All went well till ten days ago, when a violent gale carried away our foremast, and before we were to rights, the privateer ran us aboard, scrambling up our sides, uttering horrid threats if we resisted, which our gallant crew did, thinking to beat them off. My dear father, notwithstanding our tears, would join my brother in repelling the enemy; but alas! they were beat back and thrown upon the deck. I saw no more, for I was forced into this craft and left senseless in the cabin."

"Poor dear Mary, you have suffered much, but thank God you are saved, and we must hope the best. Your father and brother may be only slightly hurt; what surprises me is, that having obtained such a valuable prize as the 'Queen of the Seas,' the privateer captain should have abandoned her; for when he attacked the schooner I had command of, there was no ship in company. No doubt the 'Queen of the Seas' has pursued her voyage to Jamaica, your relatives fearfully grieved at your seizure."

"Ah! that thought distracts me," said Mary Lewellen. "If they survive, my father and brother will be frantic at the idea of my being in the power of that horrid cruel man."

"He exists no longer, Mary; I cut him down in the contest, and the negroes, despite my efforts, massacred him, and threw him overboard."

Mary shuddered, saying, "All this appears like a wonderful dream to me; your presence here, and your being in command of the vessel that took the privateer, the presence of the negroes, and then the total disappearance of privateers, negroes, and only yourself and the wounded sailor, appears incredible."

"I will explain all, dear Mary, when we have more time; we are but three aboard, and neither the mate nor myself can do much for a day or two; the wounds we received in the late contest causing much movement painful. I must go now on deck, and if the wind permits, I will steer a course for Jamaica, and perhaps we may fall in with the 'Queen of the Seas.'"

"God grant that we may do so," said Mary, fervently, "What joy if I should be restored to my beloved parents

19—2

and find them safe and well except in heart and mind; there they must suffer."

Returning on deck Cuthbert perceived the mate with a glass, examining some vessels coming towards them in the distant horizon; he could only make out the topsails of the vessels; one he said was a very large ship, the other two much smaller. Our hero took the glass, and after a steady gaze said the large ship was a vessel of war, the other a three-masted ship, and the small one he could scarcely make out, but he thought her a schooner; the man-of-war had only her topsails set; there was a stiff breeze, which would soon bring them into clear view.

"I trust it's not a French vessel of war," said the mate. "It would be too bad to fall into the clutches of Monsieur after all we have gone through."

"It's a British man-of-war," said Cuthbert Gordon, anxiously keeping the glass upon the advancing ships. "Yes, and by Jove, the other ship is the 'Queen of the Seas;' she is under a jury foremast."

"The 'Queen of the Seas,'" repeated Perkins. "What ship is that?"

"A merchant ship, belonging to a dear friend of mine; I commanded her some three years ago, when returning from New South Wales. The young lady in the cabin was seized aboard that ship, in which were her family, by that rascally privateer captain."

In half an hour more the three vessels were distinctly visible; the vessel of war was a frigate under her topsails only, the other vessels were carrying all sail.

"By Jove, there's our schooner, the 'Breeze;' I can make her out quite plain," said our hero to the astonished mate, and handing him the glass. "No doubt the frigate has the two vessels in charge. We are recognised; there goes a gun from the frigate."

The smoke could be seen curling out of the bows as the faint report reached their ears. "In half an hour they will be up with us;" and delighted, and hoping the best, Cuthbert Gordon went below to communicate the joyful intelligence to Mary Lewellen.

Frantic with joy, she sprang to her feet and followed our hero on deck, saying :

"Oh, if my dear parents are alive and well, they will be anxiously watching this vessel, which they must recognise."

The "Sans Culotte" was lying to, and she was left to do so, for the fresh breeze was bringing the vessels up. In half an hour the frigate was within pistol shot. She then shot up in the wind and lay to. As the two other vessels came up, they did so likewise. The frigate and the "Queen of the Seas" both put out boats, which rapidly pulled for the "Sans Culotte."

During these proceedings, Mary Lewellen and our hero remained in a state of intense anxiety, gazing at the approaching boats. As they neared, Mary uttered a cry of joy, clasping her hands, and weeping in excess of joy, for in the boat she recognised her father and brother, who both stood up, waving their hats, and the crew of the boat cheering.

The man-of-war's boat ran up alongside a few minutes before the "Queen's" boat, and a young officer jumped on board the "Sans Culotte ;" he looked up into Cuthbert Gordon's face, and then both young men shook each other heartily by the hand ; though belonging to different ships, they had often met at different ports, and had enjoyed many pleasant hours together.

"Well, by Jove, Gordon, this meeting is a surprise, with a vengeance," said Lieutenant Browne, of the "Narcissus ;" "we heard some account of you from the five survivors of your crew of the schooner 'Breeze ;' still we were by no means certain that the Mr. Gordon mentioned as their captain was the Cuthbert Gordon of the 'Magicienne ;' besides, we expected, if we fell in with the 'Sans Culotte,' to find no one alive in it. Thank goodness you are alive and hearty—though those pieces of sticking-plaister tell tales."

Before our hero could well reply to Lieutenant Browne, his hands were clasped in those of George Lewellen, whilst Mary almost fainted in the arms of her father.

"Oh, Cuthbert," exclaimed George Lewellen, with great

emotion, "with what joy I embrace you; these last five or six days have been periods of intense suffering. Mary restored to us—and another debt of gratitude due to you."

Cuthbert embraced his old and loved companion with a feeling of undisguised satisfaction. The delighted father, after a silent squeeze of the hand, had borne his daughter into the boat, wrapped in a mantle, to take her at once on board the "Queen," to relieve the anxious and highly wrought-up feelings of her mother.

"You must come with me, Gordon," said Lieutenant Browne; "our commander, Captain Leslie, will be most happy to see you, and lend you any assistance; for, by Jove, you are jolly short-handed. Why—one is a Frenchman."

"Yes," returned our hero, "he was cook or steward of this privateer; and to his presence of mind Miss Lewellen owes her life. But, tell me, how did you happen to fall in with the two vessels, and who is left aboard the schooner? for I was knocked senseless through the cabin skylight, and have not the slightest idea how the vessels became separated, after those confounded negroes turned upon us, and endeavoured to murder all the whites."

"I will tell you all I know," said Lieutenant Browne. "We were on the look-out for this privateer, or rather, pirate, having fallen in with two crafts plundered by her, and their crews barbarously knocked about: but we first came up with Captain Elliott in the 'Queen of the Seas,' and heard from him of the rascally and brutal conduct of the captain of the 'Sans Culotte,' and of the carrying off of Miss Lewellen. We are bound to Jamaica ourselves. Yesterday, as the fog cleared, we beheld a schooner lying to, some four miles to windward. We reached her in a short time, and put out a boat. I was in command of the boat, and on approaching the vessel, perceived a dozen or more men in the cross-trees, and a number of drunken negroes reeling about the deck, with arms in their hands, and several others also armed, threatening us if we dared approach. A man on the cross-trees of the fore-mast called out that the negroes had murdered all they could lay hands on; that the fore-cabin was defended by a number of Frenchmen belonging to the 'Sans Culotte,' privateer, and if we had not come up they would no doubt have all been murdered before night. This looked very strange; it was no use my boarding the schooner with four men. So I returned aboard the 'Narcissus,' and told our commander. He ordered out the launch, with twenty armed men, and half-a-dozen marines. So I returned to the schooner, and boarded her; but the negroes fought like infuriated beasts. The men came down from the masts, and those in the fore-cabin rushed on deck, and began cutting down the blacks without mercy. But we soon overpowered the negroes, but not before five of them were killed, and several wounded. We then bound them, and sent them down into the hold. We counted the Frenchmen, and found thirty-seven in all, part of the privateer 'Sans Culotte's' crew, and the five Englishmen belonging to the schooner. The Englishmen told me that the schooner was from the coast of Africa, and her captain, a Mr. Gordon, and the mate, a man named Perkins, were both left dead in the 'Sans Culotte' privateer; that the negroes, infuriated, had pursued the Frenchmen and Englishmen aboard the schooner to a man, during a strong squall of wind, when the two vessels instantly separated.

"The Englishmen did all they could to make the Frenchmen stand; but they were panic-struck. Many were killed and thrown overboard; the rest got into the fore-cabin and barricaded it. The five Englishmen and seven Frenchmen, after a hard struggle, were forced to run up the rigging. Some of the negroes put the schooner before the wind for several hours. They then ransacked the cabin, found some spirits, and got brutally drunk, and left the schooner to drift as she pleased. Fortunately the 'Narcissus' fell in with them the next day. Now, come aboard, Cuthbert, till we hear what Captain Leslie says. You have a famous prize, I can tell you; for the 'Sans Culotte' plundered many ships—some with specie—but she never retained any; in fact, she was more a pirate than a privateer."

Our hero was very kindly received by Captain Leslie, who offered him any assistance he might require, at the same time requesting to know how he came to be in so strange a situation.

Our hero gave a brief narrative of his adventures in Africa, &c., which pleased and surprised Captain Leslie, who congratulated him on his good fortune in getting out of such difficulties, inquiring how he intended to act.

Cuthbert Gordon said if he had his own men back he would run the "Sans Culotte" to Jamaica, in company with the "Queen of the Seas;" and if Captain Leslie would put a few hands into the schooner, she could be taken to Jamaica also, and her owners communicated with.

"Well, as we are bound to Jamaica ourselves," said Captain Leslie, "it's the best plan that can be adopted."

After some further conversation, and many kind offers from the "Narcissus'" officers, Cuthbert Gordon was put aboard the "Queen of the Seas," where he spent an hour with his dear old friends, and the now happy Mary Lewellen. By sunset all the vessels were under weigh, with a favourable breeze, for the West Indies.

CHAPTER XXIX.

Escorted by the frigate "Narcissus," the three vessels reached Port Royal, in Jamaica, without further mishap or adventure.

George Lewellen had accompanied our hero aboard the "Sans Culotte," and remained with him during the remainder of the voyage. He hoped that a year or two's residence in Jamaica would retrieve his father's affairs, who intended disposing of all his West India property, and then return to England. Two months spent in Jamaica passed very pleasantly in the country residence Mr. Lewellen had selected for his family. But our hero had a restless desire to return to England; Dora Dunskelling was ever present in his thoughts. Not for a moment did he ever forget her; her sweet, youthful face, haunted his sleeping and waking hours.

Having settled all affairs relative to the privateer and the slave schooner, and taken a most affectionate leave of the Lewellen family, and received a bundle of letters from Mary and George Lewellen for Amy and his mother, with many little tokens of affection, he sailed for Liverpool in the "Queen of the Seas," Perkins taking the berth of first mate, then vacant. The five other Englishmen also embarked in her to return to England, considerably enriched by their share of the prize. Owing to the capture of the "Sans Culotte," Mr. Lewellen recovered all the specie plundered from the "Queen of the Seas."

After a fortunate run of thirty-four days, the "Queen of the Seas" anchored in the port of Liverpool, and taking an affectionate leave of the captain and his old crew, who wished him every success and happiness in his future career, he set foot once more upon British soil, after a life of adventure and peril for two long years.

The first object nearest our hero's heart was to see his dear mother and sisters. Having provided himself with some changes of attire, he, one fine morning, at the latter end of April, took his seat on the coach-box of the "Umpire" stage coach for Shrewsbury. In those days of no steam and slow coaches, travellers had, at all events, the advantage of seeing and appreciating the beauties of the country they passed through, and ran the chance of an upset without bestowing much, if any, thought upon such an event.

At all events, they were not reminded of it so forcibly as we are now, by seeing in every station, "Accidental Death Insurance" staring us in the face when we take a ticket by rail. For our part, we always take a ticket, for two reasons; that the sum insured may benefit our heirs, and to punish the company for not taking better care of our lives.

On entering the "Golden Lion" court-yard, Shrewsbury, Gordon perceived a handsome travelling chariot, with a coronet on the panel, and two domestics, in a livery he thought he remembered, packing several articles in it. As the coach went no further than Shrewsbury, he had to stay there that night, and proceed the following morning by another coach to Newport.

Walking up to the carriage, he started as he recognised the Dunskelling coat of arms. Addressing one of the domestics, he inquired if Lord Dunskelling was then in the "Golden Lion" hotel.

"Yes, Sir," said the domestic addressed. "He is. Are you acquainted with his lordship?"

"Not personally," returned our hero, "but I know Dunskelling Castle well. I was there for some time two years ago, and——"

"Ah," said the man, interrupting him; "perhaps, Sir, you are not aware that the old lord has been dead some eighteen months."

"Dead!" repeated our hero, with a start, and a slight

change of colour. "Good Heavens! I regret to hear this intelligence. Pray excuse me. Who—"

"James! James! you're wanted," exclaimed the other domestic, from the house door. "Be quick, and bring the desk."

The valet turned round and took a desk in a leather case from the seat of the carriage, saying, "Beg your pardon, Sir, can't stop; his lordship's very impatient;" and walked away.

Our friend stood for some moments plunged in deep thought. The old lord was dead, and the title in possession of a claimant—who could that claimant be but Fitzpatrick? He remembered O'Dowd telling him that his (Cuthbert Gordon's) right to the title and estates of Dunskelling was undoubted, and that Fitzpatrick had no claim to either whilst he lived. Where was Dora? What had become of her? A thousand thoughts and ideas floated through his brain in a moment. He had often conjectured that Fitzpatrick was the instigator of his abduction, and had planned the sending him to Africa, to put him out of the way. Still he had no positive proof of his guilt, and yet no one else could have a motive for such an act.

As he returned to the hotel he resolved in his own mind to request an interview with Lord Dunskelling, and see if in reality Fitzpatrick held the title. Besides, he felt anxious to learn how and where Dora was. As he crossed the hall, and passed the foot of the principal staircase, a gentleman was coming down the stairs with a hat on his head and a walking cane in his hand. Cuthbert Gordon stopped and looked up, and beheld Lord Dunskelling, who turned deadly pale and grasped the banister, uttering the words, "Good God! Cuthbert Gordon!" and then remained, as if rooted to the stairs.

"I see you recognise me, Mr. Fitzpatrick," said our hero, quite calmly. "It is now more than two years since we met. I presume you are the person considered here as Lord Dunskelling." There were two or three waiters passing, and one or two strangers, travellers, loitering about the hall, who paused, and looked round, hearing Cuthbert Gordon's words, staring at the two young men with great curiosity.

Lord Dunskelling, as we must still call Fitzpatrick, by a great effort recovered himself, and shaking off his stupor said :—

"I am glad to see you, Mr. Gordon, though your very sudden appearance surprised me. Pray accompany me to my private room. I wish, if it is convenient to you, that you would favour me with a private interview."

"Certainly," returned our hero, following his lordship, who threw open a door, and both entered a spacious and well-furnished drawing-room.

Lord Dunskelling, though the walk to his private room occupied scarcely two minutes, completely recovered his usual nonchalant manner, and placing a chair for our hero he threw himself on the sofa. Casting his hat beside him, and looking up with an easy air of assurance, he said :—

"You, really, Mr. Gordon, came upon me like a ghost. Why, your sudden appearance was equal to your strange disappearance. Where have you been? and where have you dropped from?"

"Where I have been, Mr. Fitzpatrick; I cannot call you by a title to which you have no claim." Our hero spoke firmly, and he could see his companion change colour a little.

"Oh, my dear friend," interrupted his lordship, with a gay laugh, "there's nothing in a name—call me what you please; the law will, by-and-bye, decide upon both our titles, now that you have made your appearance. When you were not to be found in England or Ireland, and no other claimant appearing, of course, I assumed the title, and took the estates of Dunskelling; not that I think, mind you, that your claims are stronger than mine. However, this is an after question. At present I am recognised as Lord Dunskelling by the law of the land. When you prove I am not, well and good. But how is it that you have remained two years absent?"

"Mr. Fitzpatrick," said Cuthbert Gordon, sternly, "at present let us leave the question of right to the title and estates of the late Lord Dunskelling. I now ask you :— Did you, directly, or indirectly, cause me to be carried off by a party of sailors, and taken on board a vessel bound for the coast of Africa?"

"If you asked that question of your friend, Herbert O'Dowd, he might be able to give you a direct answer. What his motives were at one time in deceiving you, and afterwards having you carried out of the country, I really cannot say. But you accuse me wrongfully, when you imagine I caused you to be seized."

Gordon had his eyes fixed steadily on Lord Dunskelling's face, and in his heart he said, "That man lies ;" though his lordship looked the picture of innocence.

"Then you positively deny having had any hand in my unjustifiable seizure ?"

"Most emphatically. When you find Mr. Herbert O'Dowd, you will learn the truth."

"And where is Mr. O'Dowd to be found ?" demanded our hero, perfectly satisfied in his own mind that his lordship was deceiving him.

"Ah, that would be quite impossible to say. The rebellion in Ireland has turned the country upside down; thousands have fled. Whether Mr. O'Dowd, who was inclined to the rebel party, might, or might not have joined in the insurrection, I cannot say. Its failure— for it was a failure—forced him, no doubt, to fly into other countries, in search of the false goddess—Liberty. I should be very sorry that he should turn up anywhere in Ireland, as he would be sure to be hung, and as he is a blood connection of ours, that would be unpleasant."

"One question more, Sir, and I have done," interrupted Gordon, sternly. "Where is the only daughter of the late Lord Dunskelling ?"

"Oh, I can answer that to your perfect satisfaction," replied Lord Dunskelling, with a look of intense malice settling on his features. "I am her guardian, and have placed her in a situation where she is most happy; and only that I was robbed, yesterday, on my way home, by a most notorious highwayman, of my pocket-book, and other valuables, I could have shown you several of her letters, expressing her happiness in looking forward to our intended union—for the dear girl has promised me her fair hand—with hope of much future happiness."

Not a muscle of Cuthbert Gordon's stern features betrayed the slightest emotion. He rose from his chair, hearing a footstep in the lobby, and then a hand on the handle of the door.

"I am satisfied, Mr. Fitzpatrick," he said, in a calm, clear voice, as the door opened; "and I leave you, convinced, in my own mind, that you are not only an impostor, but a most consummate scoundrel and liar."

His lordship's valet, who stood at the doorway, remained rooted to the spot with amazement.

Lord Dunskelling, pale with concentrated rage, at being thus addressed before his servant, starting from his chair, sprung towards our hero, with his clenched hand up-raised. One look at the calm, contemptuous expression of his opponent's features, and a glance at his powerful figure, caused his lordship to pause.

"You shall pay with your life for this insult," burst from Lord Dunskelling's lips. "I shall call you to an account for these words, you—you," he paused, for the flash from our hero's eyes betokened a storm.

"Where and how you please, Mr. Fitzpatrick," replied Gordon, taking up his hat. "Now, or to-morrow morning, if it suits you."

"My lord," said the valet, bewildered, and almost stupefied. "The horses are to—"

"Curse both you and the horses," almost shouted the infuriated lord, and shaking his clenched hand at our hero, he replied, "Yes, you shall hear from me."

"I trust," returned Cuthbert Gordon, with a mocking smile, "that it will not be in the same manner as I last heard from you; but depend on it, you will hear from me," and passing the terrified valet, he descended the stairs, and entered the coffee room of the hotel. Five minutes afterwards a chariot and four, with Lord

Dunskelling inside, drove from the hotel door at a rapid pace.

Ringing for the waiter, Cuthbert Gordon requested to have a private room, to which he at once retired, leaving himself and the words he had uttered in the hall, and which were heard by some of the guests at the hotel, to be canvassed and talked over.

"Waiter, what time did the gentleman who has just left in the chariot and four arrive here, and from where?" he enquired.

"You mean Lord Dunskelling, Sir. He arrived here about four o'clock, and ordered horses for Holyhead in a couple of hours; he was attacked and robbed, Sir, on the road by the notorious——, but his lordship said, and so did his servants, that he had either severely or mortally wounded one of the highwaymen."

"For Holyhead," repeated Cuthbert Gordon; "thank you; now let me have some dinner and a bottle of sherry."

"Directly, Sir," returned the waiter, with a sweep of his napkin across the table. "Wish anything particular, Sir?"

"No, anything at hand, and soon ready," returned our hero, and then he relapsed into a deep reverie, thinking over all the words that had passed between him and Lord Dunskelling. He had certainly used strong language; but there was no doubt in his own mind that Fitzpatrick was the author of the wrong he endured; and he considered his naming Herbert O'Dowd as the instigator of his abduction a mean and lying subterfuge.

As to his assertion that Dora Dunskelling was happy under his guardianship, or had consented to an union with him, he scouted the assertion with scorn; but nevertheless, he resolved not to lose a moment after seeing his mother and sisters, in setting out for Ireland, and never to rest till he found out Dora, and learned from her own lips, her wishes and determination respecting her selected domicile; and also secure to her her rights, as the only daughter of the late Lord Dunskelling.

The next morning at six o'clock our hero left

Shrewsbury on the top of the stage coach the "Grass-hopper," a heavy lumbering conveyance, carrying six inside and ten outside passengers, besides the coachman. It was slow travelling indeed in those days, especially through Wales.

The "Grasshopper," to look at her laden with luggage and top-heavy with twelve outsiders, looked a most unlikely vehicle to traverse the cross roads from Shrews-bury to Newport.

Our hero had booked himself for an inside place, as it rained smartly during the night, and looked by no means pleasant in the early morning; but as he stood at the door of the inn, he beheld a fat old lady with a red handkerchief tied over her bonnet, a bandbox under her left arm, and a fat asthmatic spaniel under her right, get into the coach, followed by a remarkably stout old gentle-man, and then two females, each with a baby, and finally an overgrown schoolboy, with sundry articles in his arms; he abandoued the hold, as Jack would have called it, and took to the deck, offering a neat tidy Welsh girl, who wore a new glossy hat of a most formidable height and breadth of brim, his seat inside ; which apparently kind offer being gladly accepted, as she thought it would be sure to rain, he mounted on the outside. The coach proceeded at what the coachman facetiously termed six miles an hour; but as a countryman with a bundle on his back kept up with it walking for an hour, the six miles might be reduced to four, although when a descent occurred the speed reached five.

Having spent nearly an hour at breakfast, and another at dinner, besides sundry stoppages for sundry glasses of beer, the coach arrived about four o'clock at the foot of a long hill, where four roads met. In those days passengers generally walked up hill; so the coachman pulled up, and requested his "outsides and insides " to alight, as he carried a very heavy load, and his horses were blown—two hours more would bring them to Newport. Being nearly stifled inside, the passengers all got out, the old maid and her dog included. "It was time," she said, "for the poor dear to have a run," though to look at him, panting and puffing, no one could possibly suppose he had a run in him.

As the coach proceeded slowly up the hill, the stout coachman encouraging his cattle with all kinds of ejaculations, aided by a smart touch of whipcord over the flanks, the passengers followed straggling from one side to the other. Suddenly there emerged out from one of the cross roads two singularly well-mounted horsemen, in slouched beavers, and high boots, with thick belcher handkerchiefs tied round their necks ; they were powerful looking men, with red, sun-burnt, jovial-looking faces. Pulling a pistol each from their holsters, they barred the passage of all the travellers, the female portion of whom uttered sundry shrieks, whilst most of the males looked stupefied and confounded.

" Don't be alarmed, ladies, don't be alarmed," said one of the horsemen, very politely. " We won't hurt you, but merely relieve you of any trifle of cash you may have about you."

" Och, be gor," said an Irish drover, one of the outsides, " you're mighty welcome to the half-crown left me to pay my expenses ; if you had only waited till to-morrow, I'd have had twenty pounds to give you for a drove of pigs I sold in Newport."

As he spoke he kept advancing with the half-crown in his hand ; he was a very strong-looking man, with a truly good-humoured face, and a head of bushy, curly, carroty hair.

The other highwayman was urging his horse up to where our hero stood amused at the scene, amongst the frightened passengers.

Suddenly the Irish drover seized the highwayman by the leg, and with a sudden jerk threw him over his horse heavily to the ground. With an oath his comrade raised his pistol, and would doubtless have shot the pig drover, had not Gordon sprung up behind him, and pinioned his arms.

" Hurrah ! my darling, you're in a rat trap," said the drover, looking at the pinioned robber, as he grasped the fallen man by the throat, and calling to his fellow tra-

20

vellers, if they had the pluck of a calf, to help him to bind the one he held.

The moment the highwayman felt his arms pinioned, and by a grasp of iron, he dug his spurs into the side of the high-spirited horse he rode, and away he dashed, scattering the terrified travellers, killing the asthmatic spaniel, and causing its mistress to fall back, with a fearful shriek, into a deep, muddy ditch she was standing beside.

"Let go my arms, curse you," roared the highway-man, savagely, turning his head to look at his anta-gonist.

"Drop your pistol," replied our hero, coolly. The man obeyed, and then slackening his hold, our hero slid unhurt from the horse, for he had no wish to detain the man, as his own journey might be delayed. The horse continued his pace. Picking up the pistol, which was primed and loaded, our hero began hastily to retrace his steps; finding he was nearly a mile from the place he had started from. He had above a hundred pounds in notes in his pocket, and a rather valuable gold watch. To have given them up without a struggle he had no intention. He, therefore, began his walk back rather pleased; but after a few hundred yards he heard the sound of horses' feet, and looking back he perceived the highwayman returning, having mastered his horse.

"Humph!" muttered Cuthbert Gordon; "I hope I shall not be obliged to shoot this rascal." The robber, with a shout of rage, with his other pistol in his hand, urged his horse at him. Gordon was standing by a gate leading into a field, over which he vaulted. The man threw himself off his horse, and approached the gate, swearing savagely.

"Take care what you are about," said Gordon, coolly advancing; "if you put a foot on that gate, I shall be forced to blow your brains out."

"Then take that, curse you," and the robber fired his pistol within six paces of our hero, knocking his hat off.

"Not a bad shot," returned Cuthbert, approaching the gate, "I'm afraid I must shoot you." The man lost courage, and turned to regain his horse ; but as he turned, he felt himself in the grasp of a man who had sprung out from the hedge.

" Don't fire, Sir," shouted the drover, for he it was. "Be my sowl I have the beauty fast enough. Be easy, you bog-trotter, or I'll shake you out of your ugly skin ;" and true enough, he gave him a most uncomfortable shake. The highwayman ceased to struggle, as our hero, after picking up his hat, joined him.

" Be gor, he's knocked a hole in your honour's hat," exclaimed the drover.

"I wish you had it in your carroty poll," growled the robber. "What will you get by taking me to jail, eh ? "

"Faix, a deal of trouble," said the drover ; " I've saved my sixty gould guineas anyhow, my beauty."

"I'll give you twenty to let me go, and a gold watch to boot—where's my comrade ? "

" Faix, tied hand and foot, and on his way, on the top of the coach, to Newport jail."

" Let us move on," said Cuthbert to the drover, " for I suppose we shall have to walk to Newport."

"Be dad, catch the horse, your honour, and ride." This our hero did after a little trouble, and mounting, they moved on.

" You're a real beauty," said the drover to the discomfited highwayman ; " faix, you wanted to make us receivers of stolen goods. It's better you did'nt shoot this chap, Sir, because I don't think it's pleasant to have a man's blood upon one's hands."

" You are quite right, my good man," observed Gordon, just then thinking that, although he had saved his money, he was very likely to get into a deal of trouble, if bound over to prosecute.

"What is your name, friend? " questioned our hero of the drover. "I perceive we are countrymen ; from what part of Ireland do you come ? "

" Faix, I thought somehow," said the drover, quite

pleased, " that your honour had something to say to the
ould country; and be dad, when I seed you this morning,
says I, 'Dorgan Rafferty,' that's my name Sir, says I ; 'I
have surely seen that gentleman's face afore.' "

"Harkee, gentlemen," said the highwayman, requesting Dorgan Rafferty to pause—"by——I can't
stand walking in this great coat. Let me take it off,
and throw it over the horse."

"Be dad you're welcome ; it is a heavy one ; " and
Dorgan slacked his hold of the skirt.

The man took it off, and in the act he twisted it round
Dorgan's head, and then bolted, clearing the hedge as
nimbly as a highland deer. Gordon laughed; he raised
his pistol, but dropped his aim, and called out to the
enraged Irishman, who was starting in pursuit, to let
him go. "This warning may do him service—he may
mend his ways. It will do us no good to hang the
rascal, though I own we are not doing right to the community at large, in letting loose a robber."

" Well, faix, I'm glad he's gone, anyhow ; he was a
cute chap ; but he has left something behind him in this
coat."

It had become dusk ; and Dorgan Rafferty could only
perceive that the article ho pulled out of the breast
pocket of the highwayman's coat was a handsome silver-
mounted pocket-book, containing a number of things.
He put it back in the pocket, and trudged after our hero
on the horse.

"Well, Rafferty," observed Gordon, "you have not
told me where you came from. You think you have
seen me before, and, curious enough, when you got up on
the coach, I thought to myself, I have seen that face
somewhere."

"Faix, it's droll, your honour ; was your honour ever
at a place in ould Ireland called Dunskelling ? "

"Ah ! I thought so," said Cuthbert Gordon, with a
start. "Yes, I was residing or staying at Dunskelling
some years ago."

"Oh, by the immortal powers, I have it," cried the
drover; "faix, you're the gentleman as was drowned

out of Mr. O'Dowd's yacht; long life to yer. It's myself is pleased to see your honour. Lord save us; I remember all about it, and how our blessed young mistress was like one distracted, and how I myself and four others hunted the country round for hours. The Lord be good to us, your honour, Dunskelling is in strange hands now, and our dear, beautiful mistress, the blessed saints be glorified—but no one knows where she is. But where have you been, your honour? and who was it took you away to sea?"

"It's a long story, Rafferty, and won't do to tell now. Yonder are the lights of Newport; where does the coach stop?"

"At the 'Castle' hotel, your honour."

"Well," observed Cuthbert Gordon, after a moment's reflection, "I am very anxious to reach home without any delay. If I go to the 'Castle' I may be detained about this affair. Now you take this horse, and pistol, and coat, and deliver them up. If I am wanting, you know that my name is Gordon. Here is a very good inn." They were then in the town, and opposite was an inn called the "Blue Boar." "I will stop here; I have only a small portmanteau. Give this half-crown to the coachman. So if I am required, you know where to find me; and as soon as you can conveniently finish your business, come to me, I have much to ask you about, and many things to say."

"Long life to your honour," said the honest drover; "I will be sure to be with you, for by St. Patrick, if you're the son of Gorman Gordon, of Rothcrea, you're the real lord of Dunskelling."

"Don't speak so loud, my good friend; do not forget to come."

"Never fear Dorgan Rafferty, your honour; he or his would die any day for the Gordons of Rothcrea;" so, taking the horse by the bridle, he passed on across the square, whilst Cuthbert Gordon entered the "Blue Boar."

CHAPTER XXX.

CUTHBERT GORDON entered the inn, and was shown into a neat well-furnished parlour by the landlady herself, and shortly after was partaking of his tea and some broiled sewin. He was in a very thoughtful mood; the meeting with Dorgan Rafferty had awakened many recollections. He remembered that he sometimes had visited the neighbouring small farmers in the vicinity of Dunskelling ; and amongst them the widow Rafferty's well-managed tidy farm, and how fond she was of Dora, and never neglected asking after her son, who frequently went to Wales from Waterford with cattle, to sell. And now that he had so strangely met Dorgan, he longed to see him again, and to learn from him all that he knew of Dora and of Dunskelling, during the past two most eventful years for Ireland. He was within a day's journey of his own home. In twenty-four hours he might expect to embrace the tenderest of mothers and the most loving of sisters.

It was a very beautiful, clear, moonlight night ; and having finished his tea, Cuthbert Gordon took up his hat to go for a stroll through the town, telling the landlady if any one came and inquired for him, to detain the person till he returned.

Newport, sixty years ago, had very little to recommend it in a commercial point of view. The country surrounding it was pretty ; a few small colliers lay upon the immense banks of mud which lined each side of the river Usk, on its passage to the sea. Now it is one of the most, if not the most important town in South Wales, for its shipping, coal, and iron trade. Large steamers now navigate the waters of the Usk, and its population is trebled. Crossing the square he perceived a considerable crowd surrounding the door of the " Castle " inn, all discoursing vehemently, and listening—Gordon had not forgotten his knowledge of Welsh—he found all conversing about the attempt to rob the Shrewsbury coach, and the escape of both highwaymen.

"Humph! so the other rascal has got away also," thought our hero to himself. " Well, perhaps it's as well, though society may be the suffering party in the end." He did not like to ask questions; so, returning to his inn, he found Dorgan waiting for him with his valise.

Ordering up some whiskey and hot water into the little parlour, he made the honest drover sit down and help himself to his native liquor.

" Well, Rafferty, the other fellow has got off; how did he manage it ? "

" Faith, your honour, quite easy. The omadawns put him into a room in the hotel and untied his hands, locking the door, and then sending for two constables to take him to jail ; but it seems they never heeded the window, so the rascal just walked out on to the top of a shed, and into the yard, and, finding a traveller's horse hooked by the bridle to a ring in the wall, whilst its owner and the ostlers were gossiping and drinking beer at the tap, he quietly mounted, and rode off."

Our hero laughed. " Did you give up the horse and coat ? "

"Yes, Sir," said Dorgan, with a peculiarly sly look, " I gave up the horse, the coat, and the pistol, to the magistrate's clerk—but, faix, I kept the pocket-book."

"And why not the pocket-book, Dorgan ? Nothing ought to be retained."

" Faix, Mr. Gordon, when you knows why I kept the book and its contents, you'd say, may be, I was right. The pocket-book belongs to a gentleman calling himself Lord Dunskelling, and calls himself my landlord—but faix I don't."

" Lord Dunskelling ! " repeated our hero. " I recollect I saw him in Shrewsbury, and he told me he had been robbed of a pocket-book. Did you not see him when in Shrewsbury ? "

"No, Sir, I did not; I only came in from Chester late in the night, and you know I left next morning by the 'Grasshopper.' Where was he going, Sir?"

"To Ireland, no doubt; he was posting to Holyhead."

"But how did your honour come to be acquainted with him? I beg your pardon, Sir, for being so bould, but indeed myself and all my family and kin was always faithful followers of the Gordons of Rothcrea, and my grandfather often said to us—my mother and myself—that if a son of Gorman Rothcrea lived, he'd be the right lord of Dunskelling, and not the late lord. As to Mr. Fitzpatrick having any right to it, it's all balderdash. Only the ould country is in the state it is, he'd never have got the title, and made away with our young lady."

"What do you mean?" said our hero, startled, "made away with Lady Dora Dunskelling! how, and in what manner?"

"Why, you see, Sir, some twelve or fourteen months ago, she suddenly disappeared one night from Dunskelling, and it was given out that she had run away with a gentleman of the name of Maxwell, who was some time before on a visit at Dunskelling. Faix, no one believed this story, and there was a great stir made; Miss Mac-Cormack, the governess, next went off, and from that day to this Lady Dora has not been heard of. But, by gor, I have found his pretended lordship out," continued Dorgan, triumphantly, and he held up the pocket-book; "here in this little case are letters that will tell your honour all about where Lady Dora is, and they'll show what a villain his would-be lordship is."

Our hero was amazed at Dorgan's account of his cousin's disappearance or elopement with this person named Maxwell. To such a story he certainly gave no credit, but it proved to him that Lord Dunskelling would not scruple to blacken even the fair name of Dora Dun-skelling, so that he accomplished his aim. High-minded and honourable, if his own life depended on the in-spection of the pocket-book, he would have scorned the temptation. But here was a young girl dearer to him than life, at the mercy of a heartless villain. By reading the contents of the letters in the pocket-book he might save her. He no longer hesitated.

"Let me see the letters, Dorgan; she must be saved, even at the expense of my honour"

"Be St. Peter, your honour, I'd have no scruples with such a villain," replied the drover, producing the pocket-book, which was evidently a costly article, with a thick silver-plated back. There were some papers and a memoranda in the several pockets, but Dorgan, it seems, had discovered the secret of the book, for the thick-plated cover was hollow, and, by touching a particular small silver knob, the recess became visible.

"Faix, Sir, it was a mere chance my discovering the spring. Within the recess were four Bank of England notes for £50 each."

"Ah! those must in some way or other be returned to him," said our hero.

"Be gor, he has no right to them at all, at all," said Dorgan. "They belong to the right lord; but here's three letters; I only read this one," and he handed it to Cuthbert Gordon, who hastily and eagerly opened it, and read as follows :—

"Galway,
"Convent of Ursulines,
"March 24th, —

"MY DEAR NEPHEW,

"You are unjust. You accuse me of want of tact and judgment—but I think not justly. I have tried every means in my power, used even great severity, but nothing shakes Dora Dunskelling's faith, or lessens, I regret to say, her hatred of you. She has a spirit and a mind beyond her years; for the last month she has endured many privations, too many, and I will go no further, for her health, hitherto good, fails—"

Gordon paused, an angry flush came over his cheek and temples.

"Faix, they are a pretty set," put in Dorgan, who anxiously watched Cuthbert Gordon's features. "They wanted to make a Papist of our young mistress—though, glory be to the saints, I'm a holy Roman myself, it's no reason that Lady Dora should be made one against her will."

Our hero continued reading without remark.

"Thus, finding her health begin to suffer, and her heart corrupt and insensible to the truths of our holy faith, I have relaxed from my efforts. I told her, though she scorned our faith (this she denies—she scorns no faith, but she is stedfast in her own), she nevertheless was destined to become your wife. You should have seen the look of scorn that sat upon her proud, pale features. 'Sooner,' said she, ' than become the wife of Gorman Fitzpatrick, I would pass the rest of my life in this hated asylum, exposed to the cruel and perfidious schemes to subvert my religion, which have only rendered me more stedfast in the pure, unpersecuting faith, of the Protestant religion.'

"These are her own words. You may judge of her character, and the obstinacy of her disposition ; blind to the welfare of her soul, she persists in her heretical opinions and creed with all the blindness and infatuation of her sect. I will go no further. As her guardian, you placed her under my care, to instruct her in the pure faith of her ancestors, and fit her to become the wife of a Catholic gentleman. You must therefore remove her, for I find myself placed in a very painful situation. I cannot and will not outstep the law of the land.

"You know I am devoted to your interests ; but as Superior of this convent, I cannot risk its reputation ; but I have a proposal to make to you when you arrive, which I cannot venture to put on paper, so make no delay in coming here.

"Adieu, my dear Nephew.

"May the saints guide and assist you.

"Anne Madeleine Fitzpatrick."

"What detestable treachery and villany is here disclosed," said Cuthbert Gordon, excited and flushed with anger and pity. "Poor Dora ! " he mentally exclaimed, "what you must have endured! but, please God, I shall be in time to save you."

"Faix, your honour, you're not angry with me now, for opening the pocket-book?"

"No, Dorgan; as it has turned out the act is justifiable. Had you not done so, my relative would be left totally unprotected from the schemes of a traitorous villain. No time must be lost; he has the start of me by a couple of days. But earnestness and determination will do much; I must reach Galway as soon as possible; I shall only stay a single night with my family, and then proceed to Ireland."

"But, Sir, won't the Abbess of the convent in Galway be prosecuted for imprisoning our young mistress, and treating her so cruelly? It ain't clear to me that she has not some scheme in her head to make away with her."

"No, Dorgan, I do not think so badly of her as that; I know that to gain a proselyte to the Roman Catholic faith and enrich their convents is considered praiseworthy, and though the means employed to further their views may be regarded as detestable by those of the Protestant faith, it is differently viewed by the Roman Catholics themselves."

"Faix, I'm a holy Roman meself," said Dorgan, "and I don't think it's fair play, and I know our worthy priest at Dunskelling does not think so either. Faix, those convents are queer places; be gor, it's a shame to be shutting up fine young women, and making nuns of them. Be dad, if all the women were to be shut up in that way, we'd have a bad time of it."

"Well, I agree with you entirely, Dorgan," returned Cuthbert Gordon, with a smile. "Now, how are you situated? what are you going to do?"

"Well, Sir, I have business here for two or three days; I then crosses over to Waterford in a Dungarvon sloop that is loading with coal, and will then go on to my little farm at Dunskelling; but I'm ready at any moment to do your honour's bidding."

"Well, then, take this pocket-book."

"You didn't read the other letter, your honour," interrupted Dorgan. "Faix, it's in a manner as particular as the other, and shows how Lady Dora was treated by those she thought were her friends."

Cuthbert Gordon took the letter from the book; it was addressed to "Lord Dunskelling, Club House, London," and had the Dublin and London post mark. Opening it, he looked first at the signature.

"Ah !" said he, "from Julia MacCormack." He read aloud :—

"Dublin,
"Dawson Street, March 26th —

"My Dear Gorman,

"You forget how time flies ; you are leading a life of dissipation and pleasure, and you don't know at what moment title and fortune may be torn from you. Already enquiries are making in this city by certain solicitors about the only daughter of the late Lord Dunskelling.

"Yesterday, I saw MacMahon, your attorney; he said he had heard that there were steps taking to dispute your right to the estates.

"That there was a Mrs. Gordon in Dublin" (our hero started), "who was taking active measures to discover what had become of Lady Dora Dunskelling. If you intend to secure that one hundred thousand pounds, MacMahon says you must come to Dublin at once; I have no time for more.

"Ever yours devotedly,
Julia MacCormack."

"Good Heavens ! this is important, Dorgan. The Mrs. Gordon mentioned here must be my mother ; at all events it's very clear that this Miss MacCormack has all along been playing a deep game, and that she is a tool of Fitzpatrick, who, no doubt intends, if his title is disputed, to make off with this hundred thousand pounds."

"Ungrateful hussy, be dad she is," said Dorgan, "and our young mistress so attached to her."

"Well, now I see my way clearly," said Cuthbert Gordon. "I will, please God, be in Dublin in three days, and in Galway in five. I shall pass through Pembray, for fear my mother may not be the Mrs. Gordon mentioned, and then hurry on across North Wales to Holyhead. There is the pocket-book, put the letters and bank notes back, and keep them. When you get to Dunskelling, go up to the Castle, and give them into the owner's hands ; if he is not there, keep them till he is ; at all events, I shall see you before long."

"Yes; and please God, I shall have the pleasure then of seeing the real Lord Dunskelling, for Mr. Fitzpatrick has no right while you live."

"Possession is nine points of the law, Dorgan. If I have rights I will fight for them, and trust to the law ; but my heart is set upon first freeing Dora Dunskelling from her cruel persecutors."

"The blessed saints help and assist your honour," said Dorgan, fervently.

After some further conversation upon less important subjects, Dorgan Rafferty finished his whiskey, shook our hero heartily by the hand, and departed to his inn.

The night passed with Cuthbert Gordon without much sleep. The situation of his loved cousin tormented his mind ; he dreaded he knew not what, from the machinations of Lord Dunskelling. If the Mrs. Gordon mentioned in the letter was his mother, he would not delay beyond a few hours in Pembray.

A two-horse coach took him to the then little retired fishing village of Swansea, now a populous, flourishing town with railways, and copper works, and a magnificent new dock, in which ships of one thousand five hundred tons may remain always afloat.

Not liking the delay of five hours for the night mail, and knowing he would have to return by Swansea, he left his portmanteau at the inn, and started on foot to walk the sixteen miles to Pembray. A more dreary or uninteresting country scarcely exists in South Wales than from Swansea to Llanelly, over barren hills, with scanty herbage and few trees. It improves, however, on nearing Llauelly.

Many a day, many an hour, he and his twin sisters, with Mary Lewellen and her brother, had climbed to the spot on which he walked, to obtain the unrivalled view for extent and variety out-stretched before them. It was a favourite walk of theirs, and many a memory of the past stole over his mind as he gazed down upon the scene. There lay Pembray and the burrows. He could distinguish the very spot where, little more than two years before, he had fallen into the hands of the smugglers, an event, which introduced him to personages who had in those two years altered the destiny of his life. Had he not gone down that night to the wreck, he would, perhaps, have fallen in the defence of his country's flag, for undoubtedly he would have received his lieutenant's commission and gone to sea at once, and more than that, probably he would never have seen the sweet, lovely face, of Dora Dunskelling.

"Strange," thought our hero, "by what a slender thread our destinies are held." He could see the cottage, once his happy home ; and a mile from it, amidst a thick grove of trees, was Mr. Lewellen's house. What memories were associated with these two houses. He must pass Mr. Lewellen's house to reach his old home. Descending the hill with a quick step, he very shortly after reached the lodge gate. What a change ! The house was shut up ; the fine gravel sweep to the hall door was green with grass and weeds. The beautiful parasite plants that rendered the lodge a picture, were hanging, uncared for, in wild luxuriance. Three small children were playing before the door. He called to them, though they were strangers to him; but they turned round, stared at him, and ran into the lodge. A strange female came out and spoke to him in Welsh. He merely asked her if there was a family living in Rose Cottage, close by.

"No, Sir," said the woman, in very bad English, "they be gone from there."

"Thank you," returned our hero, and he passed on.

He was depressed, and yet he experienced no alarm concerning his mother or sisters, for he felt convinced it was his mother who was mentioned in the letter to Lord Dunskelling. But it was sad to see the evidence of misfortune, especially upon those he loved—Lewellen House, no doubt, was in other hands.

He passed on—the school-house was shut up; no merry voices met the ear. Mr. Lewellen was the promoter and the support of the little and well-conducted establishment. Pembray was then but a poor, unthrifty hamlet; but the iron king has changed all this.

Our hero found Rose Cottage entirely shut up. It had not had time to fall into wild neglect; and the garden and walks still looked neat—weeds here and there had in truth sprung up; and with the house had fallen into other hands, for Mr. Lewellen's property in South Wales was mortgaged, and the mortgagee had not yet determined to sell, for there was every prospect of Mr. Lewellen retrieving his affairs, and paying off the mortgage. After walking over the grounds, recalling many a pleasant hour passed in the little cottage, Cuthbert Gordon proceeded to visit the clergyman.

He passed many persons on the road, but though they stared hard at him, they did not remember him; he recollected their faces, but as they were not intimates he passed on.

The astonishment of the worthy curate, his wife and family, was great indeed, when they recognised their visitor. That night he was in a measure forced to stay with the worthy curate, who gave him a packet left by his mother previously to her departure for Ireland, for she felt sanguine that her son would yet be restored to her.

The worthy man spoke of Mr. Lewellen's sudden reverse of fortune with deep regret and sympathy, but since his departure a most valuable mine had been discovered on an estate in Glamorganshire he had purchased two or three years back, and still retained in his hands.

This iron and coal mine, it was said by an eminent engineer, would, when developed, more than double his original fortune.

The whole family listened to Cuthbert Gordon's adventures with surprise at the perils he had gone through, and admiration at the goodness of Providence in preserving him.

On retiring to his bedroom, our hero took out the packet of letters left by his mother with the curate, for his perusal, should he, as she so ardently desired, visit Pembray on his reaching England. He looked with delight upon the handwriting of a mother he so dearly loved. There were also letters from Amy and Lucy, and one or two from strangers addressed to him.

His beloved mother, in the first part of her letter, only spoke of her deep agony at his supposed loss; next, of the revulsion of feelings expressed on hearing of his safety. She then continued :—" When the first misfortune fell upon our dear and kind friends, the Lewellens, it was borne with cheerful resignation, and without any material alteration in their mode of life ; but so rapidly did one reverse follow another, and with such crushing effect, that every one in this vicinity, where he was universally beloved, and where he had spent his fine fortune liberally and well, deeply and sorrowfully grieved over his unmerited misfortunes. Still, all the family bore it cheerfully and bravely ; and finally, all determined to accompany Mr. Lewellen to the West Indies, where he hoped, by attending personally to his property, to return in a few years with his fortunes in some measure retrieved. You may imagine our grief at the separation— Lucy's especially ; but she parted with her betrothed with firmness, and with full confidence in his fidelity and honour. For a time our lives were solitary, and time passed cheerlessly; no tidings of you, my beloved boy, came to cheer us—yet we still hoped. Well, one day a letter, directed to me, and bearing the Dublin post mark, reached the cottage. Our hearts beat quicker, for we thought, though the direction was not in your handwriting, it must be about you. On opening it we perceived it was from a Dublin solicitor, of the name of Sturgeon ; the contents I copy :—

"MADAM,—I take the liberty of writing to you upon a most important subject. After considerable search, I at length procured your address. You are, no doubt, madam, aware that your late husband, Captain Gordon, was the grandson of H. Gordon, of Rothcrea, and, consequently, supposed himself, on the death of his father, to be the next to the title and estates of the Dunskelling family ; but not being possessed of certain papers and deeds to prove his right, and, indeed, not having sufficient funds to institute a proceeding to recover his rights, the will and estates were seized upon by the late Lord Dunskelling, and held by him till his death, which occurred recently. The late lord left an only daughter, who has mysteriously disappeared, whilst the title and estates have been claimed, as next heir, by Gorman Fitzpatrick, a nephew of the late lord. Now, madam, I have in my possession all the necessary deeds, documents, and papers, besides an acknowledgment in the late lord's handwriting, that your son, Cuthbert Gordon, is the real and undoubted successor to the title and estates of the late Lord Dunskelling. I would, therefore, madam, impress upon you the necessity of your immediate attention to this, and that in the absence of your son you will, as speedily as possible, come to Dublin, bringing with you any papers and letters belonging to the late Captain Gordon, and every attention shall be shown you, and steps taken to secure your son's rights.

"I have the honour to be,
"Madam, yours faithfully,
"J. W STURGEON."

"This letter, my dear boy, you will imagine, agitated and surprised me not a little, and set us all thinking and consulting what to do. At length we determined not to neglect the advice given in Mr. Sturgeon's letter ; so we at once prepared to leave for Dublin, thinking whenever you (if God spared you) arrived in England, that you would first come to us. I have briefly stated what you have now read."

The letter finished with all the kind wishes and hopes of a fond mother's heart—finally giving him directions how to find her in Dublin. Our hero having perused the letters remained a considerable time plunged in thought; and after an uneasy night's rest, he went to his friend's room, and taking a most friendly leave of the curate and his amiable family, set out for Swansea, packed up his portmanteau, and took the mail to Holyhead, and proceeded thence by packet to Dublin.

CHAPTER XXXI.

Lady Dora Dunskelling, whilst Cuthbert Gordon was traversing the wilds of Africa, was undergoing a series of trials quite sufficient to destroy the strength and health of any young girl not gifted with a naturally strong and healthy frame, and a mind of the highest intellectual cabibre.

Every species of priestly craft was exercised, to weaken her faith, for the Lady Abbess was not working alone to accomplish her nephew's views. She knew Dora was an heiress ; she was in full hopes of converting her, and imbuing her heart with devotion, and finally getting her to abjure the Protestant faith, and by skilfully working upon her mind, by terror or otherwise, get her to renounce the world, become a nun, and devote her wealth to the holy Mother Church.

It was not at all an improbable hope of the Abbess that she should succeed. She was a clever, deep, designing woman, and the Father Confessor of the convent, a thorough Jesuit, aided her with heart and soul. The convent was poor, and the *eclat* of connecting a nobleman's daughter to the true Church was not to be overlooked.

We are not going to weary our readers with details of Dora Dunskelling's trials; suffice to say, she met them with firmness and patient endurance. Calm, collected, and firm in her own faith, she defeated the wily Jesuit in his ablest arguments. Enraged at her failure, and cruel by nature, the Abbess adopted means quite unjustifiable. She tried to terrify the young girl, but she laughed to scorn the clumsy machinery of the priesthood, bore fasts and penances, being roused at all hours of the night, and forced to enter cold damp chapels, remaining for hours exposed to a cold and chilly atmosphere; but all failed; promises of luxury in her new life gave her a weapon wherewith to beat her crafty persecutors, till, finally, seeing her cheek pale, and her form grow slighter, and also some rumours reaching the Abbess's ears, that enquiries were making after the late Lord Dunskelling's daughter, frightened her, and she accordingly wrote to her nephew the letter the drover so singularly got possession of.

Dora felt her health affected, and was certain that if they persisted in their system of persecution, they would finally undermine her constitution. During these dreary weary months, the young girl never forgot him, to whom she had given her priceless heart; the remembrance of Cuthbert Gordon, and the hope that he would yet come to her rescue, went far in giving her strength to bear her trials. Determined, when she found her health impaired, to make an effort to resist the unnecessary disturbance of her nightly rest, she refused when sister Margaret (a nun of a severe and bigoted nature, who was almost always forced upon her as her companion), called her before daybreak, to leave her very indifferent couch.

"As long," said Dora Dunskelling, " as I found my strength equal to it, to avoid contention and ill-treatment, I obeyed the monstrous tyranny of your Superior. I will do so no more ; you may drag me from my bed, but of my own free will I never will endure further insults, till I regain strength and health."

Sister Margaret was astounded. "What! impiously resist the orders of the Lady Abbess! refuse to proceed to chapel with the sisterhood!"

She raised her eyes to the ceiling, and departed crossing herself devoutly, and wondering whence would the soul of the fair heretic wing its way when the time came.

She repeated Dora's words to the Lady Abbess, who heard sister Margaret quietly, and then said, " Let her be, but to-morrow let her be removed from the cell to one of the guest chambers ; do not disturb her any more at night, and see that she takes her proper exercise in the garden twice a day."

One morning, about a week after this change of regime, the Abbess came into the little parlour where Dora was sitting, reading the life of one of the saints.

"You are looking better, Lady Dora Dunskelling," said the Superior. Dora looked up.

" Yes, madam, I am better."

"I wrote, a week or so ago, to your guardian, Lord Dunskelling, to say that he had better come for you." Dora's heart beat faster ; joy at the thought of quitting the hateful walls of the convent, fear that some new peril awaited her. "You may consider, Miss Dunskelling, that I have perhaps acted somewhat harshly towards you in my earnest endeavours to correct the evils of a corrupt and evil education."

" What do you mean, madam, by such an insinuation ? The greatest care has been taken of my education, by an accomplished woman, and under my dear lamented father's own eye. Miss MacCormack may have fallen a victim to the arts and the persuasions of a bad man ; but the first years of her care of me could not be found fault with. She devoted herself to my improvement, and never for one moment inculcated into my mind any but the most virtuous sentiments."

"Then, I must say, you profited very little indeed by Miss MacCormack's teaching and morals. You eloped from your father's mansion in the dead of the night, with a gentleman with whom you had had scarcely a few days' acquaintance."

"Oh, madam," returned Dora, with a look of scorn and incredulity. "You surely cannot remain, till now, the dupe of that very shallow artifice to tempt me to quit my home. Mr. Fitzpatrick, my self-constituted guardian, with the aid of my unfortunate governess, whose happiness and comfort he has destroyed for ever—for though I think her less guilty than you do, madam, still her conscience will always reproach her, for deceiving one who truly loved her, and would have endeavoured to have made her independent for life. No, no, madam, you know my nature and disposition too well to give credit to such a monstrous fabrication."

With all her tact, the Abbess did change colour, and her eyes fell before those of the innocent and slandered maiden.

"Be it as you please, young lady," resumed the Superior after a short pause. "Such was the tale told me by your guardian, when he placed you under my care. He said he was most anxious for your future welfare; that you were reared by your father without any fixed thoughts of religion."

"That is false, madam," interrupted Dora, indignantly. "It is a slur upon the dead. My dear father was ever anxious that I should become a good Protestant and a good Christian. I had always instructions from, and attended regularly the church, where one of the best of Christian clergymen preached and taught his flock."

"Your father began life as a Roman Catholic—the creed of his forefathers," said the Abbess, bitterly. "He was always considered undecided in his opinions."

"Pardon me, madam ; you know nothing of my lamented father's opinions or of his creed. He was reared a Roman Catholic by his uncle, but not from the dictates of his own conscience. He became a Protestant, he himself told me immediately after his uncle's death, and married a Protestant lady. Her last words were to my father, 'Never, if possible, permit my child to swerve from the true Christian Protestant faith,' and my father whilst he lived, faithfully obeyed my poor mother's last request."

"I shall say no more on the subject, Lady Dora. I merely wish to show you that in my conduct towards you, I was actuated by pure and Christian motives. I wished to restore you to the true Church, in order to save your soul, and to render you happy in your union with a nobleman—"

"But, madam," interrupted Dora indignantly. "You and Mr. Fitzpatrick seem to dispose of me, as if I had no will of my own."

"Oh," returned the Superior, with a sneer. "Fourteen months' trial of your disposition has quite convinced me that you have a will of your own."

"Then, madam, rest assured that Mr. Fitzpatrick—"

"Lord Dunskelling, you mean," interrupted the Abbess.

"No, madam, I mean Mr. Gorman Fitzpatrick, who has assumed the title you give him without a shadow of right—and will never be acknowledged as my father's successor by me."

The Superior looked daggers at our heroine, as she said, "And pray, Lady Dora, who may be entitled to the distinction, if Mr. Fitzpatrick is not ? "

"That, madam, is for the law to decide, not me. I have suffered fourteen or fifteen months of cruel incarceration through his means. My name slandered by his orders and deceit—the only relative that I knew I had, was seized before my eyes, and cruelly forced away, whither I know not, and yet, the man who has committed such acts expects me to unite my destiny to his. I would sooner be shut up till death would relieve me, in one of the miserable cells in this establishment, than be the wife of a man such as Gorman Fitzpatrick."

Dora Dunskelling's cheek flushed, and her beautiful eyes, generally so mild and sweet in their expression, sparkled and flashed with the angry feelings that struggled in her breast.

The Abbess arose from her seat, pale and excited with inward rage ; had she dared, she would have instantly ordered Dora's confinement in a cell, and inflicted on her greater severity than ever. But she was frightened, for that very morning she had received a letter from Dublin, stating that great exertions were being made to discover the retreat of the late Lord Dunskelling's daughter.

"The world, young lady," said the Superior, bitterly, as she left the room, "the world has too strong a hold on your heart to permit you to take or heed the advice or the counsel of those who would save your soul and body. I wash my hands of you, and shall consider myself and my community released of a great responsibility, when I surrender you into the hands of your proper guardian." So saying she left the room.

"Cold blooded, deceitful woman," thought Dora to herself. "I can see through her plans and schemes. Save my soul and body. No, no, she had nearly crushed soul and body as it is, and now I am to be delivered a victim to that unprincipled Fitzpatrick."

A few days after this scene, about twelve o'clock in the day, a plain travelling chariot and four, with two attendants out of livery, stopped before the great portals of the convent, and in a few minutes afterwards the Abbess entered the parlour, and informed Dora that Lord Dunskelling, her guardian, had arrived, and desired her to be quick in her preparations, for he wished exceedingly to reach Dunskelling that night, where she was to remain, as he had to proceed to Dublin without delay. He was no longer her guardian ; he had made her a ward of chancery.

"Then, cannot I remain here, madam ? " asked Dora, calmly. "I do not like being left alone to travel with Mr. Fitzpatrick."

"You can tell him so, Dora Dunskelling," returned the Superior. "Here you cannot stay ; on that I am resolved, after your late unjustifiable language and accusations against me and my establishment. Your guardian awaits your presence in the parlour."

Lady Dora Dunskelling was perplexed and unhappy. She had often prayed to be delivered from the hated walls of the convent ; but she by no means wished for Lord Dunskelling to be her deliverer. She knew in her heart that he was a thoroughly bad man, and could do nothing that was honest or honourable.

"Still," she thought to herself, "he is taking me publicly from the convent. The Abbess could hardly lend herself so openly to any intended treachery." She, therefore, whilst these thoughts passed rapidly through her mind, rose, and proceeded to the visitors' parlour.

Lord Dunskelling, who was sitting gazing out at·the dismal court-yard of the convent, surrounded by its lofty wall, rose, as Dora entered the room alone, for the Abbess left her at the door. He was attired in a suit of black, looked pale, and was somewhat excited in manner, as he handed our heroine a chair, without offering his hand, or any salutation, save a slight bend of his head. He looked very serious ; and as Dora took a seat, he said :—

" I am truly sorry, Lady Dora, to hear that your health has suffered ; indeed, you are not looking very well ; but the air of your native place, as I may call Dunskelling, will soon restore you." Seeing Dora about to reply, he quickly added—" We will not now enter upon the subject of your having been placed in this establishment. I shall merely say it was not my intention that you should have been treated as you were, but simply——"

" The less said," replied Dora, coldly interrupting him, " the better ; you cannot undo what you have done. If it is your intention to proceed to Dunskelling, the sooner we leave the better ; but I must say, I accompany you with a very doubtful mind as to your projects and intentions. The Superior of this convent distinctly states that she will not permit me to remain here ; so I have no choice."

"I deserve this suspicion, Lady Dora," answered her companion, with a flush on his cheek ; " but you will be a better judge of my intentions twenty-four hours hence ; till then I must remain passive under your scorn and contempt. My carriage and servants are at the gate ; the sooner we depart the better."

"I shall not detain you ; " and Dora rose and left the parlour. In ten minutes she was ready. Not a single nun attended to bid her farewell. The Superior only, in a cold, formal manner, gave her her blessing. Agitated and uneasy, Dora crossed the court-yard ; the portal was thrown back, and then she beheld the chariot and four and two mounted attendants. It was then nearly two o'clock in the day; a domestic let down the step of the carriage, and Dora, without assistance, entered and took the seat in the far corner, Lord Dunskelling following. The postillions were mounted, and off dashed the four bays at a rapid pace. Dora, wrapped in her large mantle, uttered not a word ; a feeling of intense uneasiness rendering her nervous. As to Lord Dunskelling, he remained with his arms folded, gazing out of the window as the carriage dashed on at a very rapid pace. They passed several carts, and persons on horseback—farmers, apparently, and some vehicles going to Galway. They were then on the high road ; but when within two miles of Galway, the postillions turned out of the main road, and took a much narrower and more uneven track.

Dora saw this deviation from the main road, and started, looking into Lord Dunskelling's face, who saw the look of suspicion she cast at him; for at once he said with rather a pleasing tone :—

"Oh, you need not feel alarmed. I wish to avoid the town of Galway, and besides, this road will save us quite five miles."

The lady made no reply. The road was rough, and the pace of the horses became slower. Lord Dunskelling appeared gloomy and disturbed ; the fact was, he was baffled in almost all his schemes.

During the height of the rebellion in Ireland, when confusion and alarm were at their height, and a kind of reign of terror ruled the rural parts of the country, Fitzpatrick assumed the title, and took possession of the mansion and estates of Dunskelling, and even managed, aided by his clever, unscrupulous attorney, to get in a great part of the rents ; but as the year '98 passed away, things began rapidly to tone down into some kind of order and rule, and the law began to assert its prerogatives. Thus, when Fitzpatrick attempted to obtain the great bulk of Lord Dunskelling's wealth he met with opposition. The daughter's rights were considered—it was discovered that she was entitled to a £100,000 fortune, amassed partly in India, and partly by a life of economy from the period of the late lord's accession to the title. At length, a Mr. Sturgeon, a lawyer, of considerable talents and practice in Dublin, took proceedings in law, claimed the personal property of the late lord for his daughter, and also stated that there was a nearer claimant to the estates and title than Gorman Fitzpatrick.

Fitzpatrick passed his time in reckless dissipation and extravagance in London, but finding he had no time to lose, much as he disliked, for certain reasons, to return to Ireland, he resolved by a bold stroke to become master of £100,000, at all events.

When Cuthbert Gordon met him in Shrewsbury he was proceeding to carry out his plans, and his meeting with our hero quickened his movements. The insult he had received revived the deadly hate he bore to Cuthbert Gordon, whom he knew was the next heir to the title and estates of Dunskelling. To wound him in the dearest object of his life was now Fitzpatrick's daily schemes. Miss MacCormack he had deserted and neglected, and never intended to have any further intercourse with her. To take Lady Dora from the convent and make her his wife, would not only outwit his rival, but inflict a deadly and incurable wound upon both.

In the still troubled and unsettled state of the extreme south and west of Ireland, there was every facility afforded to carry out his scheme. He even deceived his aunt, and thus Dora was left in the power of one of the most unprincipled men in the world.

After passing the town of Galway, the carriage drove in again on the main road, and changed horses twice before it grew dark. At the last post-house, sandwiches were handed Dora and a glass of sherry, but she declined any refreshments. In fact, she felt an instinctive inclination to get out of the carriage and insist on remaining at the inn, which looked very respectable, for a feeling of dread was stealing over her. However, the horses were put to, and they drove off. As it grew dark she became more nervous, for the silence of Lord Dunskelling had something ominous in it, but at the next change the lamps were lighted, and Dora was requested to alight and partake of a cup of coffee, as the next stage would be nearly twenty miles, and a pin had got loose in the axle-tree.

Dora alighted, and followed a repulsive-looking female into a very shabby parlour; on the table was a tray with tea, coffee, and biscuits. Several doubtful-looking men were lingering about the door of what she erroneously supposed was the post-house, but they were off the main road, and the horses had been brought there by Lord Dunskelling's orders.

The look of the house was altogether mean and disreputable, so Dora, after taking a cup of coffee and a biscuit, returned to the carriage. She saw that the horses were to, and a man was knocking a linch-pin into the axle-tree.

After Dora had got into the carriage, one of the attendants came up and shut the door, and, as she thought, inserted a key and locked it. Lord Dunskelling got in on the other side, and then the carriage drove on.

CHAPTER XXXII.

SHORTLY after leaving the inn, Dora's companion took a brace of pistols from a case, primed them, and put them in the pocket under the window; after that he drew a small double-barrel pistol from his breast pocket, re-primed it, and returned it to the same place.

All these preparations rather startled our heroine; the lamps in the front being constructed so as to throw a strong light into the interior of the carriage, Dora looked at her companion, who appeared exceedingly agitated, and was continually looking out of the window.

Turning round, he perceived his companion's look of alarm; and then for the first time addressed her:

"Dora," said Lord Dunskelling, in a calm, quiet tone, "I may as well now plainly tell you, you are not going to Dunskelling."

Our heroine felt sick at heart, but with a great effort she conquered the sensation of terror she at first experienced, and in a tolerably steady voice said :—

"Then where are we going? You surely cannot mean to take a cowardly advantage of my unprotected situation, and again act treacherously towards me. What are your projects?"

"I will tell you plainly. You must be my wife—I have sworn it. I am taking you to a place where a priest is waiting. The moment the ceremony is over, we embark on board a vessel I have lying at anchor in Glengarif bay, and we sail for Spain. If you become mine willingly my whole life shall be devoted to your happiness—but willing or unwilling, in three hours more you shall be my wife."

"Never!" said Dora, "never!" and raising her hand, she said, "As sure as you sit there, so is there a just and watchful God, who will, by human means, defeat your projects; whilst the crime and outrage you seek to commit will recoil upon yourself. You tremble now." As she spoke the words a bright light shot up into the air, a hundred yards in advance of them.

Lord Dunskelling dashed down the window in front, and called out in a passionate voice, "Stop!"

The next instant two more bright flashes were seen, followed by reports. There was a violent plunging of the horses, and a shout from the postillions, and the next moment the chariot was overturned into a shallow dry ditch. The carriage went over on the side where Lord Dunskelling sat; he was precipitated with force against the side, smashing the glass to atoms. Dora instinctively grasped the two holders on her side, and saved herself from the shock. The next instant the door was broken open, and a man eagerly called out :—

"Dora! Lady Dora Dunskelling! Speak—are you hurt?"

The light of a carriage lamp fell upon those inside, and as Dora exclaimed, "Good God, that voice!" an arm encircled her waist, and drew her from the carriage.

"Oh, curse you!" exclaimed Lord Dunskelling, struggling up; and taking a pistol from the pocket, he discharged it full in the face of the man who was extricating Dora from the carriage. So close was the pistol, that Dora's garments were actually on fire, but instantly extinguished by the man supporting her, who received a slight wound on the side of the neck.

"Doul!" fiercely exclaimed several men rushing up. "Did we not tell you if you interfered you ran the risk of being shot? Where is he?"

"I never heed threats," replied Cuthbert Gordon, fiercely pushing through the six or eight armed men who crowded round the carriage door, and leading the almost insensible girl to the bank on the side of the road. She had not fainted, for as he seated her on the bank, and wrapped her shawl about her, she murmured :—

"Can this be reality? Oh, Cuthbert, Cuthbert, from what a fate you have rescued me!"

"Yes, thank God, Dora, you are rescued, but not by me; those men dragging Mr. Fitzpatrick from the carriage hold me prisoner, as well as you, dearest, but no harm will now happen to you. Are you hurt or in any way injured?"

"No, no, not hurt; only frightened by the report of the pistol that wretched man fired so close; but you are wounded," she exclaimed anxiously, "the blood is streaming from your head or neck over your clothes."

"It's nothing, dear girl," returned Cuthbert Gordon. "The ball has merely grazed the skin, but it came rather close, and we had a most providential escape."

She looked around, and by the glare of the carriage lamps, held by two of the men, she could perceive every object distinctly. There were fifteen or more men well armed; one of the horses lay dead upon the road, the two postillions were unharnessing the others. They were evidently not on a public road; it was narrow and rough, and ran amidst ranges of lofty hills.

Lord Dunskelling was held by two men, who kept their pistols to his head; his two attendants were seated on the bank with their hands bound; the night was exceedingly dark. Presently a tall man in the green uniform of the rebels, with a carbine in his hand, approached our hero and his fair companion; another man followed with a carriage lamp in his hand. The light fell upon the rebel's features, and Dora, looking up, uttered an exclamation of surprise and fear, for in the rebel she recognised Mr. Maxwell.

"I see you recognise me, Lady Dora Dunskelling," said the latter; "rest satisfied, however, that this time you will receive no injury. If I placed you in the hands of Fitzpatrick, I now release you from his detestable projects. I thought, Sir," he added turning to our hero, "you understood that you were not to interfere in this affair."

"I am not accustomed to heed threats, or receive orders," returned our hero. "You politely told me if I interfered, you or some of your companions would blow my brains out. When I saw the carriage overturned, I preferred the chance of a shot to leaving this young lady, who is a cousin of mine, unassisted."

"And very probably you would now be lifeless, had I not interfered."

"Well, Sir, I feel obliged for your interference, notwithstanding; my seizure was a risk of life also, and a faithful follower was nearly falling a victim."

"He owes his wound to your folly in resisting," said Maxwell, "and you heard me reprimand the man who fired the shot. It will be necessary for this young lady to come with us as well as yourself. You can strap one of the carriage cushions on one of those horses, and follow us, and please to recollect your pledged word."

"I shall make no effort to break it," returned Gordon: "helping Lady Dora Dunskelling out of an upset chariot, did not in any way infringe upon my word passed to you. But I candidly tell you, that to rescue her from peril or suffering, I would forfeit life as well as honour."

Dora, whilst this conversation occurred, clung to her cousin's arm, trembling with anxiety. She knew quite well how fiery and irritable, if unjustly opposed, our hero would become; she also knew something of the wild, impulsive nature of Mr. Maxwell; she therefore interrupted the conversation, by saying :—

"Lead us where you please, Mr. Maxwell. I am quite satisfied at having escaped the snare laid for my destruction."

"It was not intended, Lady Dora Dunskelling," replied Maxwell, to involve you in this desire to secure the person of Gorman Fitzpatrick ; neither was it intended to detain this gentleman a prisoner, but circumstances altered our plans. You will, however, be restored to liberty before twenty-four hours are over."

Whilst this conversation was taking place, part of the band had moved on, with Lord Dunskelling in the midst of them.

A horse with a cushion strapped on its back, with the carriage bridle to guide him, was brought for the rescued girl to mount; her large mantle from the carriage was also given to her.

"Courage, dear Dora," said Cuthbert Gordon, to his beautiful cousin; "courage, your trials will soon cease."

"I have no fear now, Cuthbert," she replied in a low affectionate voice, "that you are near me."

He pressed her hand silently, and then moved on, Mr. Maxwell and six men going before.

The party shortly after left the road, and opening a gate, followed a horse track leading seemingly across a moor in amongst the mountains.

"How providentially, Dora, this affair has terminated. Two days ago I was terrified at your situation; I dreaded your being carried off before assistance could reach you."

"I am altogether so bewildered, so astonished, most of all at your unexpected and wonderful re-appearance, and at such a moment, that I know not what to think. Five minutes before the carriage upset, I was in despair, for it was only then that Gorman Fitzpatrick made me acquainted with his terrible project. He took me from the convent, to restore me, he said, to Dunskelling; I trembled at being consigned to his care, but the Superior of the convent, where I suffered so much, positively refused me shelter under her roof."

"Ah, my poor Dora, I have no doubt you suffered all kinds of trials in that place. It was to rescue you from thence that I was coming, in advance of others, when I was seized on the road by this person in the rebel uniform you call Maxwell, who appears a gentlemanly kind of young man. It is a pity to see such a one in the ranks of those misguided men; but when, dear Dora, did you meet him before?"

"Too long a story to tell now, Cuthbert; but he it was who carried me off by Fitzpatrick's orders, and placed me in the convent in Galway. He told me he was bound by some secret oath to obey my self-constituted guardian; but though he did behave wrong, and committed an outrage, still he did it unwillingly, and conducted himself towards me in a kind and gentle manner. He told me he was a married man, and yet Fitzpatrick, to shield himself and deceive the world, spread a report that I had eloped with this Mr. Maxwell—was not this cruel ? "

" Cruel !" repeated the indignant listener ; " it was a foul and monstrous slander ; such as none but a most heartless and depraved mind could invent."

" But where, Cuthbert, can they be taking him and us ? I fear some terrible tragedy "

" We are evidently ascending the hills, no doubt to be placed in some secret retreat of a band of defeated rebels, for there are many fugitives still lurking in mountain retreats."

The difficulty of the way became so great that one of the men approached to lead the horse, whilst Cuthbert Gordon walked by the side of Dora, keeping her on its back whilst they surmounted some difficult passes.

Though accustomed to the darkness of the night, and objects consequently less indistinct, yet very little observation could be made as to the track they were pursuing ; their course lay between huge rocks, masses of boulders, tall ferns and stunted shrubs—at times exceedingly steep, and again leading along the edge of a steep precipice.

At length the path was no longer practicable, and the men paused. The rebel leader, Maxwell, came to the side of the horse, saying, " The remainder of the way, Lady Dora Dunskelling, must be performed on foot ; It is impassable for a horse, but not at all for a human being."

Cuthbert Gordon lifted Dora from the horse, which one of the men took back for some distance.

" Have we much more of this kind of path ? It is almost impassable for a female."

" I regret the difficulty of the way," returned Maxwell ; " but half-an-hour will see us at our destination ; shall some of my men carry Lady Dora ? "

" Oh, I am able with my cousin's assistance," replied Dora, eagerly, " to traverse this mountain path."

Maxwell said some words in a low voice, and passed on to the front, simply requesting our hero to keep them in sight. This was the more necessary, as a thin grey mist was creeping down over their wild mountain path.

As Maxwell passed on, Gordon wrapped Dora's mantle well about her, for the air was extremely chill, and then taking his arm, they climbed the steep and difficult path, keeping the dark forms of the men in sight.

What the young man said to the fair young girl, whom he supported on his arm, and sometimes carried over dangerous declivities, we will not lay before our readers. They were deeply attached before their separation ; time nor absence had weakened their love for each other—far otherwise—and now re-united and sharing difficulties and dangers together, the words so long kept locked in each other's hearts found form and substance, so that before one short half-hour had passed they had plighted troth, and pledged their hearts into each other's keeping. Suddenly turning an angle in the massive rocks, jutting boldly out, and leaving scarcely a foot of path to the bold climber, a blaze of light from a huge fire some distance ahead, startled them.

"Here is our destination, beloved Dora, no doubt; courage, and all will be well, I feel confident."

"Near you, Cuthbert, I feel no want of courage, still I shudder when I think what that daring bad man, Gorman Fitzpatrick, may have to endure. Depend on it, there is some terrible scene to be acted. Fitzpatrick has concealed in his breast a double-barrelled pistol. I saw him carefully examine it, shortly before we were attacked."

"We have no doubt reached our destination," returned Gordon. "See, there are a number of men drawn up on that plateau."

Dora Dunskelling could not but feel great fatigue. Her spirit and her love for our hero, however, sustained her. Previous to her incarceration in the convent, before her health became impaired, she would have felt the exertion trifling, but a whole day's travelling, scarcely any food, and the deep anxiety and terror at being alone with Lord Dunskelling, and the long, difficult trips over a wild, mountainous tract for full two hours, had tried her powers of endurance to the utmost. Cuthbert Gordon, though he cheered his loved companion, and made light of this attention to her, was still not without his secret anxiety concerning the events of the next few hours. The seizure of Lord Dunskelling, the fierce, vindictive feelings of the rebels towards him, surprised and mystified him.

Why Dora Dunskelling and himself should be forced to accompany them, also astonished him. In the meantime they had advanced, and finally halted on a considerable level space, before the mouth of an immense cavern, where there were full thirty or forty men assembled, besides those who surrounded Lord Dunskelling. The bright blaze of a turf and wood fire rendered every object around distinct; and its light fell upon the fierce, excited features of the rebels, who, leaning on their muskets, gazed at Lord Dunskelling with glances of unmistakable hatred and vengeance.

Pressing heavily on Cuthbert Gordon's arm, pale, but firm, Dora stood within a few paces of Lord Dunskelling, gazing at the various figures, upon their strange attire, wild, bearded faces, and bright arms. Almost at the moment of their halting, a tall man, leaning upon a staff, for he appeared slightly lame, advanced from the cavern with the person Dora knew as Maxwell; the stranger was attired in green uniform, a black belt, with pistols stuck in it. He had no covering on his head, but came on into the full light of the fire which one of the men stirred up into a bright blaze. The stranger stopped opposite Lord Dunskelling, and then it was that Gordon clearly beheld his features, and with a start he said, bending his head down to Dora, and speaking in a low voice:—

"That man with a staff is Herbert O'Dowd. I begin to pierce the mystery."

Lord Dunskelling fell back a pace or two, and as he shifted his position, both Dora and her companion could see he was terribly agitated and deadly pale.

"So, Gorman Fitzpatrick," exclaimed O'Dowd, in a

terribly firm clear voice, "traitor, informer, perjurer, and robber, we meet at last;" there was a murmur of execration from the group of excited men, who crowded even nearer to their leader and his once bosom associate.

"You are certainly," returned Lord Dunskelling, recovering his nerve, and folding his arms and gazing steadily into his former friend's face, "remarkably choice in your expressions, and now that we have met, what is your purpose? What do you propose doing with me?"

"Hang or shoot you like a mad dog; either mode of ridding the world of a treacherous, heartless villain is too good!"

"Take care, O'Dowd," returned Lord Dunskelling, passionately, "how you dare—"

"Dare!" shouted O'Dowd, bursting into a mocking laugh. "Dare! to Herbert O'Dowd. Stay, I will give you a chance. If you can deny, or prove to be false, any one of the atrocious deeds I will now accuse you of performing, I forgive you; nay, more, you may go from our presence with life, but with the curse of those you have sent to their doom, without a pang of remorse piercing that recreant heart. Nay," he added, in a tone that brooked no opposition, "hear me out. To suit your views, I sacrificed my honour, I outraged my feelings, and became your partner in a scheme of villany; I permitted you to send that gentleman, Mr. Gordon," motioning with his hand towards our hero, and for a second their eyes met, "I say I permitted you to send him out of the country for a time; you secretly intended he should never return. I aided you to aspire to the title of Lord Dunskelling, and for what did I commit those villanies? To ensure your co-operation in a cause dear to my heart—the liberation of Ireland from the foot of the Sassenach. As Lord Dunskelling and possessor of his wealth, your influence would be great, and your means important. You swore on the cross a terrible oath, to aid us and our cause—to keep secret whatever was confided to you. What did you do? You sold us all to the Government!"

"All these accusations sound extremely well," scornfully interrupted Lord Dunskelling; "I do not deny my oath. I see two present who witnessed my taking it; but what proofs have you that I betrayed any of you or your designs?"

"You shall have proof enough," passionately exclaimed O'Dowd. "Come forth, Gorman Purcell. Ha! you start. Your tool was not shot as you supposed, for there he stands before you."

A man, with his hands bound, was dragged forward from behind the ranks, and confronted with Lord Dunskelling.

"Here," continued O'Dowd, taking a paper from his breast, "is a list of honest, true-hearted patriots you betrayed and sold, through this miserable villain, who, to save his life, has confessed. Tucker was hung; so was McLean. Murphy McGrath, Maloney, and Timmins were shot. Even the noble-hearted Lord Edward was betrayed by you. Me you endeavoured to entrap, placing this man to watch my movements, and lead the troops into our secret haunts. On his person were found your letters and documents, to prove your guilt. This miserable victim was taken, and would have been shot; but, to save his life, he betrayed his twin-brother, who was innocent, and was shot in his stead. Here is your last letter to the Lord-Lieutenant, with your remarks; and six more victims were added to the list; and last, if not least of all your villanies, you were now carrying off Lady Dora Dunskelling, having failed in perverting her faith. Having engaged a renegade priest to unite you, and then embark with her in a sloop, now in Castletown or Glengarif, and having destroyed the happiness of your victim, who abhors you, you thought to secure her fortune, and then desert her. Such was your intention, I presume, by this letter to your accomplice, Miss MacCormack," and O'Dowd, in passionate indignation, dashed a parcel of letters at the feet of the confounded Lord Dunskelling, who, with his hand on his breast, his lips closed, and his eyes flashing with passion, glared upon O'Dowd and his men in savage rage.

"What, then, my faithful followers, does this double traitor deserve at our hands?"

"Death!" shouted the excited men, grasping their muskets.

"Stop! in God's name, O'Dowd," exclaimed Cuthbert Gordon, starting forward. But Lord Dunskelling rapidly drew his double-barrel pistol from his breast, and passionately exclaimed—"Die first, rebel and false friend," and levelled the pistol within a yard of O'Dowd's head; but the arm was dashed aside by Gordon, the pistol exploded, and O'Dowd was saved. Nevertheless, the ball found a victim, and Purcell, the informer, with a wild cry, sprung from the ground, and then fell flat on his face—a corpse.

"Oh, curse you!" exclaimed Lord Dunskelling, as he madly seized Gordon by the throat. Dora clasped her hands, and would have darted forward; but Lord Dunskelling was a child in the grasp of her lover. Before a step could be taken, he had shaken off his grasp with a violent jerk, and as he staggered back four muskets were raised, a flash and a report, and Lord Dunskelling lay dead at the feet of his wretched tool Purcell.

Dora could no longer hold up against the horrors of the scene—her powers of endurance gave way, and with a deep sigh she would have fallen fainting to the ground, had not Cuthbert caught her in his arms and, heedless of O'Dowd and his followers, pushed fiercely through them, and entered the cave. Within the cave was a wooden frame, with a straw pallet upon it. Upon this he placed her, and taking some water from a pitcher close by, he sprinkled her face and hands, and shortly after she began slowly to recover. Looking up, our hero beheld O'Dowd standing by his side, and a torch stuck in the crack in the cliff.

"I little expected," exclaimed Gordon, with a flush on his cheek, as he looked seriously into the rebel leader's calm, thoughtful features, "that Herbert O'Dowd would permit so cold-blooded a murder to take place in his presence."

"What!" exclaimed O'Dowd, the expression of his

features changing, "not shoot so execrable a villain? Why, but for you he would have taken my life. Would you have called that a murder?"

"I will talk to you by-and-bye," said Cuthbert. "This dear girl has suffered too much; such scenes were too horrible for her to witness. She ought not to have been brought here;" and stooping, he helped to raise Dora to a sitting position, and gave her a cup of water, of which she took a little.

"What you say, Mr Gordon, is quite correct, she ought not; but under the circumstances it could not be helped; too many lives were at stake to act otherwise. Lady Dora Dunskelling," continued O'Dowd, in a voice of much feeling, "will, I think, pardon me for enacting before her a scene, certainly not calculated for a virtuous maiden's eyes. But, lady, you are now freed for ever from the snares of a man without heart, feeling or principle; and who, had he not been intercepted, would have caused you a life of perpetual and bitter sorrow. To you and Mr. Gordon, my conduct and acts appear strange and criminal, but as a leader in a just and holy cause, though stigmatized as a rebel, I feel quite justified, in my own conscience, in bringing a traitor to judgment, and shooting him, as our enemies would one of us, by a drum-head court-martial. As to his being Lord Dunskelling, he never was, and never could be, even if you had ceased to exist, for the marriage of his father with his mother was illegal, and would not stand an hour's investigation. I will now leave you till Lady Dora recovers strength. I have no food to offer you, for we quit this retreat in two hours. When daylight dawns, you can descend the hill, where you will find the horse tied to a stump. I must request half-an-hour's conversation with you, Cuthbert Gordon, before we part for ever. I do not wish you to remember the name of Herbert O'Dowd with scorn and reproach."

The rebel leader was turning away, when our hero caught his hand:

"Forgive me, Herbert," he said, with considerable emotion, "our thinking differently need not create a feeling of bitterness or enmity. I know that you and

many other noble hearts imagine you are right in up-
holding the cause of Ireland's freedom ; of that say nothing.
I feel no hostility to you or them, and, believe me, there
are many things that will always render the memory of
Herbert O'Dowd dear to me."

"Thank you, Gordon, thank you," returned the in-
surgent leader with much emotion. "In other lands,
if I reach them, I shall remember you. I wronged you,
but I bitterly repented it, but now all is right, you will
gain rank and station, and"—lowering his voice, he added,
" you have gained a noble maiden's priceless heart which
is worth more than station, rank, or wealth ; I will see
you again in less than half-an-hour." He then passed
out from the cave, and a bend in the cavern shut him and
those without from the sight of the lovers.

CHAPTER XXXIII.

In order to account for our hero's so opportune appearance at the seizing of the person of Gorman Fitzpatrick,
we must retrace our narrative.

Having left Pembray, anxious and disturbed about the
mystery attending the disappearance of Dora Dunskelling,
our hero travelled as fast as travelling permitted in those
days to Holyhead ; but, unfortunately, on reaching the
packet station he found it was blowing so tremendous a
gale from the north-west, that the small sailing packet
which then carried the mails to Dublin could not venture

to sea, so there was no alternative but to remain patiently; thus two days were lost. The third brought a slight variation in the wind, which, though it still blew as violently as ever, now came from the north-east, which enabled the packet to put to sea; but so terrified were the passengers by the furious seas breaking in sheets of foam over the pier head, that only one gentleman besides our hero ventured to go on board. Though small and cramped in space, the cutters employed to carry the mails were remarkably good boats; and Captain Powell, the commander of the " Petrel," was a fine, plucky seaman, and to sea the cutter went under a close-reefed mainsail and foresail and storm-jib. Captain Powell soon found out that one of his passengers appeared to be as good a seaman as himself; for standing near the man at the helm, the cutter, just clearing the pier-head, and with but little way on her, was struck on the quarter by a tremendous sea, which swept the decks, knocking the captain and the two men at the helm against the cabin skylight, stunning the skipper, and nearly swamping the vessel, had not our hero, who was holding on by a rope from a ringbolt, seized the tiller, and before the little vessel, which broached to from the shock, had entirely lost way, put the helm up, calling out to the men on the forecastle to " hold on all," she would undoubtedly have got stern-way, and been dashed against the pier.

The captain was carried below, and had his face bathed with vinegar; the mate came up to Cuthbert Gordon, who, a most skilful steersman, was making the little " Petrel " show her abilities as a sea boat.

" Upon my conscience, Sir," he said " we have had a narrow squeak for it; you saved the craft; and by Jabers, you handled her like an angel."

Our hero laughed at the idea of one of the celestials steering a Holyhead cutter, as he replied :—

" I'm an old salt, though a young man. This is a lively boat, and if she had had sufficient way this accident would not have happened. Here, take the helm; I shall go and see how the skipper is; he had a hard knock on the head, and no mistake."

But Captain Powell was coming up the companion stairs, with a handkerchief tied round his head, but not materially hurt.

"I am glad to see you on your legs again, captain," said Cuthbert Gordon.

"Thank you, Mr. Gordon," answered the captain.

As the gentleman, who was following the skipper up the cabin stairs, heard the name of Gordon, he started, and uttered a smothered exclamation, pausing a moment on the stairs.

" My name," remarked our hero, who had observed the start and pause, and turning round he faced the stranger, " seems to surprise you ; have we met before ? "

" Name Sir, name," exclaimed the stranger, with a considerable increase of colour. " But I heard the name a year or two ago, as I happened to pass through Castle Townsend. There was a rumour through the place concerning a gentleman of that name who had mysteriously disappeared from a place, I think, called Dunskelling, or something very like it."

" Dunskelling," repeated our hero, fixing his glance upon the handsome, though care-worn features of the stranger.

" Yes," returned the young man, assuming a cool and collected manner, " that was the name ; and when Captain Powell spoke the name of Gordon, it recalled the circumstance I have just mentioned."

" There are many of my name in that part of the country," said our hero. " The Gordons, I have heard, of Rothcrca, reside somewhere in that vicinity." Then turning to Captain Powell, he continued, " I think the gale is subsiding, the wind is getting more easterly."

" I am happy to say it is," returned the skipper ; " if it remains thus, I hope to make Howth before sunset ; we can run with a slack sheet."

Our hero enquired of the captain the name of their fellow passenger, who had retired to the cabin.

" He has entered his name as Green. He's an Irishman, I think."

" Yes, I should say so," returned Cuthbert Gordon, and

feeling an inclination to have further conversation with Mr. Green, he also went below

The stranger, who was lying on one of the couches, raised his head as the young man entered the cabin, saying, "I am not a very good sailor, Mr. Gordon, at the best of times, but really this little vessel plunges so desperately, my head feels quite light."

"Well, these small craft are uneasy little things, but we are driving through a very cross sea, owing to the shift of wind, and the violence of the previous gale," returned our hero.

"You will pardon my curiosity, Mr. Gordon," observed the stranger, "but I somehow imagine that you may possibly turn out to be the same Mr. Gordon, who so strangely disappeared from Dunskelling about two years ago."

"Well, Mr. Green," answered our hero, with his gaze fixed attentively and thoughtfully upon his companion, who was not more than thirty or thirty-two years of age; "well, Mr. Green, I have no particular objection to saying I am the Mr. Gordon you speak of."

"Ha," exclaimed the stranger, "I thought so. The description then given of your personal appearance made an impression on my mind, and looking at you attentively at the time Captain Powell mentioned your name, I recalled the circumstances to my mind. The country was then very disturbed and no longer safe even for a stranger, so I travelled to Waterford and embarked for England— now that tranquillity is restored, I am returning to look after some dear relatives."

"You may think me impertinent, Mr. Gordon," continued Mr. Green, "but was your disappearance caused by any premeditated villany?"

Cuthbert Gordon was buried in profound thoughts; he heard Mr. Green's words, but his mind was bent upon the past. Suddenly looking up, and fixedly gazing into the stranger's certainly pleasing and expressive features, he asked :—

"Did you ever meet or see a gentleman whilst visiting the part of the country you mention, who was at that time called Gorman Fitzpatrick, but here recognised as Lord Dunskelling ?"

"Oh, yes !" answered Mr. Green, without the slightest hesitation, "I have seen him several times in Cork. A handsome man a nd about my age, perhaps, or a couple of years more."

Captain Powell descending the stairs preceded by the steward, who began placing a fiddle across the table to keep the articles for dinner steady, interrupted the conversation, but in his own mind Cuthbert felt satisfied Mr. Green knew more of him than he acknowledged, and that somehow or other he was connected with the past events of his life.

"Will you be able to join us at dinner, Mr. Green ? " said Captain Powell, seating himself at the table opposite our hero, who, of course, cared very little about the mysterious and troubled movements of the cutter.

"I am sorry to say I am a complete landlubber," replied Mr. Green, turning his face from the smoky viands, and quite unable to sit up.

Captain Powell and our hero made a hearty meal, and enjoyed their glass of grog after it, Mr. Green remaining as quiet as if asleep, till our hero and the skipper proceeded on deck. The "Petrel" was dashing forward, her bows buried in the foam of the sea, casting the spray in showers over her fore-deck.

The sky was beautifully clear, and the coast of Ireland distinctly visible, and not more than nine miles distant. It was scarcely dark when the "Petrel" passed over Dublin Bar, and shortly after let go her anchor off the Pigeon House Dock, Kingston, as a harbour was then unknown. Some bustle ensued in landing the mails ; boats came alongside, and as our hero was anxious to get into Dublin and, if possible, to see his mother and sisters that night, he took leave of the skipper, and throwing his portmanteau into the boat prepared to follow, when Mr. Green came on deck, and laying his hand on our hero's shoulder, said :—

"I cannot land yet, I feel so giddy ; but should you have a moment to spare there is my address ; I may be of some service to you," and he handed Cuthbert Gordon a folded paper.

"Thank you," returned our hero—"no doubt we shall meet again," and he put the paper in his pocket.

Ten minutes after he was rattling up to Dublin city in a jingle, (a vehicle long since consigned to oblivion,) and was soon safely deposited with his portmanteau at the "Packet" hotel, East-street.

It was then ten o'clock, and, resisting the impulse to visit his mother and sisters that night, he ordered his supper, and took up a morning paper; whilst reading it, he recollected the paper placed in his hand by Mr. Green, and taking it from his pocket, he opened it and read—

"SIR,—It is my earnest desire to be of service to you. You are perhaps aware that Lady Dora Dunskelling has disappeared, and is concealed in some place in this kingdom. Steps are now being taken to rescue, and restore her to her paternal home at Dunskelling. Any interference on *your part* will frustrate the purposes of those who are anxious for her liberation. You are therefore *earnestly implored* not to interfere; but wait patiently a few days, when you will hear from me again. A. GREEN."

"Ha," exclaimed Cuthbert Gordon, with a flush on his cheek. "I knew this man was a party concerned in my affairs, and no doubt in Dora's abduction also; and now possibly thinks to blind me and prevent my further interference in the completion of their schemes. This will not do, Mr. Green; I am not to be kept passive and loiter inactive whilst Gorman Fitzpatrick matures his plans. I will just see my mother and sisters, and Mr. Sturgeon, and then leave Dublin at once and proceed to Dunskelling."

Our hero passed a restless night, and after a hasty breakfast set out for Stephen's-green, where his mother and sisters had taken apartments. After five hours sacred to affection, being received by them with rapturous joy, he proceeded to Mr. Sturgeon, the lawyer, who was rejoiced to see him, and at once promised to take legal steps to release Lady Dora Dunskelling from her illegal incarceration ; at the same time it was determined that Cuthbert, taking Dorgan Rafferty with him, should depart for Dunskelling the next day, and from thence proceed to Galway, and keep a strict watch on the convent.

Having reached Dunskelling, he visited his old kind friend the housekeeper, who embraced him joyfully as the future Lord of Dunskelling, and asked a thousand questions after his beloved young mistress.

Cuthbert Gordon briefly explained how Dora had been taken to a convent near Galway, by Gorman Fitzpatrick, and that he was proceeding thither to keep watch in order to prevent her being removed by her treacherous kinsman, and to wait till the necessary power came from Dublin to obtain her release.

The next morning, Cuthbert Gordon and Rafferty started, both being well mounted and armed ; the latter having selected from his own paddock two capital roadsters. Dorgan Rafferty was in high spirits ; he having narrowly escaped shipwreck, having taken a passage from Swansea to Waterford in a deeply-laden schooner. In a gale of wind they were driven into Tramore Bay, and were forced to let go their anchor to save the vessel from being driven ashore ; and, fortunately, a very unusual case, they held on till the gale, after a night and day, subsided.

"Be gor, your lordship," (for Dorgan would persist in calling him my lord on all occasions), "I'll never set foot in a ship again ; there we were forty-eight mortal hours with the sea going clean over us ; dickens a fire could we light, and we were short of everything, especially whiskey. If we stayed below we were nigh stifled, and when we showed on deck, be gor, you had to hold on with your teeth, let alone your hands, to avoid being washed overboard. Lord save us ! it's a poor life, a sailor's."

"All of us do not think so, Dorgan," replied our hero, laughing heartily. "What should we do but for our jolly blue jackets?"

When within a few hours of their destination they were stopped by a dozen or more men, under the leadership of Maxwell, whom our hero at once recognised as his quondam acquaintance Mr. Green, but for several reasons he made no remark. Maxwell, who knew his chief ardently wished to see Cuthbert Gordon, resolved to detain him, but Rafferty making a desperate resistance, one of the men, contrary to Maxwell's orders, fired and wounded him in the side. This so enraged his master that he felled the man to the ground, and then a scuffle ensued which required all Maxwell's command over the men to quiet.

Finally, when our hero understood what the men were stationed there for, and that Dora would be in the carriage on his return from the convent, he remained passive, giving Maxwell his word of honour that he would not interfere or make any attempt to escape. Dorgan was carried to a turf cutter's cottage and his wound dressed. It was not serious, but it prevented him from further exerting himself, and therefore he was to remain where he was till rejoined by Gordon. Such was the substance of our hero's communication to Dora Dunskelling, as they sat in the cave; she on her part related briefly some of the miseries and sufferings she had endured in the convent; at length they were interrupted by the return of O'Dowd, who led our hero to some distance, where, sitting down on a rock, the former said :—

"I wish before we part—for in half-an-hour we shall all have left these mountains, and before twenty-four hours expire, I trust Maxwell and myself will be on the broad Atlantic—to give you some little explanation of the past, but it must be brief. The one grand object of my life has failed, and if I dare prophesy it will never be successfully renewed; the land will evermore wear the chains, I may say, it has forged for itself; for her faithless sons have betrayed her. After our shipwreck near Dunskelling I was laid up a considerable time in the cabin of an Irishman on the little island of Skerry. Fitzpatrick was not at all hurt, and his first exertions were made to discover what had become of you; to tell the truth he hoped you had perished. I had other designs than smuggling, but of those designs it is now needless to speak. Fitzpatrick soon found out where you were, and shortly after he heard from a spy of his, about the person of Lord Dunskelling, that his uncle had had two fits and that the doctors gave little hopes of any very long term of life, in fact, that another fit would carry him off.

"He came to me. 'O'Dowd,' said he, 'Lord Dunskelling may not live a week. They are concealing his illness from his daughter. If you will remove that Cuthbert Gordon out of the way, which you can easily do, as the rising of the United Irishmen is hourly expected, in the confusion I can grasp the title and estates ; I will bind myself to the cause, and you know what importance the wealth of the old lord will be to aid us.'

"'How do you mean, remove Mr. Gordon?' I said. 'Mark me, I will not allow his person to be injured, or any attempt on his life.'

"'Tut, man,' he replied. 'Do you think I am an assassin? I will just send him a voyage on board a schooner that will take him out of the way for six months —in that time Ireland will be free. I will hand you over thirty or forty thousand pounds at once.'

"I confess, to my shame, I was caught by the scheme, for we required money fearfully. Some two days after, (I was then near Tralee and perfectly recovered,) Fitzpatrick joined me, stated that the old lord was dead, that he had put you aboard a schooner bound to the East Indies, and that he intended assuming the title, become guardian to the daughter, and seize all that was to be had for present use, to arm and clothe my men. This detestable villain deceived me easily. I was then a leader in the insurrection under the name of D————, having discarded my own. I was afterwards made a Brigadier General, and defeated the troops sent against us in many fiercely contested fights.

"After this everything went wrong with us. Fitzpatrick, who took the most holy oaths, betrayed us, but we knew it not. My friend Maxwell bound himself to him by a fearful oath—he was, and is still a husband and father—he forced him by his oath to carry out his plans against Lady Dora Dunskelling; he managed even to make Maxwell his tool in betraying us, without his knowing he was doing so. That wretch Purcell, to whom I confided much, was also a tool of his. He wished, in fact, to get us all cut off one by one—all our plans were betrayed to the government, our leaders were led into snares, taken and hanged, after the battle of Vinegar Hill, where I was wounded in the hip.

"Still we never suspected Fitzpatrick, till Purcell fell into the hands of a party who laughed at his declaring he was a spy upon the rebels and in the employ of Lord Dunskelling. He and his two comrades, who listened to his assertions with horror, for they were staunch, were condemned to be hung—and were actually with the ropes round their necks, when Maxwell attacked the force with a strong party, and released them. The comrades of Purcell instantly related what the villian had asserted— he was searched and full confirmation of his guilt found in papers sewed in the lining of his garments. The men determined to shoot him, but Maxwell brought him and the papers to me.

"Thus I became acquainted with the whole of Fitzpatrick's villany. His last project was to carry off Lady Dora Dunskelling, having failed, through his aunt, in making her a Catholic. By a marriage with her he would become entitled to a large fortune, and his treacherous machinations against his sworn comrades would have passed unscathed, for traitors are plenty, and rewarded by the Government. I have nothing more to add. My comrades have by this time, all but Maxwell and four others, dispersed. When Maxwell met you on the packet he was returning to join me, having placed his wife and children in a place of safety. Fitzpatrick's body is beside his dupe and victim in an unhallowed grave. And now I ask you before we part, can you forgive the dishonourable, I can call it by no other name, conduct of a man who at heart wished you well, but was weak enough to be seduced by the sophistry of an unprincipled villain to lend himself to his schemes, having at heart a cause for which he would and has staked life?"

"I most freely forgive you, O'Dowd," replied his companion, warmly taking the Irish chief's hand, "for, after all, to you I shall owe the happiness of a life, but for you I should not now possess the priceless heart I can call my own—but can I, by any means in my power, secure your safe departure from this country, or secure you from ——" he hesitated, for fear of wounding the high spirit of his companion, but added, "pecuniary difficulties in a foreign land?"

"Thanks, Gordon, thanks. I shall not need it. If I once set foot on French soil, I am promised a colonel's commission in the Emperor's service, and Maxwell, whose wife and children are by this time in France, a captaincy; so with God's blessing and our good swords we shall do right well; but I cannot linger, for troops will be surrounding these hills in twelve hours, and the vessel that is to carry us to France only awaits our arrival. God bless you! Make my peace with your beautiful betrothed, and let her, when in after years she recals the scenes of the past night, let it be without a feeling of reproach to Herbert O'Dowd."

The two men pressed each other's hands warmly and affectionately, and then O'Dowd passed out of the cavern, and was lost in the gloom of night. Cuthbert Gordon returned to the side of Dora Dunskelling, who, wrapped closely in her mantle, was still seated on the rude bench, and, leaning against the rock, was dozing, completely overcome by fatigue and agitation. As she heard his footsteps, she started from her uneasy slumber with an exclamation of terror, for but a very dim uncertain light entered the cavern.

"You tremble, my beloved," said Cuthbert, taking her hand and sitting down beside her. "No wonder; you are overpowered with all you have gone through; but in another hour, as soon as it is daylight, we will descend. O'Dowd told me I should find a horse at the foot of the hill, which will in very little more than an hour take us to Kilmare. He said also that there we should find a very tolerable inn, where you could obtain rest and refreshment."

"Ah!" my dear Cuthbert, said our heroine with a sigh, "I should heed little either rest or fatigue if I could shake off the terrible vision that haunts me of the past few hours; the terrible impression of that scene weighs me down far more than any fatigue I have gone through. But where are those fierce men gone to?"

"They have gone, dearest, no doubt, into different parts of the country and dispersed, each seeking safety as he best may. O'Dowd and Maxwell and two or three others—if they can manage it—intend embarking for the coast of France."

"If it had not been for the cruel death of Gorman Fitzpatrick," observed our heroine sadly, "I should always remember the name of O'Dowd with a deep feeling of gratitude."

"Alas! love; he was the victim of circumstances. Gorman Fitzpatrick attempted his life; this so furiously enraged O'Dowd's followers that they were not to be restrained, and in their fury they shot Fitzpatrick dead."

"And what, dear Cuthbert, have they done with the unfortunate dead?" asked Dora anxiously, and with a shudder.

"They have consigned them to the earth somewhere in this vicinity," said our hero. "As soon as I possibly can I will order a search to be made for the bodies and have them removed to a Christian burial place."

In this manner the two lovers remained conversing till the faint light of early dawn began to penetrate within the gloomy recesses of the cavern; then Cuthbert Gordon, supporting his weary companion, emerged from the cavern, to behold the first rays of an unclouded sun burst over the valley beneath them. Both stood amazed at the grandeur and beauty of the scene. From the spot where they paused they overlooked a lower range of hills, and beyond these the broad Atlantic stretched itself out in its vastness, bounded only by the horizon. The

23—3

coast of Ireland, from Three Castle Head to the bold promontory marking the entrance to the Bay of Bantry, was distinctly visible. They could also trace Bear Island in all its length, the Bay of Glengarif, and its richly-wooded islands. Ships looked like dots upon the calm sea, and woods like garden shrubs, so lofty was the site upon which they stood.

"Oh, what a glorious scene!" exclaimed Dora, as she paused, struck by so unexpected and so vast a prospect.

"All this panorama was hid by the mist last evening," said our hero, as they again stopped and gazed around them. "O'Dowd, at all events, selected a most commanding spot for his retreat. From this place he could observe the approach of an enemy for miles; it commands the whole valley and its approaches."

Not a single human being met their gaze; not a remnant of the rebel band, save the consumed embers of the last night's fires.

"We must pilot ourselves, dear Dora," said our hero, in vain looking round for some trace of a path; but after searching awhile, he discovered tracks of feet winding along the side of the hill, formed by the trampling of the wild ferns and long grass between the huge masses of rock. Dora, supported by the tender care of her cousin, descended the precipitous sides of the hill, and clambered over the rocks without a murmur or complaint, till at last they had accomplished the descent, and in a very short time struck into a path, where they perceived a horse standing, fastened to the branch of a stunted tree.

"Ah!" exclaimed our hero joyfully, pressing the little hand resting in his. "O'Dowd is true to his word,— there is the horse. Courage, dear Dora. A short time will bring you to a place where you can seek repose."

"Oh, I am stronger now," she answered, than when we set out; "hope has cheered and supported me."

"You have borne a great deal of fatigue, dearest, as well as want of rest, and that after months of cruel confinement and cowardly persecution; but, please God, all this has passed away; you must look upon the past as a dream, and to the future with joy and thankfulness."

Dora pressed her lover's hand as she gazed fondly into his face.

Untying the bridle of the horse, Gordon was preparing to place Dora upon the cushion strapped upon the animal's back, when the word "halt," pronounced in a loud, harsh voice, caused him and the startled maiden to turn in the direction of the speaker, and then they perceived a soldier, with his musket presented, advance from behind a projecting rock.

Gordon, though surprised, looked at the soldier, saying calmly, "Well, my man, what do you require us to do? Are you a sentinel?"

"Yes," returned the soldier, in a sharp rough tone, "I should think I was. Now, then, follow me; my orders are strict. If you refuse," and he handled his musket in a threatening manner, "you must take the consequences."

"You can perform your duty strictly," observed our hero to the man, "and yet be civil of speech."

"Civil to a set of cut-throat croppies! that's not very likely," said the English soldier, with a laugh. "We know what you are; so come on, and don't stand giving me any of your jaw"

There was an angry flush on Gordon's cheek that caught Dora's eye, and at once she laid her hand upon her lover's arm, saying, "Let us follow this man, dear Cuthbert; he is only doing what he is no doubt instructed to do; the delay will be only trifling."

"Well, then, lead the way," said our hero to the soldier, sternly. "We are ready to follow you, though you are an unmannerly cur."

"I should think you would obey," growled the man, "or you would have an ounce of good lead in your body in half a minute."

"I tell you what, soldier," said Gordon, impatiently, "you may thank this lady, or I would break that musket on your head; as it is, I will have satisfaction from whoever commands you for your uncalled-for insolence."

As he spoke they turned the rocks, and then our hero and his fair companion perceived, not fifty yards from them, twenty or more red coats drawn up in a line, their muskets piled before them, with an officer standing in front, whilst his orderly walked his horse about. As soon as the officer perceived our hero and heroine approaching, he gave some orders to his men, who at once took their muskets and fell into rank. When within ten paces of the major, for that was the rank of the officer, the sentinel called out to our hero to halt.

But Gordon advanced close to the officer, with his fair companion. The major, a proud, haughty-looking man, first cast a contemptuous glance at our hero, and then gazed into the beautiful features of Dora with a surprised and puzzled look.

Anxious to put an end to an interview that could, he imagined, have no interest, our hero was about to address the major, when the latter said harshly, "How is this, Sir? You were ordered to halt, and yet you disregard orders. Corporal Stone," calling out one of the men, "take this man in charge."

The corporal, with four privates, immediately stepped up to our hero, and laid his hand on his shoulder.

Indignant at such rude and harsh treatment, and a lady under his protection, Gordon roughly pushed the corporal aside, saying to Major Edwards, "Sir, this harshness, in the presence of a female under my protection, is quite uncalled for. This young lady is the daughter of the late Lord Dunskelling."

"Well, Sir," angrily interrupted Major Edwards, "she shall be taken every care of. You, Sir, I believe, call yourself Cuthbert Gordon ; is it not so ? "

"My name is Gordon, certainly," replied our hero, and, with a reassuring look into the anxious face of Dora, added; "but I cannot imagine on what charge or suspicion you can possibly detain me and this lady, who is desirous of seeking shelter and repose, after the fatigue and exposure she has gone through."

"As to the lady," returned Major Edwards, "as I said before, she shall have every care taken of her. But let me ask you, Sir, were you not concerned with the party of ruffians who not only carried off this young lady, but also seized the person of the present Lord Dunskelling, whose carriage you stopped and ——"

"Oh, Sir," interrupted Dora hastily, "you must have been very much misled or badly informed respecting this affair. This gentleman, under whose protection I have placed myself, is my cousin, and he it was who rescued me from the power of Mr. Fitzpatrick, who falsely called himself Lord Dunskelling."

"And where, madam, may I ask, is Lord Dunskelling, whom you so strangely call Fitzpatrick?"

Dora shuddered, but Cuthbert Gordon at once said, "Sir, this is neither the time nor the place for this lady, so harassed and fatigued, to answer questions or enter into particulars."

"But," interrupted the major impatiently, "those questions must be answered; this lady shall immediately be conducted to Kilmare, but I arrest you on the charge of aiding and abetting rebels, and this charge you must disprove before the proper authorities; therefore consider yourself under arrest."

"I hear you, Sir, with great surprise," said our hero, calmly. "I cannot imagine who could have trumped up so false and ridiculous an accusation. I have not been a fortnight in this country, and the other night I was attacked on the high road, and my attendant severely wounded in the assault, and is now lying in a turf cutter's cottage, not a mile from here. I was carried with this young lady by a party of insurgents into the hills and detained all night, and the result of this unmanly assault upon me is, to be accused of treason, as absurd as it is unfounded."

Major Edwards' cheek flushed with anger, as he replied :—

"My conduct, Sir, may appear harsh to you and this young lady; nevertheless, I must do my duty, and act up to the orders I have received. Two servants of Lord Dunskelling were in attendance upon his carriage when attacked. They both have sworn that a person in plain clothes led the attack, and that person was the first to burst open the carriage door; that Lord Dunskelling fired, but having missed him, he seized the lady in the carriage with his lordship, and carried her out to the side of the road ; the men both swear they heard his lordship distinctly call this man Cuthbert Gordon, and declare that he was a robber and a villain. One of the servants also added, that by the light of the carriage lamp he beheld the features of the man called Gordon, and he at once re-cognised him to be the same person who had accosted him in an hotel yard in Shrewsbury, and that this person askep many questions about the Dunskelling family. He also stated that this Mr. Gordon placed the young lady he had taken out of the carriage on one of the post horses, and led the horse after the rebels, without any constraint being put upon him. Now, I do not doubt the young lady's statement—"

"But you doubt mine," interrupted our hero, angrily.

"Sir, I have a perfect right to have my own opinion, and to act as I intend doing. If I had not an idea that there may be some mistake in this affair, I would not have delayed as I have done. This young lady shall be carefully conducted to Killmare, and every attention paid to her till she can be restored to her friends or relatives. You, Sir, remain under my charge."

"Be it so, Sir," returned Cuthbert Gordon, annoyed and angry; "but at all events let this lady be no longer detained by listening to the frivolous, unfounded charges brought against me," and then, turning to the greatly distressed and chagriued young girl, he strove to reassure her, re-questing her at once to write to Mrs. Gordon, in Dublin, who would immediately come to her assistance, and take her home to the companionship of his sisters. "Another time, Major Edwards," he continued, addressing that officer, who was regarding him with rather a perplexed and dissatisfied look, "I shall request a more particular explana-tion of your unnecessary detention of my person, and also for the ungentlemauly harshness of your conduct, for I am satis-fied that there must be something more than the simple duty of an officer iu this uncalled for severity, when the proofs of the utter falseness of the charges against me have been proved by Lady Dora Dunskelling's statement, whilst the unconnected assertion of a simple domestic is maintained in preference."

Major Edwards' cheek flushed scarlet, and a fierce, angry reply was on his lips, when a murmur from the ranks caused all present to turn round.

To Gordon's intense vexation, he beheld a party of soldiers with an officer at their head, advancing round the bluff. In their midst he perceived two men with their arms tied behind them, who were in rebel uniform. On a nearer approach he with sorrow recognised in the persons of the prisoners the rebel leader O'Dowd, and his companion in arms, Maxwell.

"Ha," exclaimed Major Edwards, triumphantly, "our information was correct. No doubt, these two men are the two rebel leaders we have so anxiously endeavoured to secure." Then calling a sergeant to his side, he said— "Put this young lady on a horse, take two men, and conduct her safely to Kilmare, and let Mr. Gordon be strictly guarded; any attempt at escape may end in death."

"Sir," said Dora Dunskelling, indignantly, "I will not quit my protector; a few minutes must now prove to you the falseness of your accusations against this gentleman —or rather, I should say against the present Lord Dunskelling."

Major Edwards started and changed colour.

"Then where," he said, hurriedly, "where is the Lord Dunskelling who undoubtedly was in the carriage with you when it was stopped by the rebels?"

Dora hesitated, and appeared unwilling to name his death; but Cuthbert Gordon at once said :—

"Mr. Fitzpatrick, whom you style Lord Dunskelling, is—I deeply regret to say—no more."

"Good heavens!" exclaimed the major, but before he could utter a word the officer commanding the party stepped up to the side of the major, and recognising Lady Dora Dunskelling, he raised his hat and bowed.

The young lady at once recognised Captain Dunlop, and returned his salutation.

"We have captured," said the captain, "the famous

rebel leader, O'Donahue, and another leader named Maxwell."

"But no trace of Lord Dunskelling, not even his body? for I have this moment heard he has been barbarously murdered," enquired Major Edwards, with a dark look at our hero.

"You amaze me," returned Captain Dunlop. "Lord Dunskelling murdered! This is sad news. The rebels evidently had notice of our advance, for the entire force have dispersed and fled. The two leaders we came upon unexpectedly in a small cabin on the skirts of the bay. They were provided with a change of garments, and made a desperate resistance, killing one of our men and wounding three."

"Bring them up," cried the major. "I will glean some intelligence from the villains concerning this murder and the suspicious conduct of this person, who acknowledges to the name of Gordon, and yet pretends to be Lord Dunskelling."

"But had not the lady better be conducted from this exposed place?" asked Captain Dunlop, looking compassionately at the agitated girl.

"This lady refuses to quit Mr. Gordon's protection," returned the major, sneeringly, "and I must insist upon detaining Mr. Gordon till this mysterious transaction is cleared up. Let me examine your prisoners."

"The sooner you do so, the better," said our hero, angrily, for he felt his fair companion lean heavily on his arm. "If you only ask a single question of your prisoners you will easily understand our position. You will then find that what Lady Dora Dunskelling stated to you as facts are so."

"Confederates usually shield each other," observed Major Edwards, in a contemptuous manner. "Depend upon it, I shall require stronger proofs of your innocence than the assertions of a couple of rebel leaders."

Scarcely had the major uttered these words when the report of a volley of musketry pealed through the air. Several of the soldiers standing in the ranks fell, some were killed outright, many severely wounded. As the smoke cleared away, our hero could perceive a large body of insurgents running down from the high cliffs and rocks above the soldiers, whilst at the same moment another party in the rebel uniform rushed round the foot of the rock, and with loud shouts and cries of defiance charged the royal troops. Astounded by this sudden and most unexpected attack, in an instant O'Dowd and Maxwell were released, and then a desperate contest ensued between the rebels and the military.

Though disordered by this sudden attack, and the numbers of the assailants, Major Edwards and Captain Dunlop, both brave men, soon rallied their forces ; but the major by no means forgot his prisoner, for calling Sergeant Holloway and four men, he desired them to stand by their prisoner—should he attempt escape, they knew their duty.

As the major moved off and joined his men, Serjeant Holloway received a musket ball in his body, which stretched him at our hero's feet. At the same moment Dora uttered a stifled cry. Our hero at once took her in his arms, for the shots fell thick and fast about them, and making a rush seized the horse from the terrified groom who held him ; placing his fair burden upon the saddle he leaped up behind and, urging the startled horse into a gallop, rode rapidly from the scene of strife, escaping by a miracle the several shots discharged at him by some of the soldiers, who, when Sergeant Holloway fell, busied themselves in raising him up.

In a few minutes he was clear of the place, but still he urged the horse over the broken and irregular surface of the ground, till he came suddenly upon a well-beaten track, and then checking his speed, he perceived that the poor girl had fainted, and that the sleeve of her dress was soaked in blood. Uttering an expression of horror he leaped from the horse, and taking Dora in his arms laid her gently upon the bank, and getting a little water from a pool by his side he sprinkled and bathed her temples, and then, tearing off her sleeve, he perceived with considerable emotion that a ball had torn the flesh off her arm in a severe manner.

Thanking God that it was a mere flesh wound, he washed away the blood, and closing the flesh, bound his handkerchief tightly over the wound. Just as he finished Dora recovered consciousness, and perceiving her lover's occupation, with a sigh of relief raised her head.

"You have had a providential escape, my beloved," said our hero, tenderly; "that Major Edwards was an unfeeling scoundrel to let you stand exposed to the promiscuous firing of the two combatants."

"I was hit, dear Cuthbert, before you lifted me on the horse; I did not faint from the wound, but from complete exhaustion and fatigue. How rejoiced I feel at our providential escape from that terrible scene of contention. You cannot tell, I suppose, whether Mr. O'Dowd and his companion escaped or not."

"I saw them liberated, and fighting, and as the rebels were by far the stronger party, I make no doubt but that they escaped, knowing the ground so well. Let me now, dear Dora, place you again on the horse. We must get, as soon as we can, to some village or town, for, should the soldiers pursue and see us, in the excitement of the moment they might fire."

"I certainly long to reach a place of safety and repose," replied Dora, "and where you will be safe from the singular vindictiveness of that Major Edwards. I cannot understand his most ungentlemanly conduct."

"I cannot rightly understand his conduct myself," remarked our hero, preparing to lift his fair companion on the horse; "there is more in it than we can now comprehend."

Having re-seated Dora, he led the horse by the bridle along the path. As they were crossing the moor they came upon several tracks, evidently sheep and cattle paths, and as the moor was bounded by high hedges, they could not rightly conjecture which track to take. Whilst hesitating, two countrymen advanced towards them, driving a flock of sheep.

"This is fortunate," said Dora; "these men will put us in the right path to some town."

The men soon came up, and looked at our hero and his companion with great surprise.

On our hero's requesting one of them to put them on the nearest track to gain the mail-coach road, he offered civilly to guide them, as the path was not easy to find.

This offer was gladly accepted; from the man they learned that they were only two miles from the main road, and when there three miles would take them into Kilmare, where there was a good inn, and post chaises and horses to be had. On reaching the main road, our hero rewarded the peasant, and with hope in her heart, and increased spirits, Dora declared she felt no longer the exhaustion that before overpowered her. They both felt anxious and interested in the fate of O'Dowd, and hoped he escaped, and would be able to fly from the kingdom.

On entering the little town of Kilmare their appearance attracted considerable attention. The town was only three miles from the spot where Lord Dunskelling had been attacked and carried off. In fact that affair was the talk and wonder of the entire population. On reaching the inn, which really afforded good accommodation, our hero enquired for a surgeon to dress Dora's wound. Fortunately there was one resident in the town, and his services were soon procured.

The landlady showed our heroine every kind of attention, and the young surgeon having dressed and carefully bandaged her arm, she was forced to retire for a few hours' rest; that rest so much needed after the long hours of fatigue and trial she had undergone.

CHAPTER XXXIV.

Left to himself, Cuthbert Gordon, as he paced the little parlour of the inn, began to turn over in his mind the events of the last five hours. One circumstance greatly puzzled and annoyed him, and that was the unmistakable hostility and harshness exhibited by Major Edwards towards himself. He knew nothing of that officer; had never met him, to his knowledge; still his manner and words were hostile. Having partaken of some refreshment he determined, whilst Dora reposed, to proceed to the turf cutter's cottage, where poor Dorgan had been carried, when wounded.

On reaching the cottage he was greatly pleased to find that Dorgan was very little the worse for his wounds and quite able to accompany him back to the inn.

The worthy farmer listened with intense satisfaction to our hero's account of Fitzpatrick's death, and did not attempt to conceal his feelings of pleasure, though he perceived Cuthbert Gordon's serious countenance. By way of excusing his various exclamations of satisfaction he said :—

" Be the immortal powers, your honour, he only got what he honestly desarved ; there's an end of him anyhow."

Rewarding the honest turf cutter's wife for her kindness and attention to Dorgan, our hero and his follower left the cottage, and on Dorgan's account they walked back very quietly to the inn.

On entering the parlour they perceived a gentleman sitting at the table examining some papers. He looked at our hero with a serutinizing glance, saying :—

"I have been expecting you, Sir. My name is Blake ;

I am a county magistrate, and wish to ask you some questions. The young lady you brought here wounded, is, I understand from the surgeon, much better, and not likely to suffer much from her injury."

Mr. Blake was a short, stout, pompous kind of person —he owned considerable landed property in the county, and prided himself on the abilities he displayed as a magistrate during the troubled period of our story.

Mr. Blake had heard a very imperfect account of the stopping of Lord Dunskelling's carriage—of the seizure of its inmates and their disappearance—and the pursuit of the military, but of all else that occurred he was ignorant ; he therefore requested our hero to give him a clear account of the whole affair, as he understood that the young lady who was in the carriage was under his care and then in the house.

Cuthbert Gordon knew it was absolutely necessary that he should state facts clearly, for no doubt the murder of Lord Dunskelling would make a stir, and his being present at his death was a rather unpleasant circumstance, as he would hereafter lay claim to the title and estates. He therefore gave Mr. Blake a very distinct relation of his journey to Ireland to release his cousin from the machinations of Lord Dunskelling, his arrest with Dorgan Rafferty by the rebels, and all that occurred afterwards.

Mr. Blake looked serious, saying, "This is a terrible affair—a nobleman murdered in cold blood by a set of miscreants, and excited and instigated to commit this cruel assassination by the leader of those rebels from private motives. Why were you and the young lady brought into their retreat? Surely not to witness this brutal murder."

Now it was by no means either easy or pleasant to our hero to have to enter into such full particulars; to do so he would have to go back to his first introduction to O'Dowd and Fitzpatrick ; he therefore merely said :

"Such, as I have stated to you, Mr. Blake, are the facts. Dorgan Rafferty, a very respectable small farmer, and who was wounded in our seizure by the rebels, will, if examined, give you the same account as to the gentleman calling himself Lord Dunskelling and his miserable death. No one regrets it more sincerely than I do. I did all I could to prevent it, and the young lady suffered severely in having been present at such a scene. There will no doubt be a very strict enquiry into the whole affair, especially as I lay claim to the title and estates of the late Lord Dunskelling. I do not mean the gentleman who was so unfortunately killed, but Lady Dora's father."

Mr. Blake started, looked at our hero with a stare of amazement, and then said hastily, "May I request your name? Up to this moment I am ignorant of it."

"My name is Cuthbert Gordon," returned the person addressed, really wishing Mr. Blake's examination over, for he could see no result favourable to himself likely to come of it, without very tedious explanations, and he was very anxious to take his cousin to Dublin and place her under the protection of his mother.

"Cuthbert Gordon!" repeated Mr. Blake, starting back, and passing his hand across his eyes. "Why, good Heavens! that is the name of the person Lord Dunskelling's servant gave to Major Edwards in my presence, as one of those actually concerned in the outrage of stopping his lordship's carriage and seizing the person of Lady Dora Dunskelling, and, despite his lordship's resistance, dragging her out of the carriage and finally putting her on a horse and coolly joining the rebels in their retreat. Why, this is downright—"

"I beg you will not mystify yourself, Mr. Blake," hastily but quietly interrupted our hero, "and I must request you not to state things hastily you will regret having uttered hereafter. Major Edwards has already insulted and acted harshly in his conduct towards me, and in the presence of Lady Dora Dunskelling. He gave his attention to a man who certainly witnessed the attack upon the carriage, and who noticed my rescuing my cousin from the upset carriage, and my enforced departure with the man who committed the outrage on his lordship; but this domestic knows, in reality, nothing of the real facts.   Pray, Mr. Blake, may I ask you who is Major Edwards ?"

"Who is he ?" exclaimed Mr. Blake, his face growing scarlet and his manner excited. "Major Edwards, Sir, is my nephew—my sister's only son. He married the sister of Herbert O'Dowd, Esq., who was most unfortunately drowned when his yacht was driven ashore in a gale of wind some years ago, near Dunskelling. Major Edwards, therefore, in right of his wife, has some claim, I imagine, to feel a strong interest in the fortunes and fate of the Dunskelling family."

Cuthbert Gordon could not refrain from a smile. "Now," thought he, "here is a mystery explained. In the first place I perceived that O'Dowd permitted it to be believed that he had perished in his yacht, and when he joined the mistaken men assembled in arms against the government he assumed the name of O'Donahue. Major Edwards no doubt discovered by some means that Fitzpatrick in reality had no right to the title and estates of Dunskelling, and therefore thought his relationship on the O'Dowd side would give him claims. Vague as they were, they were worth looking after, provided that there was no such person in existence as Cuthbert Gordon." These thoughts, surmises, and ideas, required only a moment of time to pass through the brain ; therefore our hero, after a very brief pause, said to his thoughtful hearer :

"It is quite useless, Mr. Blake, for you and I to enter into the intricate consideration of the claims that will arise in consequence of the unexpected death of the old Lord Dunskelling, or the murder, for such I must myself call it, of the late presumed Lord Dunskelling. The law will decide these matters when they come to be argued in the law court. I am extremely anxious myself to proceed with Lady Dora Dunskelling to Dublin. In the proper time I will prove my claims to the title and estates of the late lord fairly and publicly ; and when the enquiries that will be sure to be made respecting the unfortunate death of Mr. Fitzpatrick are began I shall be ready with others to give evidence as to how and where it occurred. At present we can do nothing. Major Edwards and

24

Captain Dunlop I left engaged in dispersing a body of insurgents, who I presume attacked them for the purpose of releasing their leaders, whom I perceived Captain Dunlop had succeeded in securing."

Mr. Blake looked exceedingly mystified and evidently not very well pleased, but there was that in the manner and tone of his companion that satisfied him that he was quite in earnest in what he said.

"Well, Sir," observed Mr. Blake, after a short pause, "I cannot say I thoroughly understand this strange affair, and must wait till I see Major Edwards. I will now leave you, and ride over to where Captain Dunlop's detachment is quartered. I feel anxious to hear how the contest you witnessed ended, and I trust also to hear that they have secured the persons you mention as leaders, and who are, in point of fact, the murderers of the unfortunate Lord Dunskelling, as I must style him, till I see reason to call him otherwise," and with a stiff bow the magistrate left the room.

Our hero felt exceedingly glad when he departed. He rung the bell and enquired of the waiter if a chaise and pair could be had, to proceed as soon as the young lady under his charge was sufficiently recovered to bear the journey. The waiter sent in the landlady, who promised him a pair of horses to put in a chaise she had, the moment they could be brought in from the field and fed. With this promise he was forced to be satisfied; his object for a speedy departure was to avoid again at this critical juncture meeting with Major Edwards, who might notonlydetain him, but put him to exceeding inconvenience. When Dora awoke she felt greatly refreshed, the slight flesh wound on her arm causing her scarcely any inconvenience or pain. Like her lover, she also felt eager to leave the vicinity of Major Edwards and the military. She feared our hero's impetuous temper; besides which, she ardently longed to be under the protection of Mrs. Gordon.

The worthy drover was rejoiced to see his young mistress looking so well. She thanked him warmly for the service he had rendered her, and said the first person she should visit, on her return to Dunskelling, would be his kind and worthy mother.

"Please God, my lady," exclaimed Dorgan, "it won't be long before we shall see the rightful lord of Dunskelling in his natural home, and with a mistress to rule over it as good as she is beautiful."

Before another hour elapsed our heroine and her cousin drove off in the chaise got ready for them by diligent exertion; and it was fortunate that they did so, for a sergeant and ten men very shortly after arrived at the inn to arrest our hero and conduct him a prisoner to Galway, by order of Major Edwards, whose party had suffered a repulse from the insurgents, and carried off their leaders after a hotly contested fight, in which Captain Dunlop and several of his men were severely wounded, and two killed, Major Edwards himself receiving a pistol-shot in the side.

Exasperated at the escape of the two rebel leaders, Major Edwards, on reaching their quarters, despatched a sergeant and ten men to seek our hero, and to arrest him wherever he found him, and to conduct him to Galway to undergo an examination, for being a party concerned in the murder of Lord Dunskelling.

Dorgan Rafferty was to follow our hero to Dublin as soon as possible.

After resting a few hours of the night at ——, Cuthbert Gordon and his fair charge proceeded without stopping to Dublin, where Dora was received with warm affection by Mrs. Gordon and her daughters; everything was done to make her forget all she had gone through, and, in truth, she became most happy, and soon learned to love the two fair girls as sisters. We have little to relate that will interest our readers in the further fortunes of Cuthbert Gordon. Placing himself and his affairs in the hands of his solicitor, Mr. Sturgeon, in an examination that shortly afterwards took place respecting the death of Mr. Fitzpatrick—it was shown that he never had any right to the title of Lord Dunskelling—it was clearly manifested that the accusations of Major Edwards had not the slightest foundation.

Lady Dora Dunskelling created a great sensation in court when she appeared in evidence; her beauty, the persecution she had endured, and the clear and lucid manner in which she explained the seizure of Fitzpatrick and the part Cuthbert Gordon had acted in the affair, won universal admiration. Dorgan Rafferty, too, caused much amusement and applause in giving his evidence. The accusation of Major Edwards was therefore dismissed, as groundless and totally frivolous and vexatious. Finally, Cuthbert Gordon's claim to the lordship and estates of Dunskelling were fully established and allowed. Six months afterwards, Dora became the willing bride of him she had so truly loved from their first meeting. On that occasion great *fêtes* and feastings took place at Dunskelling, under the superintendence of Dorgan Rafferty.

Never was any nobleman and his bride received with more enthusiastic rejoicings than Lord and Lady Dunskelling, when three months after their union they took up their residence in the castle, which had undergone a complete transformation in its outward and inward appearance.

Every farmer and tenant on the estate was allowed six months' rent. Dorgan Rafferty was made bailiff over the Dunskelling estate, and everything was done to render the tenants and peasantry happy and contented.

Lord Dunskelling instituted a strict search for the body of Fitzpatrick without success. Neither could Lady Dunskelling discover what became of her former governess. Dora's was a forgiving heart; she wished to forget the deceptive part played by Miss MacCormack, and to place her above want or misfortune, but it was believed she had sailed for America.

Lord Dunskelling, about a year after his marriage, then the father of a fine boy, received a letter with a foreign post mark. It was from Herbert O'Dowd, a colonel in the service of Napoleon Bonaparte; in which he gave him the full particulars of his escape in a fishing boat to Bordeaux, after wonderful hardships and difficulties. Mr. Maxwell also got to France, and was then a captain in the same regiment as himself.

Mrs. Gordon and her beautiful daughter Lucy resided in Dunskelling. Amy had married the rector of Ardmore, the only son of the late rector—a very fine young man of good family and fortune, and an honour to his profession.

Lucy, true to her first and only love, was at last rewarded by her marriage to young Lewellen, whose father's fortune was fully re-established, and who, himself the pattern of fidelity, had never for a moment forgotten his beloved Lucy.

They were married by Amy's husband, and Lucy received a noble dowry from her most affectionate brother. Mr. Lewellen, tired of mercantile affairs, and anxious to be near those who were dear to him, sold his property in Wales, and purchased a very picturesque estate within seven miles of Dunskelling. Miss Lewellen remained unmarried, beloved by all the family circle, but above all by the future heir of Dunskelling, who was her delight and her joy.

THE END.